IRENE BRAND

Writing has been a lifelong interest of this author, who says that she started her first novel when she was eleven years old and hasn't finished it yet. However, since 1984 she's published more than thirty contemporary and historical novels and three nonfiction titles. She started writing professionally in 1977 after she completed her master's degree in history at Marshall University. Irene taught in secondary public schools for twenty-three years, but retired in 1989 to devote herself to writing.

Consistent involvement in the activities of her local church has been a source of inspiration for Irene's work. Traveling with her husband, Rod, to all fifty states and to thirty-two foreign countries has also inspired her writing. Irene is grateful to the many readers who have written to say that her inspiring stories and compelling portrayals of characters with strong faith have made a positive impression on their lives. You can write to her at P.O. Box 2770, Southside, WV 25187 or visit her website at www.irenebrand.com.

DANA CORBIT

started telling "people stories" at about the same time she started forming words. So it came as no surprise when the Indiana native chose a career in journalism. As an award-winning newspaper reporter and features editor, she had the opportunity to share wonderful true-life stories with her readers. She left the workforce to be a homemaker, but the stories came home with her as she discovered the joy of writing fiction. The winner of the 2007 Holt Medallion competition for novel writing, Dana feels blessed to share the stories of her heart with readers. Dana lives in southeast Michigan, where she balances the make-believe realm of her characters with her equally exciting real-life world as a wife, carpool coordinator for three athletic daughters and food supplier for two disinterested felines.

Christmas in the Air

Irene Brand
Dana Corbit

Love Inspired

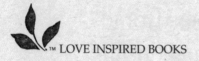

™ LOVE INSPIRED BOOKS

ISBN-13: 978-0-373-78737-1

CHRISTMAS IN THE AIR

Copyright © 2012 by Harlequin Books S.A.

The publisher acknowledges the copyright holders of the individual works as follows:

SNOWBOUND HOLIDAY
Copyright © 2005 by Irene Brand

A SEASON OF HOPE
Copyright © 2005 by Dana Corbit Nussio

This edition published by arrangement with Love Inspired Books.

® and TM are trademarks of Love Inspired Books, used under license. Trademarks indicated with ® are registered in the United States Patent and Trademark Office, the Canadian Trade Marks Office and in other countries.

www.LoveInspiredBooks.com

Printed in U.S.A.

CONTENTS

SNOWBOUND HOLIDAY

Irene Brand

You have been a refuge for the poor, a refuge
for the needy in his distress, a shelter from
the storm and a shade from the heat.
—*Isaiah 25:4*

Chapter One

A thick sheet of snow and ice blanketed the interstate. Seated in the front passenger's seat of the church van, Livia Kessler's back stiffened, and she grabbed for the handle over the door every time a gust of wind swayed the vehicle sideways. Livia prayed silently for the driver, Eric Stover, who gripped the steering wheel with both hands in his attempt to control the van. She glanced over her shoulder. The other members of their church's vocal quintet slept soundly, oblivious to the dangerous weather conditions.

The singers had made their last presentation earlier in the day at a morning worship service in a large church in Detroit. They'd eaten a light lunch and started south on Interstate 75 anticipating an easy five-or six-hour drive to their destination in Columbus, Ohio.

A mixture of sleet and rain had been falling when they left Detroit, but they'd soon left the moisture behind. When they crossed Michigan's state line into Ohio, they drove a few miles without any precipitation. As they'd bypassed the city of Toledo, however, they encountered a wind-driven, wet snow that accumulated quickly on the highway.

The flip-flap-flop of the wipers as they moved rhythmically back and forth on the windshield mesmerized Livia. She started yawning. Knowing she had to stay awake to encourage Eric, she opened the window a gap to bring fresh air into the van. The air was fresh, all right. In fact, it was frigid. She hurriedly closed the window.

"If this keeps up we won't make it back to Columbus tonight," she said quietly.

Taking a deep breath, Eric said, "I know. If the snow is heading northeast, we'll soon move past it. If not, we'd better look for a motel."

Tomorrow would be Christmas Eve, and all of them wanted to get home before then. "But Sean's plane leaves for California at ten o'clock," Livia said, knowing that the tenor member of their singing group wanted to be home for Christmas.

Nodding his head, Eric said, "I know, but I'm more concerned about our safety than his plane trip. When a strong wind gust sideswipes the van, I don't have much control over it. Can you turn on the radio? It may wake the others, but I'd like to hear a weather report."

Livia scanned the radio options until she picked up a strong FM station. They'd just missed the news apparently, because the DJ said, "Folks, sit back and listen to your favorite Christmas songs."

The gentle sounds of "I'll Be Home for Christmas" increased Livia's disappointment. Sean wasn't the only one who wanted to go home. Livia was a student at Ohio State University, and she intended to leave for her home in southern Ohio as soon as they returned from the singing engagement. In her twenty years, she had never missed a Christmas on Heritage Farm. If they had to lay over at a motel until this storm was over, she wouldn't make it home to observe Christmas with her parents, siblings and her little nephew. She couldn't miss Derek's first Christmas!

Eric slowed when they reached the city limits of Bowling Green. The change of pace awakened the passengers. Tall, thin Sean King unfolded his muscular legs, rubbed his eyes and leaned forward as a meteorologist announced, "We interrupt our musical program for a severe weather warning. A blizzard, with wind gusts in excess of forty miles per hour, is sweeping across northwestern Ohio. In some areas, a foot of snow already covers the ground, with a predicted accumulation of another foot or more in the next twenty-four hours. Stay off the highways unless it's an emergency."

"You should have gotten me up," Sean said. "Do you want me to drive for a while, Eric?"

"Yes, I'd appreciate some help," Eric said. "Visibility is poor, and I've been fighting this side wind for so long, my muscles are tied in knots. As soon as I find a place to pull over, you can drive."

Marie, Eric's wife, sat up and rubbed her husband's tense shoulders. "Oh, I didn't realize it was snowing like this. I should have stayed awake."

"You couldn't have done anything, honey, and you

were sleeping so soundly that I don't want to wake you," Eric explained.

"Will we make it home tonight?" Marie asked, voicing the major concern of all of them.

"I doubt it, unless we run out of the storm soon," Eric said. "I hope you don't miss your plane, Sean."

"Hey, man, don't worry about that," Sean said. "Depending on the direction of the storm, the Columbus airport may be closed anyway. Don't take any risks for my sake. How long before we come to another town?"

Livia took a map out of the glove compartment, and turned on the interior light. In the small ray of light, she scanned the map. "It's several miles to Findlay. We should find a motel there, but there's no town of any size before then. And if you remember from our drive on this road a few days ago, after we leave Findlay, it's mostly rural area until we approach Columbus. So that means no motels. We can't go farther than Findlay."

Livia relaxed when a highway marker indicated the next exit was two miles away. "Maybe we can find a motel at this exit," she said.

"Well, even if we don't, I'm getting off the interstate, so we can change drivers," Eric said.

But through the haze of snow, in the distance, Livia saw lights flashing. "Oh, no!" she said. "Looks like a police cruiser. There's probably been a wreck."

Eric slowed to a crawl, but the car still skidded sideways when he applied the brakes and missed hitting the patrol car by inches. An officer, bracing himself against the strong wind, held on to his hat as he approached the van.

"A pileup of vehicles has blocked the interstate between here and the next exit," the officer said. "You'll have to get off and take a secondary road south. You can access the interstate again in twelve miles. Be careful—it's a narrow road."

"Any chance we can find a motel, Officer?" Livia said.

"Not till you get to Findlay."

Another car approached behind them, and the patrolman waved them on.

"I'll keep driving, Sean. With all this snow, I can't tell where to pull off the highway." Eric wiggled back and forth in the seat and flexed his fingers before he moved forward. "Hindsight is better than foresight, I've always heard," he said. "We should have stayed overnight in Bowling Green."

Livia had been checking the outdoor thermometer on the dashboard, which registered steadily falling temperatures. Now, rather than being distressed about not getting home for Christmas, she prayed that they could find a safe shelter for the night. She'd learned the seriousness of blizzards a few years ago when a heavy snow, accompanied by an ice storm, immobilized their farm in southern Ohio. That had been Christmas week, too—the time her brother, Evan, had brought his fiancée home to spend the holidays with the family.

The headlights of the van were little help in the blinding snow, and Eric dodged twice to keep from hitting approaching vehicles on the narrow road. A large panel truck crept along the road in front of them, and Eric stayed close behind it.

"I have no sense of direction right now, but I figure that guy knows where he's going," he explained. "I'll keep him in sight."

The truck slowed to a crawl at a crossroad. The snow had covered the highway direction signs, but when the truck continued straight ahead, Eric followed. This section of road was even more narrow than the one they'd taken when they left the interstate. Fence posts and bushes covered with snow had turned the road into a narrow tunnel, and Livia couldn't see any houses or farm buildings at all. The van's bumper pushed a wall of snow ahead of it as they moved steadily forward.

Darkness had almost fallen when, with sinking heart, Livia saw the truck swerve to one side and slide into a ditch. When the driver attempted to pull out of the slide, the truck jackknifed across the road.

Livia's plummeting heart echoed Sean's words when he predicted, "It will take a wrecker to right that truck."

Gingerly applying the brakes of the van, Eric said, "Let's find out if the driver is injured."

Before Eric brought the van to a sliding halt, the truck driver climbed out of the cab, seemingly none the worse for his accident.

Knowing that they couldn't go forward, Livia rolled down her window and looked behind them to see if they could turn and retrace their route. A pickup truck and a car were following them. The driver of the pickup braked to avoid hitting the van. The old sedan behind the pickup swerved quickly to the side of the road to avoid rear-ending the pickup. The car slid sideways and stalled in a large drift, blocking the road.

"We can't go either way now," Livia said, desperation in her voice. A chilly silence enveloped the van.

Livia snatched her cell phone from her bag. A tight knot filled her throat when she saw that no service was available in this area.

"We can't use our phones, either," she said, a tremor in her voice.

Roxanne Fisher, Marie's mother, peered out the window and said, "So we're stranded."

Eric rolled down the window, stuck his head out and called to the other three travelers, who were circling their own vehicles, sizing up the situation.

"Hey, guys! Looks like we're all stuck. Get in our van, and we'll discuss our options."

Sean moved to the rear seat, sat beside Roxanne and made space for the newcomers. The three men were covered with snow when they stepped into the van. Livia gasped when the ceiling light illuminated the face of one of the men.

Quinn Damron! She turned away so he couldn't see her face. The situation was already difficult enough without encountering *this* man. Especially a man whose rejection three years ago had left her heart empty and injured—a heart that had never found room for another. Livia stared out the side window as she listened to the conversation, hoping no one had noticed her reaction and would ask her about it later.

"Any of you familiar with this area?" Eric asked. "Is there any chance of finding shelter for the night?"

One of the men, a senior citizen, said, "Yes, sir. I've lived around here nigh on to eighty years. There ain't a house in five miles of where we are."

"Any chance of getting plowed out?" the truck driver asked.

"Not until it stops snowing. I'd judge it'll be two to three days before we get any help. The snowplows will clear the interstates and major highways before they get to us. How'd you end up here anyway? This road ain't hardly ever used."

"I apparently took a wrong turn," the truck driver admitted. "I haven't made deliveries on this road before. The regular driver is on vacation. The snow had covered the road signs, and after we took several turns on that little road from the interstate, I lost my sense of direction. So I took a chance on which way to go and my luck didn't hold."

"I'm not familiar with this country, either," Eric said. "I decided this was the detour route when the truck came this way."

"Sorry I led you astray, buddy," the trucker said.

"You're no more to blame than we are," Eric assured him.

"We probably shouldn't leave the cars to find shelter," Quinn said. Livia's pulse raced at the mellow, deep voice that she still vividly recalled, erasing any doubt that he was the unforgettable man she'd met three years ago.

"And it's going to be miserable sleeping in them," Sean said.

"Especially since the temperature is supposed to drop below zero tomorrow," Quinn agreed. "I'm only twenty-five miles from home, but it might as well be a hundred miles for all the good it will do me."

"Livia," Eric said, "lower the window and try your cell phone again."

Did she hear a quick intake of breath from Quinn's direction? He'd known her as "Olivia," and there was certainly other women named Olivia out there, so it was probably her imagination. Without answering, she lowered the window, and held her phone out. But the screen still showed that she had no service. They were probably too far away for her to get a signal, and the storm certainly wasn't helping any. She shook her head at Eric, not wanting to speak, fearing that Quinn would recognize her voice. But knowing the little interest that he'd had in her, she thought bitterly, he probably hadn't given her a second thought since the last time they'd seen each other.

The elderly gentleman said, "My name's Les Holden. Since I've been around a few years longer than the rest of you, I feel free to offer some suggestions. I've lived through blizzards in this area before, and if the snow drifts, these cars could be covered. Besides, even if you wrap up, you're gonna get cold in the van."

"I think all of us know that," Sean said impatiently, "but what else can we do?"

Favoring Sean with an amused glance from under his shaggy white eyebrows, Les said, "Hold your horses, sonny, I'm coming to that." He waved his hand in the direction of the panel truck. "I almost forget. There's an abandoned church down the road a short ways, and I think we oughta move down there before it gets any darker."

"But if it's abandoned, it won't be any warmer than the cars," Sean argued. "If we stay here, we can start the motor once in a while and run the heater."

"Not if the snow gets so deep it covers our exhaust pipes," Quinn said quietly.

"There ain't been regular services in this church for years," Les continued, as if the other two hadn't spoken, "but the building is still in good shape. We use it every once in a while for funerals, so there's coal and wood on hand to build fires. We can keep a fire going. We're apt to be stranded for a day or two, so we'll be more comfortable and safer in the church than in our vehicles."

"I agree with you," Quinn said. "What do the rest of you think?"

"Wonder if there's any food in the church?" Sean said. "I'm hungry now, and fasting for a few days doesn't sound good to me."

"You'll be hungry no matter where you are," Les said shortly.

"I can help out there," the truck driver said. "My truck is full of groceries. We can take food out of it and pay my boss for whatever we use."

Marie and Roxanne voiced their approval of Les's plan, and it seemed the general consensus that they must move to the church. Apparently aware that she hadn't said anything, Eric said, "Is that all right with you, Livia?"

In a quiet voice, she said, "It's the only thing we can do. I've experienced enough snowstorms and power outages on our farm to know it's going to be unpleasant no matter where we are."

"Then if everyone agrees, you take charge, Les," Quinn said. "You're more experienced in this sort of thing than we are. Lead on to the church."

Quinn peered intently at the back of Livia's head. Could this be the Olivia Kessler he'd known at one time? Her voice sounded familiar, and she did live in Ohio, but it had been a few years. If this was the woman he'd known, and the two of them were destined to spend several days in the same building, the atmosphere might be decidedly tense. But despite the awkwardness of the past, Quinn hadn't forgotten her. He looked forward to renewing their friendship, but he wasn't proud of his past actions. He opened the car door and stepped out into the falling snow. How forgiving would Olivia be to him for breaking her heart?

Chapter Two

Quinn recalled Olivia Kessler had straight, blond hair that fell below her shoulders, just as this woman did. She'd been a tall, willowy young woman, quick and graceful. The focal point of the gentle beauty of her face had been her deep blue eyes fringed by long lashes. He wished he could get a better look at her, but this Livia woman hadn't once turned so he could see her features.

"We might have to make more'n one trip," Les said as he ducked his head against the cold wind. Quinn put thoughts of the past aside and devoted his attention to the man's instructions.

"Take everything you can the first time. Wear your heaviest coats and take blankets if you have any. Let's go single file, and keep one hand free to hold on to the person in front of you. It's easy to get separated in a blizzard. Those of you in the van, wait here until the rest of us gather what we can from our vehicles."

Livia exchanged her sneakers for fleece-lined boots and laced them securely. She shrugged into a heavy coat as she recalled the four weeks she'd spent with Quinn at a 4-H camp in eastern Ohio. She'd gone as a volunteer worker, and she'd been assigned to work with Quinn, the camp counselor.

Eight years her senior, he had been the perfect man of her dreams. They'd been together for hours every day, and Livia had developed a huge crush on him. Because of his kindness and attentiveness to her, she thought he shared her feelings. She'd been too naive to see that he treated everyone in the same friendly way. A few times, she had even imagined that he wanted to kiss her. When he didn't, she reasoned that Quinn considered it inappropriate to make any advances when they were supervising the younger campers. She'd dreamed that their relationship would deepen when they were no longer working at the camp.

The last night of the camp, she'd given Quinn an impassioned letter, the memory of which still made her face burn. She hadn't said she loved him, but she didn't hide her obvious feelings for him, writing that she didn't want him to go out of her life.

Quinn left the camp early the next morning without saying goodbye or acknowledging the note. This rejection left her feeling foolish and hurt. Livia hadn't forgotten him, however, and she'd often wondered if her infatuation for Quinn *had* been real love. She'd never found any other man to interest her. Still smarting from Quinn's rejection, she dreaded being confined with him for days.

Livia tied the hood of her fleece-lined coat below her chin. She placed her Bible, a historical novel, a notebook, a pen and a bag of trail mix in a large tote bag, which she slung over her shoulder. She carried a small garment bag in her right hand. The wind staggered her when she stepped out, and she held to the side of the van as she joined the others.

Sean was visibly shivering. A resident of southern California, he had come to OSU four years ago on a basketball scholarship. He liked the school, but had never adjusted to the climate, which differed so much from his childhood home. Regardless of how many heavy winter clothes he put on, he was always miserable when cold weather struck Ohio.

Looking like a bunch of pack animals, they huddled together in the shelter of the van until Les and the other men joined them.

"I'll go first," Les said. He pointed to Roxanne Fisher. "You fall in behind me, ma'am, and the rest of you line up behind us. Don't worry about looking forward to where you're going. I'll be your guide. Keep your eyes on the ground, follow my steps and hold on to the person in front of you."

Eric stepped into line behind his mother-in-law, and Marie stood behind him. Quinn moved behind Marie, and Sean motioned for Livia to go ahead of him. She didn't want to touch Quinn, and she had no choice but to follow him. Quinn had a large pack over his shoulder, and he carried a snow shovel in his left hand.

Sean placed a trembling hand on Livia's shoulder. She felt sorry for the guy. He was a great basketball player; he just couldn't cope with the cold and snow. Peering over her shoulder, Livia saw the truck driver take up the rear.

Above the whine of the wind, Les shouted, "Everybody ready?" Livia marveled at his foghorn voice, unusual for a man of his age. "Tug on the person in front of you, so I'll know you're in line."

When Sean squeezed Livia's shoulder, she tugged on the sleeve of Quinn's coat. It would have been simpler to tap him on the shoulder, because he was only a few inches taller than she was, but Livia couldn't bear the thought of any personal contact with Quinn.

The foolishness of her crush on Quinn had been a heavy weight on her heart for three years. How could she endure the embarrassment of facing him again?

As she trudged along in Quinn's wake, to take her mind off this man who so suddenly had come into her life again, Livia thought of Heritage Farm and her family. Christmas observance was important to the Kesslers, and she knew that, short of a sudden ninety-degree heat wave, she couldn't possibly be home for Christmas. Probably right now, her mother would be preparing the stollen, a traditional bread recipe that her ancestors had brought from Germany. Her brother Evan would have already brought the live Christmas tree into their large living room for decorating. Uncle Gavin and his wife, Emmalee, would have arrived from Florida.

Quinn stopped abruptly. Livia stumbled forward, her face landing in the middle of his back.

"We must be at the church," he said.

His words were welcome to Livia, because although they'd walked only a short distance, her face was numb from exposure to the wind-driven snow.

Inside her lightweight gloves, Livia's fingers tingled with cold.

Shielding her eyes against the icy snow, Livia saw a gray, weather-beaten frame church. Three steps led to a small porch that sheltered the front door, over which a sign was nailed, indicating that Sheltering Arms Church had been established in 1901. The church would live up to its name tonight by providing safety for eight stranded travelers. For the first time, Livia wondered if God had a reason for bringing all of them together.

Les stood in front of the door, fumbling in his pocket. Drawing out a chain holding several keys, he chose one, inserted it in the lock and pushed the door inward. He peered inside, then motioned his companions to follow him. Quinn stood aside for Livia to proceed him into the building. She nodded her thanks.

The inside of the structure was dark and uninviting. For a few moments, it seemed warm because the fierce wind and the snow-and-ice mixture were no longer stinging Livia's face. As her eyes adjusted to the dim interior, Livia noted that the building was small and neglected, although it must have been a beautiful sanctuary in its day.

The front wall of the church held a stained-glass window depicting Jesus as the Good Shepherd. The six other windows, three on each side of the church, had frosted panes. A dark wainscoting covered the lower half of the walls. Faded wallpaper reached from the wainscoting to the ceiling.

An old-fashioned pump organ was located to one side of the room with an upright piano beside it. An ornately carved wooden lectern was centered on a raised platform below the decorative window. A stove stood in the middle of the room, with a rusty stovepipe sticking through the ceiling. About twenty wooden pews completed the room's furnishings.

With a speculative glance around the room, Quinn said, "We couldn't expect any better accommodations than this under the circumstances. You said there's wood and coal available, right?" he asked Les.

"Yeah, stored in a building back of the church. There are some shovels in the supply room by the back door. We still dig graves by hand, and we keep the shovels for that. They'll come in handy for scooping coal and snow. We can shovel a path to the woodshed and carry in fuel to get the fire started."

Quinn lifted his own shovel. "I always carry a snow shovel in the truck this time of year. If the two of us can take care of scooping away the snow and bringing in the coal and wood, perhaps you other men can bring supplies from the delivery truck. It's getting dark fast."

When the other men agreed, Les said, "Just bring enough food and water to keep us through the night. Maybe the storm will run its course by morning, and we can shovel our way to our vehicles for whatever we need."

Pushing back the hood of her coat, Livia asked, "What can I do?"

"Look in the supply room for candles and holders," Les answered. He called to the men, who were leaving, "If you have any extra flashlights in your vehicles, bring them along."

Quinn took the scarf from his neck and wound it around his head to secure his cap. Pulling on woolen mittens, he followed Les out the back door. Not wasting any time, Les started shoveling. Bracing himself against the strong wind, Quinn stepped to Les's side. He'd grown up on a farm in this area, and more than once, he'd helped clear deep snow from around the farm buildings. He'd volunteered for this task, because he figured the other men hadn't had as much experience in rough living as he'd had.

Livia still hadn't made any indication that she recognized him, but he didn't doubt at all that she was the Olivia he'd met at a camp a few years ago. He had harbored some romantic thoughts of her until he'd learned that she was still in her late teens, while he was twenty-five. In addition to that problem, he still had two more years before he would receive his veterinarian's license. His busy school schedule left no time for romance. He'd shied away from dating a high school girl, but he'd often wondered if he'd made a mistake in not keeping in touch with Olivia.

Believing firmly that God intervened in the lives of His followers, Quinn thought this might not be a chance encounter. Could God have a purpose in a reunion between Olivia and himself?

It was difficult to clear the path because of the steadily falling snow. Their tracks were covered almost as soon as they moved onward. Quinn stopped, straightened, and took a deep breath.

"Pace yourself," Les shouted above the fury of the wind. "Don't overdo."

Quinn nodded his understanding. The woodshed

stood only thirty feet from the church, but his body was practically steaming when they reached the building. Stepping inside, he helped Les fill three large buckets with coal and sticks of wood.

Breathing deeply, Les said, "Which do you want to do, carry the coal inside and start a fire, or clean a path to the johnny houses?"

As he'd been shoveling, Quinn had noticed the two wooden toilets a few feet beyond the woodshed. Since the church had been abandoned for a long time, he'd figured there wouldn't be any usable inside plumbing to make life easier for them.

"I'll shovel," he said. "I haven't built a fire in a stove for a long time. You'll be better at it. Take two of the buckets. I'll bring the third one and the shovels when I finish clearing the paths."

The search of the supply room yielded about a dozen used candles and several holders, which the women placed around the room.

Marie, who wasn't often disturbed by difficult circumstances, assessed their accommodations. Laughing lightly, she said, "I can't decide which will be the most comfortable for sleeping—the floor or the wooden pews."

Marie's mother, Roxanne, who always described herself as pleasingly plump, said, "I'll opt for the floor. There's no room for me on a pew."

Les struggled into the church, carrying two buckets of fuel and shouted, "Will one of you ladies close the door behind me?"

Marie rushed to the door and strained to shut it

against the force of the wind. Livia added her strength to Marie's and they slammed the door, but a thin sheet of snow slithered across the floor before they had finished. Livia brought a rag from the supply room and mopped up the snow before it froze on the cold floor.

Les removed his gloves and blew on his hands to warm them. When he opened the door of the stove, Livia said, "I'll start the fire for you."

Les lifted his shaggy brows in surprise. "You know how to lay a fire, ma'am?"

"Sure do," Livia said. "We have a big fireplace in the living room of our farmhouse. We always have a fire in the evening during the winter. I learned to start a fire when I was just a kid."

Les watched with interest as she adjusted the draft on the stovepipe and sifted the ashes from the last fire into the ash pan. She picked up some small sticks of wood from a nearby box filled with wood and paper and arranged the kindling loosely in the stove.

"Since the church isn't used anymore, is the flue safe?" she asked. "We could have some heat we don't want if the ceiling catches on fire."

"I clean the chimney every fall, just to be sure a bird hasn't nested in it, or to see if any bricks might have crumbled and caused a blockage. It's all right."

Livia took a newspaper from the box and pushed it in around the kindling. "I'm hoping one of the men has matches or a lighter we can use."

"There's matches here," Les said. He walked into the supply room and came back with a Mason jar full of matches. "If I didn't keep the matches covered, a mouse might chew into one of them and start a fire," he explained.

"Oh, I've heard of church mice," Marie said, laughing, "or at least about people who were poor as church mice. That's our situation tonight."

"We won't be bothered with mice," Les assured her with a sly grin. "I'd judge that they've buried deep in the ground to get out of the snow."

Roxanne took several matches. "I'll light the candles."

Livia struck a match on the side of the stove and held it to the paper. She watched carefully as the paper blazed and spread to the slivers of wood. When she adjusted the damper to control the blaze, Les said approvingly, "That's a good job, miss. Let me take over now and put the coal on the fire—no need for you to dirty your hands."

Quinn smelled the smoke before he finished shoveling the paths to the "necessaries," as the pioneers had called them. He even sensed some warmth from the stove when he went inside the church.

"Come close to the stove," Les said, "and warm yourself. You had a cold job."

Quinn shivered involuntarily. "It must be zero by now." Glancing around, he saw that the men hadn't returned from the truck. "I'll go help the others with the food and supplies in a minute, after I warm up a bit."

Livia remembered that Quinn had always pulled more than his share of the load at the 4-H camp. He apparently hadn't changed.

Les cracked the front door of the church and peered

out. "With that truck over on its side, I figure they had a hard time getting into it. But I hear them coming now."

He held the door open for the men to enter. On the porch, they shook themselves like dogs to remove the snow from their clothes.

"Brrr!" Sean said. "If I ever get home to California, I'm never coming east again."

"Oh, you'll forget that after your next basketball game," Eric said. "Although I'll admit this is miserable weather, and I'd welcome some California sunshine myself."

Marie helped her husband unwrap the scarf from around his head. "Did you bring any food? I'm hungry."

"We did," Sean grumbled, "but it wasn't easy. There's almost two feet of snow already and it's still falling."

As the others made room for the three men to hover around the stove, Eric looked around the candlelit room. "It seems peaceful in here," he said. "If we had to be stranded, we could be in worse places. God made provisions for us—a dry, warm place to stay and a truck full of food."

"I'll have to keep a list of what we brought," the truck driver said, "so we can offer to pay for the supplies. But under the circumstances, I don't think the boss will charge us for what we use."

They rearranged three of the pews to circle the stove, where they crowded close together for body warmth and to eat their evening meal. Cheese, crackers, apples and cookies seemed like a banquet to a starving Livia. The men had brought several cartons of bottled water and soft drinks to supplement the meal.

Before they started to eat, Eric asked the blessing for the food and thanked God for their safety. For once, Livia couldn't be thankful for what God had given her. She was miserable. Not only did she want to be with her family, she definitely didn't want to be thrown into Quinn's company. Livia swiped away her tears. If she started crying, it would tear down the fragile defenses of the others, who were trying to make the best of a bad situation.

Livia's parents had always taught their children that God orchestrated every facet of their lives, but tonight, Livia found that hard to accept.

God, if I had to be stranded, why did Quinn Damron have to be here, too?

Chapter Three

When they finished eating, Eric said, "I firmly believe that God rules in the destiny of His creation, and for some reason, He brought us together tonight. I don't know what it is yet, and we may never know, but I suggest we accept the situation and move on. It's going to be a long night. Let's introduce ourselves, so we can at least call each other by name, instead of saying, 'Hey, you.'"

"Sounds good," Quinn said. "I'll start."

Warmth radiated from the stove now, and in the subdued light of the candles, it could have been a peaceful setting except for the dangerous conditions lurking outside the building.

The screeching wind rattled the windows and forced an occasional puff of smoke back down the chimney. Drifting snow sifted in around the doors, as if warning the travelers of potential disaster looming a few steps away.

Quinn sat directly across the circle from Livia, and she kept her eyes downcast as he talked. She hadn't yet looked directly at him. She knew she'd have to face up to her embarrassing past sometime and go on with her life. Perhaps tonight was the time.

Quinn unbuttoned the heavy coat he wore, since the room was getting warm. "My name is Quinn Damron. I'm in partnership with my father on a horse farm located about twenty-five miles from here. I'm also a farrier. Does anyone know what that is?"

Livia knew, but she didn't want to call attention to herself.

"I know," Les said. "He shoes horses."

"That's true, and some, like myself, also treat animals' diseases. I'm a licensed veterinarian, but I decided to work on the farm a year or so before I set up my practice."

"Married?" Eric inquired.

Quinn squirmed uncomfortably. "Not yet," he said. He'd been dating a neighbor for a year, but for some reason, he couldn't get serious about marrying her.

"Who's next?" Eric prodded.

The truck driver sitting to Quinn's left, said, "Might as well be me, I guess. My name's Allen Reynolds. I'm thirty, married, with two cute little daughters. I intended to be home tonight to help them trim the Christmas tree." His voice faltered, and he dropped his head, apparently unable to say more.

It was Sean's turn, and he said, "I'm sorry I've been so grumpy, but I feel better now that I'm getting warm. I'm Sean King, and I expected to go home to California tonight. After hearing about Allen's kids, I don't have any complaint, but I may complain anyway," he added with a fetching grin. "I guess that's enough about me."

"I don't think so," Roxanne Fisher said, her brown eyes shimmering in the dim light as she introduced herself. "Sean is a senior at the university, and this will be his fourth season to play basketball at OSU. You'll probably see him on national television playing in the NBA in a year or two. Besides that, he's a member of our church, and the tenor member of our quintet."

"Hey, Roxanne," Sean objected. "You're supposed to be talking about *yourself*."

"Which I will do now," the vivacious woman said, laughing. "I'm the music director at the Westside Community Church in Columbus. Sean, Marie, Eric and Livia are members of the church's quintet. I play the piano for the others to sing. In fact, we're returning from Detroit where we sang at the home church of one of our quintet members. We left him with his family for the holidays."

As Roxanne talked, Livia realized she would be next, and she didn't know what to say. If Quinn hadn't recognized her by now, he probably would when she mentioned her family. But on the other hand, he may have completely forgotten the personal information he'd learned in the four weeks they'd worked together. Obviously it hadn't meant much to him, or he would have answered her letter.

Roxanne nudged her, and Livia realized she'd been lost in thought. "I'm Olivia Kessler, but my friends call me Livia. I live on a farm in southern Ohio, near the city of Gallipolis. I'm in my sophomore year at

OSU." Her brief comments confirmed Quinn's belief that she was the young woman he had met a few years ago. He tried to catch her eye to acknowledge their former acquaintance, but without looking at him, Livia waved a hand to Eric, indicating that she'd finished.

"I'm the youth minister at Westside," Eric introduced himself. "I'm also working on my master's degree in theology."

Livia knew Eric so well that she didn't have to listen to his introduction. Her mind wandered again as she glanced around the room, thinking what a diverse group they were, not only in occupations and family background, but also in looks. Quinn had chestnut-brown hair, high cheekbones, a strong chin and a firm mouth. His long-limbed body was closer to six feet tall, and he was broad-shouldered. She couldn't see his eyes in the semidarkness, but she remembered that they were a vivid green.

Sean's eyes were a deep shade of brown, and he had light brown hair. Several inches over six feet, he moved with the easy stride of an athlete.

Allen Reynolds, a tall, massive man, was muscular rather than fat. His hair was black, and in the shadows, his dark eyes gleamed from deep orbs.

Marie Stover and her mother, Roxanne, looked alike. Both had brown hair and eyes, and their dusky, round oval faces bordered on perfection. Marie was twenty-eight, and Roxanne had been twenty when her only child was born. It was only in personality that their differences were obvious. Marie was laid-back and amiable, while Roxanne possessed a dynamic, sometimes aggressive, personality—attributes that had made her effective as the director of the musical program in a large church.

Eric was a tall, thin man who appeared frail. However, none of the teenagers he counseled could keep up with his zeal and enthusiasm in the sports and work projects he initiated.

When Les Holden started to speak, Livia gave him her undivided attention. She already appreciated the man because he'd guided them to the security of this church. Les wasn't more than five feet tall, obviously suffering with arthritis, although he wouldn't have been a big man even in his youth. Partly bald, he had a fringe of gray hair that matched the bushy gray eyebrows that extended like shingles over his faded blue eyes.

"I ain't much for making speeches," he said. "Like I told you, I'll be eighty my next birthday. I've been a widower for twenty-some years. I know how quick these storms can come, and I shouldn't have started out tonight. I aimed to spend Christmas with my daughter, who lives about ten miles away. But she won't worry when I don't show up, thinking that I'm still safe at home. That's about all, I guess."

"Les, why isn't the church used anymore?" Livia asked. "I'm grateful for its sheltering walls tonight, and it seems sad that this building is no longer a lighthouse for God in this community."

"Yes'um, I agree with you." He stood stiffly and walked around, apparently to exercise his arthritic limbs. "I remember comin' here with Mom and Dad when I was a young'un. This room would be crowded every Sunday. We sure enjoyed praising the Lord within these walls."

"If I remember right," Quinn said, "there used to be a town in this area."

"Yes, sir, that's right. The town of Bexter was built in the late 1800s. There was a railroad here, running between Akron and Chicago. Probably as many as five hundred people lived here once, but after World War II, a lot of railroad lines consolidated and little railways were shut down. The loss of the railroad killed the town. People started moving away, and finally there weren't enough left to keep the church going. A lot of my kinfolk are buried in the cemetery across the road, and some of my neighbors asked me to keep up the building and grounds. Not much else I can do anymore."

"Tell us about the stained-glass window," Marie said. "It doesn't fit with the plain architecture of the rest of the building."

"This town was named for a railroad man, Addison Bexter. He donated the window as a memorial to his parents. Because of the way Jesus is cradling the lamb in His arms, the members called their meeting house the Sheltering Arms Church. There's a little plaque on the window—you can read it in the morning."

While Les had talked, Marie had leaned her head on Eric's shoulder. When she yawned noisily, Eric laughed and said, "I think my wife is ready for bed, such as it is."

Favoring his stiff knees, Les peered out the window. "It's almost stopped snowing, but the wind's still gusty."

Quinn peered over Les's shoulder. "Looks like a good two feet of snow, wouldn't you say?"

"At least that much," Les agreed. "It's let up, but there's bound to be some drifting."

As if to reinforce his words, a gust of wind rattled the windowpanes. The gust gave way to a shrill screech that whirled around the church, making goose bumps break out on Livia's body.

"The rest of you get what sleep you can," Les said. "I'll stay up and keep the fire going. It's kinda cozy in here now, but when the temperature drops outside, it'll get colder."

"It isn't fair for you to shoulder all the responsibility," Livia objected. "I know how to stoke a fire. We're in this together. I'll take my turn."

"So will I," Quinn said.

When all of the castaways insisted that they wanted to help out, Eric said, "Let's divide into four groups of two and keep watch." He looked at his watch. "It's nine o'clock now, and it won't be daylight until seven. That's ten hours, which we can divide into two-and-a-half-hour segments. Even if she is sleepy, Marie and I will take the first shift."

"I'll watch with Sean," Roxanne said, with a fond glance at the basketball star. "I'll keep him awake."

Les looked at the truck driver. "We'd probably make a good team," he said. Allen nodded his agreement.

"Then that leaves Olivia and me," Quinn said, and experienced a quickening of his heartbeat. He darted a questioning glance at her. "Is that okay?"

It definitely wasn't okay, but what could she say?

How could she spend over two hours with a man for whom she'd harbored bitter thoughts for three years? She'd finally gotten to the point where she'd put her crush on Quinn behind her. Why had he entered her life again?

Unwilling to allow him to think that his presence bothered her, she met his eyes directly for the first time. "Of course," she said.

Perhaps these solitary hours with Quinn would erase her bitter memories and pave the way so they could become friends again.

With twenty pews at their disposal, preparations for bed were simple. They'd gathered several blankets from their vehicles, so the people who were sleeping, or trying to, could each have a covering. As cold as the room was when they moved a few feet from the stove, no one considered removing their bulky outerwear.

Since the snow had accumulated several more inches, Quinn and Allen cleared the paths to the woodshed and the johnny houses again. Eric and Les carried in more fuel to last through the night.

The trip to the outside necessary was an experience Livia would never forget. Life on the farm, and summer camping events, had prepared her for rough living, but nothing she'd experienced could prepare her for this jaunt when the wind was blowing forty miles per hour and the snow was two feet deep.

Hustling toward the necessary, Livia felt like she was in a tunnel, because the shoveled snow was heaped high on both sides of the path. The tunnel provided plenty of privacy, and Roxanne carried a large battery-driven spotlight that Quinn had brought from his truck. Despite their discomfort and unfamiliarity with this rugged substitute for plumbing, Marie and Roxanne, teeth chattering, giggled about the experience as they waited their turn in the one-person accommodation.

When all eight of them were back in the church building, Quinn warned, "Don't anyone go out alone tonight for any reason. If someone slips and falls, without any help, it could be fatal."

Preparing for the first watch, Eric and Marie cuddled under a blanket on a pew close to the stove. Livia extinguished all of the candles except two. Since they didn't know how long they'd be snowbound, they needed to conserve their small stock of candles.

Quinn and Livia were scheduled for the two o'clock shift.

Worried about being away from home and frustrated over this chance meeting with Quinn, Livia wondered if she would get any rest. Unwelcome thoughts scampered wildly through her mind. She knew that she was in for a long night of soul-searching.

Sitting on a front pew, Livia focused her attention on the stained-glass window, barely visible in the dim light. It was her custom to read the Bible and pray before she went to sleep at night. Since there wasn't enough light for her to read, she was thankful for the Scriptures that she'd memorized. Inspired by the picture of Jesus holding a lamb in His arms, she remembered the Twenty-Third Psalm, which she'd learned as a child.

"'The Lord is my Shepherd I shall not want,'" she whispered, and meditated on the rest of the psalm. She repeated quietly the verse that seemed to be the most pertinent tonight.

"'Yea, though I walk through the valley of the shadow of death, I will fear no evil: for Thou art with me; Thy rod and Thy staff they comfort me.'"

Perhaps at no other time in her life had it been necessary for her to put this promise to the test. Her life up until now had been relatively carefree. Except for her secret liking for Quinn, never before had Livia encountered any crisis when she didn't have her family to lean on.

Fortunately, their lives weren't at risk, but their situation would have been dire if God hadn't directed them along this isolated road to the Sheltering Arms Church. If they'd stayed on the interstate, they might easily have been in a deadly accident. Livia believed when anyone was wholly committed to the will of God, He directed that person's daily walk. In spite of her sorrow at missing Christmas with her family, Livia's uneasiness lessened. Whatever His reason, she believed that she was in the place God wanted her to be tonight.

Kneeling, Livia rested her head on the pew, finding comfort in being in a place where people had worshiped long ago.

God, thanks for Your protection on this stormy night. I pray that You will give my parents peace of mind. I know they are worried about me. I'm thankful

*for this opportunity to witness Your love and goodness
with my dear friends, and the ones I've met tonight
for the first time. And about Quinn, Lord? When no
other man has ever been able to replace him in my
heart, does that mean he's the one You've meant for
me all along? Is that the reason we're snowbound?
Whatever the outcome, Lord, I praise You for Your
watchful eye, yesterday, today and forever. Amen.*

Livia was warm enough in her heavy clothes, so
instead of wrapping in the blanket, she folded it under
her head as a pillow. She didn't remove her boots
when she stretched out on the hard pew. She wasn't
a large person, but the only way she found any comfort was by turning on her left side and curling up in
a fetal position. Sleepily, she wondered how anyone
the size of Quinn or Allen Reynolds could find rest
on these narrow benches.

Livia felt as if she'd just gone to sleep when Quinn
touched her shoulder. Stiff from lying on the wooden
bench, and tense from drifting in and out of sleep for
the past several hours, Livia could hardly move. She
struggled to a sitting position, rubbed her eyes and
moved quietly to sit on the bench beside the stove,
which Les and Allen were now vacating.

Les opened the door of the stove and laid several
chunks of coal and two sticks of wood on a glowing
bed of coals. "You probably won't have to do anything
for an hour," he whispered.

"We'll be fine," Livia assured him, keeping her
voice low so that she wouldn't disturb anyone who
was sleeping. "You rest and don't worry about us."

Livia propped her feet on a coal bucket because

the cold from the floor seeped through her boots. She tried to relax, although that was difficult, with Quinn sitting beside her, his shoulder touching hers. She unzipped her coat. Was it the heat from the stove, or Quinn's presence that caused the sudden flash of warmth?

Quinn hadn't been able to decipher Livia's feelings toward him. Was she angry because he'd ignored her advances when they'd been together before? Since he blamed himself for ending their relationship, it was up to him to apologize. Sensing that he'd hurt Olivia, he proceeded with caution.

Praying for the right words, he said, "I've often wondered what happened to you, Olivia."

She was tempted to answer that he knew where she lived, if he'd wanted to know so badly, but pride kept her from making the comment. Instead, she said, "You might as well call me Livia. Only my parents still use my full name."

"You've always been Olivia in my thoughts, but I'll try to change."

So, he hadn't forgotten everything!

Another long silence.

It seemed obvious that Livia wasn't going to speak, so what should he do now? Often, Quinn had wondered if he'd ever see her again, and a few times he'd considered looking her up, because he knew where she lived. But he'd always pushed aside the idea because he felt guilty about the past. Several years older than her, he should have been aware that Livia was developing a crush on him. But he'd never considered himself an irresistible man, and the thought of her being infatuated with him hadn't entered his mind.

"I've often wanted the chance to apologize for mishandling the situation between us. But you were quite a bit younger than I was, and I didn't—"

"Didn't think I was silly enough to fall in love with a man who hadn't given me any encouragement?" she interrupted bitterly.

"Oh, I'm sure it was only a crush," Quinn protested. "It couldn't have been love. You were just a kid."

"I was seventeen and old enough to know better. But, please, Quinn, that's a period of my life I'd prefer to forget. Consider yourself forgiven, if you think it's necessary, but I'd prefer not to talk about it."

"Then what can we talk about? If we just sit here and stare at the walls, time will pass mighty slowly."

"Let's talk about what we're doing now. I'm studying to be a veterinarian, too. I wanted to do something using my rural upbringing. My brother, Evan, is a county extension agent, and he also does some teaching at a nearby university. My sister is a high school teacher. I wasn't interested in teaching. But I love animals and I've worked with them all of my life. Being a veterinarian was my best choice."

"It isn't easy though, as I'm sure you're finding out."

"I know! I might as well have aspired to become a medical doctor, with all the science and other hard subjects I'm studying."

"After being in school for several years, I decided to stay on the farm for a while. Working as a farrier helps me keep up with my profession. I intend to set up my veterinarian practice in a few months."

Someone coughed, and Livia thought it was Sean. She hoped that this exposure to the severe weather didn't give him a cold. Inside the firebox, a large block of coal crumbled and the pungent smell of smoke permeated the room.

Since the wind seemed less blustery than it had earlier, she asked, "Is there any possibility we'll be rescued tomorrow?"

"I doubt it," Quinn said, with a quick glance toward her. Although Livia's features were shadowed in the dim light, the sadness mirrored on her face made her blue eyes appear almost black. "When we have bad snowstorms like this, the remote areas are always the last to get help. I hope I'm wrong, for your sake and for the others, but it could be several days before we see a snowplow."

"Doesn't it bother you to miss Christmas with your family?"

"Somewhat. But this isn't the first time I've been away from home on Christmas. I've gone skiing in Colorado with my friends several times over the Christmas holidays. My family doesn't go overboard in observing the holiday like a lot of families do. What special things does your family do at Christmas?"

As they talked, Livia realized that they were easily drifting into the close relationship they'd experienced before—a camaraderie that had turned into love on her part. Although the years had dimmed her emotions, she had no doubt that her feelings for Quinn hadn't been just a crush. He was her first, and only, love. Remembering that he'd said "not yet," when someone asked about his marital status probably indicated he was engaged or involved in a serious relationship. She had to guard her heart carefully to avoid reviving the love she'd once had for him.

Realizing that her mind had been wandering, Livia said quickly, "Our family has always had some unique ways to celebrate Christmas. I won't bore you with all the details."

"I won't be bored, I'm sure," he said.

"Mom prepares special, traditional family foods. Christmas Eve is a time for our immediate family, but on Christmas night, our aunts, uncles and cousins come to Heritage Farm, the ancestral home of the family. We sometimes have a hundred or more people. And we always go to church on Christmas Eve for a candlelight service. I'll probably miss that more than anything else."

Quinn stood, flexed his muscles, opened the stove door and replenished the fuel. The firelight glinted from his dark, curly hair as he moved his head. He held his hands out to the warmth of the stove.

"By daylight, we'll probably have a better idea of when we'll be rescued. If it's fairly obvious that it will be a few days, we should plan our own observance of Christmas. We have all we need to do that. Eric is a preacher, so he can prepare a sermon. Your friend, Roxanne, can play the piano, if it's still in good condition. Your group can sing. The rest of us will be the congregation."

Her eyes brightening, Livia said, "That's a wonderful idea! Preparing to celebrate will keep us busy, and we won't have time to feel sorry for ourselves because we're stranded."

When Roxanne and Sean started their shift, Livia went back to her hard, narrow bed with a lighter heart. Her mind was busy with the possibilities of observing Christmas and sleep still eluded her. Also, her thoughts focused on Quinn, and the wonder of seeing him again. She hadn't been mistaken in remembering him as a wonderful companion.

Livia particularly recalled the time when she and Quinn had taken a group of teenagers on a one-day canoeing expedition. A thunderstorm had come up, the creek had flooded, and they couldn't return to the camp. The twelve of them had spent a soggy, miserable night in the open, without tents or sleeping bags. The circumstances were similar to their present experience. And that time, like this one, Quinn was a bright presence for her.

On the other side of the church, Quinn also was awake. He'd recalled Livia as an energetic, fun-loving girl, but she was a woman now—an intriguing, exciting woman. How much had he missed by rebuffing her advances in the past? She'd been too young to make decisions about her future then. Still, if he'd handled the situation differently, if he'd talked to her about her crush and suggested that they remain friends, he could have kept in touch with her. That friendship might have developed into love by this time.

But since he'd discouraged her once, he had the feeling that Livia wouldn't accept if he tried to deepen their relationship now. It wasn't a matter of taking up where they'd left off, for that was apparently painful for Livia, but he definitely didn't want her to go out of his life again. Would these few days of isolation also convince Livia to start over again?

Chapter Four

Livia may have spent a more miserable night in her life, but when she turned on the narrow bench and rolled out on the floor, the night she'd just endured received high marks for misery. The sound of her fall sounded as loud as an earthquake in the church that had been silent all night, except for the noisy, penetrating wind scattering snow around their shelter.

Besides being embarrassed, Livia felt a pain in her knee. Her hope that she hadn't disturbed any of the others was dashed when Sean, who'd spent most of the night on the bench behind her, peered over the seat. His light brown hair looked as if he'd been running his fingers through it for hours. He was wide-awake.

Holding on to the seat and pulling up from the floor, Livia wrapped a blanket around herself and sat on the pew facing Sean.

"Did I wake you?"

"Are you kidding? I've spent a miserable night. I slept a little before Roxanne and I started our shift," Sean said wearily. "Les relieved us early, an hour

ago, but I haven't gone to sleep. Did you hurt yourself when you fell?"

"My knee stings a little, but it's no big deal."

Glancing around the room, she saw that some of
the others were seated in the pews or hovering around
the stove. Marie, a few seats back, caught Livia's eye,
and motioned outside. Livia shivered at the thought
of making a trip to the necessary, but she would welcome some fresh air. All night long, sporadic bursts
of wind had swept down the chimney, blowing smoke
into the room, making breathing difficult.

Livia cast the blanket aside, pulled on the heavy
coat she'd taken off during the night and picked up
her wool gloves. Marie and Roxanne waited by the
back door.

"One thing about sleeping in all your clothes, you
don't have to make a lot of preparation when you go
outdoors," Marie joked.

It took a lot to upset Marie, and Livia wished she
could be more like her. She couldn't stop worrying
about their situation, and her lack of faith in God's
providence annoyed her.

They met Quinn entering the supply room with
two buckets of fuel. His shoulders were covered with
snow.

"So it's still snowing," Livia said.

"Off and on," Quinn replied. "The worst problem
now is the drifting snow. I shoveled the paths clear
again, but the wind will no doubt fill them soon. Be
careful," he said as he stood aside to let them go out
the door.

"Wow!" Livia said as a blast of frigid air almost

took her breath away. When they left the shelter of the building, a wind surge staggered her.

"I wanted some fresh air, but this is a little too fresh." She snuggled deeper into her coat and pulled the collar over her mouth.

Marie stopped in front of her, her face showing her awe as she looked around their white world. The branches on several evergreens drooped under the weight of snow. Large mounds of snow covered shrubbery. A foot or more of snow lay on the roofs of the buildings. Livia had seen many heavy snowfalls and their aftermath in rural areas, but to Marie, who had lived in a big city all of her life, this was obviously a wondrous sight.

"The thing that impresses me the most," Marie said, "is the quietness. You know how it is in a city—we never have complete silence. But when the wind ceases for a short time, it's uncanny how quiet it is."

A brilliant cardinal whizzed past them and settled on a snow-laden branch, causing snowflakes to flutter to the ground. The red feathers of the bird stood out vividly against the white landscape.

"Oh, look," Roxanne said, pointing to the cardinal. "Our state bird in all its glory."

The ground beneath the low-spreading spruce tree was clear of snow, and a flock of chattering birds perched in the lower branches.

"If Allen has any bird feed in his truck," Livia said, "I'd like to buy some, and we can put some food out for the birds. This is a difficult time for them to find food."

The frigid wind and the swirling snow hastened

their outdoor stay. The church was empty when they returned, except for Eric, who was kneeling in prayer on the platform. The women huddled around the stove, holding out their hands for some heat.

Livia took her cell phone out of her pocket, but still no service was available. "I'll step outside and see if that will help," she said to the others.

She walked a few feet away from the church but couldn't use the phone. She waved to Sean and Quinn who were shoveling nearby. She hurried back to the semiwarm church and shook her head to Marie's questioning look.

"Livia, had you known Quinn before last night?" Marie asked, speaking quietly so as not to disturb her husband. "I sensed some sort of a spark between the two of you."

"It must have been a bright spark to last for three years," Livia tried to joke. "We met several years ago when both of us were on the staff of a 4-H camp. I hadn't seen or heard from him again until last night. It was a surprise to see him."

"Even if we have been singing together for over a year," Roxanne said, "we know so little about each other. I didn't know until last night that you were a farm girl."

Laughing lightly, Marie said, "I have a feeling that we'll know a lot about each other before we're rescued."

"Maybe even things we'd rather not know," her mother agreed.

"Let's try to prepare some breakfast," Livia said.

"My stomach is in the habit of having food three times a day."

His devotions finished, Eric joined them near the stove. He kissed Marie and said to Livia, "It's a habit you may have to break if we're here very long."

"Where are the rest of the men?" his wife asked.

"Allen and Les went to the truck to see if they could find some instant coffee. Les insists he can't function until he has his morning cup."

"So that's the reason for the pan of water on the stove," Livia said.

"Yes," Eric said. "Where he unearthed that old pot, I don't know, but he scrubbed it with snow until it was clean enough. He poured a couple of bottles of water in it."

"Good," Roxanne said. "I could use some coffee, too."

"It would be nice to have some hot water for washing," Marie said hopefully. "I don't want to wash my hands in snow."

Eric pointed to a carton of antibacterial hand wipes that Allen had brought in last night. "We'll have to make do with those. We can't risk using our bottled water for washing."

"What's Sean doing?" Roxanne asked.

"Quinn is teaching him how to shovel snow," Eric said with a lopsided grin. "They're cleaning off the steps and the porch. He's doing quite well for a guy from Southern California."

As if on cue, the door opened and Sean entered.

"I don't know how you people have survived over the years in this kind of weather," he said as he stomped his feet to remove the snow. "No wonder my family left the Midwest and moved to California. But why did my dad, who's an alumni of OSU, insist that I follow in his footsteps?"

Although Sean spoke in a light tone, Livia sympathized with him. He was suffering with the low temperatures more than the rest of them.

"Where's Quinn?" she asked.

"He went to his truck, while Allen and Les are down there. He and Les are very insistent that none of us should leave this building alone."

"Can you see the vehicles from here?" Marie asked.

"No. The visibility is less than ten feet. It isn't snowing right now, but the wind is whipping the feathery flakes until it looks like we're having another blizzard."

A smile graced Les's wrinkled face when he walked in a few minutes later. He held up a jar of ground coffee. "We had to hunt for a long time before we found it," he said. "Is the water hot?"

Roxanne laid an experimental finger on the side of the pan. "Warm, but not hot."

"I'll put another log or two on the fire," Les said. "I'm trying to be sparin' of the fuel. We might be here several days, and we don't want to run out, but I've got to have my coffee."

"A sausage biscuit would taste pretty good right now," Sean said. "Have you got one of those tucked away in your coat pocket?"

Although Les was friendly to everyone else, he seemed to dislike Sean, and he snapped, "No, city boy, you're gonna have to rough it like the rest of us."

Sean exchanged a quick glance with Roxanne and shrugged his shoulders. Livia knew Sean had been joking. In fact, under the circumstances, she thought the basketball player was adjusting quite well to the situation. She touched Sean's hand.

"He's one of those people who's grouchy before he has a cup of coffee," she whispered. "He'll probably be all right after we've eaten."

Sean responded by giving Livia a quick hug just as Quinn stepped into the door. Livia felt her face flushing as Quinn observed the gesture with obscure curiosity. Quinn's day-old stubble was frosted with snowflakes, and he looked unbelievably handsome to Livia.

She moved quickly away from Sean and joined Roxanne and Marie, who were examining the boxes of food the men had brought from the truck.

"Here are some individual boxes of cereal," Roxanne said. "We put the milk in the supply room, and it will be cold enough for us to use on our cereal." She set out a box of doughnuts.

"We have some juice in individual containers, too," Marie said. "We're fortunate to have this much."

"I started my truck and picked up a weather report on the radio," Quinn said. "I wish I had better news, but there's another round of snow coming this afternoon and twenty-below temperatures predicted for tonight."

The very thought caused cold chills to run up and down Livia's spine. The little church had been frigid *last* night, and that meant it would get worse.

"What about our chances of being rescued?" Eric asked, with a quick glance at his wife.

Quinn shook his head. "Several counties in this area are completely isolated. No rescue today, I'm sure."

"So not only will we be away from home on Christmas Eve and Christmas Day, we may not get out of here for several days," Allen said.

"Looks like," Quinn said.

"I wish there was some way to let my wife know I'm all right," Allen said. "But I suppose all of you have the same concern."

Quinn moved to Livia's side. "I'm sorry you can't get home," he said quietly.

"Yeah, me, too," she agreed. "But things could be a lot worse."

If she couldn't be at Heritage Farm for Christmas, she welcomed this time with Quinn.

"Have you said anything about our plans to celebrate Christmas?"

She shook her head. "Let's wait until they've had some breakfast. They might be more responsive to the idea then."

By the time they'd eaten their cereal and doughnuts, the water was hot enough for coffee. The coffee drinkers sipped on their favorite beverage from disposable cups, a sense of satisfaction on their faces. Marie and Livia didn't like coffee, so they drank juice.

They finished eating by nine o'clock, with a long day looming before them. The room was dim because the overcast skies kept the sun hidden. The candles had been extinguished to preserve them, as well as to improve the oxygen in the room.

In spite of heavy socks and boots, Livia's feet felt numb. She put her hand on the cold wooden floor, and knew that the heat from the stove would never warm it. The church was built only a few feet off the ground, and it was doubtful if there was any insulation underneath the building.

She went to her pack and found a comb. Even in the building, she'd kept the hood over her head most of the time. Her hair was knotted and twisted. She combed the tangles out as best she could, but wasn't making much progress when Sean sat down behind her and took the comb from her hand.

"Here, let me help," he said, "I have two younger sisters, and my mother always made me comb their hair. I got so good at it that I once considered becoming a barber." Perhaps comparing that occupation with the opportunity to become a professional basketball player, he laughed jovially. "Give me the comb and I'll be *your* big brother today." He worked gently with her hair until it flowed softly over her shoulders. When she turned toward the group near the stove, Quinn was looking at her. He turned his eyes away quickly. *What must he be thinking?*

Watching the shivering people circling the stove, Livia doubted that there'd be much interest in having a Christmas celebration. The others probably felt as miserable as she did, and she knew it would be tempting just to sit, stew and feel sorry for themselves.

Quinn raised questioning eyebrows to her, and she nodded. "You go ahead," she mouthed to him.

"Hey, folks," Quinn said. "Livia and I came up with an idea last night. Since it's pretty obvious that we can't get home for Christmas, we thought we should overcome our difficulties and celebrate Christmas here."

The other snowbound travelers looked around at each other. Seeing the dejection in their eyes, even if it wasn't necessarily showing in their facial expressions, Livia said, "Come on, everyone. Christmas is more than time spent with family. Let's make a stab at happiness. How many are willing to remember the true reason we celebrate Christmas?"

Chapter Five

Silence greeted Livia's question until Roxanne said, "Your suggestion makes sense, but I'm not sure I can get in the spirit of Christmas."

"Me, either," Sean said, and Les gave a derisive snort. Sean continued as if he hadn't heard Les. "Two days ago if anyone had told me that my most desired gift would be something as simple as a shower and a shave, I'd have thought they were crazy."

"Twon't hurt you none to go without a bath for a day or two," Les said, frowning at Sean, before he turned away. "I think you've got a good idea, Quinn." He looked around the church fondly. "It's been a long time since Christmas carols have been sung inside these walls. I kinda think the old church would welcome a Christmas Eve service."

With a shrewd glance from Sean to Les, Allen said, "Except for gifts and such, I don't know much about celebrating Christmas. However, I've learned a lot about human nature in my thirty-five years. If we sit around worrying about being cold, needing a bath, and being afraid we'll run out of food and fuel, we're going to get on each other's nerves. We'd better do *something*."

Since Eric was the only minister among them, all eyes turned to him. He stood and walked around the room. The others watched him, waiting for his decision. He lifted the lid of the upright piano and ran his fingers over the keys. Roxanne shuddered. Livia was amused that the out-of-tune piano grated on the pianist's nerves.

Eric stared at the stained-glass window. He stood behind the lectern, his hands on the dusty top.

"Until we're faced with a situation like this," he began, "we often forget the real meaning of Christmas and why we observe it." With a lopsided grin, he continued, "Standing in this pulpit brings out the preacher in me. I'm sure all of you know that the Bible doesn't say anything about celebrating the birth of Jesus. It's not His *birth,* but His death, burial and resurrection that holds the key to our salvation. We need to keep that truth foremost in our minds."

A strong blast of wind rattled the window frames. Sitting beside Sean, Livia felt him shiver.

"It was the fourth century before Christians started observing His birth, which coincided with a Roman pagan holiday, the Saturnalia, celebrated near the winter solstice. The exact date of the birth of Christ is uncertain, but by the Middle Ages, the twenty-fifth of December was generally accepted as Christmas Day."

"As I remember from Sunday school," Livia said, "early observances consisted mostly of feasting and merrymaking, a lot like the way people celebrate today."

Eric nodded. "At first, a few churches honored the nativity for one day. But during the Middle Ages, celebrations expanded to a week or two. During the Protestant Reformation, in the sixteenth century, Christmas *had* become a day of reveling more than a time of worship. The celebration was outlawed by many religious sects."

"That includes the Pilgrims and Puritans," Quinn added. "They didn't observe Christmas, but other Europeans brought the worship of Christmas to our shores. Since the Bible doesn't specifically tell us when and where, or even *if* we should observe the birth of Jesus, we can worship here as well as if we were in our own church buildings."

"As I said earlier," Eric continued, "I personally feel that God brought us together in this place for some specific reason. We can each observe the holiday in our own way, or we can join together in a unique experience that will bring us closer to the real meaning of Christmas and to each other. Are you with me?"

Everyone applauded, and Sean said, "How do we start?"

"I want to have a tree," Allen said. "I've always decorated the tree with my kids. As soon as it's light enough, I'll check outside and see if I can find anything that will serve as a tree."

"No reason you can't cut some branches off the evergreens in the cemetery," Les said. "We have to trim the trees every few years anyway."

"I've got a sewing kit in the van," Roxanne said. "If you've got any bags of popcorn in the truck, we can string that into a garland."

"I know there are some cranberries you can string with the corn," Allen said.

"Let's draw names like we did in elementary school," Livia said. "Surely, we can sort through our belongings and come up with eight gifts, even if some of the things are used. Maybe we can use whatever talents we have to give gifts that will help us remember this experience with fondness."

"I'm for that," Allen said. "I'm trying to deal with this situation positively. But I feel like an outsider. Five of you are friends. Les and I are kinda separated from the rest of you. I'm trying not to think of the negative things, like the damage to the truck and missing my family. But it's hard."

Eric stepped to Allen's side and put a brotherly arm around his broad shoulders. "My friend, we're all in this together. Don't feel shut out. Fortunately, I have my wife and mother-in-law with me. But I'm concerned about my parents, who'll be very worried about us. *We* know we're all right, but they don't. In many ways, they're going to have a worse holiday than we will. I've been praying that God will give our families peace of mind."

It seemed odd to see tears appear in Allen's eyes. His appearance suggested that he was the rugged he-man type, who wouldn't be daunted by any situation.

"Buddy," Les said, "I'm alone, too, but somehow when I'm in this old church, I feel a kinship with my loved ones who worshiped here, but who've gone on to a better place."

Perhaps considering that the conversation could turn negative, Eric said, "Shall we plan our worship service to end at midnight?"

"Good idea. We want to stay up as long as we can," Les agreed. "If we're movin' around, we won't feel the cold as much."

"While we've been talking," Quinn said, "I heard a helicopter flying over. It's probably the National Guard looked for stranded vehicles. We may have been spotted already. When we go out, we can clean the snow off the side of the church van, so the name can be seen by searchers. I've also been praying that God will reassure our families."

"I'm for making gifts for one another," Sean said. "I've got something in mind, but I doubt I can get it finished today. Let's wait until tomorrow morning to open our presents."

"I have some gifts in the truck I was taking home with me," Quinn said. "Under the circumstances, my family won't mind if I share them with you. If anyone can't think of a gift, you're welcome to anything I have."

"Don't forget to look for things in the supply room," Les said. "There might be something left from years gone by to make gifts or Christmas decorations. We used to have big Christmas programs here."

"Eric, while you plan a message," Roxanne said, "I'll see if I can get any music out of the piano. If not, we'll sing a capella."

"You might try the organ," Les suggested.

"I've already checked out the organ," Roxanne said with a laugh. "It's a pump organ. I've never tried to play one of them."

"No time like the present," Les said, as he picked up the fuel buckets and headed for the back door.

Roxanne sat on the circular organ stool, lifted the covering over the keys, and pulled out several of the regulating stops above the keyboard. Livia heard her giggling as she pumped up and down on the squeaking pedals, but her fingers picked out a melody that Livia recognized as "Silent Night."

"My boots keep sliding on these pedals. And if I forget to pump, I don't get any music," Roxanne said. "No wonder the pioneers were so hardy. This organ would make an excellent leg exerciser. But I think I'd better use the piano for tonight's service, even if it's not in tune."

"Mom," Marie said, "you know you can get music out of a washboard. It'll sound great."

And although the piano did sound out of tune to an experienced ear, in a short time, the strains of traditional Christmas music sounded through the room. Sean stood beside the piano, and he and Roxanne started singing the lyrics. The music lent a sense of gaiety to the stranded travelers, who went about their tasks humming or singing with them.

"Jingle bells, jingle bells, jingle all the way. Oh what fun it is to ride in a one-horse open sleigh," Livia sang as she rummaged in her purse for paper and pen.

Quinn came to the front pew and sat beside her. "Too bad we don't have a sleigh and the horse. We could get out of our predicament a little easier."

"We have a sleigh and plenty of horses on Heritage Farm," Livia said, finding it didn't hurt as much to talk about home when Quinn was beside her. "In fact, three years ago when my brother, Evan, brought his girlfriend, Wendy, home for a visit, they went to the Christmas Eve service in a sleigh that belonged to my grandfather. Evan and Wendy got married the following spring, and they have a little boy now."

"Someone to carry on the Kessler name then. I remember you told me about the family traditions when we met."

Livia's face flushed, and she recalled again the acute humiliation she'd lived with for years. It was time for her to stop dwelling on the negative. She must think about the good things of their past relationship rather than that last, embarrassing day.

"We've already learned that Derek has a mind of his own," she said. "He's a very strong-willed child, and he may start new family traditions, rather than carry on the old."

"Hey, Quinn," Les said when he came back with the fuel, "that extra blizzard last night brought six more inches of snow. Time to start shoveling."

Quinn groaned under his breath. "Les is a hard taskmaster. If he'd wait until the wind stops, we wouldn't have so much shoveling to do. And he shouldn't be shoveling snow at his age, but…to keep peace in our gathered family, I'll do what he says." He touched her shoulder, saying, "Keep your chin up."

The touch of his hand sent a ripple of excitement through her body.

Livia cut eight strips of paper from her notebook

and wrote the names of each of the travelers on one. What if she should get Quinn's name? For the past three years, she'd often seen gifts that she would have liked to buy for him, when shopping for friends and family.

She folded the slips of paper and dropped them into an offering tray that she found inside the lectern. She mixed the names and passed them around, then took the last paper. It was Sean's name, and she didn't know whether she was pleased or not. She would have liked an excuse to give Quinn a gift, but Sean would be more appreciative of the wool scarf she'd been knitting for her brother.

By noon, the sun was shining. The reflection on the snow was blinding, and no one dared go outside without sunglasses. Livia put hers on and stepped out on the little porch, enjoying a good look at their surroundings.

Quinn and Allen had finally persuaded Les to leave the shoveling to them, and they'd cleared an area around the front steps, as well as the area in the back where the woodshed and necessaries were located.

The landscape was awesome. Livia could see their vehicles about forty yards from the church. Across the road, a few headstones extending out of the snow marked the location of the cemetery. A large number of cedar and pine trees intermingled with the grave markers. The land was relatively flat with a few knolls toward the east.

The sun did nothing to warm the bone-chilling atmosphere. When Livia breathed deeply, the cold air nearly suffocated her. She zipped her coat high enough to cover the lower half of her face.

"We can get frostbite if we stay out too long," Quinn said quietly at her elbow. "I don't want to frighten our companions, but I'm more concerned now than I was before. We have only enough fuel to last two more days."

"That's why it's important to keep them focused on observing Christmas to get their minds off things. I keep thinking it could be so much worse."

"What's Allen doing in the cemetery?" Roxanne asked from her stance on the steps.

Livia hadn't noticed him because he was covered with snow and faded into the white landscape. Allen was cutting branches off of a cedar tree with a handsaw. Every movement of his hand dislodged a small avalanche of snow that landed on his shoulders.

"He's getting greenery for a Christmas tree," Quinn explained. "He found the saw in the woodshed. I'm going to the truck now. I have a gift that will be suitable for the person whose name I've drawn. I won't have to make anything."

"Don't stay out too long," Livia cautioned.

"I won't. My feet and hands are already cold."

He held open the door for Livia to enter the building. Their shoulders touched, their eyes met, and the sudden warmth in his gaze caused Livia to look away in confusion.

Chapter Six

Quinn closed the door and paused with his hand still holding the doorknob. An unfamiliar shiver of awareness seized his body. He knew a tense magnetism was kindling between him and Livia.

Stamping his feet to keep the circulation going, Quinn picked up a big stick that leaned against the church to use as a cane as he broke ground to his truck. When he'd been shopping two days ago for his family's gifts, he'd seen a music box with a twirling angel on top. As he'd listened to the song, "Angels We Have Heard on High," Quinn felt compelled to buy the gift, although he had no idea who he'd give it to. Now that he'd drawn Livia's name, it seemed the perfect gift for her. He'd had the music box gift-wrapped in the store, so all he had to do was put her name on it.

Quinn returned to the church in time to help Allen shape the three branches of cedar into the semblance of a tree. They used chunks of coal and wood to secure the branches in a discarded bucket they'd found in the woodshed. They wrapped the bucket in a red silk scarf that Livia provided.

Humming a Christmas tune, Marie strung the cranberries and popcorn into a garland. Les had found a box of old ornaments and some tinsel in the supply room, which Livia draped over their tree. She arranged one candle on each windowsill among some pieces of shrubbery not needed for the tree.

Laughing at their feeble efforts at making decorations, Marie said, "This just proves the old saying, 'poor people have poor ways, and lots of 'em.'"

Livia stood back to survey their handiwork. "Oh, I don't know," she said. "Our decorations are festive."

"To say the least," Marie said, with another laugh, and joined Sean and Roxanne, who were still practicing at the piano.

While the others had decorated, Eric wrapped up in a blanket and sat on a pew beneath the stained-glass window. He studied his Bible and took notes on his message for the evening service.

Food, such as it was, was set out on one of the pews, and throughout the day, people ate when they wanted to. No one seemed to have much of an appetite, but they were keeping busy, either making gifts or wrapping what they'd found in their belongings.

Eric and Quinn made another trip to the vehicles before dark to get a shopping bag of things Roxanne had bought in Detroit. She took out a package of wrapping paper and some tape. "You can all use this. I'll put it on a table in the supply room, and you can sneak in there to do your wrapping if you want to keep your presents secret."

Little by little, wrapped gifts appeared under the makeshift tree.

When the sun shone through the dirty windows of the church, Livia felt almost happy as she hurried to finish the scarf she was making for Sean. But as darkness approached, she accepted the fact that she would not be home for Christmas Day.

Her mother, Hilda, had always been the strong one of the family, the lodestar that kept her children close to home. But Hilda had also given her children freedom to be independent and make their own decisions. Livia could almost believe that she heard her mother's voice telling her to make the best of the situation.

Considering the ages of her companions, Livia realized that she was the youngest of the group, just as she always was at home. She'd rather liked being the baby of the Kessler family, but when Quinn had hinted that he hadn't pursued a relationship with her because he was older than she was, Livia would have welcomed adding a few years to her age.

When Allen brought in the bag of sunflower seeds that Livia asked him to bring, Quinn found an old can in the woodshed and filled it with the seeds. He took a shovel and went with Livia to the backyard. He scooped the snow from the ground under the evergreens, and Livia scattered the seed in several piles. Companionably, they stood shoulder to shoulder and watched the chickadees, cardinals, woodpeckers and sparrows hungrily dive into the black seeds.

"This is something else we share," Quinn said. "We have several bird feeders on our farm, and apparently you do also."

The more she was around Quinn, Livia realized that they did have a lot in common—their rural background being one of the most important.

"Yes, we feed the birds year-round, and we always have flocks of them."

When they returned to the building, Eric was questioning Les about the architecture of the church.

"There's a steeple on the church, so it must have had a bell at one time," Eric commented.

Les motioned toward a small square door in the ceiling. "It's still up there, but there ain't been a rope on it for a long time. It was a pretty-soundin' bell."

"Too bad we can't ring it," Eric said. "It would be a nice addition to our worship service tonight. Also, if we ring the bell, people living in the area might hear it and come to help us."

"That's a possibility, Eric," Quinn said. "I've got a twenty-foot rope in my pickup. And didn't I see a ladder in the woodshed, Les?"

"Yeah. It's kinda old and rickety, but I think we can use it."

With Les standing on the steps watching him, Quinn made another trip to his truck for the rope. Allen volunteered to climb the ladder and attach the rope. When he opened the trapdoor and stepped out on the timbers of the balcony, he shouted down to the others, "Let's hurry this up. It feels like the North Pole up here. We don't want to let a lot of cold air into the building."

Quinn tossed the rope up to him. Following Les's instructions on where to attach the rope to the bell, Allen soon dropped the rope through the small hole cut in the ceiling for that purpose. He closed the door and clambered down the ladder.

Handing the end of the rope to Les, Quinn said, "You do the honors, Les."

Holding the rope in his hand, Les hesitated. "I've been having second thoughts about ringing the bell. I should have told you to check the wooden structure, Allen. That bell weighs about a thousand pounds, and the timbers that hold it are old. I'm not sure how strong they are. If they give way and the bell falls through the ceiling, we'll not have a roof over our head. As the old sayin' goes, 'We'd be up the creek without a paddle.' We're gonna need all the protection we can get tonight."

"Don't ring it then, if that's the case," Eric said.

"I hate to throw cold water on the idea," Les said.

"I can go up and check out the timbers," Quinn said. "I should be able to tell if they're stable."

"That would be wise," Les agreed. "My old legs are too unsteady to climb the ladder, or I'd go. You're a muscular guy, Quinn, so watch where you step."

Fearful for Quinn, Livia said, "If it's so dangerous, maybe we shouldn't ring the bell."

He glanced her way. "It'll be all right," he assured her. "I've climbed around in barn lofts since I was a kid. This won't be much different."

Quinn's stomach was flat and his hips slender, but his shoulders were brawny. While his muscular physique stood him in good stead professionally when handling horses, cows and other large animals, Livia wondered if his shoulders were too wide to crawl through the trapdoor.

He set his right foot on the first rung. The old wooden ladder creaked under his weight, as it had under Allen's. Livia held her breath until Quinn climbed the ten feet and squeezed through the small opening. She heard his steps as he moved from rafter to rafter circling the bell tower.

Les stood under the opening, his eyes squinted tightly, trying to see what was going on.

"How does the wooden frame look?" he called.

On his hands and knees now, Quinn peered through the opening. "Solid as a rock," he assured Les. "But while I'm up here, I'll take a look at the flue and be sure it's all right. We don't want to risk a fire."

Quinn crawled carefully toward the flue, wishing he'd brought a flashlight. He ran his hands over the bricks, and while he felt some warmth, it wasn't more than would be expected after the stove had been burning for hours. Turning toward the ladder, he hit his head on a beam, his foot slipped off the rafter and he fell hard. Pain ran up his left leg as it plunged through the ceiling.

Lath and plaster fell on the group waiting below, and Livia stifled a cry as Quinn's leg, up to his knee, hung through the ceiling. Quickly, Allen climbed the ladder.

"Are you hurt, Quinn?" he called, sticking his head into the attic.

"Not much," Quinn gasped, "but I sure got a scare. I was afraid I'd come through the ceiling."

"Do you need any help?"

"I'll see if I can make it by myself," Quinn said. He wiggled backward, keenly aware of a sharp nail that tore the seat of his pants. He carefully pulled his leg out of the hole. He wiggled his foot, thankful that he didn't seem to have broken a bone. No doubt the heavy boots and socks he wore had prevented any serious damage.

"Allen, I'll crawl toward you, but before I come down, we'd better put something over that hole in the ceiling to keep the cold air out of the room. See if there's a board to cover it, or perhaps we can use one of our blankets."

Allen came down a few rungs on the ladder. "Eric, bring one of our blankets, so he can fill the hole."

Eric grabbed the first blanket he found and gave it to Allen, who in turn handed it to Quinn. Aware of the pain in his leg, and hoping he didn't have a serious injury, he crawled back to the hole and covered it.

Both Eric and Allen held the ladder as Quinn started down. When he put his weight on his left leg, a pain shot from his ankle to his hip, and he almost fell from the ladder. Gritting his teeth and holding tightly to each rung, he reached the floor without any further incident. He held Allen's arm as he walked to the nearest pew and sat down.

Alarmed by the pallor on his face, Livia hurried to him. "You've hurt your leg, haven't you?"

"'Fraid so," he admitted. "I shouldn't have been so clumsy."

She knelt beside him and started unlacing his boot. Sean joined her, and helped her pull off Quinn's boot and sock. His fingers moved quickly and gingerly over Quinn's cold foot and leg.

"Sean has had training with injuries like this,"

Livia explained. "It comes in handy in basketball training and during the games, too."

"I don't believe you have any broken bones," Sean said. "I think it's a sprain or an injured muscle. Try to stand and walk a little."

With his hand on Sean's shoulder, Quinn took several steps. "Is the pain bad?" Livia asked.

Quinn shook his head. "It's uncomfortable, but I'm sure I'll be all right. Sorry to cause such a commotion," he apologized to the others.

"I'll bet you stepped on the place where the stovepipe used to go through the ceiling," Les said. "The stovepipe went straight up then, but we decided to put a curved ell extension when we bought this new stove. We just patched the ceiling when we finished, and I forgot that place would be weak."

When Livia walked away, Quinn checked out the rip in his pants. Pointing to a pew on the other side of the aisle, Quinn quietly said to Allen, "There's a pair of jeans in my pack under that seat. Will you bring them? I tore my pants. I'll go to the supply room and change them."

Although Quinn tried to be nonchalant, the episode had embarrassed him. He didn't like to be the center of attention. But was it worth having ripped pants and a sore leg to witness Livia's obvious concern for him? Could he dare to hope that her anxiety indicated a kind feeling in her heart for him?

Chapter Seven

When her pulse stopped pounding from the trauma of Quinn's fall, Livia sat on the front pew and picked up her needlework. Quinn watched her, studying each feature of her face. Should he capitalize on her anxiety over his fall and try to lessen the tension between them?

More than a century of grime had accumulated in the attic, and as Quinn surveyed his hands, it looked as if most of it had rubbed off on him. He cleaned his hands with several hand wipes before he changed his pants. When he came from the supply room, he looked around for Livia.

He limped toward her. "May I join you?" he said. "Everyone is determined to treat me like an invalid and won't let me work. Eric and Allen are bringing in the fuel, and Sean is shoveling the drifted snow. I think we could make a country boy out of him if we tried."

Quinn was concerned about some of the gestures he'd noticed between Sean and Livia. Sean was close to her age, and so likeable that Quinn wouldn't blame any girl for choosing him.

She moved the basket of yarn from the seat, and critically examined the stitches she'd made, She found it difficult to ply the needle in and out of the yarn because her fingers were cold.

"Sit down. This gift isn't for you, so you can watch if you like."

He sat beside her and stretched out his left leg. He watched her long, sensitive fingers as she wielded the metal crochet hook through the red wool yarn.

"I was making this for my brother," Livia said, interrupting his thoughts, "but since I drew Sean's name, I'm finishing it for his gift. Evan won't mind. I've made him several scarves."

"Does Evan manage Heritage Farm?" he asked.

"Daddy and Evan are in partnership. Daddy does most of the managing, but he's semiretired. Evan and his family live on the farm. He also has a full-time job as county extension agent, so he's very busy. His wife, Wendy, has a teaching degree. She taught school for two years, but she decided to become a stay-at-home mom when Derek was born. Wendy's maternal grandparents came to spend Christmas with her, but they couldn't stay long. I hope I don't miss seeing them."

"You invited me once to visit Heritage Farm. I'm sorry I didn't make it."

Livia hesitated, not knowing what to say. She double-crocheted a few inches, made a turn, and started the last row on the scarf.

"You'd be welcome anytime. It's a good farm with

fertile river land and some hill acreage. You'd like my family, I'm sure."

"I'll take you up on that invitation before long. I hope we can stay in touch now. If you'll give me your telephone number, I can call you once in a while. And as far as that's concerned, it's not so far to Columbus that I couldn't drive in to see you occasionally."

His comment flustered Livia, and she concentrated on her needlework. She stretched out the scarf and decided it was long enough. To put on the finishing touches, she took a skein of white yarn from her basket to make a border of single crochet stitches around the whole scarf. Fortunately, she didn't need to count this simple stitch. Quinn's comments had disconcerted her, and she was tormented by confusing emotions when she sat so close to him.

Should she ask Quinn about his personal life? If he was romantically involved with someone else, she'd see to it that she wasn't at home when he visited Heritage Farm. She'd never told her family about her infatuation with Quinn, but it was hard to fool her family. Her mother had sensed something had happened at the camp, but had never asked. If they saw Quinn and her together, they would immediately know they were dating.

"When you introduced yourself last night," she said, and her fingers gripped the crochet hook tightly, "you said you weren't married *yet*. Does that mean you're intending to get married soon?"

She sure didn't want Quinn to bring his wife to Heritage Farm.

Quinn squirmed on the hard seat, conscious of the nail scratch he'd gotten in the attic.

"No, I'm not. I've been dating a neighbor I grew up with, but we're not serious. Mostly, we're just friends."

She didn't answer, seemingly concentrating on her crocheting, but her mind was whirling.

"What about you?" he asked. "I've noticed a closeness between you and Sean."

She stared at him, complete surprise on her face. "Sean! We're friends—nothing more. He has too much on his plate keeping in shape for basketball and maintaining good grades to be interested in girls. Not that a lot of women wouldn't welcome his attention."

"Including you," Quinn persisted.

Livia crocheted several more stitches, her mind spinning with bewilderment. Could he possibly be jealous of Sean? The thought was heartening.

She shook her head, repeating, "Sean and I are friends. I haven't dated since I was in high school."

"Why?"

She shrugged one shoulder and managed to say casually, "I haven't met anyone I wanted to date."

He laughed slightly. "That a good reason, I suppose."

He stood cautiously, and she believed he was hurt more than he'd admit. "I won't bother you anymore so you can finish your work."

She let him go without further comment.

Roxanne had humorously appointed herself as the chef, and she asked Allen to bring a case of canned vegetable soup from his truck.

"Every time I see how much eight people can eat,"

she said to Livia, "I'm thankful for that truckload of food. Those few snacks we had in the car wouldn't have lasted long."

Les contributed a large pan that he was taking as a gift to his daughter, and they opened ten cans of the soup and dumped it into the pan. It took more than an hour before the soup was edible, and then it was only lukewarm.

The soup, along with cheese, bread, crackers, apples and cookies, sated their hunger temporarily. Livia had never been a big eater, but she knew she would be hungry before morning. They had divided the soup into eight equal shares, and she figured it did little to appease the appetites of Quinn and Allen, both big men, who would obviously require more food than the others.

The little church, with the smell of smoke and food aromas, seemed oppressive for a moment to Livia, and she wanted to be alone. She opened the door and stepped out on the porch. A quarter-moon shed a soft silvery radiance over the little valley where they were marooned.

Although the exact date of Jesus' birth was unknown, it was not inconceivable to believe that He was born on such a night as this. It took only a few minutes for the intense cold to seep through her clothes, and Livia hurried back inside. Quinn slanted a questioning, concerned glance toward her. His gray eyes held hers until she nodded that she was all right.

In preparation for the worship service, Marie and Livia lit the candles in the windows and set another candle on the piano to give Roxanne enough light to find the right keys. The men pulled the piano close to the stove.

"We have our quintet music in the van," Roxanne said, "but it's a difficult arrangement, and I can't see well enough to read the notes. All of us will sing traditional carols, which I can play without music. There are hymnals in the pews, and you can use those if you don't remember the words. Sean will solo 'O Holy Night' at the end of our service."

They all hovered as near the stove as they could when Eric started the service.

"My friends," he said, "I'll ask you first of all to recall a Christmas of the past that's still vivid in your memory."

Livia didn't even have to take a second thought. It was the one they were without electric power several days before Christmas. It was the same year Wendy came to meet the Kessler family. At first, they'd thought it was a disaster to be without electricity. But the days without modern conveniences had drawn them closer together than if circumstances had been normal. Livia thought the same thing was happening in this little forsaken church tonight.

"I can tell by some of your expressions," Eric continued, "that you're having difficulty recalling any specific Christmas that stands out in your memory. Most of my Christmases have been the same. But it goes without saying that this Christmas will never be forgotten. Every year, we'll remember what happened here tonight. We'll talk of it to our children and grandchildren, and they will in turn pass the story on to their families. So it's important that we remember, not only the hardships we endured, and the fellowship we have, but also that we commemorated the birth of Jesus."

Eric prayed, and then he turned to Roxanne.

"Go ahead with your music."

As cold as it was in the room, Livia wondered how Roxanne could play the piano. She wore a pair of thin leather gloves, but they would provide little warmth against the cold black and white keys.

Roxanne's fingers did stumble a little. Livia noticed that she hit several wrong notes, which seldom happened, but the music seemed more beautiful to Livia than when she listened to Roxanne play the Steinway Grand in their church sanctuary. They moved from one well-known carol to another, most of them singing from memory because the candlelight was dim.

More than ever before, Livia envisioned the actual events of the birth of Christ, as Eric read from the second chapter of Luke.

"'And Joseph also went up from Galilee, out of the city of Nazareth, into Judæa, unto the city of David, which is called Bethlehem; to be taxed with Mary his espoused wife, being great with child. And so it was, that, while they were there, the days were accomplished that she should be delivered. And she brought forth her firstborn son, and wrapped Him in swaddling clothes, and laid Him in a manger; because there was no room for them in the inn.'"

Mary would have endured the same pain that any other mother would experience during the birth of her son. Compared to present-day hospital conditions, the Son of God had come into the world under dismal circumstances. But, since He was God in the *flesh,* it was fitting for His birth to be a natural one.

As Eric continued reading the account of Jesus' birth, Livia imagined herself walking with the shepherds as they left the fields and hurried to the stable to see the Christ Child. Tonight, when they were worshiping in a cold, abandoned building, she fully comprehended the pathetic conditions surrounding Joseph and Mary, and their newborn child.

"The focus of my message tonight is based on a verse in the fourth chapter of Galatians," Eric said, interrupting her thoughts. He then read out, "'But when the fullness of the time was come, God sent forth His Son, made of a woman, made under the law.'"

"The Jews had been watching centuries for the promised Messiah," Eric said, "and some had given up hope of His coming. Although men had despaired of His arrival, Jesus came to earth at the *right* time, the *best* time.

"I pray that tonight's message will make a lasting impression on all of us. Always remember that when God does a work in our lives, it's at the *best* time for us."

A candle in one of the windows tipped over, and Quinn moved quickly to extinguish it before the greenery caught fire. Everyone was conscious of the need to prevent a fire tonight. Eric paused until he returned.

"I don't know where some of you are in your walk with God, but if you feel comfortable in doing so, please kneel with me to worship the newborn King.

Each time we worship Jesus, He's born again in our hearts. While we're kneeling, Sean will close our service by singing, 'O Holy Night.'"

When she slid to her knees, Livia realized that Quinn was kneeling beside her. It seemed natural for them to clasp hands.

Before he sang, Sean said, "Although I thought I really wanted to be home in California tonight, I've realized that there's no place I'd rather be than where I am. I've never understood before what the shepherds must have experienced as they knelt before the infant Jesus. I feel sure that the rest of my life, each Christmas Eve, my heart and my thoughts will return to this place."

Livia felt the same way, and the way Quinn squeezed her hand, she knew his thoughts were in harmony with hers.

Singing without musical accompaniment, Sean's strong tenor voice sounded loud and clear in the quiet of the little sanctuary. The only other sound was the popping of coals in the stove.

As he sang the words of the second stanza, Livia's heart sang with him.

"With humble hearts we bow in adoration before this Child, gift of God's matchless love. Sent from on high to purchase our salvation—that we might dwell with him ever above."

When the last strains of the music ceased, a hush fell over the room.

When they stood, Eric said, "Again, don't feel uncomfortable or obligated if it this isn't natural for you, but in our church, we always give hugs of fellowship." He turned to Sean. They embraced and thumped one another on their backs. Livia quivered at Quinn's nearness, wanting him to embrace her, but hardly daring to hope that he would.

"May I?" he asked quietly.

Livia had often fantasized about what it would be like to be held in Quinn's arms. Her body trembled when he pulled her close, and she locked her arms momentarily around his waist.

Quinn sensed that she was trembling, and he wondered if the cold had caused her to shake, or if she also experienced the exhilarating sensations he felt. Uncertain of Livia's feelings, he didn't tighten the embrace as he wanted to do.

Exercising a lot of willpower, Livia removed herself from Quinn's arms and moved to hug the members of her church. Allen and Les were obviously ill at ease with being hugged, though they didn't invite nor rebuff the fellowship gesture.

"Since we're sure that the bell is stable now, how about ringing it to acknowledge the birth of our Savior?" Les said. "I doubt anyone will hear it except us, but we ought to have bells of some kind ringing."

"I keep thinking how God sent angels to the shepherds to tell them the good news of Jesus' birth and where to find Him," Quinn said. "Maybe God will use the ringing bell as a message to people in this area that someone is stranded in the church. By the way, how far is it to nearest house?"

"Oh, no more than five miles," Les answered. "Actually, it's only seven or eight miles west, as the crow flies, to the main highway."

"As clear and still as it is now, the sound of that bell should carry well," Eric said. "Give it a try, Les, and we'll see what it sounds like."

"Stand back, just in case," Les said as he positioned himself under the bell tower and tugged on the rope. The swaying of the bell shook the ceiling, and Livia held her breath, fearing that the bell might fall through the roof.

After a half dozen or so tugs on the rope, the mellow tone of the old bell resounded loud and clear through the church.

"Sounds just like old times," Les said, when he handed the rope to Quinn. "Give it a tug or two, buddy. It's hard pullin' and takes my wind."

As Quinn continue to ring the bell, Roxanne said, "Doesn't it sound beautiful! It's what we needed to bring our worship to a close."

"We should ring it at intervals tomorrow," Quinn said as he let go of the rope. "That bell may bring us some rescuers."

"Since we're running low on fuel," Les said, "I'm thinkin' we'd better bank the fire tonight while we're asleep. We can wrap in blankets and stay warm."

"I've got an idea that might keep us warmer," Quinn said. "Why don't we put the seats of these pews together and two of us sleep side by side? Body heat will make all of us more comfortable. Eric and Marie can share a set of pews. Livia and Roxanne could sleep together. Sean and I could pair up, as could Allen and Les. It's just an idea, so no one should feel forced to participate."

"I'd rather be where I can check the stove once in

a while," Les said. "I won't disturb anyone if I'm by myself."

"I'll stretch out close to you," Allen said, "so you can call if you need help."

But the rest of them agreed that they'd like some extra warmth. When Livia lay back-to-back with Roxanne, she was more comfortable than the night before. Wedged together as the seats were, there wasn't any danger of falling out of bed as she'd done last night.

Although she was physically and mentally tired, Livia's mind was too busy to go to sleep. The pain of being separated from her family during one of the special times of the year was a blow to her. Still, she was pleased to spend this Christmas season with Quinn. Perhaps she'd read more into his embrace than she should have, but she sensed his feelings toward her in that brief hug went beyond the spiritual regard of one believer to another. If she'd had to choose between being at Heritage Farm tonight or in this abandoned church building with Quinn, which one would she have chosen? She really didn't know. Perhaps God had spared her the choice.

Livia did sleep finally, but her slumbers were fitful. She was aware every time that Les slipped out of his blankets and checked the stove. But she knew that the elderly man slept some because he snored intermittently.

Roxanne was a good sleeping partner, because she seldom moved during the night, and her deep, even breathing, whether asleep or awake, comforted Livia. She woke up when the dawning of the day filtered some light into the building. Her face felt frigid. If Les or Quinn didn't stir the fire soon, she intended to.

Trying not to wake Roxanne, Livia sat up. She peered over the back of the pew and saw Allen sitting up in bed. Les's blankets were empty.

When Allen saw that she was awake, he lifted his hand in greeting. Quinn's head appeared over the top of the pew where he'd spent the night with Sean beside him. He looked toward Livia, and quietly mouthed the words, "Merry Christmas."

"You, too," she whispered back.

Allen walked over to Quinn. Whispering, he said, "Quinn, I'm worried about Les. I woke up an hour ago, and he was gone. I figured he'd gone out for fuel, and I dropped back to sleep. He's still not here. Shouldn't we look for him?"

Chapter Eight

"How long has it been daylight?" Quinn asked, throwing back the blanket and vaulting out of the seat.

"I don't know," Allen answered. "My watch says eight o'clock. I peeked outside, and it feels a lot warmer, but we're fogged in. Kind of a strange weather phenomenon, I think."

Quinn had awakened Sean when he'd gotten up. "What's wrong?" Sean asked.

Quinn explained quietly.

"What are you going to do?" Sean said, yawning and standing up.

"I'm going to find him. It's dangerous for anyone to be out in this weather for very long."

"I'll go with you," Sean said. "I've had all of this church pew I can stand."

"It *would* be safer if two of us go," Quinn said.

"Quinn," Allen protested, "I'll go with Sean. I see you're still favoring that leg."

"It needs to be limbered up," Quinn said. He put on the heavy coat he'd shed before trying to sleep and limped toward the door. After taking a quick glance outside, he said, "Apparently there's a warm front moving in from the south. A man could easily get disoriented in this thick fog. Only two of us should go out at a time. Sean and I can go first. We'll look around in the back first."

"I can do that myself," Sean said, as he shrugged into his fleece-lined coat, zipped it up to cover the lower half of his face and tied the hood securely.

"We should stay together, because we can easily get separated in this fog," Quinn said. "I'll go with you."

"You'd better take a light," Allen said. "And here's a piece of rope that we had left from fixing the bell yesterday. It wouldn't be a bad idea to tie it around your waists. That fog is so thick, you won't be able to see one hand in front of the other."

Believing it was sound advice, Quinn secured the rope around his waist, and handed the other end to Sean. Six feet of rope separated them, allowing them freedom of movement.

They covered the back area where the woodshed and johnny houses were, but they didn't see any sign of Les.

"I don't believe he's been out here," Sean said. "The wind has covered our tracks from last night, and there aren't any new tracks in the snow."

"I agree," Quinn said. "So that means he went out the front door. Fortunately, it's not as cold as it was at midnight, but the temperature is still below freezing. We must find him as soon as possible."

When they went back inside, everyone was up.

Marie still sat in the pew she'd shared with her husband, her eyes befuddled with sleep.

"No sign that he's been in the backyard," Quinn reported. "We'll go out front and see what we can find."

"I'll help look, too," Eric volunteered.

Quinn shook his head. "No, only two of us at a time. I can't believe an old-timer like Les would slip away like this. He can't have gone far, but let's do this in shifts. When Sean and I get tired, we'll come back, and you and Allen can go. It might be a good idea for you to ring the church bell every fifteen minutes—that way we can keep our bearings."

Livia walked to the door with them. When she saw the thick fog, she laid her hand on Quinn's shoulder. "Be careful," she said.

He covered her hand with his gloved fingers. "We'll be all right. I just hope that Les is."

All of them had grown fond of Les, and when the door closed behind Quinn and Sean, Eric said, "Let's pray for the safety of all three of them. And then build up the fire so they'll be more comfortable when they bring him back."

He took hold of Marie's and Roxanne's hands. Livia joined hands with Marie and reached for Allen's hand. With only a slight hesitation, he joined their prayer circle.

"Why don't you lead us in prayer, Livia?" Eric said.

"God," Livia prayed, "Your Word teaches that even a sparrow can't fall to the ground unless You are aware of it. We believe You know where Les is, even if we don't. Guide Quinn and Sean as they search for him—lead them in the right direction. Protect them, too, God. Reward them for their willingness to risk themselves for others. For what You have done and what You will do in this situation, we thank You. Amen."

Quinn took the lead when they stepped off the church's steps. They'd gone only a short distance when the building was lost to view. Because the fog hovered about a foot off the ground, it was possible to see where they walked.

"I see footprints in the snow," Sean said.

"Yes, and only one set, so they must be Les's. Looks like he's heading for the vehicles."

"We may be making a mountain out of a molehill. We'll probably find him sitting in his car."

"Let's hope," Quinn answered.

The steps led past the delivery truck and the Westside Community Church van and stopped at Les's car.

"The snow is brushed off the trunk," Sean said. "He must have come down here for something."

Studying the footprints intently, Quinn said, "That's probably true, but where do his tracks go from here? I still can't believe he'd go out alone, when he's been warning us to stay together."

They tramped around in the snow, checked drifts, and peered inside the car, but they didn't find Les.

"Oh, look," Sean said. "We walked over his tracks. He's heading back toward the church."

Giving the younger man a pleased look, Quinn said, "You may not be a country boy, Sean, but you've got good eyes. That's good tracking. The snow didn't drift in this area between his car and the church van, and our tracks are still there from when we got things yesterday. But I see now, there are fresher tracks that don't have any snow in them at all."

"I'm having a little trouble breathing," Sean said. "This fog is thick, and I seem to take in a mouthful of moist, arctic air every time I say anything."

"Then we'll talk only when necessary."

The tones of the church bell sounded across the snow, and Quinn turned toward the sound, knowing they were heading in the right direction. But when they neared the church, Les's tracks veered off to the right.

"He must have gone into the cemetery," Sean said, and they headed in that direction.

Huge drifts lay throughout the cemetery, but Les had circled most of them. At one place, he'd stumbled into a drift and had crawled out of it. They came to a gravestone, where the snow had been swept away. A bouquet of artificial red poinsettias had been laid at the base of the stone.

The inscription read Ray Holden. The birth and death dates indicated that the boy had died at eighteen.

"Must have been Les's grandson," Quinn commented.

A short distance away, they came to a plot beneath a tall spruce tree close to a woven-wire fence. Again the snow had been brushed away from several Holden stones. A spray of flowers leaned against the marker of Sarah Holden's grave.

"The age would be right for these to be Les's wife and his parents," Quinn said.

Covering his mouth with his hand to keep out the

cold air, Sean mumbled, "I suppose he wanted the flowers on their graves for Christmas Day, and preferred to mourn alone. He took a big risk, though."

"He didn't think he could get lost."

The church bell rang again.

Quinn and Sean exchanged worried glances because instead of turning toward the church, Les's steps led through a gap in the fence into a pasture.

"He must have gotten disoriented in the fog," Quinn said. "Are you up to going farther? Or shall we go back, rest up, and send the other guys out?"

Taking a deep breath, Sean said, "We'd better keep going on. If he's down, we need to find him as soon as possible."

The bell rang again, indicating they had walked fifteen more minutes. They found Les face down in a deep drift. He looked lifeless, and Quinn feared to touch him.

Sean turned troubled eyes toward Quinn, who knelt beside Les and touched his face. It was cold, but his body was warm beneath his coat. An erratic pulse beat in the man's forehead. Quinn shook his shoulder, and Les opened his eyes.

"I'm just tuckered out—lost my way in the fog," he mumbled.

Quinn and Sean took his arms and lifted Les to his feet.

"Think you can walk to the church?" Quinn asked.

"Of course I can," Les said, took one step and fell again.

"I'll carry him," Sean said.

"No, I can walk, I tell you," Les said testily in a

weak voice. Ignoring his comments, Sean knelt and easily picked him up.

Quinn checked to be sure the rope was still taut between them. "I'll go ahead and break trail," he said. Glancing over his shoulder at Sean, he asked with a slight grin on his face, "Were you a Boy Scout?"

"Yes. For about ten years. I guess it paid off today."

"Put me down, I can walk," Les said querulously, and he grumbled all the way to the church. "Treating me like I was an old man. I don't want to be carried."

"Hush," Sean said. "There comes a time when everyone needs to be carried. Stop squirming around— you're making my work harder."

The bell rang again, and Quinn breathed a silent prayer. They'd almost reached the church. When he could see the building, he called out a greeting, and the door opened immediately. He untied the rope from his waist to give Sean more freedom to carry Les into the building. They entered, and Sean lowered him to a sitting position on a church pew close to the stove.

Roxanne and Livia hurried to Les's side and removed his gloves, checking his fingers for frostbite. They were cold, but not blue.

"What about your feet?" Roxanne said.

"Not much feeling in them," Les admitted.

Allen knelt and removed Les's shoes and socks. Using a blanket they'd been warming, Allen wrapped Les's feet and propped them on a coal bucket so they'd be close to the stove.

"Why did you go out alone?" Allen scolded. "You know better than that. At least, you could have told us where you were going. We've been worried about you."

"If it hadn't warmed up, you could easily have died," Quinn said.

"I know, but I thought I could go out and be back in before any of you woke up. I would have, too, but that fog didn't come until I started into the graveyard. I couldn't see at all for a while, and I just got turned around. My feet's starting to sting, so I may pay for my folly by losing a toe or two."

Examining his feet, Sean said, "I don't think so."

"The water is heated," Allen said, "so you can have a cup of coffee. That should warm you up. Quinn, you and Sean had better have a cup, too."

Taking a swallow of the lukewarm coffee, Quinn said, "That bell really helped us. When neither Sean nor I had been in the cemetery before, we might have gotten lost just like Les. The snow had broken down the fence, and there wasn't anything to warn us not to go into that big pasture."

Eric went for more fuel, and he returned with one bucket of coal.

"I hate to be the bearer of more bad news," he said, "but there's only a few more buckets of coal left, and not a great deal of wood."

"But we'll be all right," Quinn said. "It's getting warmer outside, so we won't freeze although we may be uncomfortable."

His teeth still chattering, Les said, "If we have to, we'll tear down the woodshed and burn it. I can re-build it as soon as the weather clears up."

Even though Livia didn't like coffee, she drank a

cup, merely to have a warm beverage with the dry doughnuts she ate for breakfast. She was beginning to feel hungry now, because they'd not had much to eat for two days.

"Let's plan our Christmas dinner," she said. "Allen, can you think of anything else we can buy from your truck?"

"Preferably something that can be considered holiday food," Roxanne added.

"How about a canned ham?" Allen said. "And there's a case of canned sweet potatoes and some cranberry relish. Do I need to bring more bread? It's probably frozen by now, but I'll go get it."

"Before you go, I've got something to say," Les remarked. "I'm thankful to Quinn and Sean for rescuing me, especially Sean, for I ain't treated him very good."

"Oh, that's no problem," Sean answered easily. "I figured you thought I was a city kid."

"That's part of it. I did think you were a spoiled kid that didn't know much except basketball. But the real reason I didn't cotton to you was because you remind me of my grandson."

Quinn and Sean exchanged glances.

"He died when he was still a teenager, and I guess I kinda resented that you were here and he wasn't. This is the first Christmas without him, and I ain't come to terms with my grievin' yet. The reason I was traveling this way when the storm hit was to put some flowers on his grave. There's a better road to my daughter's house, but I just had a hankering to be with my loved ones that have passed on. I didn't know I'd cause any trouble by going to put the flowers on their graves. So, sonny, I'm sorry I've been mean to you. May the Lord forgive me for it."

Sean closed the distance between them in two long steps. He grasped Les's hands in his. "Don't blame yourself. I didn't make a good first impression because I don't like winter weather, and I was irritated that I couldn't go home."

"While we're in a confessing mood," Allen said, "I need to say something." He stood and walked around the room, and with his back toward them, he said, "Probably you've guessed that I don't have the same faith the rest of you do. I've not had much use for church people, and I wasn't keen on spending this time with you. But you've taught me that I've been wrong. Seeing the way you handled this change in your plans has taught me a thing or two."

Allen turned to face them, his expression serious and confused. "After the rest of you were sleeping last night, I lay awake doing a lot of thinking. I'm bewildered now, and I don't know where I'm going from here, but I do know I want to be like you people. I hope you'll pray for me."

"We're all praying people," Quinn said. "Give us your telephone number, so we can call and check on your spiritual progress to encourage you."

"I'll need all the help I can get."

"As I said last night, God had a purpose for bringing all of us together," Eric commented. "We're beginning to see the reasons. The future will probably tell us more," he added, with a speculative glance between Quinn and Livia.

"Wouldn't this be a good time to open our presents?" Marie said, to spare Livia the embarrassment that reflected in her eyes. "We should do that before we start to fix our food."

"Suits me," Eric said. "I'll do the honors and pass the gifts around. Let's open our gifts by age—oldest ones go first. We know lots of things about each other, so we might as well tell our ages. Is that okay with everyone?"

They soon sorted out their ages, so that Les was the first to open his gift, with Roxanne in second place. As the youngest in the group, Livia wouldn't open her gift until last.

Only two of the packages were professionally wrapped. The others showed the absence of expert handling.

Sorting through the eight gifts, Eric picked up a flat, loosely wrapped gift, which he handed to Les.

"To Les from Sean," he said.

Les threw a smile Sean's way. "As mean as I've been to you, hard to tell what this might be."

"I just wanted to show you I can do something else besides play basketball," Sean said, returning the smile.

"Oh, my," Les said when he tore the paper away. He held up a pen-and-ink drawing of the interior of the Sheltering Arms Church, focusing on the chancel—the way it must have looked in its heyday. The dirt and cracks had been removed from the windows, and the furniture and floor shone as if they were new, giving a splendor to the old building.

"Sonny, I'll treasure this all the days of my life. Thanks."

"Well, mother-in-law," Eric said. "You're next. 'To Roxanne from Lester.'"

Her gift was wrapped in a brown paper bag, and Roxanne took out a carved wooden dog. "So that's what you were making yesterday," Roxanne said. "Thank you so much. It looks like the little terrier I had when I was a child."

"I always did like to whittle," Les said, embarrassed.

"Allen," Eric said, "I had a gift for you—a pair of gloves that I've only worn a few times. But in light of what you've just told us, I'm going to give you something else."

He handed his Bible to Allen. "I've used this Bible for several years, and it's well-marked with my favorite verses. It's something I cherish, but I want you to have it with my blessings."

It seemed odd to see tears brighten Allen's eyes.

As the rest of the thoughtful gifts were passed to the recipients, it was difficult to remember that they were stranded travelers. Goodwill and love filled the old building as a few rays of sunshine brightened the room.

Roxanne had her daughter's name, and she gave her a set of pearls that she'd bought and had wrapped in Detroit. Marie gave Quinn a set of cologne and aftershave lotion that she'd bought for Eric. "Sorry, honey," she said to her husband, as Quinn unwrapped the gift.

Sean appreciated Livia's scarf, and immediately

tied it around his neck. "Wish I'd had this when we were on our rescue mission this morning," he said.

Livia received the last gift, and she'd already figured out that Quinn had pulled her name. Her hands moistened as she unwrapped the beautifully wrapped box that had obviously been bought before they'd been stranded. Whose gift was she getting?

The box contained a music box, with a twirling silver angel on top of the revolving base. With trembling hands, she wound the tape, placed the music box on the table and as the angel revolved slowly, the music of "Angels We Have Heard on High" swirled throughout the room.

Meeting Quinn's eyes briefly, Livia said with all the warmth she could muster, which wasn't much, "Thank you. It's a beautiful gift."

She wanted to say, "Did you buy this for the woman you've been dating? Because if you did, I don't want it."

She knew her thoughts were mean-spirited, because others had received gifts bought for someone else. But her heart was still vulnerable where Quinn was concerned, and she was unsure of herself.

And of Quinn's feelings.

Chapter Nine

By humming "Jingle Bells," and moving in time to the music, the stranded travelers created a festive air, as they heated the sweet potatoes on the stove and sliced the cold ham for sandwiches. As a surprise, Allen had brought two pumpkin pies and one cherry pie to top off the meal.

"As good a Christmas meal as I've ever had," Eric said, with an apologetic look toward Roxanne. "When we've eaten with you on Christmas Day, Mom, I've never really been hungry. I was hungry today."

Roxanne laughed at him. "No need for an apology. I agree with you."

They were sitting around, relaxing after the meal, when Quinn stood suddenly. "Do you hear what I hear?"

And Sean broke into the lyrics of a traditional song. "Do you see what I see?"

Quinn shook his head. "No, I'm serious. I hear a tractor."

They all rushed out on the porch as a huge tractor plowed to a noisy stop before the steps. A burly farmer, dressed in a red woolen coat with a knit cap pulled over his ears, jumped down from his enclosed cab.

"I thought there must be somebody stranded over here," he said. "I heard bells ringing in the night and thought Santa's Rudolph had a bell around his neck." He laughed heartily at his joke. "But I got to studying on it this morning, and I told my missus I'd better have a look-see."

The fog had lifted slightly, and he glanced toward the snowbound vehicles. "Looks like you had trouble. Anybody hurt in the accident?"

Recognizing the farmer, Quinn stepped forward.

"Why, Quinn Damron, what are you doing here?" the farmer exclaimed.

Quinn shook hands with him. To his companions, he said, "I've been to Mr. Dunlow's farm several times, doctoring his animals. He lives over near the interstate, so the bell carried a long way."

Briefly, Quinn explained what had happened to them, how they'd taken shelter in the church, and he introduced his companions. Quinn said, "Come inside, if you have time."

"I won't come in, but is there anything I can do for you? You got anything to eat?"

Quinn motioned to the upended truck. "We've had plenty of food, because that's a grocery truck. Depending on how long we'll be here, we may run out of fuel. Are the roads being plowed now?"

"Yes, the interstate is pretty well cleared, and if the

sun shines like they're predicting for the afternoon, there will be some thawing."

"Then we can last through the rest of today and to-night," Les said, stepping from behind Allen.

"Hi, there, Lester," Dunlow said. "How'd an old-timer like you get stranded in a snowstorm?"

Les shrugged his shoulders. "The best of us makes mistakes sometime, Dunlow, although in light of the fellowship we've been havin', I'm not sure this was a mistake."

"Well, you do look hale and hearty," Dunlow said. He reached in his tractor and pulled out a chain saw.

"I'll see to it that you're plowed out as soon as possible," the farmer said, "but there's no reason for you to be cold." He motioned to a dead tree along the roadbed, not far from the church. "I'll saw that tree up for you, and you won't run out of fuel."

More optimistic now that they knew rescue was near, they laughed and joked as they followed Dunlow to the tree. He quickly felled the tree and cut it into lengths that would fit the stove. The snowbound travelers carried the wood to the woodshed and several armfuls into the church, singing as they worked. The extra exertion made Livia feel warmer, and she was perspiring before the last chunk of wood was taken inside.

Before Dunlow climbed back on his tractor, he said, "We've been using our telephones right along, and soon's as I get back, I'll report your whereabouts to the state road workers. Do you want me to call your families and tell them you're all right?"

"That would be wonderful!" Livia exclaimed. "Our

families don't have any idea where we are, and I get no cell phone reception out here."

"My wife likes to talk on the phone, 'specially now that she's snowbound. You write down the telephone numbers and names. She'll notify your kin."

Livia got her notebook and wrote down the numbers as each one dictated.

"Just one call will do for the three of us," Roxanne said. "I'll give you the name of my sister."

The farmer absolutely refused to take the money they offered him for the long distance calls. "Nope. I'd be a miserly creature if I can't help my fellowmen once in a while without being paid for it."

Dunlow tucked the paper in his coat pocket, climbed back into the tractor cab and shouted above the noise of the engine, "Merry Christmas!"

He waved, and went roaring back the way he'd come. Knowing that their rescue was imminent, the group returned to the church building with a lighter heart.

Despite the warmer weather, when the sun went down, the building was cold, and they again took shifts keeping their sanctuary warm. A lot had changed since Quinn and Livia had sat together two nights ago. Although Livia was anxious to get home, she had mixed feelings about being rescued because she was enjoying her time with Quinn.

Although they'd sat silently for a long period, Quinn must have shared her thoughts, because he said, "Sounds as if this time tomorrow night, we'll be going on to our respective homes," Quinn said.

"Livia, it's been wonderful running into you again. Will we continue to see each other now?"

"Do you want to see me?" she asked.

"Well, of course," he said quickly. "I just said I'd enjoyed seeing you again."

"But you're dating someone."

"Yes, but we're really more like friends keeping each other company for dinners and things."

"Did you buy the music box for her?"

His green eyes widened in amazement. "No, I didn't. I bought her a gift, but it wasn't the music box."

"Then who did you buy it for?"

"You."

"Me! You didn't know you'd even see me!"

"No, I didn't know it, but God knew we'd be together for Christmas. I saw the music box in a jewelry store display case when I was shopping in the mall. I thought it was a beautiful thing. I bought it on impulse, not having any idea what I'd do with it. When I met you again and was fortunate enough to choose your name, I was sure the gift was meant for you."

Shamefaced, Livia said, "I'm sorry I jumped to the wrong conclusion. Thinking you'd bought it for someone else, spoiled the gift for me. I'll really treasure it now."

"Since we got started off on the wrong foot once before let's start over. I won't ask for any commitments now, but I'd like to see where this leads. God seems to have thrown us back together for a reason. Will you let me come and visit you at Heritage Farm? After that, I'll have my mother invite you to come to our home. Then if we still enjoy being together, it's an easy trip for me to drive to OSU every other weekend. Does that sound like a good plan to you?"

Livia didn't know why she hesitated. He was offering what she'd wanted for three years. Was she going to be foolish again and drive Quinn away from her forever?

"Yes, it does. I've always wanted you to see Heritage Farm and meet my family. Let's exchange phone numbers, and we'll arrange a weekend visit as soon as possible. I find it hard to forgive myself for the awkwardness of the past and our lost friendship."

He took her hand. "Don't be hard on yourself. I was at fault, too. Let's forget it."

"I'm not sure it's best to forget what happened. We need to learn from our mistakes. I don't want to go through again what I have for the past three years."

"These few days we've been together, and they seem like weeks, I've kept playing the 'What Might Have Been' game, wondering where we'd be today if we hadn't lost track of each other."

She looked at him, amazement on her face. "I've been doing the same thing," she said. "I've wondered if we'd still be seeing each other, or if a few months of dating would have shown us that we aren't compatible at all."

He shook his head. "I don't really believe that would have happened." He pulled her into the shelter of his arm, and kissed her forehead. "I've felt kinda sad when I've noticed how much Eric and Marie love each other, wondering how much I've missed by not continuing to see you."

Livia didn't answer, and he realized she was crying. Tears slowly found their way down her cheeks, and she swiped them away. He didn't think he should ask her why she was crying, but he wrapped his arms around her and rocked her gently back and forth.

Livia yielded to the driving sobs that shook her body as the tears washed away the rejection and unhappiness that had dominated her heart. In Quinn's arms, she put the indecisive period of her past behind her. Someday she would tell Quinn how she felt, but not tonight. All she wanted now was to continue to enjoy the security of his arms.

When she quieted, with a tender hand, Quinn lifted her face. Tears still trembled on her eyelids, and he wiped them away. Quinn's lips caressed hers tenderly until he realized that Livia was responding. His lips were warm and sweet on hers, and Livia knew that today marked a new beginning for them.

After the interlude with Quinn, Livia thought she would sleep, but the pews she occupied with Roxanne seemed harder than the night before. How easy it had been, in Quinn's arms, to put the past behind her and bury the disappointments and embarrassments which had made her miserable for years.

She realized now that her faith had been weak, or she wouldn't have let one bitter incident distress her for so long. Her parents had taught their children from infancy that God had a plan for each individual's life. To find true happiness, one had to submit *personal* will to *God's* will. She hadn't done that. She had made up her mind three years ago that she wanted Quinn, and instead of waiting for God's timing in the matter, she'd planned her own agenda to get him.

Now she fully understood it had been God's will all along for her and Quinn to be together. Considering her immaturity at age seventeen, if she had started dating Quinn, their relationship probably wouldn't have lasted. Eight years difference in age now didn't seem nearly as much as it had been when they'd first met.

What would her parents think when she sprung Quinn on them suddenly? She'd never mentioned him to any of her family, although she'd often wanted to confide in her brother. But her ego had been so wounded that, like an old dog, she had crawled off by herself to lick her wounds. Probably her mother had known all along that something was bothering her youngest daughter, but Hilda Kessler was a wise woman. She'd raised her children to be self-reliant, and she hadn't pried into her daughter's emotional problems.

God, forgive me, for not trusting You to guide my life. I'm grateful that You brought Quinn back into my life. I won't try to outrun You again. You lead the way—I'll be happy to follow.

Livia sensed a marked difference in the attitude of her companions when she woke up the next morning and stepped stiffly off of the church pew. For one thing, the sun was shining, which seemed to add to their hope that they would be rescued before the day was over.

They grouped around the stove for breakfast, and

Marie must have echoed all of their thoughts. As she chewed halfheartedly on a cold doughnut, she said, "I hope the Lord will forgive me for an ungrateful attitude, but once we get out of this predicament, I don't think I'll ever eat another doughnut."

Her comment brought a universal laugh from her companions.

"The same thought was rolling through my mind," Sean said, "but I've complained so much, I decided to keep my mouth shut for once."

"Matter of fact," Les said with a mischievous grin, "I never did like store-bought doughnuts. My missus used to make doughnuts that would melt in your mouth. I'd sure like to take a bite of one of them."

"Please," Sean said, "don't talk about home-cooked food. My mouth had been watering two days for a large slab of turkey, mashed potatoes, bread stuffing and hot rolls. Lead me to it." He rubbed his stomach and groaned.

"Don't forget about the rest of basketball season," Eric warned. "If you gain a lot of weight, the coach will keep you sitting on the bench."

"You can't gain a pound by dreaming," Sean retorted. "Besides, by the time I get home, my family will be tired of turkey and dressing and will probably be eating pizza."

"That's another no-no word," Quinn protested. "I've been so hungry for a slice of pizza that I even dreamed about eating some last night." Swallowing the last bite of doughnut, he stood. "I'm going to take the broom from the supply room and sweep the snow off of my truck. That way, the sun won't have so much to melt. I'll sweep yours off, Les."

"Thanks," Les said, "but hadn't you better stay off that sore leg."

"I'm having very little trouble with it. I think it was only a pulled muscle."

"I'm convinced that we'll be plowed out today," Roxanne said, "so we need to straighten up this room. Les, can you tell us where everything is supposed to be?"

"Sure. I'll give you a hand on moving the pews back in place."

"I'll take the candles out of the windows and put them back in the supply room." Livia said. "What should we do with the greenery we brought in?"

"There's a place in the back where we burn trash, so I'll pile the branches beside the woodshed. When the snow melts, I'll get rid of the trash."

Marie picked up all the empty cartons, water bottles and other trash—enough to fill two large garbage bags. "We'll put those in my trunk," Les said. "I'll take them to my daughter's—she has garbage removal service."

By ten o'clock, Sean, who had been outside, threw the door wide open.

"Here comes the snowplow. Listen to the engine— that's more beautiful than Handel's 'Messiah,' to my ears right now."

They collided with each other in their haste to hurry outdoors. When the snowplow opened a road to their stranded vehicles, they gave a great shout of welcome.

"Hey," Sean said, "you guys should come to my basketball games. You're making more noise than the fans do when I make a jump shot and win the ball game."

The driver of the snowplow turned the vehicle before he stopped and jumped down from the cab. The men crowded around him, shaking his hand, pounding him on the back. He was bundled against the cold and a heavy beard covered his face. Only his eyes peered out from his woolen stocking cap.

"We're really glad to see you," Quinn said.

"Had a rough time of it, have you?" the man said sympathetically in a kind drawl.

"Not as bad as it could have been," Quinn answered. "We've had food and drinks, as well as a place of shelter."

"How are the highways?" Eric asked.

"The interstate has been plowed, but it's slick in spots. Most of the secondary roads are still covered with snow. We're trying to rescue stranded motorists. Which way are you heading?"

"To Columbus," Eric said.

"You might be better off to take I-65 to Dayton and go east on I-70. That will add distance to your trip, but Highway 23 probably has snow cover in spots. The interstates are safer. The blizzard swept northeast toward the Great Lakes, where some places have two feet of snow. There's only a few inches of snow in Columbus."

"Three of us live locally," Quinn said, "so we can find our way home now that you've plowed the roads."

The plowman walked to the delivery truck. "I can't

do much for you," he said to Allen, "except call a wrecker. I'll have one sent as soon as possible. If the rest of you want to follow me as I leave, I'll be handy in case you have any more trouble, which I don't think you will."

"Oh, we don't want to leave Allen behind," Roxanne said.

"You go on your way," Les said. "I ain't in a hurry. I'll stay until they've pulled the truck out."

"I'm not leaving, either," Quinn said. Turning to Allen, he continued, "You'll need a ride to your home after they right the truck. I doubt you should try to drive it until a mechanic checks out the damage. I'll take you home. Those of you going to Columbus can follow the snowplow, since you have the farthest to go."

The eight of them had bonded so quickly during their brief time together that it was like leaving old friends to say goodbye. With helpful directions from Quinn, Eric turned the van around on the narrow road, while Sean and the women went into the church for their luggage.

When he saw that the other church passengers were storing their gear in the van, Quinn realized that Livia was in the church alone. He stepped inside just as she picked up her luggage.

"Will you leave for home as soon as you return to Columbus?"

"Yes. I already have my things packed. I'll go as soon as possible."

"For how long?"

"It will be two weeks before I return to OSU."

"I'd like to see you before then."

"Call me at home," Livia said. She gave him her cell phone number, as well as the house number at Heritage Farm. "Unless it interferes with plans my folks have already made, would you want to come for New Year's weekend?"

"I'd love to. I'll be in touch in a few days."

He didn't want to delay her companions, but Quinn needed the reassurance that Livia had a place in his future. He opened his arms wide, and she rushed inside. It was too soon to say, "I love you," but Quinn knew that his heart had found a lodging place in the woman he gathered close.

Livia's heart lurched with happiness, knowing that the love of her life was within her grasp. She felt like that breathless girl of seventeen who'd fallen so completely for Quinn. She put her arms around his neck and lifted her face for his kiss. Livia's eyes closed as their lips touched, filling her heart with warmth and peace.

By noon the next day, Livia turned her small car into the curved driveway that led to Heritage Farm. The Kesslers had settled this land prior to the Civil War, and the brick house, now painted white, had been built a few years later. The magnificent house was situated on a rounded knoll that overlooked the Ohio River.

Livia's foot pressed on the gas pedal as she climbed the hill. Home had never looked so good! When she brought her car to a halt at the rear of the original house, the door opened, and her mother stepped out.

Hilda Kessler's blond hair was streaked with gray, but her blue eyes gleamed serenely. Livia couldn't remember a time when she'd been away for any length of time that Hilda hadn't been standing in that door to welcome her home.

Turning off the ignition, Livia jumped out of the car and ran to her mother.

"I've been thanking God for keeping you safe. It's good to have you home," Hilda said in her soft voice. "We've missed you."

"Oh, Mom, it's been the most incredible experience I've ever had! I can't wait to tell you all about it."

On the last day of the year, Livia stood at that same door and watched Quinn's truck turn off the highway into her family's private driveway. It pleased her that all of the Christmas guests were gone, and that her parents were on an errand into town. A few days of absence made her somewhat unsure of Quinn's feelings for her, and she preferred to be alone when she saw him again.

When he stopped the truck, Livia walked toward him, her hands outstretched. "Welcome to Heritage Farm."

Quinn kissed her gently on the cheek. "I've missed you, Livia."

"Yes, when our group spent three days together, it seemed unusual not to look around and see you or one of the other six. Come inside."

Quinn took a minute to survey the broad fertile fields located along the Ohio River with the appreciative eyes of a farmer.

"This is a beautiful farm. I can see why it means so much to your family."

She led him into the large, cozy family room. "Mom and Daddy had to be away for the afternoon." With a sheepish grin, she said, "Actually, I think it was a contrived errand to give us a little time to ourselves. My immediate family will all be here for supper."

"I look forward to meeting your folks, but I wanted to see you alone first. Have you told your parents about us?"

"Not everything, but I did fill them in on our meeting at camp a few years ago. I hesitated to say too much—I was afraid that our emotions may have been overworked when we were stranded together. I thought I'd better be sure you hadn't changed your mind before I said anything."

"I had to explain to my parents why I was making this visit, but I couldn't go into any details. I know I said that we'd take some time before we made any decisions, but I don't have any doubt. I've made up my mind—I want to marry you, Livia."

"Is that a proposal?" she said, her heart fluttering at his words.

He grinned sheepishly. "Yes, but not a very romantic one, I guess. It sounded more like a demand than a proposal. So let me start over. I love you, Livia, and if you can find it in your heart to love me, too, we ought to get married."

Her eyes glistened mischievously, and he laughed aloud. "That's even worse than my first attempt," he said.

Livia laughed with him. "Why don't you propose like my grandfather did? When he met my grandmother, he knew right away that she was the one for him. A week later, he went to her house. When she came to the door, he said, 'Let's get hitched.' That seemed to work. They were together for over fifty years."

"Do you want to?" he asked.

"Want to what?"

"Get hitched?"

Smothering a laugh, Livia said, "Yes."

Hearing a car approaching the house, Quinn guessed her parents were returning. He had hoped for more time alone with her before he met the others, but taking advantage of the situation, Quinn pulled Livia into a bear hug.

"Then that's all I need to know," he said. "We'll work out the details later."

They were still kissing when Livia heard the outside door open. She broke the embrace and looked quickly toward her parents as they stood in the doorway. She frantically tried to think of an explanation until she noted the expressions on their faces. Karl and Hilda Kessler didn't seem at all surprised to see the tall, dark-haired man kissing their youngest daughter.

Epilogue

A balmy breeze blew across the area, but the sun was shining as Quinn and Livia turned off the interstate and took the secondary road to Sheltering Arms Church. After they'd been married three years ago, Livia and Quinn had set up their veterinarian practice in Bowling Green. Livia took care of the small-animal end of the business, while Quinn devoted his time to farm stock.

Since they lived nearby, they'd often driven by the church where they'd been reunited five years ago. But today they'd come for a reunion with the travelers with whom they'd shared three anxiety-filled yet exhilarating days. The snowstorm that stranded the eight of them at Sheltering Arms Church had gone down in the history books as one of the worst blizzards in northwestern Ohio.

Turning in her seat to be sure that six-month-old Ruth was still cozy in her car seat, Livia said to her husband, "Quinn, I'm so excited. Won't it be wonderful to see everyone again?"

"Sure will. I feel like we're going to a family reunion."

"I feel closer to these people than some of my own relatives, so it *is* a family reunion. I'm a little sad though that Les won't be with us."

"Yes, but he left his mark on the old church. I'm sure we'll be aware of his presence."

Six months ago, Quinn and Livia had attended Les's funeral in the church. Livia looked toward his grave marker as Quinn parked their van.

Annie Colver, Les's daughter, who'd taken on the role of looking after the church since her father's death, came out to greet them.

Livia carried Ruth's car seat into the church, while Quinn brought in two picnic baskets.

"I've pushed the seats forward and put up these folding tables in the back to hold our food," Annie said. "We won't need much heat tonight, but I built a fire in the stove to remind you of your wintery sojourn here."

The next to arrive were Roxanne, Marie and Eric, who led their two-year-old son into the building. Eric was now the senior pastor of a church in Illinois, and the Damrons hadn't seen the Stover family since Livia had graduated from OSU.

Soon after their forced stay at Sheltering Arms Church, Allen Reynolds had moved to the Cincinnati area. Quinn had kept in touch with Allen as a spiritual mentor, and they looked forward to meeting his wife and two daughters.

Sean was the last to arrive, and his friends cheered as he drove up in his late-model Jaguar. With his first check from his NBA contract, Sean had bought Sheltering Arms Church from the denomination that owned it and established a trust fund for the permanent upkeep of the building and cemetery. He had invested stewardship of the property in a board of local citizens with the stipulation that the original architecture of the building be maintained.

The windows had been repaired and the walls painted and papered. The exterior of the building had been repaired and painted, and the sign refurbished.

As they took a tour of the premises, the friends noticed that the woodshed and the johnny houses had new roofs. Otherwise, the area seemed unchanged.

Livia shivered and, pointing to the johnny houses, she whispered to Marie, "I can still feel the cold air and blowing snow we had to endure to make our trips to this building."

"Yes," Marie agreed. "But it doesn't look like it will snow tonight."

Motioning to the sun setting in a clear sky, Livia said, "I don't think there's any danger of that."

They gathered around the two folding tables Annie had provided, filled with turkey and ham, vegetables, salads and desserts. Marie had brought two dozen doughnuts as a comical reminder of how many of them they'd eaten when they were snowbound. As they enjoyed the food, their conversation centered nostalgically on the past.

Electricity was still not available in the building, so Annie lit candles as dusk fell. When Roxanne started playing the piano, now in tune and melodious, the others took their seats.

Sitting in the pew beside Quinn, holding Ruth in her arms, Livia reflected on the past five years. She and Quinn had been engaged two years before they were married, giving her time to finish college. Their marriage had been the love match she'd always dreamed of having. And the thing that made it so special was their mutual commitment to the Lord's service.

Eric stood behind the lectern and read the Scripture he'd used for his text five years ago. "'But when the fullness of the time was come, God sent forth His Son.'"

Livia was thankful that God had worked His will in her life at the right time. She had wanted to be with Quinn when she'd met him as a teenager. But it wasn't God's timing. She'd often wondered if they had been married when she was so immature, if their marriage could have survived.

A sob filled her throat when Livia thought how blessed she was tonight. She lifted her hand and caressed Quinn's face. He shifted his eyes from Eric to look at her. He took her hand and kissed the palm, then he bent over and pressed a light kiss on her lips. Marveling at the love she felt for him, Livia realized that they were sitting in the same pew where he'd kissed her for the first time.

Quinn continued to hold her hand as Sean stood to sing "O Little Town of Bethlehem." The words found lodging in Livia's heart as if she were hearing them for the first time.

"No ear may hear His coming, but, in this world

of sin, where meek souls will receive Him still, the dear Christ enters in."

Livia bowed her head and worshiped the Child in the manger who'd become the Savior of all mankind.

* * * * *

Dear Reader,

In every life there comes a time when we need a refuge, a shelter in the time of storm. Christians have that refuge/shelter in the Holy Spirit, who dwells in our hearts. As you read my story of eight stranded people, perhaps you've already found a refuge in our Lord, Jesus Christ. If not, I pray that the message of the book will find lodging in your heart, and that you will seek a security to strengthen your faith through bad and/or good times.

It has been a pleasure to share this second book with Dana Corbit. We count it a privilege and blessing to have produced these stories for your reading pleasure. Thanks to the Love Inspired editors for giving us the opportunity.

Irene B. Brand

A SEASON OF HOPE

Dana Corbit

It is not for you to know the times or the seasons,
which the Father has put in His own power.
—*Acts* 1:7

To my dear friends Maija Anderson, Toni Brock, Joy Golicz, LuAnn Taylor and the two Melissas— M. Baxter and M. Lucken. I have been so privileged to know real, amazing women like all of you. I'm blessed to call you friends. Thank you for always believing in me and in my stories. My life and those stories are richer because of you.

Chapter One

The world was filled with two kinds of people as far as David Wright was concerned. In the first group were the lucky jokers who actually learned from their mistakes. Those in the second group were doomed to repeat theirs with the regularity of a three-legged dog addicted to traffic hopscotch.

David would have preferred to include himself in the first group since rehabilitation was a cornerstone in his line of work. But as he stared down at the flared sleeves of his scratchy robe and rubbed at the itchy adhesive securing his grizzled beard, he saw the evidence that he was a card-carrying member of the group that never learned.

"David, are you ready?" Martin Rich called as he stuck his head inside the men's room door at New Hope Church.

"Be right out."

Bustling sounds filtered through the open door, carrying a whistled version of "I'll Be Home for Christmas." Obviously, somebody was a lot happier than he was spending the last two days before Christmas in Destiny, Indiana, taking a fictional journey from Nazareth to Judaea. He wished Martin would close the door and shut out the holiday spirit. He wasn't in the mood for it.

Instead, the lanky middle-aged banker stepped inside. In a Wise Man getup rather than one of his tailor-made suits, Martin looked as ridiculous as David did, though the older man seemed blissfully unaware of it.

"Here, let me help." Before David had time to resist, Martin had stuffed an ugly striped hat on his head. "Now that really *tops* off the costume."

David ignored the bad pun as he frowned into the mirror. "Gee, thanks."

"No problem." Martin paused to adjust his own Bethlehem-chic chapeau. "Destiny's second annual live nativity scene would be a bust without you. If not for Joseph, who would get Mary to the inn on time?"

David shrugged. Who indeed? And he wasn't talking about the Biblical story, either. No one else would have been gullible enough to be coerced into wearing this robe not once, but twice. He should have known better after last year's performance, when an abandoned baby girl was discovered in the manger and chaos erupted. But he hadn't *known better,* and now if the last-minute cast replacement was the worst thing to happen, he would consider himself blessed.

Martin pulled the door open again but looked back over his shoulder. "She got to you, too, didn't she?"

David nodded, not bothering to ask who the *she* was

when they both knew how persuasive Allison Hensley—now Chandler—could be when she set her mind to something. As her best friend, David hadn't stood a chance against those puppy dog eyes.

"She had this big idea that I should reprise my role as Joseph to her Mary." And he'd given in, knowing full well what a farce it was for him to play a member of the Holy Family when Allison was his only connection to the church these days.

"She pulled one over on you then."

It sure felt like she had, though in his heart, David knew she never would have intentionally bailed on him. Besides, no one became that sick on purpose. He would have defended his friend's honor if Martin's hearty laughter hadn't suddenly filled the room. It sounded so much like the cartoon version of the Jolly Old Elf that David was tempted to say, "Wrong story, bud."

But because the whole situation was a mess, he added a little Charles Dickens to the mix. "Bah. Humbug!"

He felt more like Ebenezer Scrooge than the Christ child's earthly father anyway, and dreaded the rehearsal, the performance and the introduction to the stand-in Mary. Especially that. Though the Biblical Joseph probably had plenty on his mind, such as the heavy responsibility of parenting God's son, David figured that at least he hadn't had to worry that the stable scene was part of a friend's matchmaking scheme.

Already, David could use his dating honor roll to paper the walls of the refurbished warehouse he called home. After four years of playing the field since law school, even he was getting sick of himself. So why did his friend insist on trying to set him up with another woman—especially her twenty-five-year-old cousin?

A pang of guilt struck him for the self-centered jerk he was. Allison was probably too busy chasing after her adopted year-old daughter and suffering bouts of morning, noon and night sickness with her problem pregnancy to make his love life her top priority. She'd only asked her cousin to fill in because she was too sick to get out of bed.

"Yo, David, are you with me?" Martin called out. "Quit daydreaming so we can get this rehearsal over before New Year's."

As David slumped after him out the church door, the frigid east-central Indiana wind and the farm stench from hay and livestock bombarded his senses. Even with the long underwear he'd remembered this time, the wind clawed at his clothes and invaded his bones. His ears and fingers already ached, and his cheeks burned. If it was this cold under the steel gray helmet of daylight, he wondered what it would be like after dark.

"Have you met our new Mary?" Martin asked as they crossed the field toward the makeshift stable.

"Not yet."

"Then now's as good a time as any. Hey, Sondra."

Guessing that this time was no *worse* than any other, David glanced at the woman whose head came up when she heard her name. Even if she hadn't strode toward them, her costume would have given her away.

Instead of waiting for Martin to introduce them, she shot out her hand in a practiced businesslike manner. "Hi. I'm Sondra Stevens."

"David Wright."

She had a firm handshake despite her fingers being so icy cold that they must have felt numb. He tried to ignore the tickle in his palm when he released her.

"You might recognize David's name from the political signs outnumbering Christmas lights this year." Martin chuckled. "If he wins next month's special election, at twenty-eight he'll be the youngest Superior Court judge in Cox County history."

"That's quite an accomplishment," she said.

Funny, the bank teller he'd had dinner with last week had appeared more impressed when he'd shared that news with her.

"Sondra is the assistant human resources director at Tool Around, Kentucky's largest RV manufacturer. She's on her way up in that company."

His introduction duties finished, Martin excused himself to join the other Wise Men. David didn't like the strange feeling that he'd been left to fend for himself as he turned back to Sondra.

From beneath the costume's head covering, huge mahogany-hued eyes stared out at him. Those eyes trapped him under their intelligent and evaluating gaze, making him wonder if Sondra was in the habit of studying others to determine their worthiness for her attention. That she looked away and readjusted her shawl clued him in that she'd found him lacking. On some elemental level, it bothered him that she could dismiss him so easily.

"I'm playing Joseph," he said needlessly.

Laughter lit her eyes, but it stopped at her mouth. "I figured it was that or you had interesting taste in clothing."

"I have great taste in clothes...and everything else." Why he'd said it David wasn't sure, other than that he'd felt a sudden need to defend himself.

"So I've heard."

"My reputation precedes me."

Most days it didn't bother him to have a reputation as the local bachelor attorney who'd dated most of Destiny's single women—none more than twice. Since he'd long ago accepted that he wasn't cut out for the deep stuff, he'd always been decent to his dates, keeping things casual so nobody got hurt. It was strange, but today he wished the reputation didn't follow him so closely, ruining his chance for a good first impression.

"Yes, it does. Impressive."

Her tone suggested she wasn't really impressed by whatever she'd heard. She paused long enough to make him squirm, if he were the type to shift under cross-examination. He wasn't.

"Allison said you made a good Joseph." She lifted an eyebrow and lowered it.

"Touché." He smiled, letting her have her joke and resisting the urge to wonder what she'd really been hinting at before. "If I know Allison at all, she proba-bly said my performance was fabulous or stupendous."

"Something like that, but I like to stick to the facts and forget the flowery words. Allison and I are op-posites that way."

She had that right. Even having just met her, he sensed that the two of them were different in a lot of ways. They wore the same blue costume and both had oval-shaped faces, but that was all they appeared to have in common.

Allison was the perfect woman to play Jesus' mother. A nurturer, the former social worker was so kind and warm that she drew people the way flowers turned to sunshine. Sondra, on the other hand, was an unlikely Mary. She seemed tough and arrogant instead of submissive to God's will, the way Jesus' mother had been.

Even in appearance, Sondra was as dark as Allison was light. Allison's blond tresses streamed down her back, while her cousin cut her nearly black hair short in a no-nonsense style. His friend had always fought the height-weight battle, but Sondra was willowy and so tall her costume only brushed her ankles.

She was also tall enough to nearly look a man in the eye, particularly one like him who lacked two inches to reach six feet. And any man wouldn't have had a tough time looking back at the exotic beauty, with her flawless light bronze skin and sculpted features.

He was already admiring her eyelashes, that never in a million years would require mascara, when she drew her eyebrows together as a huge clue that he'd been staring.

David cleared his throat. "Uh, thanks for filling in at the last minute. Not that anyone can fill Allison's shoes completely. She came up with this whole idea last year and pulled it together."

"I'm not trying to fill her shoes, but I did want to be here for her. Allison needed me."

She might as well have tossed a bucket of water over him, as effectively as her comment woke him up. What was he thinking, noticing any woman right now, especially Allison's cousin? Didn't he have enough on his plate with an election to win, messed-up priorities to get in order and a sick puppy of a friend to help out?

That was another thing. If Allison needed anyone right now, she needed *him*. Okay, she just might need Cox County Sheriff's Deputy Brock Chandler, too. Brock was, after all, her husband. But if Allison needed a friend, David had already dug in the trenches and was ready for battle. He didn't need any reinforcements from Allison's Kentucky relatives.

Sondra rubbed her hands together. "It's freezing out here."

"That's Indiana for you. They're predicting four to six inches of snow before Christmas morning."

"Too bad I won't be around long enough to see it."

She sure didn't sound disappointed about missing Indiana's white Christmas. He got the idea that she wanted to see Destiny in her rearview mirror as quickly as possible. That was a good thing. He would be more than happy to help her to her car.

"I couldn't believe it when Allison called me," she said, breaking the silence that had stretched too long. "I've never heard of a pregnant woman being so sick that she had to have a portable IV."

"The doctors call it hyperemesis, which means that she threw up a lot. Constantly, in fact. Finally, the nurse put in a PIC line—or percutaneous invasive catheter—to fight dehydration. You probably aren't aware of this, but in the first twelve weeks of her pregnancy, she's lost ten pounds instead of gaining any weight."

He took smug satisfaction in the shock registering on Sondra's face. She didn't know about Allison's condition or any of the fancy medical terms that he could spout now. She hadn't been there. He had.

"If only she'd called…" She let her voice trail off, her regret unmistakable.

He had poised his hand to squeeze her shoulder in comfort before he realized what he was doing. It wasn't his business. This case wasn't his to judge, even if the cousins weren't as close as Sondra wanted him to believe.

Having turned away to collect her pillow from a nearby haystack, Sondra fortunately missed his lapse. When she turned back, though, her shoulders were straight, as if she'd overcome her own weak moment.

"But as she said, 'The show must go on.'" She rested her hands on a pillow stomach that looked more like she'd swallowed a basketball than she carried a baby inside.

"Do you think they need us over there yet?"

"You know the story, don't you? Joseph and Mary arrive late, when all of the rooms in the inn are full."

"I know the story."

He shrugged. "We do need to get over to the donkey, though."

"That donkey?" She pointed to the Shetland pony someone was leading across the grass.

"That's the one."

"We really are doing some acting here."

The corners of his mouth pulled up. "Stella has the toughest role. She's doing a pony encore performance."

David decided he needed to focus on his own encore. Whenever he'd needed Allison, she'd dropped everything for him. She'd never asked much of him in return. Well, she was relying on him this one time to make the show go off without any more hitches. She needed him to do this, and he wouldn't let her down.

Leading Sondra across the churchyard to the mark for their theatrical entry into Bethlehem, David couldn't resist shooting a glance back at the wooden stable. As long as the child in the manger remained a doll, they could handle anything.

Chapter Two

Sondra settled herself sidesaddle on their "donkey" and wondered where her life had taken the wrong turn that had landed her in this place. It must have been the moment she took the ramp onto Interstate 65, heading north to Indiana. Or well before it, when, during a moment of weakness, she'd agreed to participate in Allison's harebrained plan.

Who was she kidding? She would have done almost anything for her cousin whom, along with Aunt Mary and Uncle Bruce, she owed for all the normal experiences of her childhood. Every trip to Indiana Beach or Brown County State Park came as a backseat passenger in the Hensleys' car. She was indebted to them for so much more—for freely given hugs and for little-girl trinkets her single mom couldn't afford—but working with David Wright was stretching the limits of her gratitude.

The least she could expect was a little appreciation for her dropping everything, crossing a state line and driving past acre after acre of flat, Hoosier farmland to reach Destiny. But David didn't even give her credit for her trouble. In fact, he seemed to resent her for just being there. What did he plan to do, play Mary and Joseph all by himself? Maybe he could crawl into the manger and play the Baby Jesus while he was at it.

Sondra couldn't help smiling at the image of big strong David curled up in the hay. Or sporting her costume and pillow belly for that matter.

A disloyal part of her figured it would be a waste for him to hide all his dark wavy hair beneath her heavy head shawl. Even with his hair clipped short on the sides, he couldn't hide its tendency to curl. If David wore her strange costume, the blue robe would only accentuate his light blue eyes. Translucent eyes that seemed to see everything yet reveal nothing.

Not that she'd noticed or anything. Or if she had noticed, she hadn't wasted any time dwelling on what she'd seen. Or if she had dwelled just a bit, then she at least was too smart to let a pretty face turn her head.

That the pony chose this moment to whinny and flip its mane, forcing her to tighten her grip on the reins, only annoyed her. David certainly wasn't harboring any attraction for her; he'd made that clear enough with the way he'd treated her. And from what her cousin had told her about him, he wasn't especially selective in choosing his many dating partners. What did it say about her that the skin on her arms tingled just because of David's nearness as he stood next to the pony? She wasn't that desperate for dates. Maybe long-term relationships weren't her thing, but she'd had her share of dinners and movies.

Again, Stella whinnied and stomped her foot.

David glanced over and frowned. "You're not going to lose control, are you? We don't need you galloping into Bethlehem tonight like a bad cowboy wanna-be."

Sondra narrowed her gaze at him and patted the pony's neck. She crooned to the horse instead of speaking to him. "Don't you listen to that old grouch, Stella. You and I know you'll pull this off like an old pro."

She looked at David. "I'm from Louisville, remember? I know how to sit a horse." Okay, she hadn't ridden more than a half-dozen times in her life, but she could ride, and that was all he needed to know.

"Glad to hear it. Wouldn't want the show to turn into a media event like last year." His smile was smug enough to make her fist her fingers over the reins. The teeth he flashed were straight and white, a fact that only annoyed her further. How could she find a man like him attractive?

"There won't be a problem from me, but I can't speak for anyone else." She raised both eyebrows.

He only kept smiling and continued his habit of grating on her nerves. For someone she'd known less than a half hour, he sure was a quick study at it.

Why did she let him get to her? And why couldn't she resist baiting him in return? She could answer those questions no more than she could figure out why she was so determined to prove herself to him. On her own turf at the office, she no longer had to prove anything to anyone. No one could match her sixty-hour workweeks and the sacrifice of her already limited social life. Now her dream job was within her grasp—human resources director—if only she continued to keep up the pace.

"That's our cue," David told her as the last strains of "O Holy Night" filtered through the sound system. "We might as well get this over with."

He had that right. She needed only to get through this one day and she would fulfill her promise to Allison. Then she would sprint to her car and be across the Indiana-Kentucky border before the first snowflakes fell.

Still, her annoying co-star was just one of the reasons that she wanted her immediate destiny to be far away from Destiny. Just as she remembered from her childhood visits, Destiny seemed to close in around her, trapping her in its suffocating neighborliness.

Give her a big city any day. She'd been gone from Louisville less than a day, and yet she longed for her impersonal apartment in its impersonal complex in an impersonal area just outside the city. At least she figured missing home was what had caused the dull ache inside her as she'd passed by some of Center Street's tiny, holiday-decorated homes. People inside them were probably peeking out their shades as she drove by, picking her out for the stranger she was.

How people could survive in such a small town where everyone knew each other's business, she couldn't imagine. Two-bit towns like this one were where some women ended up when they gave up their dreams for a man. Others just became lonely, bitter women like her mother. She would never repeat her mother's mistakes.

Because the only way out of Destiny was to get this rehearsal and the final performance over with, Sondra reluctantly handed David her pony's reins and let him lead her onto the set. Letting a guy lead her anywhere, now that was a first—and last if she had anything to say about it. At least this was only theater.

"This is the life, isn't it?" David said softly as they neared the stable. "Just a man taking care of his little family."

Sondra had to grip the saddle horn to keep from hopping down and tackling him. Worse than his guessing she would be uncomfortable letting a man take her horse's reins, David seemed to enjoy her discomfort.

"It took a special man to be the adoptive father of Jesus," she whispered back. "Most men couldn't have handled the job."

She couldn't resist stressing the words "most men" or including him in that category, because David Wright was a jerk with a capital "J." If she did an Internet search for the word "jerk," his picture and resume would probably appear as top match. She couldn't believe Allison had offered last year to set her up with him. Didn't her cousin like her at all?

Well, she refused to let him bother her any longer. She wouldn't let his rudeness get to her, and she wouldn't allow herself to be affected by his good looks. She'd promised Allison, and that's all there was too it. She wasn't like her father; she kept her commitments. Unlike him, she didn't escape in a big rig when the times got tough, leaving the people he allegedly loved in a cloud of diesel exhaust.

No, she wasn't leaving, so David could just forget about pushing her buttons. She would get through this night if it killed her. Or him. Or maybe the both of them.

David yanked the poufy hat off his head and rubbed his frozen ears as he trudged over to his car. If his ears were frostbitten and were amputated, would he still be able to hear cases from the bench? Chances were he'd still be able to hear claims from the prosecution and pleas from the defense, but he would sure look funny doing it.

Settling behind the wheel of Reba, his seasoned sedan with rust-pattern detailing, he turned the key and blasted the heat. Usually he would have taken time to appreciate how the old gal's engine whined and then purred, but then he wasn't usually so rankled with himself.

At the thump of something beating the window, he jerked his head. Martin stood in the wind yelling something outside the glass. If only David had not given Reba a chance to warm up and had driven right off the lot, he could have avoided facing anyone from the cast, but now he was stuck. He cranked open the window.

Martin reached in to pat David's shoulder with his gloved hand. "Well done, young man. Everyone felt the true meaning of Christmas right down to their toes."

"They probably couldn't feel their toes. I know I can't."

Martin demonstrated his full-belly laugh again and nodded. "Okay, maybe a few had frostbitten toes. But if they were watching and listening at all, they also got hearts shock full of praise tonight. You and Sondra did a great job, particularly under such short notice."

David lifted a shoulder and let it fall.

The side of Martin's mouth came up. "That's exactly what Sondra did when I said it to her."

Martin glanced out at the nearly empty field they'd used as a parking lot. "She's probably close to Indianapolis as quickly as she left after the show. Can't say as I blame her. She had a long drive back to Louisville. But it's too bad she couldn't spend the holidays with her cousin."

"That is too bad," David conceded.

Allison probably would have liked that since she no longer had any extended family around. It would have been special to her since it was the first Christmas for Allison and Brock since they'd married and Joy's adoption had become final. Since they'd become a real family. But he'd heard Sondra himself—nothing could have kept her in town.

"Anyway, I'm sure Allison is proud of you, David. You really came through for her."

David swallowed hard, somehow still managing to nod before the Wise Man left to return to his banker's life. If David's actions could be called coming through for Allison, then he wondered to what extremes he would have to go to fail her.

Though the performance had been nearly flaw-less—if less exciting than last year's chaos—he couldn't take credit for it. He'd done as much to sab-otage the show as any of the other performers had done to make it work.

None of the cast or the audience had frozen to death, the livestock hadn't bit anyone or stampeded, and the sound system had managed not to pick up signals from local baby monitors. Best of all, though, the child in the manger stayed plastic and kept quiet during the whole performance.

Despite him, rather because of him, the show had been serene and worshipful. It spoke to everyone there. For a few seconds, it had even affected him, and noth-ing spiritual had touched him in years. The event had reminded him of his childhood, when all of this—the star, the shepherds, the manger and its heralded occu-pant—had really meant something.

Fortunately, only the animals had been close enough to see the dramatic subplot that had unfolded right on stage. From up close, audience members would have recognized that the character Mary never met her husband's gaze during the whole performance, and though her shoulders were curved in submission and praise, her hands were fisted.

David knew because he kept looking over at her, hoping to catch her eye and whisper an apology. She didn't give him the chance. Not that he'd deserved one. He'd tested her patience all afternoon.

But she'd pushed him, too. Every word out of her mouth hinted that she didn't think he was good enough for her, whether she came right out and said it or not. He should have been pleased that she was every bit as disinterested in him as he was in her and yet he'd found her aloofness unsettling.

None of that mattered. He still doubted Allison would be proud of him for any of this. Ashamed— that was a better word. He was ashamed enough for the both of them. He sure hadn't gained any votes by his behavior tonight.

First thing in the morning, he would call Allison to apologize. He would even offer to write a letter to Sondra and apologize to her, too. If he were fortunate, when he threw himself on her mercy, Allison would volunteer to tell Sondra how sorry he was.

He had it in his favor that his best friend was always gracious in accepting apologies. He'd been on the receiving end of her forgiveness enough to know. But this time he probably would have to count on the fact that it would be Christmas Eve when he faced her. He knew, at least he hoped, that no one could stay angry over Christmas.

Chapter Three

David had to ring the doorbell three times before anyone answered, but the moment the door swung open, he knew why he'd been asked to apologize in person. Been set up was more like it.

"Good morning, David." Sondra's greeting sounded forced, but she still wore a victorious smile.

She looked fresh and comfortable in a yellow sweater and jeans, with her short hair tucked behind her ears. Fuzzy slippers covered her feet, suggesting she wasn't on her way out the door.

Surprise must have thrown him off, but for a fleeting second, David couldn't decide whether to give her a nasty look or grab her and kiss her. Fortunately for him, he did neither. "Hello."

"Hey you guys, catch her, will you?" Allison called from the other room.

As if on cue, a munchkin with a mess of dark curls toddled through Sondra's legs and shot for the door.

David whisked the baby into his arms before the bottoms of her footed pajamas got wet.

"And where do you think you're going, sweetie pea? And where did you get that?" A shaggy teddy bear he'd never seen before dangled from her hand. The toy had matted brown fur and only one remaining button eye.

Joy Chandler clutched the bear to her and answered in the gibberish she still preferred to her limited repertoire of words such as "mama," "dada," "ice cream" and, the one he liked best, "Dabe."

He pushed past Sondra and closed the door before swinging Joy around in his arms. She rewarded him by screeching the coveted word, "Dabe."

"I bet you were coming out to see me. Well, I was coming in to see you." He turned her so she was sitting upright on his hip.

"David, Sondra, can you bring her in here?"

"Just a minute." He released the bundle of energy so he could take his boots off and then followed her padding feet into the family room. Behind him, Sondra hesitated for a second and then followed.

In the comfortable room with overstuffed couches, built-in bookshelves and a TV that wasn't on, Allison rested on a love seat, with a plumped pillow behind her back and an afghan over her knees. Attached to her arm was the long clear tube that connected to the portable IV stand.

"Aren't you thrilled with my surprise?" Allison gestured unnecessarily toward her cousin.

David nodded because his lungs might have exploded if he tried to repeat the word "thrilled."

"Now you said you wanted to apologize to me for your strange behavior last night. And to someone else. I wanted to give you the opportunity." She smiled at him, but she didn't gloat.

Was this how animals caught in live cages felt, trapped inside four walls but with the promise of freedom once it was all over?

He looked back and forth between them and finally began. "Ladies, I'm sorry for being a jerk last night. It was stressful enough without me making it worse."

Allison glanced over at Sondra and then back to him. "Okay, I forgive you, but you probably won't be asked to be Joseph again next year."

David managed to control his temptation to do a happy dance, as it wouldn't make him appear properly contrite. He turned to Sondra.

She spoke before he had the chance. "I'm sorry, too. I wasn't being very nice, either."

"Thanks." He was surprised to realize he wasn't just being polite. Her apology and her acceptance of his gave him a strange relief that he chose not to analyze. "I thought you were trying to leave before the snow came."

"That's the best part," Allison interjected.

David jerked around to face his friend, who looked as excited as a child who'd opened all her presents early.

"Sondra volunteered to stay and to help me over the Christmas holidays. Isn't that great?"

"Great." No one could have missed his lack of enthusiasm, so he rushed to add, "That will be nice for you to have family around." The last sounded authentic because he really wanted it for her.

Allison's grin widened. "It's going to be so much fun spending Joy's first real Christmas—well, one that she's awake for anyway—together." Her eyes filled as she likely remembered last year's Christmas day that she'd spent searching with Brock for Joy's birth mother.

"I'm looking forward to it," Sondra said. "Here, sweetheart, let me help with that." She rushed over to the tree to *help* Joy with the half-dozen ornaments the toddler had already thrown on the floor.

He spoke to Sondra while her back was still turned. "I thought you had to get back to work."

"I don't." She turned back to him, the pillow-type ornaments gathered in her arms. "My office is on shutdown until January third."

"And she's going to stay the whole time." For a woman who'd felt lousy for weeks and was using an IV as an accessory, Allison looked downright giddy. "It will be such a help since Brock's going to have to pull extra holiday shifts at the sheriff's department. It's been tough handling Joy by myself lately."

David sat on the far arm of the love seat and rested his hands on his thighs to keep them from fisting. If she needed help, she could have come to him. Not this cousin who was never around. "Why didn't you say so, kiddo? You know I could have—"

"David William Wright, you've been doing enough for me lately. More than I ever should've let you."

"I haven't done anything. Besides—"

She interrupted him again, this time waving the arm that was free of a tube. "*Besides,* you're busy. The election is coming up. Don't you want to get elected?"

He chuckled at that. "I won't get elected if I work right through Christmas. This is a Christian town, and you know it. No one would appreciate me going door-to-door on Christmas Eve unless I was singing carols, and we both know that wouldn't get me any votes."

She smiled at Sondra conspiratorially. "He's right about that."

She rubbed her chin for a few seconds, appearing to think it over. "Okay, David, you can help if you want. With all I need to finish, I can't afford to turn down any offers. As behind as I am, I'll never catch up."

But Sondra shook her head. "We don't need to put David out. Not when I have the time off. I'm sure if you and I work together, we'll get everything done."

David shook his head just as hard. "She can't help. She needs to rest even if the doctor does agree to take out her IV at this afternoon's appointment."

"Okay, then I'll do it all myself. The list you wrote isn't too long." She glanced at David. "Besides, most of the stuff—decorating, cleaning, wrapping gifts—probably isn't up his alley."

Sondra was doing it again. First, she'd thought she was too good to be set up with him, though he wasn't the slightest bit interested. Now she didn't think he was qualified to do mindless chores. Enough was enough.

"No, I can't promise perfection," he said, pausing to suggest that someone else was pledging just that, "but I'll do whatever you need."

He gave an exaggerated salute as he turned to Allison. "Your Christmas slave, reporting for duty."

Christmas slave indeed, Sondra thought as she brushed out the house's second and final toilet bowl. A proprietary butler was a better description of David's job title. Every time she started a job, he gave her tips about how her cousin liked things to be done in her house.

"Allison likes her towels tri-folded instead of just in half."

"Allison likes honey in her tea instead of sugar."

"Allison wants Joy to have her nap at one-thirty, not one-fifteen, so she'll wake up later."

Sondra had to admit that he did his share, and he did a good job of cleaning, but if he gave her one more suggestion about what Allison wanted, needed or preferred, she would scream. Besides, he was a guy. How did he even know this stuff about her cousin?

But the answer was simple: time. David had spent far more of it with Allison in the last five years than she had. Her career often had kept her too busy to be with her friends or family, but today it seemed a poor excuse.

She should have been around, especially in the last

year when she could have been getting to know Joy. "Dabe" had been there, so the baby loved him instead.

"Are you done with the throne yet?"

Sondra jerked at the sound, hitting her head on the toilet lid. Lifting up, she turned to find him leaning on the doorjamb with his arms crossed. Nothing like adding *injury* to *insult*. But as much as her head smarted, she wouldn't give him the satisfaction of seeing her rub it.

"Yes?" She raised an exaggerated eyebrow.

"Oh, sorry about that. I was just going to tell you that I think Allison likes her bathroom—"

She shot out her rubber-gloved hand to interrupt him. "Clean? Yeah, most people do."

Standing up from the commode, she stepped over to the sink and took her time removing the gloves. "I'm finished. I probably haven't done it just the way she likes, but I'm sure Allison will appreciate having a clean house."

Instead of pressing forward with whatever advice he'd been about to give, he nodded. "What does that leave?"

"If you've finished dusting in the living room, then the only room left is the kitchen. But we need to get the rest of those gifts in the closet wrapped before Joy wakes up and has a heyday playing in the bows."

"She'll have plenty of time for that tomorrow."

For the first time all afternoon, they agreed on something. Sondra couldn't wait to spend this special Christmas with the one-year-old, seeing the excitement in those golden brown eyes. It crossed her mind that this might be the closest she ever came to sharing experiences like that with her own children, but she tucked the notion in the back of her mind where it belonged. No sense dwelling on what she didn't have.

"I'll get the packages and meet you in the family room." Before he could offer any suggestions, she added, "I'll be quiet so I won't wake Allison or Joy."

He nodded and turned the opposite way down the hall. When he was out of sight, Sondra inhaled deeply to calm herself. It was a relief since the air seemed extra thin whenever he was near her.

She found him again in the family room, scissors and cellophane tape already on the floor next to him. With a grunt, she dumped several shopping bags and rolls of wrapping paper on the floor and plopped down next to them.

"You should have let me get all of that."

"I could handle it myself," she shot back.

"I know you could."

She swallowed. "Oh." How was someone who questioned the motives of chivalrous men supposed to take that? Especially when she was tempted to like it. Unable to resist, she glanced at him.

He wasn't laughing. He looked right back at her, not so long as to be called leering but long enough to transform her legs to gelatin. Fortunately, she was already sitting cross-legged on the floor, so she didn't have the humiliation of having her limbs fold under her. Because she was having a hard time breathing again, she turned away and started wrapping a sweet-faced baby doll.

David set to work, too, creating a wrapping paper and tape glob, topped off with a bow. By his second masterpiece, Sondra couldn't help watching him work.

"What?" he asked with an annoyed expression.

"Ever wrapped presents before?"

He shrugged. "Yeah, sure. Hasn't everyone?"

She glanced at his completed pile, and a chuckle bubbled in her throat before she could contain it.

"What are you, the quality inspector?"

"I could have asked you the same question earlier."

He laughed as he attached a long piece of tape over an awkward-shaped package. "Yeah, forget I asked that. How come you get all of the nice square and rectangle boxes while I get all this round stuff?"

"Just lucky, I guess." Swallowing a giggle, she secured a fancy bow on her last package and curled the ribbons with her scissors. When she caught him staring at her package, she explained, "Mom and I compete to have the prettiest wrapped gifts under the tree."

"So that's it. The kinds of gifts you see at my parents' house come professionally wrapped from the jeweler. Mother always pretends she doesn't know where they're from, and we sit around wearing suits and ties and chuckling at her guesses."

"It sounds as if you'll have a blast tomorrow then."

"I will. I'll be here."

"Here?" she repeated, ignoring her racing pulse. The last thing she needed was to spend another day with David.

"You don't think I would miss seeing Joy open her presents tomorrow, do you?"

Her lips pulled up. "Of course not. But your parents live in town. Won't they be upset that you won't be there? Mom is sulking that I won't be in Louisville."

"We'll get together later. They'll barely miss me at dinner since Mother is counting on a meal for twenty-five. It wouldn't be Christmas at Lloyd and Evelyn Wright's home without the mayor, the sheriff, the town board. Mother's serving squab, I hear."

"Does your mother pull off a dinner party like that all by herself?"

"Absolutely." David winked. "Well, she does have the caterer's number on speed dial, and she's careful to set the menu with him by September first."

"Sounds elegant."

"Always."

"And dull."

"Always."

Sondra chuckled. "No wonder you're coming here."

"I can't wait. I'm going to videotape."

He sounded so excited that she couldn't help smiling until another thought struck her. "Wait. You said dinner. I haven't even talked to Allison about what she wants for the Christmas meal."

Panic had her hands sweating. She'd had plenty of titles behind her name, but cook was never one of them. Her only claims to fame in the kitchen were abilities to burn water *and* overcook minute rice.

David waved away her concern with his hand. "Don't worry. It's under control. Allison accepted my offer to make the whole dinner."

She'd just been getting comfortable with him, and

here he went again with his one-upmanship best-friend thing. She didn't even know when he would have found time to volunteer to be the holiday chef between completing his own list of chores and critiquing hers. Well, if he'd been confident enough of his cooking skills to offer to do the whole job then they would at least have a decent meal.

At the sound of footsteps, Sondra turned to see Allison padding through the doorway, her IV stand in tow.

"The place looks great, guys."

David crossed to her and placed his hand under her elbow to steady her. "Sweetie, you're supposed to be in bed. If you needed something, you should have called me."

"I'm fine. Really. I need to get cleaned up before my doctor's appointment."

"Uh, okay." He rolled his lips inward, clearly embarrassed that he couldn't help his friend with her personal care, too.

Allison smiled. "Oh, David, I was thinking more about Christmas dinner."

"Don't worry. I've got it all under control. Borkley's Market has a fresh sixteen-pound turkey and yeast rolls waiting for me, and I've got the grocery list ready."

Allison settled back on her sofa daybed. "That's great, but I was thinking—"

"Turkey, sweet potatoes, stuffing, mashed potatoes, rolls, peas, pumpkin pie and chocolate chip cookies for Joy. Can you think of anything else?"

Sondra didn't know about her cousin, but she couldn't think of anything. She was in awe of anyone who could pull a holiday meal together. David apparently could do that with one hand while planning a winning court strategy with the other.

She'd never felt so outdone. He'd finally proven he was a far better choice to help Allison than she could ever hope to be. She should just pack up her bags and give him space to work.

"No, that sounds like a complete menu," Allison said. "But, as I said before I was interrupted, I was thinking that you could use some help in the kitchen. You and Sondra should cook Christmas dinner together. Isn't that a wonderful idea?"

Their answer came as a simultaneous "wonderful" that was as unenthusiastic as David's earlier comment.

David kept staring at Sondra as if expecting her to gracefully decline. *Over my dead body,* a competitive and, this time, dangerous side of her declared. There might be dead bodies, if she did anything more than stir the dinner pot. But the way David was taunting her, she couldn't have backed down now, even for an immediate job promotion. She was in, and she was sticking.

Well, she had about twelve hours to become a cook at least half as incredible as David seemed to think he was. Improbable but not impossible. There was only one thing she knew for sure: This would be a Christmas to remember.

Chapter Four

David closed the door to the wall oven and wiped his hands on his apron. Daylight had barely taken hold on Destiny's Christmas morning, and he and Sondra had already been slaving over a not-yet-hot stove for more than two hours.

Outside the kitchen, the Chandler house was silent as Brock had already left for work and Joy was still snoozing contentedly in her crib. David's gift to Allison this morning would be a few extra hours of shut-eye.

He peeked through the window of the double oven, satisfied to see the dark spices dotting the skin of the still-pink bird.

"Well, that's one thing down."

"One down and ninety-nine to go?"

He turned to see Sondra watching him from the table where she'd been peeling and chopping potatoes and tossing them in a big pot for the last twenty minutes. Already her face was smeared with what looked like flour, and she hadn't even started baking yet.

"You don't have to help, you know," he told her. "It's Christmas morning. Why don't you just relax and let me take care of everything?"

He waited for the sparks to fly since he'd been itching for a fight ever since she'd let him in the front door, looking bright-eyed and fresh-faced.

A not-on-your-life-buddy glare crossed her features before her expression softened to a smile. "I wouldn't dream of deserting you with all of this work, especially on Christmas Day."

Go ahead. Desert me. Make my day. But he managed to contain his version of the famous Clint Eastwood line since he'd only have to apologize for it anyway. He doubted his idea that the only way Sondra could really help him would be to wait outside until she became the ice sculpture wouldn't go over well, either.

"It would be difficult, but I could probably limp along on my own."

"Good thing you won't have to try."

Her smile was a gloating one, so it only annoyed him further that he couldn't help noticing how much prettier she looked when she smiled.

If she thought she was the best "man" for this job just because she could look downright inviting in a frilly apron that said, "Honey the Chef," then she had another think coming. This Christmas dinner was his gig, and he was only letting her play along because it seemed so important to Allison. He hadn't had the heart to tell his friend that it would take a lot more than baking with sugar and vanilla to make her cousin seem sweet to him.

Sondra dropped the last of the potato peels into the garbage and crossed to the sink to wash the potatoes. "So what's next?"

How do I know? What had he been thinking, offering to make the whole meal when he'd never even eaten a homemade Christmas dinner, let alone cooked one? His mother's catering plans didn't sound so bad now.

Why had Allison taken him up on his offer anyway, when she knew perfectly well that his culinary abilities were limited to spaghetti sauce out of a jar and anything with instructions on the box? He shrugged. She probably figured that a Christmas dinner à la canned pasta was better than none at all.

"Why don't you check on Joy while I go over my list?" he asked, to buy some time.

As Sondra left, he released the breath he'd been holding and turned to his notes, which were really only parts of last night's shopping list. Sure, he'd known what to buy from the pictures on the grocery story circular, but beyond that, he was at a loss.

Where exactly did one *stuff* stuffing? How did a candied yam get candied? And what did he do with that can of stuff that looked like cranberry gelatin that he'd already opened by mistake?

What he wouldn't have given if his parents had left him a step-by-step holiday dinner manual under the tree that morning. Still, he would rather let someone *tie* his legs together and bake *him* before he would let Sondra know that someone besides the turkey was winging it here.

"Pie crust," he said when she returned. "Why don't you get started on that?"

Her eyes widened as if he'd just spoken to her in a foreign language, but she squared her shoulders and nodded. "I can do that."

Then she reached into one of the kitchen drawers and pulled out a cookbook.

She answered his questioning glance with a shrug. "Found this last night. Figured it might come in handy."

"Just might." More than she knew. He turned to wash his hands in the sink, trying not to let his relief show.

That he'd been beginning to question their competence suddenly annoyed him. He and Sondra were both college graduates. That meant they had managed to learn a thing or two from books. They could handle this. At least he could.

"Are you making the filling?" she asked as she poured a cup of flour into a mixing bowl.

"Of course." He held up a can of pumpkin that he was pleased to see had a recipe right on the label. He used it as his guide to set the temperature on the lower oven.

"Good. Then it's a team effort."

Well, not exactly a team. More a chef and his kitchen crew. But he decided to keep that to himself, because as much as he hated to admit it, he just might need Sondra's help to get all of this done.

Just as he scraped the pumpkin into a bowl, Allison padded into the kitchen, already dressed in slacks and a loose-fitting blouse instead of her pajamas. She still looked pale, the way she had for the last several weeks, but she was wearing a bright smile.

"Merry Christmas you two. Aren't you guys ready?" she asked as she dragged a hairbrush through her damp hair.

"Happy Christmas, cousin." Sondra waved a flour-covered hand but barely looked up from her mission.

"Merry Christmas. What do you mean, *ready?*" David cocked his head. "Dinner won't be finished for a few hours." How few or how many hours he didn't know for sure, but he didn't want to worry her.

Allison shook her head. "I mean for church. Christmas service. You didn't forget, did you?"

As a matter of fact, he had, and from the way that Sondra jerked her head up from her work, he wasn't alone.

Sondra shrugged. "I usually go Christmas Eve. That's when our church in Louisville has its service. But sure, we can go."

David only frowned. He should have known if he were going to escape the drudgery of his family's picture-perfect Christmas to hang with the Chandlers, it would cost him. The price: church attendance. As if the whole manger event hadn't been a big enough dose of the true Christmas spirit for one year.

This was going to require a different tack. He

crossed to Allison and rested his hands on her fore-arms. "Are you sure you're feeling well enough to go? The doctor said—"

She jerked out of his reach. "I know what he said. That I'm just fine. He even released me from my IV ball and chain."

"Still, he told you to take it easy, to listen to your body…for your sake and for the baby's sake."

Okay, he'd been over the top to mention her unborn child, but he didn't think his action warranted the evil eye she was giving him.

"Of course, you're fine," Sondra interjected in a soothing voice. "He's just concerned about you. We both are."

How did Sondra know *what* he was? And since when did he need a third party intervening for him with his best friend? That answer was simple: since Sondra blew into Destiny. Okay, the evidence was circumstantial, but he was willing to hand down his judgment anyway.

"I'm fine. I don't even feel nauseated this morning. I've missed so much church lately. You're not going to keep me from going on Christmas, are you?"

At the same time, David and Sondra shook their heads. He didn't know what Sondra's excuse was, but he'd already established that he couldn't deny his friend anything.

Allison grinned. "Good. I'll get Joy ready. Can you two be ready in a half hour?"

David shot a glance at Sondra, who lifted an eye-brow before returning to her mixing. Clearly, she was expecting him to answer, to *know* what to answer. He was just going to have to, that was all.

"We'll just toss this pie in the oven and get ready."

Having mixed in the shortening and shaped her flour mess into a ball, Sondra looked up again. "Yeah, it will only take a few minutes."

"Great." Allison rolled her lips inward as if she was holding back a smile as she hurried out of the room.

"She doesn't think we can do this," Sondra said as soon as her cousin was out of earshot.

"Well, she's wrong." Annoyed, he cracked an egg on the side of his bowl and then had to dig a good-sized piece of shell out of the mixture. He frowned at Sondra as she fought back a grin. "Well, she is."

"Okay."

"Is that crust about ready?"

"I guess." Sondra lifted her rolling pin to show him the uneven oval of dough on the counter. "I just have to get it in the pie pan now."

That particular chore required both of them, and some water added to repair the tears in the dough, but before long they had orange-brown filling in the shell and he was settling the creation in the oven. Only a little filling sloshed over the side of the plate and landed on the oven element before he closed the door.

"Well, we did it." Sondra peeked in the oven door and smiled.

"It will be done by the time we get home from church."

They washed up and turned off the kitchen lights. David felt just a little smug with their accomplishment. This Christmas dinner thing was going to be a piece of cake. The best part of all was they would be able to have that cake and eat it, too.

Chapter Five

An acrid scent escaped from the kitchen when Sondra turned Allison's key in the lock and pushed open the side-entrance door.

"The oven!" Sondra shrieked as she rushed into the kitchen. She stared at the oven door, though she couldn't see inside it.

"Aw, man!"

David pressed Joy into her mother's arms, but he must have not heard Allison's helpless "wait" because he rushed over and threw open the lower oven door. A cloud of black smoke rolled upward, and he had to jump back to avoid singeing his eyebrows. Next to him, Sondra shot out of the way, as well.

"Wait," Allison said a second time, and the other two turned to stare.

Balancing a wide-eyed toddler on her hip, she crossed to the back door and propped it open. She turned to face them with a hint of a smile on her lips.

Sondra's reaction was swift and startling. It was all

she could do not to throw herself between her cousin and her cooking partner to shield him from criticism. And Allison hadn't even criticized. She'd only smiled when they should have been laughing together. It was funny, wasn't it?

Since when had she and David become allies instead opponents? He certainly hadn't asked for her support, so she couldn't understand her temptation to side with him whether he liked it or not.

As if the situation wasn't chaotic enough, the kitchen smoke alarm started blaring. Sondra grabbed a dishtowel and flapped it below the detector, but the machine continued to squeal.

David pointed to the oven. "You get the pie. I'll get the alarm." He stretched up and pulled the case off the smoke alarm and fiddled with the battery.

While he was still working, Sondra grabbed a pair of oven mitts and reached into the oven. At least she could see inside now well enough to retrieve what was left of the pie. No longer a festive orange, the pastry was charred and oily looking on top, and its crust was so overcooked and brown that parts of it crumbled as she pulled it from the oven. She carried it out the back door and set it on the sidewalk. When it was cool enough not to melt the bag, it would go in the garbage where it belonged.

Behind her, the squawking stopped. David was opening the kitchen window when she came back through the door.

"I don't really like pumpkin pie anyway," she said.

"We torched it just for you." Despite his sardonic tone, David's lips turned up as he said it.

"Wow, my first Christmas present. Thanks."

"You're welcome."

"Was this oven my present?" Allison asked from behind them.

Both turned to see Allison examining her empty oven. Inside it, the liquid filling that had spilled over the sides of the pie had burned all over the heating element and the bottom.

Sondra shook her head. "No, cleaning it will be our present."

"Do you think you could spill something in the garage? Brock needs a present, too."

David curled his lip at her. "I've just crossed you both off my holiday list." He went to her and relieved her of her child. "But this one," he paused to nuzzle the baby, "she can have anything she wants."

Sondra found it sweet the way David stared down at Joy with such adoration, as if he loved her to the bottom of his heart. The man was such a contradiction: someone with a reputed fear of commitment, but clearly his ties to his friends were deeply fused. He was committed. A small part of her wished she could be on the receiving end of David's friendship.

"Hey, Sondra."

She flinched as she realized her cousin had spoken to her. She turned to see Allison studying her. Knowing.

Shaking her head, Sondra tried to cover her slip. "I just can't get over how beautiful Joy is." She approached Allison and took her hand. "I'm so happy to become a part of her life and to have found my way back into yours."

Allison squeezed her hand, her eyes misting. "Well, you need to know that we're pretty selfish with the people in our lives. I'll have Brock handcuff you and extradite you if you try to slip away again."

"I'll keep that in mind."

Sondra glanced over at David, whose attention was now on the two of them rather than the baby who was playing with the designs in his sweater. To her surprise, he didn't appear jealous of her new relationship with her cousin, but perhaps pleased for her.

"Okay, Allison, it's time for you to lie down so Sondra and I can get Christmas dinner on the table," he said, already returning to his list of details. "It might have to be more simple than we planned, but we should have something together by the time that Brock gets home from his shift."

Sondra nodded. "Sure, we still have a lot of things—turkey, peas, rolls, mashed potatoes. I just have to get the potatoes started."

Moving to the stovetop, she stared into the pan of peeled potatoes. Red and shriveled-looking peeled potatoes.

Her jaw dropped. After several seconds, she finally was able to speak again. "Um…turkey, peas and rolls anyway."

David and Allison crowded up behind her and peered into the pan. When David looked up, he frowned.

"Oh," Allison said before looking up. "They turn colors just like apples if you don't put them in water soon enough after cutting them."

It was Sondra's turn to say "oh." David didn't say anything at all. No condemnation. No *Allison likes her potatoes this way.* He wasn't even laughing. As Sondra kept studying him and expecting him to say something, answers to a few of her questions accumulated in her mind.

Allison cleared her throat. "You know, I am a little tired. Maybe Joy will cuddle up and rest with me until dinner." She reached out her arms for Joy, who went willingly into them. Allison couldn't seem to get out of the room fast enough, and what sounded suspiciously like laughter followed her down the hall.

Sondra waited until her cousin closed her bedroom door before she faced David. "You have no idea what you're doing, do you?"

"What are you talking about?"

"Don't act so innocent with me. You've been dominating the cooking like the next Wolfgang Puck, and you're as clueless in a kitchen as I am. Otherwise, you would have known that potatoes turn red and pumpkin pies can't bake for two-and-a-half hours."

She expected a vehement denial, but David only turned away and dumped the ruined potatoes into the garbage can. When she was certain he wouldn't answer her question, he straightened and met her gaze.

"Guilty."

She shook her head. "Why did you do it?"

He shrugged. "Your guess is as good as mine."

"You wanted to prove to Allison that you could be more valuable to her than some interloping cousin from Kentucky?"

"Okay, your guess is better than mine."

She smiled at that. "Or at least as good. Are you going to let Allison in on your little secret, or am I?"

"She knows."

Sondra stared at him incredulously. "And she was going to let us bang around in the kitchen all day and let me believe you knew what you were doing?"

"As she said, she wasn't in a position to turn down offers. I offered."

I didn't, she wanted to say, but she hadn't exactly refused, either.

David looked in the upper oven at the now golden bird. "At least we'll be able to have a dinner of some kind. The little white thing popped up, so it's supposed to be done. Just pop the peas in the microwave, we'll slice the turkey and, voilà, Christmas dinner."

She stood beside him and peered in. "It looks right, and it smells the way it should, so it's probably okay."

"Sure, it's okay. I always heard that only an idiot could mess up a turkey."

"I would have thought the same thing about potatoes."

He shook his head. "No, never potatoes. Those are hard to make."

She laughed with him then, surprised by both his kindness in letting her off the hook and how good it felt to laugh with him. A voice inside her whispered that she could get used to this, but she tucked it to the back of her mind where it belonged.

"One time I watched a sitcom where the character did something really dumb with a turkey."

He was still laughing. "What did she do?"

"You know that plastic bag thing inside the turkey—the one with the bird's neck, heart, liver and gizzard in it? Well she actually cooked it inside the bird."

David wasn't laughing anymore. In fact, he couldn't have looked more shocked if she'd slapped him.

She stared at him for several seconds. "You didn't!"

He only shoved his hands back through his hair, grumbling things best left unrepeated under his breath.

"You left it inside?"

"I can't believe it. I just can't believe it."

He looked so desolate that she couldn't help feeling sorry for him. She glanced back and forth between David and the turkey that still might have been edible, but there was no way they would be able to serve it. The yuck factor on the entrée would be far too high.

"David, it was just a mistake."

"What are we supposed to feed everyone? Now because of me, there'll be no Christmas dinner."

"Well, they might not have a picture-perfect dinner, but they'll definitely have something to eat."

He met her gaze and lifted a questioning brow.

"You put the peas in the microwave, dump that cranberry sauce in a bowl and put the rolls on the table." She paused until he looked back at her from the microwave. "I'll call for pizza delivery."

Chapter Six

Following the dinner prayer, David lifted his head and opened his eyes. Everyone around him was smiling—Joy, Allison and Sondra. Even Brock had a big grin on his face, probably because he was comfortable out of uniform and dressed in jeans and a sweatshirt.

"'God bless us every one!'" Sondra called out in her best Tiny Tim imitation from *A Christmas Carol.*

Bah. His own traditional Dickens line was on the tip of his tongue again, but he glanced at his friends and took a drink of water instead. They all were his friends now, even Sondra, though it had taken a Christmas dinner of horrors to cement their bond.

He couldn't help smiling at her suggestion that they order out and her determination to find at least one place open on the holiday. Only one had been, but she'd been great—first in not blaming him for the turkey fiasco and then in working with him instead of against him to find a solution. He met Sondra's gaze as he raised his water glass.

"Yes, every one," he said finally.

"I don't know about you guys, but I'm starved," Brock said as he threw open one of the boxes and lifted out a slice of pizza. "It's been a long day— what with booking bank robbers and solving a stack of cold cases."

"Hand out a lot of tickets to families going a little too fast on their way to grandma's house, did you?" David even managed to keep a straight face when he asked it.

The deputy grinned. "Just a lot of warnings. Have to make sure everyone gets there in one piece." Finally, Brock took a bite of the pizza, and his expression was one of pure bliss. "Everything but anchovies. How'd you know that was my favorite kind?"

"How do you know there aren't anchovies on that pizza?" Allison asked her husband nonchalantly as she cut up tiny bites and set them on Joy's high chair tray.

Brock looked suspiciously at the pizza for a few seconds before frowning at her.

"You're safe," Sondra told him. "Your wife promised another round of toilet hugging if we put fish on her pizza."

Though Allison had taken special pains with her makeup and hair to look her best before Brock came home from work, she appeared a little paler than before. The dark circles beneath her eyes were a little more pronounced. She'd been resting for quite a while earlier. Was she sick again?

"Are you okay, pal?" David studied her across the table as he asked.

Allison smiled, but her gaze didn't quite meet his. "I'm fine. Our outing to the services just took more out of me than I expected. I'll probably make it an early night."

"Of course she's fine." Brock grinned. "She's beautiful. But she's got a tough job carrying around our baby while chasing after our big girl. God's got some great plans for this little one."

He touched his wife's abdomen for a few seconds and then lifted her hand. Their fingers laced as if they'd practiced that very gesture daily just to make it appear so effortless now.

David smiled over the love his friends had been so fortunate to find. Suddenly, though, he found himself staring down at Sondra's hand as it rested on the table next to him. The same hand that had gripped his in a firm but cold handshake the night of the nativity performance.

Now he could see that it wasn't a fragile hand. It appeared strong, with fine long fingers and short-trimmed nails. It would probably be warm, too. He wondered how it would feel to fold his fingers around hers and feel them closing over his in a gesture that would be more about sharing than leading or following.

"Hey, good thing these two messed up Christmas dinner. I like pizza better than all that froufrou stuff anyway."

David startled at Brock's words and took a drink of his water to cover his discomfort. What was wrong with him? When had he gone from not liking Sondra at all to definitely not *not* liking her? He was about to damage his reputation as a ladies' man if he let this particular woman get under his skin.

If Sondra noticed his slip, she didn't make any indication, but the hand he'd been regarding slipped gracefully into her lap to grip her napkin. "Hey, Brock, don't accuse us of not being froufrou. We still have Aunt Mary's china and crystal, and a whole batch of chocolate chip cookies that we made with Allison's help."

"I stand corrected then. I just want to compliment the chefs on our great Christmas dinner."

"I'm partial to peanut butter toast myself," Allison replied.

Sondra lifted an eyebrow and looked back and forth between the two of them.

David leaned his head toward her to explain. "That's supposed to be an inside joke about their first date, which really was a makeshift Christmas dinner after they'd been searching all day for Joy's birth mother."

"Remind me never to confide in you again because you can't keep a secret." Allison's attempt at a scowl failed when her lips turned up.

David grinned back at her. "Um, Allison, never tell me anything again because I can't keep a secret."

Sondra straightened in her chair, her slice of pepperoni pizza still dangling in her hand. "I, however, am available should you need a good listening ear that doesn't belong to a blabbermouth."

"I'll keep that in mind," Allison answered, but she

looked back and forth between her cousin and friend, as if waiting for the next round of ammunition to be discharged.

David raised both of his hands, palms up. "What? Do you think I'm going to wrestle her to the floor until she cries uncle and says she'll stay away from my friend?"

"It crossed my mind," Allison said in a small voice.

Brock chewed on his pizza, trying not to smile. Sondra looked away, appearing determined not to make eye contact with any of them.

David pressed his lips together but just couldn't keep a straight face. Once he started laughing, he couldn't stop that, either. "Okay, I deserve that."

Sondra raised her hand. "Me, too."

And she started laughing. Brock and Allison followed. Even Joy got in on the action with her high-pitched tinkling laugh, as she clapped her hands in delight.

When he could finally talk again, David turned back to Allison. "So why'd you do it? Or rather why'd you let *us* do it?"

"I already told you, I wasn't in a position to turn down offers as much as I still had to do to get ready for Christmas." She paused to smile at Sondra and David by turns. "You two were competing so hard that this house is cleaner than it's been in a long time."

"Except the oven," Brock chimed.

She nodded. "Except that."

Sondra waved her fork to get a turn. "I'll be cleaning that tomorrow, remember?"

"We," David said simply.

"Right," the other three chimed.

Allison waved her hand. "Anyway, with me out of commission and with Brock out protecting holiday travelers, we couldn't have done all this without you guys. You've made our first Christmas as a family so special."

Brock nodded his agreement. "Yeah, thanks, you two. We really appreciate it. I hated not being here when Allison needed me, but you really came through for us."

They had, hadn't they? But as much as the praise flattered David, it embarrassed him, too. Didn't they realize that even with competing against Sondra, he'd had the best Christmas of his life with them?

The holiday felt different at the Chandler house, as if it was about faith and family, giving and cherishing. If the celebration had touched his heart, just imagine what an impact it would have had on him if he still believed all the lessons he'd been taught in Sunday school.

Disquiet filled him, so David pushed the thoughts away and glanced over at Sondra. She was staring down at the table and twirling her fork in a puddle of pizza sauce and peas on her plate. Clearly, Brock and Allison's praise had affected her, perhaps even humbled her the way it had him.

"Joy sure loved all her toys, especially her baby doll," Sondra said to fill the lull.

Brock laughed. "Not as much as she loved the boxes, the wrapping paper and the bows."

Sondra's head came up, and she quipped, "Even the ones that David wrapped."

"There's nothing wrong with my wrapping ability."

But one side of Allison's mouth popped up, and soon they were all laughing again. Though a fire crackled in the fireplace in the family room, no one in the Chandler house needed it for warmth. It was all around them.

David's chest tightened. He'd always told himself he didn't want or need any of this—a home, a family, something more permanent than the stacked crates of law books and the pressed board dressers in his apartment. But now he wasn't so sure.

Had Sondra changed his mind? No, they barely knew each other. Still, the fact that he was having these thoughts told him he needed to step away and get his head on straight. To sequester himself in a jury room under lock and key. He certainly couldn't do it while Sondra was sitting right there beside him—close enough to touch.

When the snickering finally settled, David pushed away from the table and stood. He stacked several plates to carry into the kitchen.

"Here, let me get those."

Instead of grabbing for her own stack, Sondra reached for the dishes in David's hands. The brush of her fingers over his was unintentional, yet downright electric. David pulled his hand away but not before he shot a glance across the table to see if the sparks had burned anyone else.

Allison had looked away at the right time to miss

the exchange, but Brock was staring at him. He lifted a brow.

As if she recognized a tense moment about to become even more strained, Joy spoke up then, her loud babbling filling the room again. As soon as she had all of their attention, the one-year-old reached up her arms and said a brand-new word: "Tonda."

Sondra glanced back over her shoulder as she carried an armload of dishes into the kitchen. Close behind, David balanced heirloom china in one hand and an empty pizza box in the other.

Taking up the rear, Brock carefully carried four water glasses.

"Okay, you guys, just set them on the counter and get out of our kitchen," Brock said. "I'll take care of all this as soon as I get Allison and Joy settled."

Sondra shook her head. "It will only take us a few minutes to get this put away. By the time they're both in bed, we'll be done and you can relax."

Brock set the dishes down and crossed his arms, his legs in the wide stance of a standoff, and the deputy probably wasn't in the habit of losing those.

"You two have done more than your share today. The least I can do is clean up."

David tilted his head at an odd angle and lifted his eyebrow. "Does this mean you're cleaning the oven?"

"Not a chance. You two can take that one on tomorrow. But for now, I want you to vamoose."

David nodded. "Okay. I guess I'll go home then."

"And I'll help Allison get ready for bed," Sondra said. They both started toward the dining room.

"Wait," Brock paused until they stopped. "I was just thinking that there's a really cool Christmas lights display at Hope Park. We'd planned to take Sondra to see it, but since Allison's a little tired, why don't the two of you go together?"

The deer-in-the-headlights look on David's face would have been funny if it hadn't hurt so much. Was being alone with her really such a horrifying idea, especially when Brock's suggestion had sounded like a fine one to her? Too fine for her own good sense.

"It would be great, but I shouldn't. It's getting late, and I need to get home."

Brock cocked his head, seeming to enjoy watching his guest squirm. "Oh, it's not that late. You could walk around the park for an hour and still be at home by ten."

Backing away a step, David tried again. "I still haven't stopped by to exchange gifts with my parents yet."

"Didn't you say your mother would have a houseful of guests and that you could go by tomorrow?"

"Sure, but—"

"I'd really appreciate it. Allison would, too."

David was trapped, and they all knew it. He shrugged and turned to Sondra. "It is a really clear night, so the displays will look great. Want to go see them?"

It was Sondra's turn to be horrified. She couldn't bear the idea of forcing him to escort her. She'd never had to coerce a man into taking her out before, and she wasn't about to start now.

She rolled her lips, too embarrassed to look at him, so she glanced at Brock instead. "You know, I'm kind of tired, too. Maybe I'll just turn in early."

Taking a deep breath, she gathered her courage and faced David. "Thanks so much for the offer, but I think I'll have to—"

She didn't even have the word "decline" formed in her mouth before Brock stepped between them. "You guys are really disappointing me. If you two early-to-bed homebodies are the best examples of quality singles we have around here, then the future for Destiny looks dim."

Instead of responding to Brock, David turned back to Sondra again. "Come on. It will be fun. We can't disappoint the old married folk, can we?"

"Well, with an offer like that, how can I refuse?" And how could she be so pathetic as to have a tripping pulse and sweaty palms over *an offer like that?*

Brock let out an audible sigh. "Good then, that's settled. I didn't think I would ever get the two of you out of my house so I could be alone with my wife."

When both of them jerked their heads to face him, Brock grinned. "Tomorrow's our anniversary, you know."

Sondra was glad this outing would make someone happy because, whether he'd painted on a smile for it or not, David didn't wanted to be with her. But hadn't this whole week been about doing something for her cousin's benefit instead of hers? Her thoughts settled, she grabbed her parka and headed for the door. This would be a night they would probably both remember—as a torture for him and a humiliation for her.

Chapter Seven

Sondra leaned her head back and stared up into the cloudless night sky above Hope Park, awed by the huge black canvas dotted only by a dusting of stars. Though the frigid temperature was a telltale sign that winter had taken up long-term residence in the Hoosier state, the wind wasn't blowing now, so the drifts of powdery snow held their shape rather than constantly transforming.

"It's beautiful, isn't it?" Sondra's question came out as a sigh.

"You mean the lights? They're great."

Under the illumination of the displays and the park safety lights, Sondra could see him clearly, so she was well aware he'd been studying the celestial display rather than the earthbound one just as she had been.

"No. All this." She spread her hands wide and looked up again, inhaling the Christmas air. Her lungs ached over its chill, but she barely noticed. Inside, she felt warmer than she had in days.

"You're right. It's beautiful."

She smiled at his words as they trudged along the park path, the hard-packed base of snow crunching beneath their feet. They passed displays formed of multicolored lights, but these images of Santa Claus and his eight tiny reindeer, Christmas trees and Frosty the Snowman couldn't compare to God's creation displayed above them in twinkling lights.

How ironic that the closest she'd felt to God during the season celebrating Jesus' birth was with David, who Allison had told her was in a "questioning period" about his faith.

"Do you think the shepherds saw a clear sky like this the night Jesus was born?" She swept a hand wide and twirled around to follow it. "Except for the huge star, that is?"

"If I remember the story correctly, in the Book of Luke, it wasn't a star that brought the shepherds to the manger. Wasn't it an angel who showed up in the fields, scared them to death and told them the Good News?"

Sondra chuckled. Speaking of irony, he sure had a good handle on the Scriptures for someone who wasn't sure he believed them. She was reminded of another time when he'd questioned her knowledge on the story of Jesus' birth, but that seemed like a lifetime ago rather than days. A lot could happen in a few days—to perceptions and even to feelings.

"I know. I know." She shook her head. "The only mention of the star in the east came in the Book of Matthew, when the Wise Men were following it. It's strange how we think we know the nativity story, but it has changed so much in the retelling."

He nodded as they passed a particularly large light display with a *Babes in Toyland* theme.

"For instance, if we were being strictly Biblical in the live performance, we wouldn't have had Martin and his fellow Wise Men near the manger since they visited some time later at a house," he said.

"And we wouldn't have had the cows and sheep that the Bible never specifically mentions," she added.

David stood still and looked up at one of the light displays, this one with of a manger scene just like the one they'd performed. He stared at it for several long seconds before turning back to her. "Our donkey-slash-Shetland pony wasn't Scriptural, either, but we liked her anyway."

Sondra couldn't help smiling. She'd expected some awkwardness between them after the way David had been coerced into bringing her, but he'd been really nice.

"Maybe we don't tell the story perfectly, but at least we tell it."

With a nod at her words, David turned back to study the crèche again. Sondra stood admiring it as well, until the wind picked up and sent a chill through her. She pulled her hood tight over her ears.

"If you're cold, we can go."

"No, I'm fine. Allison's boots are great." She caught him glancing at the heavy cold-weather boots. "See Allison and I do have a few things in common. Including really big feet."

"More than a few."

His words brought her head up again, but David looked away before she could study his expression. Were these commonalities good things in his opinion or further reasons to convince him he shouldn't have come tonight?

Neither said anything for several seconds, and when David did speak again, he changed the subject.

"I really didn't want to come here tonight."

"No." The word was out of her mouth, dripping with sarcasm, before she had a chance to censor herself.

The side of his mouth that she could see in profile lifted. At least he thought her outburst was funny instead of pitiful.

"But not for the reasons you must be thinking."

"Which are?"

Both of his shoulders lifted and then dropped. "I don't know. You have to think I didn't want to come here because it was with you."

Sondra had to hold her breath to keep from sighing her relief. As if her sarcastic "no" hadn't been enough of a giveaway.

"I mean, it *was* because I didn't want to go with you, but…"

He let his words fall away just as the nearly inaudible "oh" slipped past her lips. Any lingering hope that he hadn't heard it evaporated when he faced her.

"Look, I'm not saying what I mean here."

He held his hands wide in a plea for understanding, but it was pretty hard to oblige him when she was so busy trying to guard feelings that should never have been this vulnerable in the first place.

"Are you always this eloquent as a speaker in court?"

He chuckled. "Sometimes more so. But let me try, okay?" He didn't wait for her to answer but pressed on as if he couldn't afford to lose momentum. "What I'm saying is I didn't want to come here with you—to be anywhere alone with you—because I wanted…"

What? That she managed not to shout it loudly enough to wake the park's hibernating creatures amazed her. Still, she didn't have to wait long for his answer.

"This." He lifted her gloved hand and laced his leather-clad fingers with hers.

Time must have passed, individual sparkling lights must have blinked on and off a few dozen times in synchronization, but her world paused as she saw nothing but their joined hands. Through his gloves and hers, she could still feel his warmth, and instead of anxiety, his touch brought her peace.

When she glanced up from their hands, David was staring at her. He wasn't laughing or even grinning. If anything, the Casanova of Destiny looked uncertain, and that newest irony of the night made her chuckle.

"If my moves are that funny, then I must be losing my touch."

Somehow she guessed that David had tamed his *moves* on her behalf. She shook her head. "Not funny."

His lips curved up. "Good. I never wanted to be a comedian."

He lifted her hand into the crook of his arm and started walking again. If this was how wonderful it felt to be a part of a couple, then she wondered why she'd made a habit of keeping her distance.

"From your live nativity performance, I'm guessing you also don't want to be an actor."

"Not if I can help it."

They walked on in a comfortable silence past displays of snowflakes, hammering elves, a trio of Wise Men on camels and a Madonna scene of Mary and the Christ child.

"This isn't your average Christmas lights display, is it?" Sondra said after the last.

"So you noticed. Hope Park is privately owned so there aren't any of those church and state issues. That way many of the displays can show what the owner sees as the true meaning of Christmas."

She couldn't help giving him a sidelong glance to see if he was serious. "What the owner sees? You don't believe Jesus' birth is the true meaning?"

"I used to believe it all." He looked past her to a wooded area. "I don't know what I believe anymore?"

"How could you have played the part if you didn't believe?"

"What can I say? I'm a sap, and my best friend coerced me into doing it."

Sondra glanced at him again. "Didn't it feel dishonest?"

"Sometimes. It did feel a lot like acting."

"But you know the Scriptural nativity story so well."

He glanced up into that clear sky once more. "Knowing and believing aren't the same things."

Sondra stewed on that as they continued on the path. He was right; those things were devastatingly different when it came to eternity. For the first time since he'd taken her hand, she felt cold, but the sensation was inside rather than on her skin's surface, and more for his sake than hers.

"What made you question? I know you were raised in a Christian home. Allison told me your parents go to her church."

"Now there's some acting for you." He looked straight ahead as he walked, his jaw tight. "My parents were too busy being seen in their third-row pew at church and funding events for their high-profile charities to remember they had two boys waiting for them at their so-called Christian home."

"You have a brother?"

"Michael. He's four years older. After college, he bought a ticket to Seattle and never came back."

A lot of things about David were beginning to make sense. "But you did, even if you did join a small law firm known for pro bono work instead of working at the practice your grandfather started in the thirties."

He turned his head to look at her. "How do you know all that?" Then he answered his own question. "Allison."

She made an affirmative sound in her throat. "So part of your protest against your parents is to boycott the faith they taught you."

He appeared to consider it several seconds before answering. "Maybe."

That was likely the closest thing to an admission she would get, so she didn't push it. Instead, she tilted her head back and studied the patterns of stars above her. "What do you see up in the sky?"

"You mean other than the Big Dipper, Little Dipper and Orion?"

She smiled. "I see God's creation. It's amazing. Maybe it sounds naive, but I really believe He placed those stars up in the sky for us to enjoy."

"Not naive." He stared at those same spots of light.

His words surprised her, but she didn't tell him so. "I have the same kind of feelings about Christ's birth. The live nativity was so poignant to me because it made God's sacrifice real to everyone there."

"The aroma sure was real."

She shook her head at his comment. "Can you imagine the enormity of it? God was sending his son, not to be a little darling asleep on the hay. He was sending Jesus to grow up in the real world and then to die for our sins."

Instead of answering her, he gently pulled away, causing her hand to fall back to her side. He turned to study one of the displays, this one of a choir of angels rejoicing. While he looked, Sondra studied him, trying to ignore how cold her hand felt no longer tucked in the crook of his arm.

"I don't buy it," she said finally.

David glanced over his shoulder in surprise. "Buy what?"

"That you don't believe. You speak of your faith in the past tense, and yet you stare at the stars, just as amazed as I am. I think your faith is still important to you, but maybe you've just lost your way a little."

When he turned back to her, he gave her his endearing half smile. "A little?"

"Okay, maybe a lot, but no matter how far you've traveled, God's always there, waiting for your return."

"It must be comforting to be so certain."

"God's the only certainty I've ever had in my life," she admitted, surprising herself by being so frank. Opening to him felt dangerous in some ways and freeing in others. She didn't know how to reconcile those feelings, and she wasn't prepared to try.

David stepped toward her and took her hand again. "I'm glad you've had your faith to rely on then, because I wouldn't want you to be alone."

Sondra drew in a breath. Just as he'd touched her hand, now he'd caressed her heart. She could almost feel it warming and stretching, opening to him in a way she hadn't expected, hadn't planned. Suddenly, she wanted to touch his heart, too, in a spiritual and a personal way. She didn't want him to be alone, either.

"Are you afraid to let God closer in your life?" she asked him.

His smile was slow, thoughtful, as he rubbed his thumb over the back of her hand. "Sure, I guess. But aren't we all afraid of something?"

Their gazes caught. Held. When he broke the connection, he lowered his gaze to her mouth. He was going to kiss her, and she was going to let him. She felt it with a clarity she'd seldom felt in her life.

But then his words filtered into her thoughts, muddling them. Yes, they both had fears. Her own question came flying backing into her face. Was she afraid? No, she was terrified. Not of her personal relationship with God, but of allowing anyone else to get that close.

Panic had her shoulders tightening, her elbows pressing into her ribs. This was a mistake. Sure, David seemed wonderful now, but what if he were just like her father. He already had a reputation as a scoundrel of sorts. Could she bear to be left again? No, the risk was too great. How would she gather up the pieces of her broken heart when he left?

Unaware of the war inside her, David leaned in so close that she could feel his warm breath on her cheek. Releasing her hand, he instead rested both of his hands on her shoulders. He studied her expression, waited. He was asking for permission. It was so sweet and endearing. But it was also something she couldn't give.

"Uh, David, I can't do this."

Hurt flashed alongside the flickering lights in his eyes before he released her, his expression carefully blank. "Can't or won't?"

She only shook her head. Could she even explain her choices when her heart's survival depended on it? For self-preservation alone, Sondra had pulled back from the only kiss she'd ever truly wanted.

Chapter Eight

That next afternoon David rang the doorbell of the Chandler household for the third time in as many days. Dreading this visit most of all, he wiped some of the new snow off his coat and stomped the gray slush off his boots.

Lord, please let Allison answer the door instead of Sondra. He startled, surprised by how easily he'd reopened his dialogue with God, particularly when he needed something. And he needed something, all right. He needed to know what to say when he had to face Sondra again.

Unfortunately, he didn't have time to wait for divine inspiration as the woman in question opened the door.

"Hello." Sondra kept glancing up at him from under her lashes, looking as embarrassed as he felt.

"Sorry I'm late. I had breakfast with my parents so we could exchange gifts."

She cocked her head. "What are you doing here?"

"Aren't we supposed to clean the oven?"

"I've already started it. Didn't Allison tell you it's self-cleaning?"

She pressed her lips together, the same lips that he'd come so closing to kissing last night. If he were honest with himself, he would have to admit that he still wanted to kiss her, too, right there on the porch. But admitting it was more than his pride could handle.

By now she was wringing her hands and balancing her weight first on one foot and then the other.

"Are you going to come in out of the cold?"

He grinned. "I guess I could."

Sondra let him in and closed the door behind him, but she seemed to be looking beyond him or beside him. Anywhere but at him.

"I have to get back to the kitchen. Joy's having a snack."

As if on cue, the sound of metal pounding on plastic poured out of the kitchen.

David recognized the sound. "She has her spoon again."

"She loves to beat it on the tray." Sondra led the way into the kitchen where Joy, buckled safely in her high chair, was performing a drum solo with a teaspoon.

Joy paused from beating on the tray and causing Cheerios to bounce to the floor long enough to turn to him and point. "Dabe. Dabe. Dabe."

"Hey there, kiddo," David said.

Sondra bent to pick up some of the mess. "Okay, Joy, we're going to have to eat some of these, too. The ones that haven't hit the floor yet."

David smiled, knowing Sondra couldn't see him and wouldn't ask what he found so amusing. At least they had one safe subject—Joy—in their conversation filled with awkward pauses. He had a pretty good idea that the subjects of their trip to the park and a kiss that didn't happen were off-limits.

Maybe they were better off if they didn't discuss those things anyway. At least it saved him from wondering when he had transformed from a successful social angler to one who could only wonder about the fish who got away.

Even after getting to know him, Sondra apparently still didn't think he was good enough for her. All night the reality of it had eaten at him. But worse than being bothered by it, something inside him made him want to prove her wrong. He wanted to tell her he could be different with her. How could he promise that, though, when even he didn't know whether he would desert her before the never-never land of the third date?

Because that question had no answer and it only exhausted him to search for it, he turned to another safe subject. "Where's Allison?"

"She's resting." She glanced over at him and lowered her voice. "I think she's still recovering from yesterday's excitement."

Concern had him stepping closer to press Sondra for the details he craved. "You're sure she's okay?"

Sondra nodded. "I was worried, too, but she assured me she's just tired."

David felt his body relax. "Well, okay. At least she's taking care of herself."

She smiled at him, the first comfortable expression since he'd arrived. "My cousin is very fortunate to have a friend like you."

"She didn't do so badly in the relative department, either."

"I can't decide if that's praise or not since she didn't exactly choose me." She tilted her head and studied him. "You were talking about *me,* right?"

When she started laughing, David joined in, and Joy giggled and clapped her hands. They were finally over their discomfort from last night, and he didn't want to cause more awkwardness between them, so he decided it would be best for them to just remain friends. Then when she returned to Kentucky, he could wish her well and get back to his own life.

"I'm so glad you talked me into doing this." Sondra spun around on the sidewalk late that afternoon, holding her hands out to catch snowflakes and feeling like a child seeing snow for the first time. "It's beautiful out here."

"I just wanted to get out of the kitchen and away from the smell of the self-cleaning oven burning off the pumpkin pie stuff." He broke into a feigned coughing fit, covering his mouth with one hand and pushing the stroller with the other.

She nodded. "It was pretty bad, but that whole room shone by the time we were finished with it."

"Joy needed to get out of the house for a while, too." He glanced down at the baby, who was asleep and covered with a tiny quilt.

Sondra followed his gaze to the cherublike face. "Looks like she's getting a kick out of the outing."

"The cool air's good for her." He bent to tuck the quilt up to her chin. "We wore her out with all of those swing and slide races."

And they had. They'd built a tiny snowman on the neighborhood school's playground and had shown Joy how to make snow angels, and then David had pushed Sondra on the swing with the child in her lap. They'd even taken a few goofy snapshots on David's digital camera to share with Brock and Allison.

The afternoon would have been perfect if only Sondra could have relaxed and enjoyed it. Instead, she'd spent the whole time watching David with little Joy and wishing for things she'd never dared to before. A husband. Children of her own. She'd always believed those things were only for other women—ones who weren't independent, successful businesswomen like she was. Women who didn't have her particular scars.

Her internal arguments, though, had fallen as flat as the farmland surrounding Destiny. Though an unlikely choice, David was the one who'd made her thoughts about as clear as the mud on those fields. When her feelings for him had metamorphosed from rival to friend to something more, she wasn't sure, but they had changed, and she had to decide what to do about it.

"We should get back to the house," David said as he turned the stroller around. "Allison's probably awake by now and will be getting hungry."

"My hands are getting numb, too."

He glanced down at her gloved hands but didn't say anything. Still, words he hadn't said—that he'd warmed her hand the night before—hung heavily between them.

"You've got snowflakes on your eyelashes." He stopped the stroller, pulled off his glove and reached over to gently brush them away.

Her face tingled where he'd touched her skin, and she didn't seem to have any breath left, so she was surprised she was able to get out a rough "thanks."

"Glad to be of service."

Only when he'd pushed the stroller past could she finally begin to breathe normally again. Just being near him made her feel alive in a way she'd never experienced before, as if she could do anything just because he was near her. But could she overcome her fears? Could she put her trust in any man and open her heart to him completely? Was she made of the right stuff to trust like that?

Even if she could trust, was David a man she could rely on? He could be a good friend; he'd proven that with Allison. But the trail of broken hearts he'd probably left in his wake suggested that friendship was the most she should ask of him. Could she risk asking for more?

The house was dark when they reached it as, lately, dusk had started stealing daylight before the dinner hour.

"Allison forgot to turn on the Christmas lights," David said as they ascended the walk. He parked the stroller beside the porch and took out Allison's keys.

"Maybe she's still sleeping or reading in her room."

He nodded, but he still hurried to unlock the door. "I just want to check in on her. She's been awfully tired all day." As he pushed the door open, he looked back over his shoulder. "Have you got Joy?"

"Yeah." She moved to the stroller and unbuckled the toddler, who immediately awakened with a moan and a stretch. "Go ahead. I'll be right in."

David didn't wait for further encouragement before he rushed into the house, heading straight for Brock and Allison's room. By the time that Sondra had wrestled Joy's snowsuit from the stroller harness and had reached the room with the still bundled child in her arms, David was sitting on the side of the bed. Allison lay on her side under the covers, her knees drawn up to her middle.

Sondra crossed the room in the three long strides. "What is it? What's the matter?"

"I knew it. I just knew something was wrong," David mumbled as he patted his best friend's shoulder. "You've been sick again, haven't you?"

Allison grimaced, her hands pressed against her barely rounded tummy. A soft moan escaped her before she finally forced out the word "cramping."

Sondra blinked. She knew she should do something, but her feet felt rooted to the floor. She should say something, but she didn't have any words. Even with her limited knowledge of pregnancy issues, she knew what cramping signaled: miscarriage. Or maybe something else, equally horrible. After all of Allison's hard work taking care of her body and even after Sondra and David's battles to be the best care provider to her, she was going to lose her child anyway.

"I paged Brock. Hasn't called back."

"I should have been here," David grumbled again. "I shouldn't have—"

"You've got to stop it, David." Sondra words surprised him as much as they had her. She glanced down at Joy's wide eyes and started swaying so the child didn't cry.

David shook his head, his thoughts appearing to have cleared. "You're right." He turned back to Allison and pushed her hair back from her face as he might have done to a sick child. "We've got to get you to the hospital."

"But Brock—"

"We'll call him. He can meet us at the hospital."

David's clear focus helped Sondra to form a plan of her own. "You get Allison to the car, and I'll see if one of the neighbors can take Joy for a few hours. I'll meet you at the car."

Having a plan helped her keep her thoughts clear as she jogged out the front door with the toddler in her arms. *Lord, please be with Allison and her baby. Hold both of them in the palm of Your hand. Amen.*

Sondra had to knock on three doors before she found someone at home, but Allison's friend down the street offered to keep Joy as long as they needed.

David had her cousin stretched out in the back seat of her car where the infant car seat had been before, and he was waiting in the driver's seat by the time that she came running across the snow-covered lawn to meet them. As soon as she'd climbed in the seat next to Allison and had gathered her close, David threw the gearshift into Reverse.

"Be careful," Sondra told him after he took a fast turn. "You don't want to cause her any more pain."

"I'm doing the best I can, okay?" Without waiting for her answer, he grumbled under his breath, "I should have been there."

Allison's grunt of pain interrupted whatever further self-criticism he would have said next.

"Where's Brock?" Allison murmured.

Sondra squeezed her cousin's arm. "Don't worry, sweetie, he's meeting us there."

"I need him."

"I know you do."

Allison's groan filled the car. "Joy?" she managed.

"She's fine. Jill's watching her."

"The baby…"

At least Allison hadn't phrased the last as a question because Sondra couldn't have answered her if she had. Only God had those answers. Still, she wished there was something she could say to give her cousin hope.

David answered instead. "God's with your baby right now, kiddo. The little one's in good hands."

Sondra tried not to look at him, tried not to lend too much importance to a comment he'd surely made just to comfort his friend. But she couldn't help hoping that David was listening to his own words and that he was aware that God was there to support him, too.

He was going to need the support only God could

give. Already, David was holding himself responsible for something over which he had no control. If something happened to Allison or her baby, he would never forgive himself.

Chapter Nine

Just before midnight Sondra leaned back in a stiff vinyl seat at Cox County Hospital, dangling in that void between sleep and wake. But something bumping against her shoulder made her instantly alert.

Next to her, David's head bobbed again and hit her shoulder harder. He woke with a jolt and shot a glance her way. "Sorry."

She smiled. "It's okay. Why don't you just rest for a while?" She patted her shoulder in the silent offer of a temporary resting place.

"Thanks. I'm okay."

It shouldn't have surprised her that David wouldn't allow himself to risk sleep, not when he'd spent the night being strong for everyone else. He hadn't budged from that chair just outside the emergency room entrance since the medical staff had rushed Allison through it. After Brock had arrived to be at his wife's bedside, David had insisted on staying, at least until they were sure his friend would be all right. Even now he stared at the wooden double doors, as if by doing so he could will them open and could wrestle answers from the closed-lipped hospital staff.

Steadfast. That was the best word Sondra could find to describe his actions tonight. She would never be able to think of that word again without being reminded of the last few hours. Without thinking of David Wright.

Strange, she didn't even mind that he'd stayed for Allison's benefit rather than hers. He'd been there for her, too. Strong when she'd felt vulnerable. Solid when her hope had been riddled with holes. The least she could do was offer a brace when his wall of strength wavered.

She reached over and squeezed the hand he'd set on the armrest. This time he accepted her support, which surprised and pleased her.

They were still holding hands when Brock pulled open one of the double doors and approached them, his hair sticking up where he'd been worrying it with his hands. Brock's face appeared as wan and exhausted as Sondra felt.

And then he smiled.

"She's going to be all right." The words spilled from his lips in a rush. "Praise God, she's going…to be fine." Tears that had been close to the surface from his first word trailed down his cheeks unchecked.

Sondra came out of the seat and gathered Brock into her arms. Another question burned in her mind, but how could she ask it? David stood, as well, and squeezed Brock's shoulder.

Finally, Sondra pulled back, but she still gripped Brock's forearms. "The baby?" Her words came out only as a whisper, but Brock stiffened, signaling that he'd heard.

"Oh." He stepped back and shoved his hand through his hair again. "He's just fine. The doctor said it was severe dehydration that caused the cramping. They're pumping his mommy full of liquids right now, and they're going to have to spend the night here, but he's a real trouper."

Sondra was smiling by then and crossed her arms before she answered him. "You mean he or *she,* don't you?"

Brock shook his head and laughed. "After all tests my wife has undergone today, I can tell you that he is a *he.* Joy's going to have a baby brother."

"Congratulations, buddy."

The somber mood of minutes before evaporated as David and Brock were shaking hands and trading pats on the back. Usually, such male antics would have annoyed her, but now she only smiled. *Thank You, Lord, for protecting them.* Then, as an afterthought, she added, *And thank You for sending David...to all of us.*

David returned to the kitchen after transporting Joy from the portable crib at the neighbor's house to her own bed. He would have expected to be relaxed now, to feel exhaustion pooling in his brain like a pothole in a downpour, but he was keyed up instead, his heart and mind racing.

Sondra looked up from the teakettle she was just placing on the stove. "Did she go down easily for you?"

"She grunted a few times, stuck her backside into the air and crashed."

"I doubt it's going to be that easy for me tonight." She indicated the teakettle with a tilt of her head. "I thought some chamomile might help."

"You, too, huh?"

"Would you like to stay and have some?"

"Do you have anything else without caffeine? Chamomile's only for when you're sick, and I'm never *that* sick."

She pointed to the canister on the counter marked "tea" where he found several herb varieties.

"What a night," Sondra said on a sigh when she finally took a seat next to him, her mug in her hand.

"You can say that again."

"What a—"

He raised his hand. "No, don't."

Still, he smiled. Sondra looked as overwhelmed as he felt. He sensed that she understood him, too, and was surprised that the idea of it didn't terrify him. Neither spoke for several minutes, as words felt extraneous to the situation, but finally the need to share filled him.

"I thought I might lose her tonight. My best friend and her baby."

Sondra rested her elbows on the table and steepled her fingers together. "I know." She didn't have to say it aloud for him to know she'd shared his worries and now shared his relief.

"I haven't prayed the way I did tonight in years."

"Me, neither, and I've been going to church all along." She smiled over the rim of her cup. "Did it feel good?"

"Yeah." He pondered that. Even as far as he'd traveled from God the last few years, the Father had still been there with him, giving him comfort he didn't deserve. "I realized a lot of things tonight."

"What do you mean?"

"I relied on Allison a lot more than I knew."

Instead of pressing, Sondra took another sip of her tea, giving him the freedom to elaborate in his own good time. It was as if she understood that he was admitting these truths to himself for the first time, too, and didn't want to rush him.

"If I let my friend fulfill my need for companionship, I didn't have to risk letting anyone else in. To get close. It was easy to change women like I traded dirty socks when I knew that Allison would always be there for me no matter what."

He took a deep breath, as the last was the hardest to admit. "I was lying to myself."

"I'm pretty good at that, too."

He'd been stirring honey into the tea he wasn't really drinking, and his surprise caused him to clink the teaspoon on the porcelain.

"Has Allison told you anything about my father?"

He shook his head. "I'd assumed he died when you were young or something like that."

"Yeah, something like that." The side of her mouth pulled up, but she still looked sad. "He deserted my mother and me when I was seven. Mom gave up her life and her dream of being a professor of literature for this over-the-road trucker who couldn't bear the constraints of marriage, both in its requirement of making a home somewhere and in that pesky fidelity requirement."

The last surprised him, but it also gave him some insight into Sondra's background. He hurt for the betrayal and abandonment she must have felt as a child.

"Mom never really got over any of it," she continued. "She's still bitter, though she did manage to make a home for us by herself and even teaches literature now at the local community college."

He knew of another person who hadn't recovered from the man's collateral damage, but he didn't mention it. "So how does all of that make you a liar?"

"I use my father as an example of why I should never let anyone get close. Plenty of men in this world are just like him."

Not all, he was tempted to say, so he pushed away the thought. "Your theory sounds reasonable." And it did. Hadn't he used his family for the very same purpose?

She took a sip of her tea and set it aside. "You know that teddy bear Joy's been dragging around? It's mine. The last thing Dad ever gave me before he left."

David couldn't stop picturing that poor little girl she probably still was in many ways. A knot lodged in his throat at the thought of that child, clinging to that teddy bear—then and now.

"Where is he now?" he managed when he'd been sure he couldn't speak.

"Letters have come from Chattanooga and Baton Rouge and even Salt Lake City—usually one every few years or so. But his only true home is the open road."

"You were better off without someone like him. You probably wouldn't be the strong, capable woman you are if he'd stuck around."

"I also wouldn't be the dating nightmare that I am."

They both laughed at that until David finally stopped himself. "You think you're bad. You're talking to a man who's never had a third date with anyone."

She studied him. "Does a third date feel like a marriage proposal or something?"

Surprise had him drawing in a breath. "Something like that."

More like *exactly* like that, but this wasn't the time for specifics. Sondra just *got* him. He wasn't used to women who understood him, except for Allison, who'd always been a friend to him and nothing more.

Sondra shrugged. "I've gotten a few dates beyond three, but not too far past it. I know it's silly, but I figure if I'm always the first to leave, then I'm safe."

"It's not silly."

He understood and, in a lot of ways, had used a similar plan in his own life. His fear was different from hers though. A part of him always wondered if that fear-of-intimacy gene his parents both seemed to carry was hereditary. Until now, it hadn't mattered so much whether he had it in him to really love someone, but Sondra was different than all the others. She tempted him to try.

David didn't realize how quiet he'd become until he glanced at Sondra and found her studying him. An amazed expression shaped her features as though she was just seeing him for the first time, and this time, she'd found him worthy. Funny, he'd never felt less so.

"Your dad really hurt you, didn't he?"

Her only answer was a sad smile.

The rush of emotion came so suddenly and with such intensity that David had to draw in a breath to steady himself. He couldn't stop the words, though, because they came from the heart.

"I would never hurt you."

The need to reach for her was so overwhelming that he had to fist his hands beneath the table to prevent it. He longed to touch her full lips with his, but her refusal from the other night was still fresh in his mind. It had to be her wish that they be together, not just his. So he could do nothing but wait for her to tell him what she wanted.

Sondra drew in an audible breath and chewed her lip. Well, he had his answer, and it wasn't a green light. His disappointment was tinged with other emotions he couldn't define as he gripped the table, preparing to stand.

But the feel of Sondra's fingers covering his stopped him where he sat. "I know" was all she said before she leaned slightly toward him. The trust he saw when he looked into her eyes was his undoing.

Resting his hands on her forearms, he closed the remaining distance between them and pressed his lips to hers. As soon as they touched, he realized his mistake. This was so different from the empty embraces he'd shared with a parade of women. Kissing Sondra felt like an answer to prayer, and he hadn't realized he'd been praying.

He tilted his head and caressed her mouth again, smiling against her skin as her hands traced up his shoulders to his nape. Even after the kiss ended, she didn't pull away but rested her cheek against his.

David closed his eyes, breathing in the sweet scent of wildflowers in her hair. "I could get used to this."

"Me, too," she answered on a sigh.

Because he longed to be a gentleman with her even if he hadn't been one with the women of his past, David came to his feet.

"I'd better get going."

Sondra stood next to him and raised a hand in protest, but he only clasped that hand and drew it to his lips. Then he leaned over and brushed his lips over hers once more. "Good night."

She smiled as he pulled away. "Good night."

Even after David had closed the door behind him and headed out into the frosty night, Sondra remained with him, in his thoughts and in his senses. She'd touched him in a place he'd thought untouchable before—his heart.

Chapter Ten

Just over a month later, Sondra turned off Interstate 69 onto the maze of state roads and county roads leading her back to Destiny. Her chest ached with increasing anticipation as each mile brought her closer to town. Closer to David.

Just outside the town limits, she saw the first of the political signs that made her smile: Be Right—Vote Wright for Superior I Judge. She'd promised David she would make a return visit on his election day, even if she was an out-of-towner and couldn't vote for him. At least the late January weather had cooperated enough to make the journey north from Louisville pretty painless.

"Next time it's your turn to come to my stomping grounds, Mr. Wright," she said to her car's interior. She and David had already agreed as much when he'd first asked her to come the day of the special judicial election. Until now he'd been too busy campaigning to have time for a social life. He had stiff competition in two other local attorneys, both with more legal experience than he had.

More political signs, some for each of the three candidates, dotted the front yards as Sondra reached the center of town. She pulled into the parking lot of New Hope Church, where David had rented the hall for what he hoped would be a victory celebration.

As she climbed out of her car, her gaze went to the open field where their lean-to stable stage had once stood. The stable had still been in place when they'd stopped by during their momentous third real date on New Year's Eve to revisit the location of their unusual first meeting.

What a poignant night that had been, even if David had been more nervous than she'd ever seen him. But then he'd been traveling uncharted waters in his dating experience, so she'd cut him some slack. She'd been ambivalent herself that night, as it was her last evening in town.

She'd also expected that date to be their last.

"Well, look who's rolled out of the big city just to crash the voter polls in Destiny."

The voice that she knew so well from their many phone conversations filtered up behind her, drawing her out of her nostalgia. She turned to see David approaching her.

Trying to ignore her quickening pulse at just the sight of him, she grinned. "I already voted for you three times under three identities. Is that enough?"

He quirked his head. "Just three?"

Instead of waiting for her to come up with another

pithy comment, he rushed right up to her, wrapped her in his arms and lifted her, down parka and all, off the ground.

"You're a sight for sore eyes."

"Why, are your eyes sore?"

"No, but my heart sure is."

She blinked over his comment, but she didn't have time to analyze it because as soon as he'd let her feet touch the ground, he covered her mouth with his. The same sweet tremor, the burst of hope and joy that had wrapped itself around her heart the first time they'd kissed, returned with a vengeance. As she had every time she'd thought about it in the last few weeks, she wondered what she'd been afraid of.

After several seconds, she finally caught her breath. "Are you feeling confident about the election results?"

"I am now." He pulled her close enough that they could touch foreheads.

"You mean you were questioning before? I don't believe it." She'd never once questioned whether David would win the election or whether he belonged in Destiny. Her only uncertainties had been over whether, or even how, she would fit into his life.

"No, I've been sure of everything, especially after that great pep talk last night."

"And the night before that and the night before that." She laughed. "Good thing that you had that one-rate long-distance plan."

The fact was they hadn't missed a single night of talking to each other since she'd driven out of Destiny on the first of January, tears streaming down her face and her heart in her hands.

With one hundred and sixty miles between them, it had been easier for her to convince herself that their relationship was simply casual, a friendship really. But now that he was here in the flesh, the lie she'd been telling herself stood out like muddy footprints on a pristine, white carpet.

"Are you cold? We should get inside." Even as he spoke, he flipped up her collar and zipped her coat to her chin. Then he gathered her to him again. "I'm not ready to share you yet."

She closed her eyes and soaked in his warmth, his soap-fresh scent and the comfort of being encircled in his arms. Only after several seconds of bliss did the questions come. Share her? Did that mean he wanted her to be his alone? No, she had to be reading something into his words, was worrying unnecessarily when he hadn't asked her to give up a single thing for him. She was talking about David here. David, who'd dated more women than could crowd into that church hall. But none as many times as he'd been out with her.

Still, they'd had only three real dates that hadn't involved coercion, not nearly enough to constitute a relationship. It didn't matter that she could add to that number twenty-eight daily phone calls, some lasting long into the night. Nor could she let it count that sometimes she felt so connected to him that her arm might have reached out with his hand or her brain might have received messages with his eyes.

They had lives in two different states with careers that mattered to them and people who counted on them. Only someone without a survival instinct wouldn't have recognized that any long-distance relationship between them would be doomed.

They could date as friends and nothing more. She had to be smart. She had to do anything she could think of to keep herself from falling in love with him. But a sinking feeling inside her told her it was already too late.

David glanced around at his cheering friends and political supporters as he stood at the lectern. They wouldn't have to wait long into the night to know the election results after all. Early returns from the three largest voter precincts were so decisive that he could have declared victory an hour before, but he'd delayed out of respect for his worthy opponents.

Nothing could dampen his joy tonight, not even his parents' presence or the fact that his new job would earn them bragging rights with the country club set. He was the new Superior Court judge. He'd even won by a landslide. And if things went his way, the rest of his life would fall neatly into place before the night was over.

He raised his hands to quiet the applause. "Thank you for coming tonight. I appreciate all of you for your support, your friendship and most importantly, for today anyway, your votes."

Getting the laugh he was hoping for, he pressed on, even if his palms were so sweaty that they kept slipping off the wood at the edge of the lectern. "Now that most of the votes are in, the people have spoken, and all I can say is I am privileged and honored to serve as Cox County's newest Superior Court judge."

Brock Chandler popped up on stage then, carrying Joy. Both of them sported "Be Right—Vote Wright" T-shirts, though Joy's covered her to her toes. "Let's hear it for Judge Wright."

The small crowd erupted in cheers and applause that went on for so long that David started to fidget. He'd never been this nervous speaking before, even in front of a judge, prosecutor, a seated jury and a room packed with spectators. But then, though those other speeches had been important to him and critical to a client's freedom, he'd never had so much personally riding on his words.

"Hey, Judge Wright, can you fix my speeding ticket?" a voice on the far side of the room called out.

David jerked his head toward the sound to find Judge Hal Douglas relaxing in one of the room's few armchairs with a satisfied grin on his face. The heart attack that had caused him to retire early certainly hadn't taken any of the old codger's spunk.

"Sorry, wrong court—you know that. Besides, I won't be sworn in for three weeks. You'll have to take that one up with Deputy Chandler."

"He gave me the ticket," Hal called out.

"So quit it with the lead foot, Judge," Brock responded.

All of the levity around him only made David more agitated. If he didn't speak up now, the perfect moment he'd planned would have passed him by. It might have taken him a lifetime, but he'd finally found the love he'd always craved. Sondra was everything he could have wanted in a woman and more. All of his life, he had proceeded with caution, always kept up his guard to prevent an uppercut to the chin. But tonight of all nights, he no longer wanted to be cautious. He wanted to tell the world about the woman who'd stolen his heart.

He raised his hands to quiet the crowd again. It took several minutes, but finally the volume lowered a fraction.

"I know you've all been patient, but if you'll humor me just a moment longer, then you can spend the rest of the night enjoying all this good food and great company."

He paused but only long enough to draw his breath and gather his courage. "If any of you haven't met her, I wanted to introduce you to my friend, Sondra Stevens." With a hand, he motioned toward her. "Sondra, could you please come up here?"

Her shoulders stiffened and her eyes went wide before she shook her head slightly and mouthed the word "no."

David only grinned. "Come on, now. Don't be shy." Then he turned back to audience members who were looking at him with odd expressions and beginning to whisper. "Everyone, Sondra needs a little encouragement."

Applause broke out again, until a reluctant Sondra approached the lectern. When she reached him, David stepped down and took her hand. He tilted his head toward her. "This is Sondra. We met over a manger."

A few "Hi, Sondra's" drifted from the crowd before its members became quiet. Expectant. Sondra looked so shocked and uncertain that he longed to take her in his arms and tell her everything would be okay. It was too soon, though. The embrace would come in time, but he had to do this right.

"I have a little something I'd like to say to Sondra, if you all don't mind."

A few chuckles broke the silence as he lowered to one knee. The color had drained from her face. He'd expected laughter from her, maybe even a few tears, but this reaction surprised him. That was okay. He had a lifetime to learn to anticipate her moods and reactions.

"Sondra Stevens, you've made me a changed man. You've shown me how happy my life can be."

She held up her free hand and opened her mouth as if to interrupt him, but he shook his head.

"Please, just let me get this out before I explode." He reached up and clasped her second hand. "I love you, Sondra. I didn't even realize I was capable of that, but it was before I met you."

Her eyes flooded then. Now that was more the reaction he'd expected. It hadn't even hurt to say the words out loud that he'd been hiding for weeks in his heart, so he braced himself for the most important ones he would ever speak.

Releasing her hands, he reached into his suit jacket pocket and produced a tiny felt box. Inside was an emerald-cut solitaire diamond. "I want to build a life with you here in Destiny—to work with you, worship with you, raise children with you. Will you be my wife?"

Sondra lowered her gaze to the ground. Her eyes and her throat burned. She couldn't seem to get enough air to stop the empty ache in her lungs. Tears she'd been fighting from the moment he'd called her up front spilled over her lower lids.

She couldn't look at him or the ring he offered because she might see the hope in his eyes. Then she would be lost. She wouldn't have the strength to deny him, even if it cost her.

"Are you okay?" David asked, perhaps for the first time realizing that all was not well.

She didn't even try to stop the tears anymore as they poured down her cheeks and dripped off her chin. Her chest heaved with the hopelessness that settled around her.

"What is it, Sondra?"

She could hear the concern, the fear in his voice, but she didn't reach out to help him. Couldn't.

David came up from his knee and set the box on the lectern. Though he rested his hands on her shoulders, his touch offered no comfort now.

He probably didn't realize that his offer was just like her father's when he'd asked her mother to let go of her life just to be a part of his. Would David also leave as her father had? Would she be like her mother, alone and bitter?

She was so confused. Her fears crowded in so

close about her that she felt smothered by them. David wasn't like her father; she had to believe that. She wouldn't have loved him if he were. Obviously she didn't love him enough though to give up what she wanted for him. He deserved better. Maybe they both did.

Whispers in increasing volume brought her gaze up from the floor. She only wished they didn't have an audience. Forcing herself, she finally met David's gaze. He was still waiting, though his stark expression showed his hope had deserted him.

"Sondra," he began again, but she raised a hand to stop him.

Each word brought a fresh ache to her heart, but she made herself say them anyway.

"I'm sorry, David. I can't marry you."

Chapter Eleven

David was brooding in his office again that Friday morning. He'd mastered the skill in the last three days since he'd been humiliated in front of most of Destiny. As uncomfortable as he'd often felt about his playboy reputation, it was far worse to know that the whole town knew for certain he was a loser at love.

A call from the law office's administrative assistant saying that he had a guest only annoyed him further. He hated that his pulse tripped at the possibility that Sondra might be the one waiting for him outside. Whether he liked it or not, she'd walked away from him, and she probably wasn't coming back.

Allison was standing outside his office door when he opened it.

"Hey, sweetie." She stood on tiptoe to hug him and then stepped past him into the office. Without asking if he was busy, she lowered herself into the upholstered chair opposite his desk.

"Why don't you have a seat?" he grumbled as he returned behind his desk and sat.

"Thanks. I will."

For once, David couldn't muster a smile for his best friend. "What are you doing here?"

"I was just at the obstetrician's." She patted her softly rounded tummy. "I've gained nine whole pounds now."

"That's great."

She nodded, then frowned. "Are you doing okay?"

"Why wouldn't I be?"

"Oh, I don't know. Maybe because Sondra ripped your heart out in front of all your friends and neighbors?"

He brushed his hand through the air and dropped it back on the desk. "Oh, that. It wasn't a big deal."

"Then why did everyone in this office warn me that I was entering a hazardous area by coming in here with you? And why do you look like you haven't slept in a week?"

David shook his head. "I've just been busy getting ready to turn my cases over to the partners before I leave the practice."

"Don't deny that she hurt you, David. Not to me."

He opened his mouth to produce another excuse, but then he clicked it shut. What was the point when his friend could see through him?

"I was wrong about her, that's all."

"Wrong how?"

"To think I could put my trust in her. I know now why I'd never done that before." He shook his head. "I won't make that mistake again."

Allison leaned forward in her chair so that her elbows touched his desk. "Did you think at all about what you were asking of her?"

"Of course I did." He leaned back and crossed his arms. "I asked her to marry me."

"No, it was more than that. In front of everyone, you asked the woman you said you loved to give up her career, her independence and the life she's made for herself."

"I didn't realize—"

"You knew about her scars, and still you put her on the spot before an audience."

David blinked. She was right. He had known, but it hadn't stopped him from making a fool of both of them. He shook his head at his ignorance.

"Here I was thinking I was making the big gesture, and I was just being a jerk."

"Not a jerk exactly." She paused for a few seconds, as if considering what he'd said, before she spoke again. "But there's something you might want to think about. Love isn't just about having someone to fulfill your need for companionship. It's about being the person that *she* needs. About putting her first."

Having said what she'd intended to, Allison hugged him and left him alone to his brood. Only he couldn't work up the steam anymore. He'd been so selfish. He'd thought only of how loving Sondra could better his life when he should have been worried about how his love could improve hers.

Agape. He remembered the Greek word for God's type of sacrificial love from church, but he'd never before seen how it could apply to his life. He understood now, and he wanted to truly love Sondra, putting her hopes and dreams before his own.

But even love couldn't change the fact that he was tied to Cox County now, and her life was in Kentucky. The distance seemed an insurmountable obstacle between them. Was a compromise even possible, and if it was, then how could he find it?

But the realization struck him that the situation wasn't in his hands. It never had been. *Lord, I know You have all the answers here. If it's Your will for the two of us to be together, I know You'll show us the way. Amen.*

David straightened at his desk, feeling confident for the first time since election night, probably even longer than that. It was a relief from the weight of the embarrassment and resentment he'd been carrying.

The experience of giving up control to God was going to take some getting used to, even if any result had to be better than the mess he'd created all by himself. Still, there had to be something he could do in the meanwhile, instead of simply sitting on his hands. Finally, after all this time, he had an idea that might make a difference.

Of course, God would be in charge from kickoff to the final minute, but the Father probably wouldn't mind if he gave a little help from the sidelines. The idea probably had originated from above, anyway, and he was taking credit for it.

No matter its source, at least his plan gave him something to focus on besides missing Sondra. His energy would have to be divided in three ways, though. The first part would go to prayer, an activity he planned to become an expert in during the next few weeks. The second would go to setting a plan into action. Last, but far from least, he would concentrate on doing something he should have done all along—becoming the kind of man Sondra deserved.

Sondra closed the door to her apartment and flipped on the lights, immediately shrugging out of her suit jacket and kicking off her heels. The flat eggshell walls and neutral décor that she used to find so clean and unencumbered mocked her now, just like the comfort she'd once taken in the anonymity of the city.

Trying to ignore the way the apartment's walls closed in about her, she padded into her bedroom to trade the rest of her work clothes for comfortable sweats. If only she could shake off her malaise inside as easily, because it felt as if nothing could comfort her heart since she'd walked out of David's life.

She didn't have to ask herself how much time had passed since she'd made what might have been the biggest mistake of her life. A clock marking the time elapsed—just two hours short of twenty days now— seemed to have been implanted in her mind. The same way David had imbedded himself in her heart.

As Sondra pulled her favorite Kentucky Wildcats sweatshirt over her head, she wondered what David was doing right then. Did he feel as lonely in his huge warehouse apartment as she did in her tiny flat? No, she would never wish that kind of aloneness on him, or anyone for that matter. She preferred to think of him celebrating tonight with friends before tomorrow's swearing-in ceremony.

Still, when the phone rang, her pulse leaped and again she hoped. Why he would bother calling now, she wasn't even sure. He'd proposed, even if his offer had been unconventional. She was the one who'd said no.

"Hello?" She hoped whoever was on the other end of the line couldn't hear the desperation in her voice.

"Are you finally home from work? Any reason you were there late again?" Jane Stevens never bothered with formal greetings since she spoke to her daughter regularly.

"Hi, Mom. Just paperwork due before that QS 9000 certification inspection."

"It's always something, isn't it? Are you okay?"

Her answer was automatic and at least as honest as Sondra had been with herself lately. "Yeah, I'm fine."

She held her breath, hoping they could drop the subject this time. Discussing her broken heart with her mother just didn't feel right. Sure, Jane could relate, but her bitterness felt toxic. *You see, men are all the same.* Her mother's words still rang in Sondra's ears, yet they didn't ring true. David wasn't the same. He couldn't be.

Her mother made a scoffing sound into the phone, and Sondra braced herself.

"Honey, you're not fine. You're not fine at all."

She couldn't listen to it, couldn't bear to hear "I told you so" again. "Mom—"

"And it's all my fault," Jane continued.

Sondra started. "What...what are you saying?"

"I was wrong." An audible sigh came through the phone line. "I was hurt, but I've hurt you most of all."

"No, Mom, it was Dad. He hurt us."

"Sweetheart, listen to me. You can't base decisions about your life on our mistakes—your father's and mine."

Sondra was tempted to argue, to defend her mother's honor, but something stopped her. Maybe her mother was ready to let some of her anger go.

"Marriage is about giving and taking, about loving even on days when your spouse is unlovable. If only I had trusted God with the situation, things might have been different."

Sondra had to disagree this time. "You can't hold yourself responsible for his desertion, his infidelity."

"I couldn't forgive. I taught my own daughter not to trust people. I became a bitter, lonely woman."

"You loved me, Mom. You raised me the best you could, all by yourself."

Again Jane's breathing was audible. Resigned. "Do you love him, Sondra?"

She didn't even hesitate. "Yes. I love him."

"Then don't close the door so easily. Don't be alone...like me."

Jane said nothing for several seconds, and when she did speak, her voice sounded gravelly, as if she were crying. In all her life, Sondra had never seen her mother cry, even in the days after her father had left. Jane had only remained stoic and icy cold.

"Please, please put the situation in God's hands," Jane told her.

Sondra barely heard the other things her mother said before Jane ended the call. As if her thoughts hadn't been muddled enough since the election-night fiasco when she'd rushed back to Louisville and tried to bury her hurt in her work.

She couldn't imagine a more unlikely source for relationship advice, but her mother was there giving it. That was only one of the contradictions she was beginning to recognize in her life. Another was her career. Had power in the corporate world ever really been her dream, or had her career only been a safe haven from real world personal relationships? She wasn't sure.

And did she even want to *have it all* in terms of job titles and prestige and to *have nothing* when she returned home at night?

Sondra didn't have to ask herself that question twice. No, she didn't want that. She wanted a life that was filled with smiles and laughter, with faith and love. And she wanted all those things with David.

Before she realized what she was doing, she was throwing clothes and cosmetics in a bag. She would have to call into work from the road, but that wouldn't be a problem since she had plenty of flextime available from all her overtime work lately.

She wasn't sure what would happen when she reached Indiana or even whether David had changed his mind about her. He hadn't called, but then neither had she. Still, she had to go, had to follow God's urging and her heart. For her, it seemed that all roads led back to David and to her Destiny.

Chapter Twelve

The next morning David stood with his right hand raised and his left hand on a Bible as he was sworn in as the new judge for Cox County Superior Court I. David shifted in his long black robe, feeling uncomfortable in the garment. It would grow on him and he would grow into the role it represented in the coming months.

The courtroom looked different somehow, though he'd spent plenty of hours on the other side of that gleaming mahogany desk where he would now preside. The twin desks where the prosecution and the defense made their cases appeared smaller than he remembered.

Judge Douglas leaned on a cane as he swore in his replacement. "I would like to present the Honorable David William Wright."

The sound of applause around him only added to the surreal feeling that came with achieving a goal of being judge two years before his thirtieth birthday.

Several of his supporters had taken time out from their busy lives to share his achievement with him. Allison waved when she caught his attention. She and Brock stood next to David's parents. David could pick out fellow defense attorneys, friends from the prosecutor's office and even Martin Rich from the live nativity among the guests.

Only one person was conspicuously absent, but he shouldn't have expected Sondra to show. After his too-public proposal and her humbling refusal, she would probably feel too conspicuous anyway. He hadn't realized how much he'd still hoped, until disappointment filtered through him. Maybe he was just as mistaken in believing there was a chance for them at all.

And then someone pulled the courtroom door open and there she was.

David's breath caught in his throat. It seemed as if it took forever to reach her as he wound his way through the crowd, shaking a few hands as he passed, but finally they came face-to-face.

"Hey."

"Hi." She still wore her parka and a stocking cap, and both were wet with snow. "Um…sorry I'm late."

"I'm glad you came. Thanks." David kept his hands to his sides instead of reaching out to grip hers. He'd never in his life wanted to touch another human being more than he wanted to gather her into his arms right then, but he wasn't entirely sure he'd be able to let her go.

"The drive was rough."

"You just drove up this morning?"

"Well, I started last night, but it was slow trip on Interstate 65 with the snow blowing."

David swallowed. "You shouldn't have taken that kind of risk just to be here for this." He didn't know what he would have done if she'd been in an accident while making her way north to the event. To him.

"I really wanted to be here for this."

He lifted an eyebrow, still not certain what statement she'd made by coming. "Then I'm glad you made it in one piece."

Sondra was looking about nervously as if she'd noticed that they had a crowd. It shouldn't have surprised her after their very public last meeting. He was sorry about that. He was sorry about a lot of things. Because having an audience had been a mistake last time, and he didn't want to repeat it, he took her by the arm and ushered her into his new judge's chambers.

"Sondra, I—"

"David, I—"

Because they both began at the same time and in the same way, they laughed, but the sound died away quickly.

"Really, Sondra, let me—"

She shook her head to stop him. "You have to give me the chance—"

"No, I need you to understand that I didn't mean to embarrass—"

"Please, David. Let me say I'm sorry."

The side of his mouth pulled up despite his best effort to remain serious. Only the two of them were competitive enough to battle about anything, even being the first to apologize.

"Okay, you win." David indicated with his hand for her to take one of the guest chairs opposite his new desk, and he sat in the other. "You go first, but you don't have anything to be sorry about."

Sondra pressed her lips together, and her eyes shone too brightly. After several seconds, she finally spoke. "I'm so sorry about what happened the night of the election. Your question just took me by surprise."

"Hit you broadside is more like it."

"That, too." She shrugged. "I was surprised and terrified and...just not ready. All I could think about was what I would be giving up. Not what I would gain."

Gain? He studied her face, looking for hidden meanings in her words. Had she found his offer worth considering, even before, when it was so one-sided? Even though he knew it was risky, he still was tempted to hope.

His words came out in a rush. "I shouldn't have asked in front of everyone. I didn't even realize what I'd asked you to sacrifice. I shouldn't have expected you to give up your whole life for me. I had no right."

Though her eyes were still shiny, a smile appeared on her lips. "I thought you said I could go first."

He held his hands wide and opened his mouth to explain but then closed it again. "Okay, go ahead."

She nodded but didn't speak right away. Her smile vanished, and she chewed her lip. His stomach tightened as his already tenuous hope wavered, but still he waited.

Sondra's heart beat so furiously in her chest that she was convinced David could hear it. Her eyes burned with the emotion dwelling so close to the surface. How could she tell him what was in her heart? Could she lay herself bare that way? What if— No, she wouldn't allow her fears to keep her from having what she needed. Not this time.

Taking a deep breath, she began. "I'm sorry I humiliated you in front of, well, everyone. I was scared. I'm still scared."

Strange, as she spoke the words aloud, her feelings inside contradicted her. She didn't feel frightened anymore. Inside her was this strange calm assurance that all would be well. "I didn't know if I was ready to give up my plans, my dreams, for anyone."

He leaned forward in his chair. "You see, you don't have to—"

"David, are you going to let me finish this here, or will I have to go deliver it as a speech from the judge's seat where you won't interrupt?"

He closed his mouth and waved with his hand for her to proceed, but from his expression, it appeared that whatever he had to say was making him crazy. She could relate to that, yet she had to slow her thoughts if she wanted to do this right. And she wanted that in the worst way.

"What I didn't realize was that since I'd met you, my dreams had changed. I didn't want the same things anymore. So I wouldn't have to give up anything to have everything I wanted."

David opened his mouth, preparing to interrupt

her again, but he must have remembered because he shook his head and stopped himself.

Sondra only smiled. Always the courtroom attorney, David would forever try to get the last word in during their unavoidable debates, but she looked forward to their disagreements and to the opportunity to make up after them.

"What I want, David, is you. I'm in love with you, and I want to build a life with you right here in Destiny. That is, if the offer still stands."

Facing her, David leaned so close that she could see every facet of his translucent blue eyes and could feel his warm breath on her cheek. Her hands were already trembling before he reached for them. As their fingers laced, Sondra felt a tremor that made her wonder if hers were the only hands that had been shaking.

But then the side of David's mouth lifted. "Now you're all done apologizing, right? Because I wouldn't want to develop a reputation as a man who can't take turns."

The emotion that had been clogging her throat dislodged in a nervous giggle. "I'm all done."

"Sure?" At her nod, he smiled. "Okay, now, what was I apologizing for? Oh wait, I remember. I'm sorry I proposed to you in front of everyone in town."

He paused, his expression becoming serious as he peered so deeply into her eyes that he must have been able to see into her heart as well.

"But my proposal was real. The offer, flawed as it is, will be there whenever you're ready to accept it. You're the only woman I've ever loved or will ever love. I know it's God's plan for us to be together, so I'll be waiting until you're ready."

Sondra wasn't sure whether she had moved her head first or if David had shifted, but suddenly his lips were touching hers, sealing those promises with his kiss. She folded her arms behind his neck, feeling strength in acquiescence, freedom in entrusting him with her heart.

When David pulled away, he was wearing one of his mischievous smiles. "Are you prepared to hear my proposal again? I've just added an element that I'm sure you'll find will really sweeten the deal."

Sondra shook her head, and, in case he hadn't gotten the message, she said it aloud. "No."

He rested his hands on her forearms, and his grip tightened reflexively. "What do you mean? No, you don't want to hear my proposal again? Or are you saying 'no' to my proposal?"

She blew out a breath, amazed that after all she'd told him, he could still worry that she would shoot him down.

"Neither. I don't need to hear the proposal again, though I would probably enjoy hearing those words in private instead of over a public address system. And, no, I don't need you to sweeten the offer. The only thing I need is you."

David just looked at her for so long with his eyebrows drawn together in confusion that she took pity on him.

She cleared her throat. "Are you going to ask me again, or aren't you?"

"Well, when you put it like that…." He let his words trail off, but he still slipped out of his chair, black robe and all, and came to rest on one knee in front of her.

Déjà vu had her drawing in a sharp breath, but the man she loved only continued to smile. That smile was so appealing that she couldn't help returning it.

"Sondra, if you agree to be my wife, I'll spend every day making sure you know you made the right decision." He took a deep breath. "Will you marry me?"

The word "yes" had barely crossed her lips before he lifted up to press his mouth to hers. His arms came around her in a fierce hug, and then his lips caressed hers again in a kiss of hope, of permanence. Moving back from her, he stood and crossed to the corner of his office where his suit jacket hung on a coat tree. He reached in the pocket and produced a felt box Sondra recognized.

He pointed to the box and raised an eyebrow, and at her nod, opened it. The emerald-cut diamond ring was still nestled inside it. David returned and crouched in front of her, finally lifting out the ring and slipping it on her finger where it belonged.

Sondra stared down at her hand, as amazed by the promise the ring represented as by its glimmering beauty. But then she lifted her head to look up at him again. "You had the ring with you. How did you know I'd be here?"

"I didn't. I was only hoping. If you hadn't come today, I was planning a road trip to Louisville."

She feigned a shocked look. "You mean I could

have saved myself a treacherous journey on icy Indiana roads if I'd only waited a few days?"

"Guess so." He stood up and pulled her with him, gathering her into his arms once more. "I also guess we have some news to share with the crowd out there." He indicated the door with a tilt of his head.

"Wouldn't they have all gone back to their own busy lives by now?"

David rolled his eyes. "With the two of us in here? Are you kidding? I guess I'll have to teach you a thing or two about life in a small town."

"So I take it we're big news?"

"The newspaper photographer should be arriving at any minute."

Chapter Thirteen

As it turned out, the photographer was already waiting when they came out of the door. And just as David had predicted, most of the ceremony guests were still milling around, munching on the light snacks and waiting for news.

David grinned at his new fiancée's shocked expression. He supposed he could have told her that the *Destiny Post* photographer was just late showing up for his swearing-in ceremony, but he enjoyed seeing her surprise.

He hoped his announcement would shock her just as much and please her a whole lot more. No doubt the *Post* photographer, who'd been at the paper since Lyndon Johnson was president, would be happy he'd been tardy, too, since he would get to break the story that would eventually make statewide news.

"May I have everyone's attention please," David said needlessly, since the room was already becoming quiet as he crossed to the lectern where defense and prosecution usually made their cases.

He gestured for Sondra to come nearer, and her shoulders tightened at the repeat of the earlier fiasco, but she came to him and took the hand he offered. "I wanted to announce to you all that the population of Destiny, Indiana, is about to become seven hundred and one. I have asked Sondra Stevens, the love of my life, to marry me—again—and she has agreed."

A whoop that could only have been from Brock Chandler rose up from the crowd.

"You sure she said yes this time?" Judge Douglas called out from the chair where he was resting.

"I'm sure." He lifted the hand he held, which happened to be the one on which she wore his ring.

"What'd ya have to promise her?" Hal Douglas prodded.

"That I'd be an incredible husband." In effect, he had said that, and he was determined to keep that promise. "I even offered to sweeten the deal to convince her to stay here with me in Destiny, but Sondra wouldn't hear of it. I'm thanking God for my blessings because she agreed to marry me without any perks.

"That makes my gift to her and to the community that much more special." Unable to resist, David pulled Sondra to him and kissed her, right there in front of his parents and everyone.

Sondra waved her hand in front of her face, clearly embarrassed, but she was smiling, too. He watched her until she drew her eyebrows together in a questioning expression.

"Spill it, Wright, or we'll be here until next Christmas," Brock called out.

He waved at the deputy, who held little Joy in his

arms. "I didn't think it was fair to make my wife-to-be give up her life to come to Destiny, but I also couldn't move Cox County Courts across the state line. A compromise was to bring at least part of Sondra's work with her."

David glanced once more at Sondra's perplexed expression before his big announcement.

"With a little help from that trust fund from my grandparents that was languishing at First National, I have purchased the site of the now-defunct Clear View Motel and surrounding properties. On that site, if my fiancée agrees to it anyway, I hope to build the largest recreational vehicle dealership and parts and service center in east-central Indiana."

Because Sondra appeared more shell-shocked than thrilled as she stared into the crowd, David rushed on anxiously. Why did he insist on continuing to surprise her in public? He was still a member of the group that never learned from its mistakes—just him and that three-legged dog. But he was ready to burn his membership card.

He spoke to the crowd but watched her in his peripheral vision, hoping to see her eyes light up, or a smile or anything to suggest that his idea wasn't a big mistake.

"A combination facility like this could provide job opportunities for Destiny residents as well as bring tourism dollars to Cox County. There might even be a possibility for an RV park near Clemens Reservoir...."

His words trailed off as he caught sight of Sondra staring at him now, her expression incredulous. "Are you kidding?" Her words were just above a whisper.

He continued, this time meeting her gaze. "But all of that would be up to the dealership's owner and operator: Sondra Stevens—soon to be Wright."

She shook her head. "You can't be serious."

"I am." But her comment made him second-guess whether he should be.

Whatever she'd been about to say after that was drowned out by applause that flooded the room. Everyone around them recognized that the idea would benefit Destiny. The court was still out on whether it would be a good thing for the woman he loved.

"If you get the approvals, do you have a name in mind for the place?" the photographer called from the rear of the room.

He shook his head. "Not at all. That and the rest of the decisions would be up to the owner/operator."

"How about Clear Rolling?" Judge Douglas supplied.

"I know," Allison called out. "Clear Roads Ahead."

Soon names were being bandied about over a business that was still no more than a pipe dream. Only Sondra hadn't contributed, hadn't said anything more.

David backpedaled as quickly as he could. "All of this is very preliminary. We won't go forward with it at all if it's not what's best for Sondra."

"We'll call it the Road to Destiny RV Center."

He turned at the sound of her voice, and she was smiling back at him. "You did this for me?" she whispered.

Then she turned back to the crowd of people who had supported him and would accept and support her just the same. "Does anybody here wonder why I'm in love with this guy?"

After several few minutes and a lot more excited ramblings about the proposed dealership, the crowd began to dissipate. As soon as they were alone in the courtroom, David led Sondra back to his chambers. He removed the judge's robe from over his shirt and tie and hung it on the coat tree.

He was only halfway into his suit jacket before Sondra threw herself into his arms. She pressed her lips to his and pulled back, still resting her hands on his shoulders.

"I still can't believe you did all of this for me. Where did you even get the idea?"

"It started with Allison giving a lecture about what real love was. God put His two cents in, as well, and I listened."

"Looks like you mastered the skill."

Tilting his head, he lowered his mouth to hers and kissed her with all the hopes, dreams and promises in his heart. So this was what it felt like to have everything he'd ever wanted in life—even the parts he'd never realized he could ask for.

When he pulled away, he rested his forehead against hers. "Loving you is the best thing I've ever done. I'm determined to do it well for the rest of our lives."

She smiled back at him. "Don't worry, I'll be here to see that you do."

On a snowy Sunday afternoon in early March, Sondra processed down the aisle of New Hope Church toward the man who had earned her heart. His eyes were shining with tears as she approached him in her simple white gown. She had to blink back tears of her own when he smiled at her.

"You're so beautiful," he said, not bothering to whisper.

"You're pretty handsome yourself."

Until she heard the chuckles behind her, Sondra had almost forgotten they weren't alone in the sanctuary. Still, the ceremony was private, just the way she wanted it. She insisted that it had been enough that they'd met in a stable stage, and he'd proposed during an acceptance speech.

As she glanced back at their few guests—the Chandlers, her mother and his parents—she was convinced she'd made the right decision.

When she turned back to him, David held out his hand. Without hesitation, she placed her hand in his, just as she was entrusting him with her heart and her future. *Thank You, Father, for sending David to me.*

"Do you take this man to be your lawfully wedded husband?" Reverend Jeff Reed asked.

"I will."

The words she'd never expected to say came so easily. She wasn't afraid, and she knew she never needed to fear while in the security of David's arms. His love was steadfast and sure.

"David, will you love, honor and keep her, forsaking all others, keep you only to her, as long as you both shall live?"

"You bet I will," David answered to laughter from their audience.

Soon the formalities were over, and David drew her into his arms.

"This is for forever," he whispered as he lowered his head for their first kiss as husband and wife.

Bliss. That was the only way she could describe feelings welling inside her as he took her hand and led her up the aisle.

They'd come so far to reach this point, these vows, and a faith they could share in a life together. It felt as if they'd run a marathon coming from opposite directions to the same finish line. Only the race didn't end here. It was only the beginning. From this point on, they would run side by side.

* * * * *

Dear Reader,

My friend Irene Brand and I wish you joy this Christmas season as we celebrate God's great gift to a dark world in the form of His son, Jesus. For the two of us, writing *Christmas in the Air* has been like a warm holiday visit with old friends. In our novellas we have revisited characters from our earlier stories in *A Family for Christmas,* sharing with them as they open their hearts to the peace of the Christ Child.

In my novella "A Season of Hope" the characters learn about the perfection of God's plan and His timing, even in the unlikely location of a stable stage. Ladies' man David Wright must finally face his fear of commitment during a face-off with independent businesswoman Sondra Stevens, who harbors her own emotional scars. Can they open their hearts to love's possibilities without receiving more visible wounds? Anything's possible in this season of hope.

Dana Corbit

REQUEST YOUR FREE BOOKS!

2 FREE INSPIRATIONAL NOVELS
PLUS 2
FREE
MYSTERY GIFTS

Love Inspired®

YES! Please send me 2 FREE Love Inspired® novels and my 2 FREE mystery gifts (gifts are worth about $10). After receiving them, if I don't wish to receive any more books, I can return the shipping statement marked "cancel." If I don't cancel, I will receive 6 brand-new novels every month and be billed just $4.49 per book in the U.S. or $4.99 per book in Canada. That's a savings of at least 22% off the cover price. It's quite a bargain! Shipping and handling is just 50¢ per book in the U.S. and 75¢ per book in Canada.* I understand that accepting the 2 free books and gifts places me under no obligation to buy anything. I can always return a shipment and cancel at any time. Even if I never buy another book, the two free books and gifts are mine to keep forever.

105/305 IDN FVW5

Name	(PLEASE PRINT)	
Address		Apt. #
City	State/Prov.	Zip/Postal Code

Signature (if under 18, a parent or guardian must sign)

Mail to the **Reader Service:**
IN U.S.A.: P.O. Box 1867, Buffalo, NY 14240-1867
IN CANADA: P.O. Box 609, Fort Erie, Ontario L2A 5X3

**Are you a subscriber to Love Inspired books
and want to receive the larger-print edition?
Call 1-800-873-8635 or visit www.ReaderService.com.**

* Terms and prices subject to change without notice. Prices do not include applicable taxes. Sales tax applicable in N.Y. Canadian residents will be charged applicable taxes. Offer not valid in Quebec. This offer is limited to one order per household. Not valid for current subscribers to Love Inspired books. All orders subject to credit approval. Credit or debit balances in a customer's account(s) may be offset by any other outstanding balance owed by or to the customer. Please allow 4 to 6 weeks for delivery. Offer available while quantities last.

Your Privacy—The Reader Service is committed to protecting your privacy. Our Privacy Policy is available online at www.ReaderService.com or upon request from the Reader Service.

We make a portion of our mailing list available to reputable third parties that offer products we believe may interest you. If you prefer that we not exchange your name with third parties, or if you wish to clarify or modify your communication preferences, please visit us at www.ReaderService.com/consumerschoice or write to us at Reader Service Preference Service, P.O. Box 9062, Buffalo, NY 14269. Include your complete name and address.

LIDIR12

Love Inspired® SUSPENSE

RIVETING INSPIRATIONAL ROMANCE

Watch for our series of edge-
of-your-seat suspense novels.
These contemporary tales
of intrigue and romance
feature Christian characters
facing challenges to their faith...
and their lives!

AVAILABLE IN REGULAR
& LARGER-PRINT FORMATS

LARGER-PRINT BOOKS!

GET 2 FREE LARGER-PRINT NOVELS PLUS 2 FREE MYSTERY GIFTS

Love Inspired

Larger-print novels are now available...

YES! Please send me 2 FREE LARGER-PRINT Love Inspired® novels and my 2 FREE mystery gifts (gifts are worth about $10). After receiving them, if I don't wish to receive any more books, I can return the shipping statement marked "cancel." If I don't cancel, I will receive 6 brand-new novels every month and be billed just $4.99 per book in the U.S. or $5.49 per book in Canada. That's a savings of at least 23% off the cover price. It's quite a bargain! Shipping and handling is just 50¢ per book in the U.S. and 75¢ per book in Canada.* I understand that accepting the 2 free books and gifts places me under no obligation to buy anything. I can always return a shipment and cancel at any time. Even if I never buy another book, the two free books and gifts are mine to keep forever.

122/322 IDN FVXH

Name _____ (PLEASE PRINT)

Address _____ Apt. #

City _____ State/Prov. _____ Zip/Postal Code

Signature (if under 18, a parent or guardian must sign)

Mail to the **Reader Service:**
IN U.S.A.: P.O. Box 1867, Buffalo, NY 14240-1867
IN CANADA: P.O. Box 609, Fort Erie, Ontario L2A 5X3

Are you a current subscriber to Love Inspired books and want to receive the larger-print edition?
Call 1-800-873-8635 or visit www.ReaderService.com.

* Terms and prices subject to change without notice. Prices do not include applicable taxes. Sales tax applicable in N.Y. Canadian residents will be charged applicable taxes. Offer not valid in Quebec. This offer is limited to one order per household. Not valid for current subscribers to Love Inspired Larger Print books. All orders subject to credit approval. Credit or debit balances in a customer's account(s) may be offset by any other outstanding balance owed by or to the customer. Please allow 4 to 6 weeks for delivery. Offer available while quantities last.

Your Privacy—The Reader Service is committed to protecting your privacy. Our Privacy Policy is available online at www.ReaderService.com or upon request from the Reader Service.

We make a portion of our mailing list available to reputable third parties that offer products we believe may interest you. If you prefer that we not exchange your name with third parties, or if you wish to clarify or modify your communication preferences, please visit us at www.ReaderService.com/consumerschoice or write to us at Reader Service Preference Service, P.O. Box 9062, Buffalo, NY 14269. Include your complete name and address.

LILPDIR12

FAMOUS FAMILIES

YES! Please send me the *Famous Families* collection featuring the Fortunes, the Bravos, the McCabes and the Cavanaughs. This collection will begin with 3 FREE BOOKS and 2 FREE GIFTS in my very first shipment—and more valuable free gifts will follow! My books will arrive in 8 monthly shipments until I have the entire 51-book *Famous Families* collection. I will receive 2-3 free books in each shipment and I will pay just $4.49 U.S./$5.39 CDN for each of the other 4 books in each shipment, plus $2.99 for shipping and handling.* If I decide to keep the entire collection, I'll only have paid for 32 books because 19 books are free. I understand that accepting the 3 free books and gifts places me under no obligation to buy anything. I can always return a shipment and cancel at any time. My free books and gifts are mine to keep no matter what I decide.

268 HCN 0387   468 HCN 0387

Name _____ (PLEASE PRINT) _____

Address _____ Apt. # _____

City _____ State/Prov. _____ Zip/Postal Code _____

Signature (if under 18, a parent or guardian must sign)

Mail to the **Reader Service:**
IN U.S.A.: P.O. Box 1867, Buffalo, NY 14240-1867
IN CANADA: P.O. Box 609, Fort Erie, Ontario L2A 5X3

* Terms and prices subject to change without notice. Prices do not include applicable taxes. Sales tax applicable in N.Y. Canadian residents will be charged applicable taxes. This offer is limited to one order per household. All orders subject to approval. Credit or debit balances in a customer's account(s) may be offset by any other outstanding balance owed by or to the customer. Please allow 4 to 6 weeks for delivery. Offer available while quantities last. Offer not available to Quebec residents.

Your Privacy— The Reader Service is committed to protecting your privacy. Our Privacy Policy is available online at www.ReaderService.com or upon request from the Reader Service.
We make a portion of our mailing list available to reputable third parties that offer products we believe may interest you. If you prefer that we not exchange your name with third parties, or if you wish to clarify or modify your communication preferences, please visit us at www.ReaderService.com/consumerschoice or write to us at Reader Service Preference Service, P.O. Box 9062, Buffalo, NY 14269. Include your complete name and address.

FFBPA12

EXILES OF THE STARS

ANDRE NORTON

SF

ace books

A Division of Charter Communications Inc.
A GROSSET & DUNLAP COMPANY
360 Park Avenue South
New York, New York 10010

EXILES OF THE STARS

Copyright © 1971 by Andre Norton

An ACE Book
by arrangement with
The Viking Press, Inc.

Cover art by John Rush

First Ace printing: July 1972
Second Ace printing: February 1975
Third Ace printing: June 1979

Manufactured in the United States of America

Chapter 1

KRIP VORLUND

There was an odd haze in the room, or was it my eyes? I cupped my hands over them for a moment as I wondered, not only about trusting in my sight, but about this whole situation. For the haze might be the visible emanation of that emotion anyone with the slightest esper talent could pick up clearly—the acrid taste, touch, smell, of fear. Not our own fear, but that of the city which pulsed around us like the uneven breathing of a great terrified animal.

Sensing that, I wanted to run out of the room, the building, beyond the city walls to such security as the *Lydis* had to offer, where the shell of the Free Trader which was my home could shut out that aura of a fear fast approaching panic. Yet I sat where I was, forced my hands to lie quietly across my knees as I watched those in the room with me, listened to the clicking speech of the men of Kartum on the planet Thoth.

There were four of them. Two were priests, both past middle life, both of high standing by the richness of their deep-violet over-mantles, which they

5

had not put aside even though the room was far too warm. The dark skin of their faces, shaven heads, and gesturing hands was lightened with designs in ceremonial yellow paint. Each fingernail was covered with a claw-shaped metal sheath set with tiny gems, which winked and blinked even in this subdued lighting as their fingers, flickering in and out, drew symbols in the air as if they could not carry on any serious conversation without the constant invocation of their god.

Their companions were officials of the ruler of Kartum, as close to him, they averred in the speech of Thoth, as the hairs of his ceremonial royal beard. They sat across the table from our captain, Urban Foss, seemingly willing enough to let the priests do the talking. But their hands were never far from weapon butts, as if they expected at any moment to see the door burst open, the enemy in upon us.

There were three of us from the *Lydis*—Captain Foss, cargomaster Juhel Lidj, and me, Krip Vorlund, the least of that company—Free Traders, born to space and the freedom of the starways as are all our kind. We have been rovers for so long that we have perhaps mutated into a new breed of humankind. Nothing to us, these planet intrigues—not unless we were entrapped in them. And that did not happen often. Experience, a grim teacher, had made us very wary of the politics of the planet-born.

Three—no, we were four. I dropped a hand now and my fingers touched a stiff brush of upstanding hair. I did not have to glance down to know what—who—sat up on her haunches beside my chair, feeling, sensing even more strongly than I the unease of spirit, the creeping menace which darkened about us.

Outwardly there was a glassia of Yiktor there,

black-furred except for the tuft of coarse, stiffened gray-white bristles on the crown of the head, with a slender tail as long again as the body, and large paws with sheathed, dagger-sharp claws. Yet appearances were deceiving. For the animal body housed another spirit. This was truly Maelen—she once a Moon Singer of the Thassa—who had been given this outer shape when her own body was broken and dying, then was condemned by her own people to its wearing because she had broken their laws.

Yiktor of the three-ringed moon— What had happened there more than a planet-year ago was printed on my mind so that no small detail could ever be forgotten. It was Maelen who had saved me—my life if not my body, or the body I had worn when I landed there. That body was long since "dead"—spaced to drift forever among the stars—unless it be drawn some day into the fiery embrace of a sun and consumed.

I had had a second body, one which had run on four legs, hunted and killed, bayed at the moon Sotrath—which left in my mind strange dreams of a world which was all scent and sounds such as my own species never knew. And now I wore a third covering, akin to the first and yet different, a body which had another small residue of the alien to creep slowly into my consciousness, so that at times even the world of the *Lydis* (which I had known from birth) seemed strange, a little distorted. Yet I was Krip Vorlund in truth, no matter what outer covering I might wear (that now being the husk of Maquad of the Thassa). Maelen had done this—the twice changing—and for that, despite her motives of good, not ill—she went now four-footed, furred, in my company. Not that I regretted the last.

I had been first a man, then a barsk, and was now outwardly a Thassa; and parts of all mingled in me. My fingers moved through Maelen's stiff crest as I listened, watched, sucked in air tainted not only with queer odors peculiar to a house of Kartum but with the emotions of its inhabitants. I had always possessed the talent of mind-seek. Many Traders developed that, so it was not uncommon. But I also knew that in Maquad's body such a sense had been heightened, sharpened. That was why I was one of this company at this hour, my superiors valuing my worth as an esper to judge those we must deal with.

And I knew that Maelen's even keener powers must also be at work, weighing, assaying. With our combined report Foss would have much on which to base his decision. And that decision must come very soon.

The *Lydis* had planeted four days ago with a routine cargo of pulmn, a powder made from the kelp beds of Hawaika. In ordinary times that powder would have been sold to the temples to become fuel for their ever-burning scented fires. The trade was not a fabulously handsome payload, but it made a reasonable profit. And there was to be picked up in return (if one got on the good side of the priests) the treasures of Nod—or a trickle of them. Which in turn were worth very much indeed on any inner world.

Thoth, Ptah, Anubis, Sekhmet, Set; five planets with the sun Amen-Re to warm them. Of the five, Set was too close to that sun to support life, Anubis a frozen waste without colonization. Which left Thoth, Ptah, and Sekhmet. All those had been explored, two partly colonized, generations ago, by

Terran-descended settlers. Only those settlers had not been the first.

Our kind is late come to space; that we learned on our first galactic voyaging. There have been races, empires, which rose, fell, and vanished long before our ancestors lifted their heads to wonder dimly at the nature of the stars. Wherever we go we find traces of these other peoples—though there is much we do not know, cannot learn. "Forerunners" we call them, lumping them all together. Though more and more we are coming to understand that there were many more than just one such galaxy-wide empire, one single race voyaging in the past. But we have learned so little.

The system of Amen-Re turned out to be particularly rich in ancient remains. But it was not known yet whether the civilization which had flourished here had been only system-wide, or perhaps an outpost of a yet-unclassified galactic one. Mainly because the priests had very early taken upon themselves the guardianship of such "treasure."

Each people had its gods, its controlling powers. There is an inner need in our species to acknowledge something beyond ourselves, something greater. In some civilizations there is a primitive retrogression to sacrifice—even of the worshipers' own kind—and to religions of fear and darkness. Or belief can be the recognition of a spirit, without any formal protestation of rites. But on many worlds the gods are strong and their voices, the priests, are considered infallible, above even the temporal rulers. So that Traders walk softly and cautiously on any world where there are many temples and such a priesthood.

The system of Amen-Re had been colonized by ships from Veda. And those had been filled with refugees from a devastating religious war—the persecuted, fleeing. Thus a hierarchy had had control from the first.

Luckily they were not rigidly fanatical toward the unknown. On some worlds the remnants of any native former civilization were destroyed as devilish work. But in the case of Amen-Re some farsighted high priest in the early days had had the wit to realize that these remains were indeed treasure which could be exploited. He had proclaimed all such finds the due of the god, to be kept in the temples.

When Traders began to call at Thoth (settlement on Ptah was too small to induce visits), lesser finds were offered in bargaining, and these became the reason for cargo exploitation. For there was no local product on Thoth worth the expense of off-world shipping.

It was the lesser bits, the crumbs, which were so offered. The bulk of the best was used to adorn the temples. But those were enough to make the trip worthwhile for my people, if not for the great companies and combines. Our cargo space was strictly limited; we lived on the fringe of the trade of the galaxy, picking up those items too small to entice the bigger dealers.

So trade with Thoth had become routine. But ship time is not planet time. Between one visit and the next there may be a vast change on any world, political or even physical. And when the *Lydis* had set down this time, she had found boiling around her the beginnings of chaos, unless there came some sharp change. Government, religion, do not exist in a vacuum. Here government and religion—which had always had a firm alliance—were together under fire.

A half year earlier there had arisen in the mountain

country to the east of Kartum a new prophet. There had been such before, but somehow the temples had managed either to discredit them or to absorb their teachings without undue trouble. This time the priesthood found itself on the defensive. And, its complacency well established by years of untroubled rule, it handled the initial difficulty clumsily.

As sometimes happens, one mistake led to a greater, until now the government at Kartum was virtually in a state of siege. With the church under pressure, the temporal powers scented independence. The well-established nobility was loyal to the temple. After all, their affairs were so intertwined that they could not easily withdraw their support. But there are always have-nots wanting to be haves—lesser nobility and members of old families who resent not having more. And some of these made common cause with the rebels.

The spark which had set it off was the uncovering of a "treasure" place which held some mysterious contagion swift to kill off those involved. Not only that, but the plague spread, bringing death to others who had not dealt with the place at all. Then a fanatical hill priest-prophet began to preach that the treasures were evil and should be destroyed.

He led a mob to blow up the infected site, then went on, hot with the thirst for destruction, to do the same to the local temple which served as a storage place for the goods. The authorities moved in then, and the contagion attacked the troops. This was accepted by the surviving rebels as a vindication of their beliefs. So the uprising spread, finding adherents who wanted nothing more than to upset the status quo.

As is only too common where there has been an

untroubled rule, the authorities had not realized the seriousness of what they termed a local outburst. There had been quite a few among the higher-placed priests and nobles who had been loath to move at once, wanting to conciliate the rebels. In fact there had been too much talk and not enough action at just the wrong moment.

Now there was a first-class civil war in progress. And, as far as we were able to learn, the government was shaky. Which was the reason for this secret meeting here in the house of a local lordling. The *Lydis* had come in with a cargo now of little or no value. And while a Free Trader may make an unpaying voyage once, a second such can put the ship in debt to the League.

To be without a ship is death for my kind. We know no other life—planetside existence is prison. And even if we could scrape a berth on another Trader, that would mean starting from the bottom once again, with little hope of ever climbing to freedom again. It would perhaps not be so hard on junior members of the crew, such as myself, who was only assistant cargomaster. But we had had to fight for even our lowly berths. As for Captain Foss, the other officers—it would mean total defeat.

Thus, though we had learned of the upsetting state of affairs within a half hour after landing, we did not space again. As long as there was the least hope of turning the voyage to some account we remained finned down, even though we were sure there was presently no market for pulmn. As a matter of routine, Foss and Lidj had contacted the temple. But instead of our arranging an open meeting with a supply priest, they had summoned us here.

So great was their need that they wasted no time

in formal greeting but came directly to the point. For it seemed that after all we did have something to sell —safety. Not for the men who met us, nor even for their superiors, but for the cream of the planet's treasure, which could be loaded on board the *Lydis* and sent to protective custody elsewhere.

On Ptah the temple had established a well-based outpost, mainly because certain minerals were mined there. And it had become a recognized custom for the hierarchy of the church to withdraw to Ptah at times for periods of retreat, removed from the distractions of Thoth. It was to that sanctuary that they proposed now to send the pick of the temple holdings, and the *Lydis* was to transport them.

When Captain Foss asked why they did not use their own ore-transport ships for the purpose (not that he was averse to the chance to make this trip pay), they had a quick answer. First, the ore ships were mainly robo-controlled, not prepared to carry a crew of more than one or two techs on board. They could not risk sending the treasure in such, when tinkering with the controls might lose it forever. Secondly, the *Lydis*, being a Free Trader, could be trusted. For such was the Traders' reputation that all knew, once under contract, we held by our word. To void such a bond was unthinkable. The few, very few, times it had happened, the League itself had meted out such punishment as we did not care to remember.

Therefore, they said, if we took contract they knew that their cargo would be delivered. And not only one such cargo, but they would have at least two, maybe more. If the rebels did not invest the city (as they now threatened) too soon, the priests would continue to send off their hoard as long as they could. But the cream of it all would be on the first trip. And they would pay—which was the subject of the present meeting.

Not that we were having any wrangling. But no man becomes a Trader without a very shrewd idea of how to judge his wares or services. Thus to outbargain one of us was virtually impossible. And, too, this was a seller's market, and we had a monopoly on what we had to offer.

There had been two serious defeats of the government forces within a matter of ten days. Though the loyal army still stubbornly held the road to the city, there was no reason to believe that they could continue to do so for long. So Foss and Lidj made the best of their advantage. There was also the danger of an uprising in Kartum, as three other cities had already fallen to rebels working from within, inciting mobs to violence and taking advantage of such outbursts. As one of the priests had said, it was almost as if a kind of raging insanity spread from man to man at these times.

"Trouble—" I did not need that mind-alert from Maelen, for I could feel it also, an ingathering of darkness, as if any light was swallowed up by shadows. Whether the priests had any esper talents, I did not know. Perhaps even this aura of panic could be induced by a gifted enemy at work. Though I did not pick up any distinct trace of such interference.

I stirred; Lidj glanced at me, picked up my unspoken warning. Those of the *Lydis* had learned, even as I, that since my return to the ship in this Thassa body my esper powers were greater than they had once been. In turn he nodded at the priests.

"Let it be so contracted." As cargomaster he had the final decision. For in such matters he could overrule even the captain. Trade was his duty, first and always.

But if the priests were relieved, there was no lightening of the tension in that chamber. Maelen pressed against my knee, but she did not mind-touch. Only I noted that her head tuft was no longer so erect. And I remembered of old that the sign of anger or alarm with the glassia was a flattening of that tuft to lie against the skull. So I sent mind-seek swiftly to probe the atmosphere.

Straight mind-to-mind reading cannot be unless it is willed by both participants. But it is easy enough to tune in on emotions, and I found (though at a distance which I could not measure) something which sent my hand to the butt of my stunner, even as Maelen's crest had betrayed her own concern. There was menace far more directed than the uneasiness in this room. But I could not read whether it was directed against those who had summoned us, or against our own ship's party.

The priests left first with the nobles. They had guardsmen waiting without—which we had not. Foss looked directly to me.

"Something is amiss, more than just the general situation," he commented.

"There is trouble waiting out there." I nodded to the door and what lay beyond. "Yes, more than what we might ordinarily expect."

Maelen reared, setting her forepaws against me, her head raised so that her golden eyes looked into mine. Her thought was plain in my mind.

"Let me go first. A scout is needed."

I was loath to agree. Here she was plainly alien and, as such, might not only attract unwelcome attention but, in the trigger-set tension, even invite attack.

"Not so." She had read my thought. "You forget— it is night. And I, being in this body, know how to use the dark as a friend."

So I opened the door and she slipped through. The hall without was not well lighted and I marveled at how well she used the general dusk as a cover, being gone before I was aware. Foss and Lidj joined me, the captain saying, "There is a very wrong feel here. The sooner we raise ship, I am thinking, the better. How long will loading take?"

Lidj shrugged. "That depends upon the bulk of the cargo. At any rate we can make all ready to handle it." He spoke in code into his wrist com, giving orders to dump the pulmn to make room. There was this much the priests had had to agree to—they must let us, at the other end of the voyage, take our reckoning out of the treasure already stored in the temple on Ptah. And a certain amount must be in pieces of our own selection. Usually Traders had to accept discards without choice.

We headed for the street. By Foss's precaution our meeting had been held in a house close to the city wall, so we need not venture far into Kartum. But I, for one, knew that I would not breathe really easily again until my boot plates rang on the *Lydis*'s entry ramp. The dusk which had hung at our coming had thickened into night. But there was still the roar of life in the city.

Then—

"'Ware!" Maelen's warning was as sharp as a vocal shout. "Make haste for the gates!"

She had sent with such power that even Foss had picked up her alert, and I did not need to pass her

16

message on. We started at a trot for the gate, Foss getting out our entry pass.

I noticed a flurry by that barrier as we neared. Fighting. Above the hoarse shouting of the men milling in combat came the *crack* of the native weapons. Luckily this was not a planet which dealt with lasers and blasters. But they had solid-projectile weapons which made a din. Our stunners could not kill, only render unconscious. But we could die from one of those archaic arms in use ahead as quickly as from a blaster.

Foss adjusted the beam button of his stunner; Lidj and I did likewise, altering from narrow ray to wide sweep. Such firing exhausted the charges quickly, but in such cases as this we had no choice. We must clear a path ahead.

"To the right—" Lidj did not really need that direction from Foss. He had already moved into flank position on one side, as I did on the other.

We hurried on, knowing that we must get closer for a most effective attack. Then I saw Maelen hunkered in a doorway. She ran to me, ready to join our final dash.

"Now!"

We fired together, sweeping all the struggling company, friend and foe alike, if we did have friends among those fighters. Men staggered and fell, and we began to run, leaping over the prone bodies sprawled across the gate opening. But the barrier itself was closed and we thrust against it in vain.

"Lever, in the gatehouse—" panted Foss.

Maelen streaked away. She might no longer have humanoid hands, but glassia paws are not to be underestimated. And that she was able to make good use of those she demonstrated a moment later as the

17

side panels drew back to let us wriggle through.

Then we ran as if the demon hosts of Nebu brayed at our heels. For at any moment one of those projectile weapons might be aimed at us. I, for one, felt a strange sensation between my shoulder blades, somehow anticipating such a wound.

However, there came no such stroke of ill fortune, and we did reach the ramp and safety. So all four of us, Maelen running with the greatest ease, pounded up into the *Lydis*. And we were hardly through the hatch opening when we heard the grate of metal, knew that those on duty were sealing the ship.

Foss leaned against the wall by the ramp, thumbing a new charge into his stunner. It was plain that from now on we must be prepared to defend ourselves, as much as if we were on an openly hostile world.

I looked to Maelen. "Did you warn of the fight at the gate?"

"Not so. There were those a-prowl who sought to capture you. They would prevent the treasure from going hence. But they came too late. And I think that the gate fight, in a manner, spoiled their plans."

Foss had not followed that, so I reported it to him.

He was grimly close-faced now. "If we are to raise that treasure—they will have to send it to us. No man from here goes planetside again!"

Chapter 2

KRIP VORLUND

"So, what do we do now? We're safe enough in the ship. But how long do we wait?" Manus Hunold, our astrogator, had triggered the visa-plate, and we who had crowded into the control cabin to watch by its aid what happened without were intent on what it could show us.

Men streamed out onto the field, ringing in the *Lydis*—though they showed a very healthy regard for her blast-off rockets and kept a prudent distance from the lift area near her fins. They were not of the half-soldier, half-police force who supported authority, though they were armed and even kept a ragged discipline in their confrontation of the ship. However, how they could expect to come to any open quarrel with us if we stayed inside, I could not guess.

I had snapped mind-seek; there were too many waves of raw emotion circling out there. To tune to any point in that sea of violence was to tax my power near to burn-out.

"They can't be stupid enough to believe they can overrun us—" That was Pawlin Shallard, our engineer. "They're too far above the primitive to think that possible."

"No." Lidj had his head up, was watching the screen so intently he might be trying to pick out of that crowd some certain face or figure. Hunold had set the screen on "circle" as he might have done at a first set-down on an unexplored world, so that the scene shifted, allowing us a slow survey about the landing site. "No, they won't rush us. They want something else. To prevent our cargo from coming. But these are city men—I would not have believed the rebels had infiltrated in such numbers or so quickly—" He broke off, frowning at the ever-changing picture.

"Wait!" Foss pushed a "hold" button and that slow revolution was halted.

What we saw now was the gate through which we had come only a short time ago. Through it was issuing a well-armed force in uniform, the first sign of a disciplined attack on the rebels. The men in it spread out as skirmishers to form a loose cover for a cart. On that was mounted a long-snouted, heavy-looking tube which men swung down and around to face the mob between them and the ship. A fringe of the rebels began to push away from the line of fire. But that great barrel swung in a small arc, as if warning of the swath it could cut through their ranks.

Men ran from the mass of those besieging us—first by ones and twos, and then by squads. We had no idea of the more complex weapons of Thoth, but it would seem that this was one the natives held in high respect. The mob was not giving up entirely. But the ranks of the loyal soldiery were being constantly augmented from the city, pushing out and out, the mob retreating sullenly before them.

"This is it!" Lidj made for the ship ladder. "I'd say they are going to run the cargo out now. Do we open to load?" Under normal circumstances the loading of the ship was his department. But with the safety of the *Lydis* perhaps at stake, that decision passed automatically to Foss.

"Cover the hatches with stunners; open the upper first. Until we see how well they manage—" was the captain's answer.

Minutes later we stood within the upper hatch. It was open and I had an unpleasantly naked feeling as I waited at my duty post, my calculator fastened to my wrist instead of lying in the palm of my hand, leaving me free to use my weapon. This time I had that set on narrow beam. Griss Sharvan, second engineer, pressed into guard service and facing me on the other side of the cargo opening, kept his ready on high-energy spray.

The barreled weapon had been moved farther out, to free the city gate. But its snout still swung in a jerky pattern, right to left and back again. There were no members of the mob left in front of us within the now-narrowed field of our vision, except several prone bodies, men who must have been picked off by the skirmishers.

Beyond, the gate had been opened to its furthest extent. And through that gap came the first of the heavily loaded transports. The Thothians had motorized cars which burned liquid fuel. To us such seemed sluggish when compared to the solar-energized machines of the inner planets. But at least they were better than the animal-drawn vehicles of truly primitive worlds. And now three of these trucks crawled over the field toward the *Lydis*.

A robed priest drove each, but there were guards

aboard, on the alert, their heads protected by grotesque bowl-shaped helmets, their weapons ready. Between those, we saw, as the first truck ground nearer, more priests crouched behind what small protection the sides of the vehicles offered, their faces livid. But they arose quickly as the truck came to a halt under the swinging lines of our crane, and pawed at the top boxes and bales of the cargo. It seemed that they were to shift that while the guards remained on the defensive.

Thus began the loading of the *Lydis*. The priests were willing but awkward workers. So I swung out and down with the crane to help below, trying not to think of the possibility of a lucky shot from the mob. For there was the crackle of firing now coming from a distance.

Up and down, in with the crane ropes, up—down. We had to use great care, for though all were well muffled in wrappings, we knew that what we handled were irreplaceable treasures. The first truck, emptied, drew to one side. But the men who had manned it remained, the priests to help with the loading of the next, the guards spreading out as had the skirmishers from the gate. I continued to supervise the loading, at the same time listing the number of each piece swung aloft, reciting it into my recorder. Lidj by the hatch would be making a duplicate of my record, and together they would be officially sealed in the presence of the priests' representatives when all was aboard.

Three trucks we emptied. The load of the fourth consisted of only four pieces—one extra-large, three small. I signaled for double crane power, not quite sure if the biggest crate could be maneuvered through the hatch. It was a tight squeeze, but the men there managed it. When I saw it disappear I spoke to the priest in charge.

"Any more?"

He shook his head as he still watched where that large crate had vanished. Then he looked to me.

"No more. But the High One will come to take receipt for the shipment."

"How soon?" I pressed. Still I did not use mind-touch. There was too much chance of being over-whelmed by the raw emotion engendered on a battle-field. Of course the *Lydis* was such a fort as could not be stormed, but I knew the sooner we raised from Thoth the better.

"When he can." His answer was ambiguous enough to be irritating. Already he turned away, calling some order in the native tongue.

I shrugged and swung up to the hatch. There was a stowage robo at work there. My superior leaned against the wall just inside, reading the dial of his recorder. As I came in he pressed the "stop" button to seal off his list.

"They won't take receipt," I reported. "They say that there is a High One coming to do that."

Lidj grunted, so I went to see to the sealing of the holds. The large crate which had been the last was still in the claws of two robo haulers. And, strong as those were, it was not easily moved. I watched them center it in the smaller top hold, snap on the locks to keep it in position during flight. That was the last, and I could now slide the doors shut, imprint the seal which would protect the cargo until we planeted once more. Of course Lidj would be along later to add his thumb signature to mine, and only when the two of us released it could anything less than a destruct burner get it out.

I stopped in my cabin as I went aloft. Maelen, as was usual during cargo loading, lay on her own bunk there. Her crested head rested on her two forepaws, which were folded under her muzzle as she stretched out at her ease. But she was not sleeping. Her golden eyes were open. At a second glance I recognized that fixity of stare—she was engaged in intense mind-seek, and I did not disturb her. Whatever she so listened to was of absorbing interest.

As I was backing out, not wanting to trouble her, the rigid tension broke. Her head lifted a little. But I waited for her to communicate first.

"There is one who comes, but not he whom you expect."

For I thought of the high priest coming for the receipt.

"He is not of the same mind as those who hired our aid," she continued. "Rather is he of an opposite will—"

"A rebel?"

"No. This one wears the same robe as the other temple men. But he does not share their wishes. He thinks it ill done, close to evil, to take these treasures from the sanctuary he serves. He believes that in retaliation his god will bring down ill upon all who aid in such a crime, for such it is to him. He is not one who tempers belief because of a change in the winds of fortune. Now he comes, because he deems it his duty, to deliver the curse of his god. For he serves a being who knows more of wrath than of love and justice. He comes to curse us—"

"To curse only—or to fight?" I asked.

"Do you think of the one as less than the other! In some ways a curse can be a greater weapon, when it is delivered by a believer."

To say that I would scoff at that is wrong. Any far rover of the sky trails can tell you that there is nothing so strange that it cannot happen on one world or another. I have known curses to slay—but only on one condition, that he who is so cursed is also a believer. Perhaps the priests who had sent their treasure into our holds might so be cursed, believe, and die. But for us of the *Lydis* it was a different matter. We are not men of no belief. Each man has his own god or supreme power. Maelen herself had him she called Molaster, by whom and for whom she fashioned her way of life. But that we might be touched by some god of Thoth I could not accept.

"Accept or not"—she had easily followed my thought—"believe or not, yet a curse, any curse, is a heavy load to carry. For evil begets evil and dark clings to shadows. The curse of a believer has its own power. This man is sincere in what he believes and he has powers of his own. Belief *is* power!"

"You cry a warning?" I was more serious now, for such from Maelen was not to be taken lightly.

"I do not know. Were I what I once was—" Her thoughts were suddenly closed to me. Never had I heard her regret what she had left behind on Yiktor when her own body had taken fatal hurt and her people, in addition, had set upon her the penance of perhaps years in the form she now wore. If she had any times of longing or depression, she held them locked within her. And now this broken sentence expressed a desire to hold again what she had had as a Moon Singer of the Thassa, as a man would reach wistfully for a weapon he had lost.

I knew that her message must be passed on to the captain as soon as possible and I went up to the control cabin. Foss sat watching the visa-plate, which at present showed the line of empty trucks on their way back to Kartum. The snouted weapon still sat just outside the gate, its crew alert about it as if they expected more trouble.

"Hatch closed, cargo sealed," I reported. Though that was only a matter of form. Lidj was in the astrogator's seat, slumped a little in the webbing, as he chewed thoughtfully on a stick of restorative slo-go.

"Maelen says—" I began, not even sure if I had their full attention. But I continued with the report.

"Cursing now," Foss commented as I finished. "But why? We are supposed to be saving their treasures for them, aren't we?"

"Schism in the temple, yet," Lidj said in answer to the captain's first question. "It would seem that this High Priest has more than one complication to make life interesting for him. It is rather to be wondered at why this was not mentioned before we accepted contract." His jaws clamped shut on the stick.

The visa-plate pictured new action for us. Though the trucks had gone through the gates, the guards there made no move to fall back. However, there was a stir at that barrier. Not more of the army, rather a procession which might have been honoring some feast day of the god.

We could see plainly the dull purple of priestly robes, brightened by dashes of vivid crimson or angry bursts of orange-yellow, as if flames sprouted here and there. We could not hear, but we could see the large drums borne by men on the outer edges of that line of march, drums being vigorously beaten.

"We have that on board which might be as fire to a fuse," Lidj remarked, still watching the screen, chewing at his slo-go. "The Throne of Qur."

I stared at him. One hears of legends. They are the

foundation for much careless talk and speculation. But to see—actually to lay hands on the fabric of one, that is another matter altogether. That last, the largest crate we had hoisted aboard—the Throne of Qur!

Who had been the first, the real owners of the treasures of Thoth? No one could set name to them now. Oddly enough, though the remains found were obviously products of a very high civilization, there had never been discovered any form of writing or record. We had no names for the kings, queens, nobles, priests, who had left their possessions so. Thus the finders, of necessity, had given the names of their own to the finds.

The Throne had been discovered all alone, walled away in a section by itself at the end of a blind passage in one of the early-located caches. The adventurer who had bossed the crew uncovering it had been not a native to Thoth, but an archaeologist (or so he claimed) from Phaphor. He had named his discovery for a deity of his home world. Not that that had brought him luck, perhaps the contrary. For such christening had offended the priests. The adventurer had died, suddenly, and the Throne had been speedily claimed by the temple, in spite of the fact that the priesthood had earlier sold excavation rights. For that find had been made in the days before the complete monopoly of the priesthood had been enforced. To uncover the Throne he had given his life, as he must have known, for he had made a vain attempt to reseal that side passage, perhaps hoping to smuggle the Throne away. Only it was far too late for that as soon as it was found.

The Throne had been fashioned for one of a race who had physically resembled us. The seat was wrought of a red metal, surprisingly light in weight for its durability. Guarding this were two side pieces, the tops of which furnished arms, and those reared as the heads of unknown creatures, all overlaid with scales of gold and burnished green, with eyes of milky white stones. But it was the flaring, towering back which was its chief marvel. For it seemed to be a wide spread of feathers so delicately fashioned of gold and green that they might once have been real fronds. And the tip of each feather was widened to enclose a blue-green gem, a full one hundred of them in all by count.

But the real peculiarity of the piece, apart from the skill and wonderful craftsmanship, was that those blue-green stones and the milky ones set in the arms were, as far as anyone had been able to discover, not only not native to Thoth but unknown anywhere else. Nor were their like set into any other object so far found on this planet.

Once revealed, the Throne had been moved to the temple in Kartum, where it formed one of the main attractions. Since a close inspection was allowed only after endless waiting and under strict supervision, not much had since been learned of it—though images of it appeared on every tape dealing with Thoth.

The procession by the gate moved out toward the *Lydis*. And those bright red and yellow touches were now seen as wide scarves or shawls resting about the shoulders of the center core of marchers, strung out behind a single man. He was tall, standing well above those immediately about him, and so gaunt that the bones of his face were almost death's-head sharp. There was no softness in that face, nothing but deeply graven lines which spelled fanaticism. His mouth moved as though he were speaking, shouting, or chanting along with the drums which flanked him.

His eyes were fastened on the *Lydis*.

I was aware of movement beside me—Maelen was there, her head strained at an angle to watch the screen. I stooped and picked her up that she might see more easily. Her body was more solid, heavier, than it appeared.

"A man of peril, a strong believer," she told me. "Though he is not like our Old Ones—yet he could be, were he properly schooled in the Way of Molaster. Save that such as he have not the open heart and mind that are needful. He sees but one path and is prepared to give all, even life, to achieve what he wishes. Such men are dangerous—"

Lidj glanced over his shoulder. "You are right, little one." He must have picked up her full mind-send. To my shipmates Maelen was all glassia, of course. Only Griss Sharvan had ever seen her in her Thassa body, and even he now seemed unable to connect animal with woman. They knew she was not in truth as she seemed, but they could not hold that ever in mind.

The procession of priests formed a wedge, with their leader at its tip—a spear point aimed at the ship. We still could not hear, but we saw the drummers rest their sticks. Yet the lips of the tall priest still moved and now also his hands. For he stooped and caught up a handful of the trampled, sandy soil. This he spat upon, though he looked not at it, but ever to the ship.

Having spat, he rolled it back and forth between his palms. And now and then he raised it higher, seemed to breathe into what he rolled and kneaded so.

"He curses," Maelen reported. "He calls upon his god to curse that which would take from Thoth the treasures of the temple, and all those who aid in the matter. And he swears that the treasure shall be returned, though those who take it will then be dead and blasted—and for its return he shall wait where he now stands."

The priest's lips no longer moved. Two of his followers pushed forward, one on either side. They whipped from beneath their cloaks two lengths of matting, and these they spread upon the ground one over the other. When they had done, though he never looked once at them but only to the *Lydis*, the priest knelt upon that carpet, his hands crossed upon his breast. Nor did he afterward stir, while his followers, drums and all, withdrew some paces.

Now from the gate came a small surface car which detoured around the kneeling priest in a very wide swing. And it approached the *Lydis*.

"Our take-off authorization." Lidj climbed from his seat. "I'll go get it—the sooner we lift the better."

He put the uneaten portion of his slo-go back into its covering, stowed it in a seam pocket, and started from the cabin. With take-off sure to follow soon, we all scattered, making for our posts, ready to strap down. Maelen I aided into her upper berth, laced the protective webbing which she could not manage with her paws, then dropped into my own place. As I lay waiting for the signal I thought of the kneeling priest.

Unless we did make a second trip to pick up more cargo, he was going to have a long wait. And what if we did return, having made our first delivery to Ptah? Would such a return prove him so wrong that he would not only lose his followers but be shaken in his own belief?

"Let us return first—" Maelen's thought came.

There is no betraying intonation in thoughts as there sometimes is in voices. Yet there was something— Did she really believe some ill luck would come to us?

"The Scales of Molaster hang true and steady for those of good will. Any evil in this matter is not of our doing. Yet I do not like—"

The signal for blast-off cut across that. She shut her mind as one might shut his mouth. We lay waiting for the familiar discomfort as the *Lydis* headed up and out—not to the stars this time, but to the fourth planet of the system, a pale crescent now showing in the western sky.

Since we did not go into hyper for such a short trip, we unstrapped as soon as we were on stable speed. Also we were now in free fall, a condition which is never comfortable—though we had been accustomed to it practically from birth. Maelen did not like it at all and preferred to spend such periods in her take-off webbing. I saw that she was as comfortable as might be under the circumstances and then pulled my way along to Lidj's quarters.

But I found, to my amazement, that my superior was not alone. Though he had discarded the robe and cape of his calling, the shaven head of the man lying on the cargomaster's own bunk was plainly that of a priest. We had not been prepared for any passenger; at least I had not been informed of one. And it was so seldom that a Free Trader carried any but a member of the crew that I looked quickly to Lidj for enlightenment. The priest himself lay limp, held by take-off webbing still, appearing totally unconscious.

Lidj waved me outside the cabin and followed. He pulled shut the sliding panel to seal the cabin.

"A passenger—"

"He had orders we had to accept," Lidj informed me. I could see he had little liking for the matter. "He not only brought a warning, to rise as soon as we could, but authorization from the high priest for him to see our cargo to its destination and take charge there. I do not know what pot has boiled over down there—but our Thothian charterers wanted us away as fast as rockets could raise us. At least we can do with one extra aboard, as long as he is going no farther than Ptah."

Chapter 3

MAELEN

I lay in my assigned resting place in this ship and fought once again my weary battle, that battle which I could never share with another, not even with this outlander who had fought a like one in his time. I who was once Maelen, Moon Singer, and (as I know now) far too arrogant in my pride of deed and word, believing that I alone had an accounting with fate and that all would go according to my desire.

Well do we of the Thassa need to remember the Scales of Molaster, wherein the deeds of our bodies, the thoughts of our minds, the wishes of our hearts, will be weighed against truth and right!

Because I had been so weighed and found wanting, now I went in other guise, that of my small comrade Vors. And Vors had willingly given me her body when my own had failed me. So I must not belittle or waste the great sacrifice she had made. Thus I willed myself to endure and endure and endure—to fight this battle not once but again and again, and again and again.

I had chosen, as a Moon Singer who must learn to

be one with other living things, to run the high places of Yiktor in animal guise, and had so fulfilled my duty. Yet that had been always with the comfortable knowledge that my own body waited for my return, that this exile was only for a time. While now—

Always, though, I was still Maelen—myself—ME; yet also there was an occupying part which still held the essence of Vors. Much as I had loved and honored her for the great thing she had done for me, yet also I must struggle against the instincts of this body, to remain as much as I could only a temporary indweller. And always was the brooding shadow of a new fear—that there would be no escape ever, that through the years Vors would become more and more, Maelen less and less.

I longed to ask my companion—this alien Krip Vorlund—whether such a fear had ridden him when he had run as a barsk. Yet I could not admit to any that I carried such unease in me. Though whether that silence was born of some of my old pride and need to be mistress of the situation, or whether it was a curb which was needful, I did not know. It remained that I must play my role as best I could. But also I welcomed those times when it was given me to play some necessary part in the life of the *Lydis*, for then it seemed that Maelen was wholly in command again. So it had been that during those last hours on Thoth I had been able to forget myself and enter into the venture of the ship.

Yet I lay now and my thoughts were dark, for I remembered the priest who had ceremoniously cursed us. As I had told Krip, there is power in the pure belief of such a man. Though he had used no wand or staff to point us out to the Strengths of the Deep Dark, still he had called upon what he knew to encompass us. And—I had not been able to reach his mind; there had been a barrier locking me out as securely as if he had been an Old One.

Now I lay on the bunk, held snug by the webbing (for with all my shipboard life I have never been able to adjust well to free fall)—I lay there and used mind-seek.

Those of the *Lydis* were as always. I touched only lightly the surface of their thoughts. For to probe, unless that is desperately needed, is a violation to which no living being should subject another. But in my seeking I came upon another mind and—

I swung my head around, reached with my teeth for the lacing which held me. Then sane reason took control, and I sent a call to Krip. His reply was instant —he must have read my concern.

"What is it?"

"There is one on board from Thoth. He means us ill!"

There was a pause and then his answer came clearly.

"I have him under my eyes now. He is unconscious; he has been so since the ship lifted."

"His mind is awake—and busy! Krip, this man, he is more than all others we met on Thoth. He is akin, closely akin, to the one who cursed us. Watch him— watch him well!"

But even then I did not realize how different he was, this stranger, nor just how much we had to fear him. For, as with him who had cursed us, there was a barrier behind which he hid more than half his thoughts. And though I could not read them, I did sense peril there.

"Do not doubt, he shall be watched."

It was as if the stranger had heard what had passed

between us. Perhaps he did. For there followed a swift subduing of the emanations of his mind. Though that could have come from a bodily weakness also. But I was on guard, as if in truth I walked a sentry's beat in the belly of the *Lydis*.

There is no night or day, morn or evening, in a ship. Which was something I had found hard to adjust to when first I came on board. Just as the narrow spaces of the cabins, the corridors, were prison-like for one who never had any home save the wagons of the Thassa, had always lived by choice beyond man-made walls. There was always an acrid scent here. And sometimes the throbbing of the engines which powered us from star to star seemed almost more than I could bear, so that my only escape was into the past and my memories. No night or day, save those which the Traders arbitrarily set for themselves, divided into orderly periods of sleep and waking.

Once the ship was in flight and set on course, there was little which had to be done to keep her so. Krip had early shown me that her crew did not lack occupation, however. Some of them created with their hands, making small things which amused them, or which they could add to their trade goods. Others busied their minds, learning from their store of information tapes. So did they labor to keep the ship from becoming their prison also.

For Krip—well, perhaps it was for him now as it was for me, and the body he wore influenced him a little. Because he was outwardly Thassa, he asked of me my memories, wanting to learn all he could of my people. And I shared with him freely, save for such things which could not be spread before any outlander. So we both escaped into a world beyond the throbbing cabin walls.

Now a little later he returned, ready for the sleep period. Was there any change in what I had learned about our passenger, he asked. Lidj had taken it upon himself, after my warning, to give the man a certain drug which was meant to ease lift-off and which should keep him in slumber for much of our voyage.

No, no change, I answered. And so accustomed had I become to the ship's pattern that, I, too, felt the need of sleep.

I was sharply awakened from my rest, as sharply as if a noose of filan cord had closed about my body, jerking me upright. I found myself in truth fighting the webbing which held me fast to the bunk, even as my mind steadied.

For a dazed moment or two, I could not guess what had so roused me. Then I knew that I no longer felt the ever-present beat of the engine, but rather there was a break in the smooth rhythm. And only a second later a shrill sound came from above my head, issuing from the intercom system of the ship—a warning that all was not well with the *Lydis*.

Krip rolled out of the lower bunk. Since we were in free fall his too-swift movement carried him against the other wall with bruising force. I heard him give a muttered exclamation as he caught at a wall rack and clawed his way back to where I lay. Holding on with one hand, he ripped loose my webbing.

Now that the first warning had awakened us, words came from the intercom, booming like a signal of doom.

"All off-duty personnel, strap down for orbiting!"

Krip paused, his hand still on my webbing, while I clung with my great claws to the bunk so I would not float away, unable to govern my going. Then he responded to orders, pushing me back, making me secure again before he returned to his own place.

"We cannot have reached Ptah!" I was still shaken from that sudden awakening.

"No—but the ship—"

He did not need to continue. Even I, who was no real star voyager, could feel the difference. There was a catch in the rhythm of the engines.

I dared not use mind-touch, lest I disturb some brain needed to concentrate on the ship's well-being. But I tried mind-seek. Perhaps it was instinct which aimed that first at the stranger in our midst.

I have no idea whether I cried out aloud. But instantly Krip answered me. And when he read my discovery his alarm was near fear.

I am—was—a Moon Singer. As such, I used the wand. I could beam-read. I have wrought the transfer of bodies under the three rings of Sotrath. By the grace of Molaster I have done much with my talent. But this that I now touched upon was new, alien, dark, and destructive beyond all my reckoning.

For there flowed from that priest as he lay a current of pure power. And I could slip along it, as I did, drawing Krip's thought with me, through the *Lydis*, down to something that lay below those engines which were her life—something in the cargo hold.

And that mind power released the force of what lay in hiding, which had been cunningly attuned to the thought of one man alone. So that there now emanated from that hidden packet a more powerful force than any thought, and a deadly one, acting upon the heart of the *Lydis* to slow the beat of her engines, make them sluggish. And in time it would bring about their failure.

I tried to dam that compelling force flowing from

the mind of the priest. But it was as if the current of energy were encased in the Rock of Tormora. It could be neither cut nor swayed from its purpose. Yet I sensed that if it might be halted, then the packet would fail in turn. Learning that, Krip sent his own message:

"The man then, if not his thought—get to the man!"

Straightway I saw he was right. Now I ceased my fight against that current and joined with Krip to seek out Lidj, who should be nearest to the stranger. And so we warned the cargomaster, urging physical action on his part.

It came! That current of feeding energy pulsed, lessened, surged again—then sparked weakly and was gone. The vibration in the ship steadied for perhaps four heartbeats. Then it, too, flickered off. I could feel through the *Lydis* the surge of will of those in her, their fear and need to hold that engine steady.

Then came the return of gravity. We were in orbit —but where and—

My glassia body was not fashioned to take such strains. Though I fought frantically to retain consciousness, I failed.

There was a flat-sweet taste in my mouth; moisture trickled from my muzzle. That part of me which was Vors remembered blood. I ached painfully. When I forced open my eyes I could see only through a mist. But the roof of the cabin was steadily up and I was pulled to the bunk by a gravity greater than that of Thoth.

We had set down. Were we back on Thoth? I doubted it. Hooking my claws against the sides of the bunk, I was able in spite of the webbing to wriggle closer to the edge, look down to see how it had fared with my cabinmate.

As he pushed himself up his eyes met mine. There was a sudden look of concern—

"Maelen!" he said aloud. "You are hurt!"

I turned attention to my body. There were bruises, yes. And blood had issued from my nose and mouth to bedaub my fur. Yet all hurts were small, and I reported it so.

Thus we planeted, not on Thoth, nor on Ptah, which had been our goal, but on Sekhmet. Strange names, all these. Krip had long since told me that the early space explorers of his race were wont to give to suns and their attendant worlds the names of gods and goddesses known to the more primitive peoples of their own historic past. And where those worlds had no native inhabitants to use a rival name, those of the Terran explorers were accepted.

These of the system of Amen-Re were so named from legend. And Krip had shown me the symbols on the map edge to identify each. They had come from the very far past. Set, too fiery to support life, had the picture of a saurian creature; Thoth, that of a long-beaked bird. Ptah was human enough, but Sekhmet was represented in that company by the furred head of a creature which Krip knew and had seen in his own lifetime and which he called a "cat."

These cats had taken to space voyaging easily and had been common on ships in the early days—though now they were few. Only a small number were carefully nurtured in the asteroid bases of the Traders. A cat's head had Sekhmet, but the body of a woman. What powers the goddess had represented, Krip did not know. Such lore was forgotten. But this world she had given her name to was not of good repute.

It had heavier gravity than Thoth or Ptah, and was so forbidding that, though there had been attempts to colonize it, those had been given up. A few prospectors came now and then, but they had discovered nothing which was not present also on Ptah and much more easily obtained there. Somewhere on its land mass was a Patrol beacon for the relaying of messages. But for the rest it was left to its scouring winds, its lowering skies, and what strange life was native to it.

Not only had we set down on this bleak world—which act was a feat of skill on the parts of our pilot and engineer—but we were in a manner now prisoners here. For that energy which had played upon our engines had done such damage as could not be repaired without supplies and tools which the *Lydis* did not carry.

As for the priest, we had no answers out of him, for he was dead. Lidj, aroused by our warning, had struck quickly. His blow, meant to knock the Thothian unconscious, had not done the harm; rather it was as if the sudden cessation of the act of sabotage had recoiled, burning life out of him. So we did not know the reason for the attack, save that it must have been aimed at keeping us from Ptah.

What was left to us now was to make secure our own safety. Somewhere hidden among these roughly splintered hills (for this land was all sharp peaks and valleys so deep and narrow that they might have been cut into the planet by the sword of an angry giant) there was a Patrol beacon. To reach that and broadcast for help was our only hope.

Within the shell of the *Lydis* was a small two-man flitter, meant to be used for exploration. This was brought out, assembled for service. Over the broken terrain such a trip in search of a beacon which might lie half the world away was a chancy undertaking. And though all the crew were ready to volunteer, it was decided that they should draw lots for the search party.

This they did, each man drawing from a bowl into which they had dropped small cubes bearing their rank symbols. And chance so marked down our astrogator Manus Hunold and second engineer Griss Sharvan.

They took from the stores, making packs of emergency rations and other needs. And the flitter was checked and rechecked, taken up on two trial flights, before Captain Foss was assured it would do.

I had said that this was a planet of evil omen. Though I found nothing by mind-seek to indicate any menace beyond that of the very rugged nature of the surface and the darkness of the landscape. Dark that landscape was.

There are many barren stretches of waste on Yiktor. The high hill country, which is the closest thing to home territory the Thassa now hold, is largely what the lowland men term desert waste. Yet there is always a feeling of light, of freedom, therein.

But here the overpowering atmosphere was one of darkness. The rocky walls of the towering escarpments were of a black or very dark-gray stone. What scanty vegetation there was had a ghostly wanness, being of a pallid gray hue. Or else it nearly matched the rocks in whose crevices it grew, dusky nodules so unpleasant to look upon that to touch them would require a great effort of will.

Even the sand which rose in dunes across this open space where Captain Foss had brought us in for a masterly landing was more like the ashes of long-dead fires—so powdery and fine (save where our deter rockets had fused it) that it held no footprint. Clouds of it were whirled into the air by the cold winds—winds which wailed and cried as they cut through the tortured rock of the heights. It was a land which was an enemy to our kind and which made plain that hostility as the hours passed.

It was those winds which were the greatest source of concern for the flitter. If such gusts grew stronger, the light craft could not battle a passage over dangerously rough country.

Some rewiring and careful work on the com of the *Lydis* had brought a very weak suggestion of a signal. So our com-tech Sanson Korde was certain that there was a beacon somewhere on the land where we had set down. A very small piece of doubtful good fortune.

For me there was little enough to do. My paws were not designed to work on the flitter. So I set myself another task, prowling around among those grim rocks, listening with every talent I had—of body and mind—for aught which might live here and mean us ill.

Sekhmet was not devoid of animal life. There were small scuttling insects, things which hid in the breaks between stones. But none of them thought, as we measure mind power. Of larger creatures I discovered not a trace. Which did not mean that such could not exist somewhere, just that if they did they were beyond the range of my present search.

Though I picked up no spark of intelligent life, there was something else here which I could not explain—a sensation of a hovering just beyond my range of conscious search. It was a feeling I had never known before save in one place, and there I had good reason to expect such. In the highest lands of Yiktor the Thassa have their own places. Once, legend tells us, we were a settled people even as the lowlanders are today. We knew the confinement of cities, the rise of permanent walls ever about us.

Then there came a time when we made a choice which would change not only those alive to make it then, but the generations born to follow them—to turn aside from works made by hands to other powers, invisible, immeasurable. And it was the choice of those faced by such a splitting of the life road to take that which favored mind over body. So gradually it was less and less needful for us to be rooted in one place. Possessions had little meaning. If a man or woman had more than he needed he shared with the less fortunate.

We became rovers, more at home in the lands of the wilds than those which had held our forefathers rooted. But still there were certain sacred sites which were very old, so old that their original use had long since vanished even from the ancient tales. And these we resorted to on occasions when there was a need that we gather for a centering of the power—for the raising up of an Old One, or a like happening.

These sites have an atmosphere, an aura, which is theirs alone. So that they come alive while we abide there, welcoming us with a warmth of spirit as restoring as a draft of clear water is to a man who has long thirsted. And this feeling—of vast antiquity and purpose—was something I well knew.

But here— Why did I have something of the same sensation—of an old, old thing with a kernel of meaning, a meaning I did not understand? It was as if I had been presented with a record roll which must be learned, yet the symbols on it were so alien they sparked no meaning in my mind. And this feeling haunted me whenever I made the rounds of our improvised landing field. Yet never could I center it in any one direction so that I might explore further and discover the reason of its troubling. I felt it only as if it were part of the dry, grit-laden air, the bitter wind wailing in the rocks.

I was not the only troubled one, but that which occupied the minds of my companions was a different matter. That the priest had triggered the device which had brought about our disaster they knew. The device itself had been found, and in a surprising place. For a careful search had led them to the Throne of Qur. First they thought that what they sought would be within the crate which covered that. But that was not so. They fully exposed the Throne and discovered nothing. Then they began a careful search, inch by inch, of the piece itself, using their best detector. Thus Lidj had uncovered a cavity in the towering back. Pressure upon two of the gems there had released a spring. Within was a box of dull metal.

The radiation reading was such that he put on protective gloves before he forced it out of its tight setting, transferring it into a shielded holder which was then taken out of the ship to be put among the rocks where whatever energy it broadcast could do no harm. These Traders had traveled far and had a wide knowledge of many worlds; yet the workmanship of that box and the nature of the energy it employed were unknown to them.

Save that they agreed on one thing, that it was not of Thothian making, since it was manifest that the technology there was too primitive to produce such a device.

"Unless," Captain Foss commented, "these priests in their eternal treasure-seeking have uncovered secrets they are not as quick to display as the other things they have found. It is apparent that that hollow in the Throne was not lately added, but must have been a part of it since its first fashioning. Was this also left over from that time? We have a dead man, a secret which is dangerous. We have a weapon used at just the right point in our voyage to force us to Sekhmet. And this adds up to a sum I dislike."

"But why— We could have been left derelict in space—" Shallard, the engineer, burst out. "It was only by the favor of fortune we were able to make a good landing here."

Foss stared across the rocks and the shifting dunes of powdery sand.

"I wonder—on that I wonder," he said slowly. And then he turned to the two who had drawn the lots for the beacon search. "I am beginning to believe that the sooner we contact authority the better. Prepare to take off in the next lull of the wind."

Chapter 4

MAELEN

So did they wing off in the flitter. In that was a device which kept them in contact with the *Lydis,* though they did not report more than passing above the same landscape as we saw. However, Foss kept in contact with them by the com unit of the ship, and his unease was as clear as if he shouted his thoughts aloud.

That we had been sabotaged it was unnecessary to question. But the reason remained unclear. Had we been delayed before take-off on Thoth, that would have been simple. Either the rebel forces or that fanatical priest could have done so. Only this stroke had come in mid-flight.

Had we been meant to land on Sekhmet? The captain was dubious about that—such depended too much on chance. He was more certain the attack had been meant to leave the *Lydis* helpless in space. And the rest of the crew agreed with him. At least on-planet one had more of a fighting chance; we might not have been given even that small advantage. In either case the threat was grave, so that even before he gave his orders to Korde, the com-tech had opened panels, was studying the maze of wiring behind them. There was a chance that these elements could be converted to a super-com, something with which to signal for help if the voyage of the flitter failed. The Traders were well used to improvising when the need arose.

Night was coming—though the day on Sekhmet had been hardly more than pallid dusk, the cloud cover lying so thickly across the riven hills. And with that flow of shadows the cold was greater. So I bushed my fur, not consciously, but by instinct.

Krip summoned me back to the ship, for they planned to seal themselves within, using that as a fort, even as it had been outside Kartum. I made one more scout sweep—found nothing threatening. Nothing which I could point to and say, "This is danger." Yet—

As the hatch closed behind me, the warmth and light of the *Lydis* giving a sense of security, still I was troubled by that other feeling—that we were ringed about by— What?

I used my claws to climb the ladder which led to the living quarters. But I was opposite the hatch of the hold wherein sat the Throne when I paused, clinging to the rungs. My head swung to that closed door as if drawn by an overwhelming force. So great was the pull that I hunched from the ladder itself to the space by the door, my shoulder brushing its surface.

That box which had wrought our disaster was now safely gone; I had watched its outside disposal. But from this room flowed a sense of—"life" is the closest I could come to describing it. I might now be in the field of some invisible communication. There was not only the mental alert, but a corresponding tingle in my flesh. My fur was rippling as it might under the touch of a strong wind. I must have given forth a mind-call, for Krip's answer came quickly:

"Maelen! What is it?"

I tried to reply, but there was so little of which I could make a definite message. Yet what I offered was enough to summon them to me with speed—Krip, the captain, and Lidj.

"But the box is gone," Captain Foss said. He stepped to one side as Lidj crowded past to reopen the sealed hatch. "Or— Can there be another?"

Krip's hand was on my head, smoothing that oddly ruffled fur. His face expressed his concern, not only for what danger might lurk here, but in a measure for me also. For he knew that I could not tell what lay behind the door, and my very ignorance was an additional source of danger. I was shaken now as I had never been in the past.

Lidj had the door open. And, with that, light flashed within. There sat the Throne, facing us squarely. They had not recrated it as yet. Only the cavity in the back was closed again. The captain turned to me.

"Well, what is it?"

But in turn I looked to Krip. "Do you feel it?"

He faced the Throne, his face now blank of expression, his dark Thassa eyes fixed. I saw his tongue pass over his lower lip.

"I feel—something—" But his puzzlement was strong.

Both the other Traders looked from one of us to the other. It was plain they did not share what we felt. Krip took a step forward—put his hand to the seat of the Throne.

I cried aloud my protest as a glassia growl. But too

late. His finger tips touched the red metal. A visible shudder shook his body; he reeled back as if he had thrust his hand into open fire—reeled and fell against Lidj, who threw out an arm just in time to keep him from sliding to the floor. The captain rounded on me.

"What is it?" he demanded.

"Force—" I aimed mind-speech at him. "Strong force. I have never met its like before."

He jerked away from the Throne. Lidj, still supporting Krip, did the same.

"But why don't we also feel it?" the Captain asked, now eyeing the Throne as if he expected it to discharge raw energy into his very face.

"I do not know—perhaps because the Thassa are more attuned to what it exudes. But it is broadcasting force, and out there"—I swung my head to indicate the wall of the ship—"there is something which draws such a broadcast."

The captain studied the artifact warily. Then he came to the only decision a man conditioned as a Free Trader could make. The safety of the *Lydis* was above all else.

"We unload—not just the Throne, all this. We cache it until we learn what's behind it all."

I heard Lidj suck in his breath sharply. "To break contract—" he began, citing another part of the Traders' creed.

"No contract holds that a cargo of danger must be transported, the more so when that danger was not made plain at the acceptance of the bargain. The *Lydis* has already been planeted through the agency of this—this treasure! We are only lucky that we are not now in a drifting derelict because of it. This must go out—speedily!"

So, despite the dark, floodlights were strung, and

once more the robos were put to work. This time they trundled to the hatches all those crates, boxes, and bales which had been so carefully stowed there on Thoth. Several of the robos were swung to the ground and there set to plowing through the dunes, piling the cargo within such shelter as a ridge of rock afforded. And there last of all was put the Throne of Qur, its glittering beauty uncovered, since they did not wait to crate it again.

"Suppose"—Lidj stood checking off the pieces as the robos brought them along—"this is just what someone wants—that we dump it where it can be easily picked up?"

"We have alarms rigged. Nothing can approach without triggering those. And then we can defend it." The captain spoke to me. "You can guard?"

It was very seldom during the months since I had joined the ship that he had asked any direct service of me, though he acknowledged I had talents which his men did not possess. What I had I gave willingly, before it was asked. It would seem now that he hesitated a little, as if this was a thing for which I ought to be allowed to volunteer.

I answered that I could and would—though I did not want to come too close to that pile of cargo, especially the glittering Throne. So they rigged their alarms. But as they went into the ship again, Krip came down the ramp.

His adventure in the hold had so affected him that he had had to withdraw for a space to his cabin. Now he wore the thermo garments made for cold worlds, the hood pulled over his head, the mittens on his hands. And he carried a weapon I had seldom seen him use—a blaster.

"Where do you think you're—" the captain began when Krip interrupted.

"I stay with Maelen. Perhaps I do not have her power, but still I am closer to her than the rest of you are. I stay."

At first the captain looked ready to protest, then he nodded. "Well enough."

When they had gone and the ramp was back in the ship, Krip waded through the drifting sand to look at the Throne—though he kept well away from it, I was glad to note.

"What—and why?"

"What and why, indeed," I made answer. "There are perhaps as many answers as I have claws to unsheathe. Perhaps the captain is wrong and we were indeed meant to land here, even to unload the cargo. Only that dead priest could answer us truly what and why."

I sat up on my haunches, balancing awkwardly as one must do in a body fashioned to go on four feet when one would be as erect as one ready to march on two. The wind curled about my ribs and back in a cold lash, yet my fur kept me warm. However, the sand-ash arose in great choking swirls, shifting over the Throne of Qur.

Now I squinted against that blowing grit, my gaze fixed upon the chair. Did—did I see for an instant divorced from true time what my eyes reported? Or did I imagine it only?

Did the dust fashion, even as if it clung to an invisible but solid core, the likeness of a body enthroned as might be a judge to give voice upon our affairs?

It was only for an instant that it seemed so. Then that shadow vanished. The wind-driven dust collapsed into a film on the red metal. And I do not think Krip saw it at all.

There was nothing more in the night. Our lights continued to shine on the air-spun dust, which built small hillocks around the boxes. My most alert senses could not pick up any echo among the rocks or in the near hills. We might have dreamed it all, save that we knew we had not. A fancy that it had been done to force the cargo out into the open settled so deep in my mind that I almost believed it the truth. But if we had been so worked upon to render the treasure vulnerable, no one now made any move to collect it.

Sekhmet had no moon to ride her cloudy sky. Beyond the circle of lights the darkness was complete. Shortly after the ship was sealed again, the wind died, the sand and dust ceased to drift. It was very quiet, almost too much so—for the feeling that we were waiting grew stronger.

Yet there came no attack—if any menace did lurk. However, in the early morning something occurred, in its way a greater blow at the *Lydis*, at our small party, than any attack of a formless evil. For this was concrete, a matter of evidence. The flitter's broadcast suddenly failed. All efforts to re-establish contact proved futile. Somewhere out in the waste of hills, mountains, knife-sharp valleys, the craft and her crew of two must be in trouble.

Since the *Lydis* carried only one flitter, there was no hope of manning a rescue flyer. Any such trip must be done overland. And the terrain was such as to render that well-nigh impossible. We could depend now only on the improvised com in the ship. To gather volume enough to signal off-world, Korde must tap our engines. Also, for any such broadcast there would be a frustrating time lag.

As was customary among the Traders, the remaining members of the crew assembled to discuss the grim future, to come to an agreement as to what must be done. Because Free Traders are bound to their ships, owning no home world of earth and stone, water and air, they are more closely knit together than many clans. That they could abandon two of their number lost in the unknown was unthinkable. Yet to search on foot for them was a task defeated before begun. Thus caught between two needs, they were men entrapped. Shallard agreed that the *Lydis* might just be able to rise from her present site. But that she could again make a safe landing he doubted. All his delving into the engines did not make plain just what had hit her power, but important circuits were burned out.

Again, as was the custom, each man offered what suggestions he could. Though in the end there was only one which could be followed—that the off-world com must be put into operation. It was then that Lidj voiced a warning of his own.

"It cannot be overlooked," he told them, "that we may have been pulled into a trap. Oh, I know that it is just on the edge of possibility that we were meant to fin down here on Sekhmet. On the other hand, how many cases of actual looting of ships in space are known? Such tales are more readily found on the fiction tapes, where the authors are not bound by the technical difficulties of such a maneuver. I think we can assume that the cargo is what led to sabotage. All right—who wants it? The rebels, that fanatic of a priest? Or some unknown party, who hopes to gather in loot worth more stellars than we could count in a year—if they could lift it from us and transport it out?

"Once away from this system, it would be a matter

of possession being nine-tenths of the law. Only here are the claims of the priesthood recognized as legal. You have heard of the Abna expedition, and the one that Harre Largo managed ten years back? They got in, found their treasure, got out again. The priests yelled themselves near black in the face over both, but the finds were legitimate, made by the men who ran the stuff out—they were not stolen.

"Then there are the laws of salvage. Think about those carefully. Suppose the *Lydis* had crashed here. That would cancel our own contract. Such an accident would open up a neat loophole which would be easy to use. Anyone finding a wrecked ship on an unsettled world—"

"That would only apply," cut in Captain Foss, "if all the crew were dead."

He did not have to underline that for us. A moment later he added: "I think we can be sure this is sabotage. And certainly this idea of a third party is logical. It could explain what happened to the flitter."

As he said, it all fitted together neatly. Yet, perhaps because my way of thinking was Thassa and not Trader, because I depended not upon machines and their patterns, I could not wholly accept such an explanation. There was something in what I had felt by the Throne of Qur, in that lowering feeling of being watched, which did not spring from any ordinary experience. No, in an indefinable way it was oddly akin to the Thassa. And I was sure that this affair was of a different nature from those of the Traders.

But because I had no proof, nothing but this feeling, I did not offer my suggestion. Those on the *Lydis* believed now that they were under siege, must wait for the unknown enemy to show his hand in some manner. And they voted to turn all their efforts to the broadcast for aid.

However, only two of them could provide the knowledgeable assistance Korde needed. For the others, Captain Foss had another task. That cargo now piled in open sight was, he decided, to be hidden as quickly as possible. Once more he disembarked the working robos, while Krip and I went out from the immediate vicinity of the ship in search of a good cache site.

There were plenty of possibilities in this very rough country. But we wanted one which would fulfill the captain's needs best—that being a site which could be sealed once the treasure was stowed. So we examined any narrow crevice, surveyed carefully any promising hole which might give entrance to a cave or other opening.

I was no longer aware of any current flowing between the Throne and some place beyond the valley. In the morning's early light that artifact, now shrouded in dust which clouded its brilliance, was only an inanimate object. One might well believe that imagination had supplied the happenings of the night before, except that it had not. Had that emanation been a kind of beacon, informing others of our position?

If so, once they were sure, they could well have turned off that which made a magnet of the cargo. So, as we went, I mind-searched as well as I could, even though to beam-read properly and at a goodly distance I did not have what I needed most, my lost wand of power, plus the chance for complete concentration—shutting all else out of my mind.

We came at last to a ridge taller than those immediately around our landing site. And the light was brighter, the sullen clouds less heavy. Along the wall—

Some trick of the light, together with a filmy deposit of sand which clung in curve and cut and hollow—I rose to my haunches, straining back my short neck, longing for a better range of vision.

Because the dust and the light made clear something of those lines on the stone. I saw there a design, far too regular in pattern for me to believe that it had been formed by erosion alone, the scouring of the wind-driven sand.

"Krip!"

At my summons he turned back from where he had gone farther down that cut.

"The wall—," I drew his attention to what seemed clearer and clearer the longer I studied it—that pattern so worn by the years that at first it could hardly be distinguished at all.

"What about the wall?" He looked at it. But there was only open puzzlement on his face.

"The pattern there." By now it was so plain to me I could not understand why he also did not see it. "Look—" I became impatient as I pointed as best I could with a forepaw, unsheathing claws as if I could reach up and trace the lines themselves. "Thus—and thus—and thus—" I followed the lines so, in and out. There were gaps, of course, but the over-all spread was firm enough not to need all the parts long weathered away.

He squinted, his eyes obediently following my gestures. Then I saw the dawn of excitement on his face.

"Yes!" His own mittened hand swung up as he, too, traced the design. "It is too regular to be natural. But—" Now I sensed a whisper of alarm in his mind

—as if something in the design was wrong.

It was when I looked again, not at the part closer to me, but moving back even farther to catch the whole of it, that I saw it was not the abstract design my eyes had first reported. What was really pictured on the cliffside was a face—or rather a mask. And that was of something neither human nor of any creature I knew.

But into Krip's mind flashed one word—"CAT!"

Once he had so identified it I could indeed trace a resemblance between it and the small symbol on the old map of the Amen-Re system. Yet it was also different. That head had been more rounded, far closer to a picture one could associate with a living animal. This was a distinctly triangular presentation with the narrowest angle pointing to the foot of the cliff.

In the area at the wider top there were two deep gashes set aslant to form eyes. Deep and very dark, giving one the disturbing impression that they pitted a skull. There was an indication of a muzzle with a lower opening, as if the creature had its mouth half open, while a series of lines made upstanding ears. There was nothing normal about the mask. Yet once it was called to my attention, I could see that it had evolved from a cat's head.

I had felt nothing but interest when I had seen the cat on the chart, a desire to see one of these animals for myself. But this thing—it was not of the same type at all.

The hollow which was the mouth held my interest now. And I went to explore it. Though the opening was so narrow that anyone of human bulk must crouch low to enter, I could do it with ease. In I padded, needing to know the why and wherefore, for so much effort had been expended in making the carving that I was sure it had a purpose.

The space was shallow—hardly more than half again the length of my glassia body. I raised one of my paws and felt before me, for it was too dark here to see. Thus I touched a surface which was smooth. Yet my seeking claws caught and ran along grooves, which I traced until I was sure that those marked divisions of blocks which had been carefully fitted into place.

When I reported this to Krip I was already sure of what we might have discovered by chance. While Sekhmet had never been known to house any treasure (perhaps it had never been well searched), we could have discovered such a hiding place. Though we had little time to prove or disprove it.

I tried to work my claw tips between the stones, to see if they could be so loosened. But it was impossible. When I scrambled out, Krip had his wrist com uncovered, was reporting our find. Though the captain showed some interest, he urged us now to carry out our original task and locate a place where the cargo could be cached.

"Not around here." Krip's decision matched mine. "If they—whoever they may be—do come looking, we need not direct them in turn to that!" He gestured to the cat's head.

Thus we turned directly away from that, heading to the northwest. So we came upon a crevice which the light of Krip's torch told us deepened into a cave. And since we had found nothing so good closer to our landing site, we selected that.

So rough was the terrain that the passage of each laden robo had to be carefully supervised. Foss wanted no cutting or smoothing of the way to the hiding place. It took us most of the remaining daylight hours to see all into the crevice. Once the cargo was stowed, rocks were built into a stopper, well under the overhang of the outer part of the crevice, where they might be overlooked unless someone was searching with extra care.

Then a small flamer, such as is used for ship repairs, was brought in and the rocks fused into a cork which would take a great deal of time and trouble to loosen.

Lidj made a last inspection. "Best we can do. Now —let's see this other find of yours."

We led them to the cliff face. It was difficult now, though they shone working lights on it, to see the lines which had been more distinct in the early morning. I thought perhaps the dust had largely blown away. Lidj at first professed to distinguish nothing. And it was only when he hunched well down and centered a torch into the mouth, located that inner wall of blocks, that he was convinced the find was not some far flight of imagination.

"Well enough," he admitted then. "What this may lead to"—he held the torch closer to the wall—" can be anyone's guess. Certainly nothing we can explore now. But who knows about later?"

However, I knew that beneath his outer calm he was excited. This was such a find as might return to the *Lydis* all the lost profit from this voyage—perhaps even more.

Chapter 5

KRIP VORLUND

"Men who go looking for trouble never have far to walk." Lidj leaned back in his chair, his hands folded over his middle. He was not gazing at me, but rather at the wall over my head. In another man his tone might have been one of resignation. But Juhel Lidj was not one to be resigned or lacking in enterprise in any situation, or so it had been so far during our association.

"And we have been looking for trouble?" I dared to prod when he did not add to that statement.

"Perhaps we have, Krip, perhaps we have." Still he watched the wall as if somewhere on it were scrawled or taped the answer to our puzzle. "I don't believe in curses—not unless they are my own. But neither do I know that that priest back on Thoth did not know exactly what he was doing. And, to my belief, he was playing some hand of his own. When the news comes that we are missing, then his credit will go up. The efficiency of his communication with their god will be proven."

"Temple politics?" I thought I followed him. "Then

you believe that that is at the bottom of it, that we don't have to be worried about being jumped while here?"

Now he did glance at me. "Don't put words in my mouth, Krip Vorlund. Perhaps my suggestion is just another logical deduction. I'm not a theurgist of Manical, to draw lines on my palm with a sacred crayon, pour a spot of purple wine in the middle, and then read the fate of the ship pictured therein. To my mind there is the smell of temple intrigue in this, that is all. The question which is most important is, how do we get out of their trap?"

That brought back what was uppermost in our minds, the disappearance, if not from the sky of Sekhmet, at least from our visa-screen, of the flitter. This was, judging by the terrain immediately about us, a harsh world, and forced down on such, Hunold and Sharvan would be faced by a desperate choice—if they still lived. Would they struggle on, trying to reach the beacon, or were they already attempting to fight their way back to the *Lydis?* Perhaps it all depended upon how far they judged themselves to be from either goal.

The Traders stand by their own. Such is bred in us, as much as the need for space, the impatience and uneasiness which grips us when we have been too long planetside. It was only the knowledge that without any guides, we ourselves might wander fruitlessly and to no useful purpose, which kept us chained to the *Lydis* and not out searching for our lost shipmates.

"Korde can do it, if it can be done. There is a Patrol asteroid station between here and Thoth. If he can beam a signal strong enough to reach either that or some cruise ship of theirs, then we're set."

Patrol? Well, the Patrol is necessary. There must be some law and order even in space. And their men are always under orders to render assistance to any ship in distress. But it grated on our Free Trader pride to have to call for such help. We were far too used to our independence. I spun the case of a report tape between thumb and forefinger, guessing just how much this galled our captain.

"One thing on the credit side," Lidj continued. "That find which your furred friend turned up out there. If there *is* a treasure cache here, the priests cannot claim it. But we can."

He was once more staring at the wall. I did not have to mind-probe to know what occupied his thoughts. Such a find would not only render the *Lydis* famous, but perhaps lift us all to the status of contract men, with enough credits behind us to think of our own ships. Even more so since the find was made on a planet where exploration was not restricted, where more than one such could be turned up.

I had been thinking ever since Maelen had drawn my attention to those cliff-wall carvings. And I had done some research among my own store of tapes.

A Free Trader's success depends on many things, luck being well to the fore among those. So luck had been with us here, good as well as bad. But the firm base of any Trader's efficiency is knowledge, not specialized as a tech must have, but wide—ranging from the legends of desert rovers on one planet to the habits of ocean plants on another. We listened, we kept records, we went with open minds and very open ears wherever we planeted, or when we exchanged news with others of our kind.

"When Korde is through with this com hookup, do

you suppose he could rig something else?" I knew what I wanted, but the technical know-how to make it was beyond my skill.

"Just what, and for what purpose?"

"A periscope drill." The term might not be the right one, but that was the closest I could come to describing what I had read about in the tapes. "They used such, rigged with an impulse scanner, on Sattra II where the Zacathans were prospecting for the Ganqus tombs. With something like that we might be able to get an idea of what *is* back in the cliff. It saves the labor of digging in where there may be nothing worth hunting. As on Jason, where the tombs of the Three-eyes had already been looted—"

"You have information on this?"

"Just what it does, not the mechanics of it." I shook my head. "You'd have to have a tech work it out."

"Maybe we can—if we have the time. Bring me that note tape."

When I returned to my cabin to get that, Maelen raised her head from the cushion of her forepaws, her gold eyes agleam. Though I saw a glassia, yet when her thoughts met mine it was no animal sharing my small quarters. In my mind she was as I first saw her, slender in her gray-and-red garments, the soft fur of her jacket as bright in its red-gold luxuriance as the silver-and-ruby jewel set between the winging lift of her fair silver brows, her hair piled formally high with ruby-headed pins to hold it. And that picture I held closer because somehow, though she had never brought it into words between us, she found comfort in the knowledge that I saw her as the Thassa Moon Singer who saved my life when I was hunted through the hills of Yiktor.

"There is news?"

"Not yet." I pulled down one of the seats which snapped up to the wall when not in use. "You cannot contact them?"

But I need not have asked that. Had she been able, we would have known it. Her gifts, so much the less compared to what they had once been, were always at our service.

"No. Perhaps they have gone too far—or perhaps I am too limited now. But it is not altogether concern for those of our company missing which lies in your mind now."

I clicked one tape cover against the next, hunting that which had the notation I wanted. "Maelen, is there any way to thought-see through the cliff—behind the cat mask?"

She did not answer me at once. She must have been considering carefully before she did.

"Mind-send must have a definite goal. If I knew of some spark of life there I could focus upon it. As it is—no. But—you have thought of some way?" She had been quick to pick that up from me.

"Something I heard of—a periscope drill. It might just work here, so we could learn if we have found a treasure cache or not. Yes, here it is." I snapped the tape into my reader, ran it along impatiently, seeking the pertinent section.

She shared my absorption in that the rather vague report which a fellow Trader, who had been chartered to supply the Zacathan expedition, had furnished me.

"It seems a complicated machine," she commented, not entirely with favor. Her reaction might have arisen from the Thassa distaste for machines and any need to depend upon them. "But if it works, then I can see it in use here. Also, I believe you are correct in your guess that if this is a treasure cache it will not be the only one to be found on Sekhmet.

"Krip, do you remember how once, long ago it now seems, we spoke of treasure and you said that it could be many things on many worlds, but that each man had his own idea of what it was? Then you added that what would be precious to you was a ship of your own, that that was what your people considered true treasure. Suppose this cache, or another, were to yield enough to give you that. What would you do with such a ship—voyage, as does the *Lydis*, seeking profit wherever chance and trade call you?"

She was right in that a ship was the Trader standard of treasure. Though it would take a sum beyond perhaps even the value of the cargo from Thoth to buy a ship for each member of the *Lydis*'s crew. And all finds would be shared. But a ship of my own—

Dreams can be dreamed, but to bring them alive calls for logic and planning. I was in training as a cargomaster and, as I well knew and admitted, a long way from being ready to take full responsibility for top rating even in that berth. I was no pilot, engineer, astrogator. What would I truly do if I had credits in my belt tomorrow which would buy me the ship of my daydreaming?

Again she followed my thoughts.

"Do you remember, Krip Vorlund, how you spoke when I told you *my* fancy—of taking my little people in a ship to the stars? Could such a treasure buy that ship?"

So she still held to *her* dream? Though perhaps it had now even less chance of realization than mine.

"It would have to be a treasure past all reckoning," I told her soberly.

"Agreed. And I have not gone a-voyaging these

past months with a closed mind. The Thassa know Yiktor in width and length, but they know not space. I have learned that there are limits of which I was unaware when I claimed to be a Moon Singer of power. We are but a small people among many, many races and species. Yet to recognize that is a good beginning. With your delving machine do you go hunting, Krip—if the time is given you."

"Lidj thinks—" I told her what the cargomaster had said. But before I had finished, her furred head moved from side to side.

"Such a conclusion is logical. But there is this. Since I first took sentry duty here, I know we have been watched."

"What! By whom—from where?"

"It is because I cannot answer just such questions that I have not given a warning. Whatever it is which forces my unease, it lurks beyond the edge of my probe. I can no longer far-beam-read. The Old Ones took much of my power when they reft from me my wand. There only remains enough to warn. What is here only watches; it has yet made no move. But—tell me, Krip—why is it that a cat face is upon the cliff wall?"

Her sudden change of subject startled me. And I could not give her an answer.

"This is what I mean." Her thought-send was impatient. "The cat is an ancient symbol of Sekhmet, for whom this planet is named. That you told me. But—were not this sun and its attendant worlds given their names originally by some Scout of your people who landed here in exploration? Therefore the cat is an off-world symbol.

"Yet here we find it—or a pattern enough like it so that you say 'cat' at once when you trace it—marking something *not* left by settlers of your kind. Why did these unknown and forgotten earlier ones use the cat mask?"

I had not really thought of that before.

"It must be something left by the first settlers. Perhaps they tried to colonize Sekhmet before the other planets."

"I think not. I think this is far too old. How many years has this system been settled? Do you have such a record?"

"I don't know. If they were of the first wave, perhaps a thousand years, a little less."

"Yet I would judge that carving to be twice, maybe thrice that age. To erode stone so deeply takes a long time. At our places on Yiktor that is so. And the rest of the treasures are not of settler making; they were found by the first men to land. Still we have here a cat mask! Who, and how old, were the gods for whom this system was named—this cat-headed Sekhmet?"

"They were Terran and very old even on that world. And Terra took to space a thousand years ago." I shook my head. "Much history has been forgotten in the weight of years. And Terra is halfway across the galaxy from here. When such gods and goddesses were worshiped, her people had no space travel."

"Perhaps your species did not then go forth from their parent world. But did any visit them there? The races of the Forerunners—how many such civilizations rose and fell?"

"No one knows, not even the Zacathans, who make the study of history their greatest science and art. And nowadays even Terra is half legend. I have never met a space-farer who has actually been there, or one who can claim clear descent from its people."

"Fable, legend—in the core of such there exists a small kernel of truth. Maybe here—"

The com over my head crackled and Foss sounded a general message.

"Broadcast now possible. We are sending off-world."

Though whether that effort would avail us, who could tell? I took my tape and went back to Lidj, playing the pertinent portion for him and then again for Shallard. The latter did not seem very hopeful that he and Korde could produce any such instrument, but went off again at last to consult his own records.

Waiting can be very wearying. We set up a watch which did not involve either Korde, always on com duty, or Shallard. Maelen and I shared a term. We made only the rounds of the valley in which the *Lydis* had finned down, not venturing beyond its rim, however much we would have liked to explore near the cat mask or prospect about that for other indications that long-ago men, or other intelligent beings, had been there.

We saw no one, heard nothing; nor was Maelen able to pick up any thought waves to suggest that this was more than a deserted stretch of inhospitable land. However, she continued to affirm that there was an influence of some kind hanging about which puzzled and, I think (though this she did not admit), alarmed her.

Maelen had always been much of an enigma to me. At first her alienness had set a barrier between us, a severance which had been strengthened when she had used her power to save my life by the only method possible—making man into beast. Or rather moving that which was truly Krip Vorlund from one body to another. That the man body had died through mischance had not been her fault, hard as my loss had seemed to me at the time. She had given me the use of a barsk's body. And she had brought me to the one I now wore in turn.

Thassa I walked, though Thassa I did not now live. And perhaps that outer shell of Thassa moved me closer in spirit than I had been before to the Moon Singer, Mistress of Little Ones, that I had known. Sometimes I found myself deliberately trying to tap whatever residue of Thassa might linger in my body, so that I could better understand Maelen.

Three guises I had worn in less than one planetary year—man, beast, Thassa. And the thought ever lurked in the depths of my mind that each was a part of me. Maquad, whose body finally became mine, was long dead. As a Thassa undergoing instruction he had taken on beast form, and in that form he had been killed by an ignorant hunter from the lowlands, poaching on forbidden territory. In his humanoid form the beast spirit had gone mad after a space, unable to adjust—so that what remained was a living husk. I had displaced no one when I took that husk.

But the body which had been Maelen's—that had died. And only because Vors, one of her Little Ones, had offered her spirit a dwelling place had she survived. The Old Ones had condemned her to live as Vors for a time they reckoned by a reading of the stars which hung in Yiktor's skies. But when that time had passed—where would she find a new body?

That question troubled me from time to time, though I strove to hide it from her, having a strange feeling that such speculation would be forbidden, or was wrong to mention, until she herself might clear such uncertainty. But she never had. I wanted to know more of the Thassa, but there was a barrier still raised around certain parts of their lives, and that I dared not breach.

Now we stood together in the early morning, having climbed to the cliff top which was part of the valley rim. Maelen faced out, her head pointing in the direction the flitter had taken as it bore off into the unknown. The wind ruffled her fur just as it also curled about my thermo jacket.

"Out there—it abides," came her thought.

"What does?"

"I do not know, save that it lies there waiting, watching—ever. Or—does it dream?"

"Dream?" Her choice of word surprised me. Though I strove with all the esper talent I had to catch that emanation which appeared so clear to Maelen, I had never yet touched it.

"Dream, yes. There are true dreams which can be foreseeing. Surely you know that." Once more she was impatient. "I dreamed—that I know. Yet the manner of my dream I cannot recall—save in small snatches of light, color, or feeling."

"Feeling?" I sought to lead her on.

"Waiting! That is the feeling!" There was triumph as she solved a problem. "I was waiting for something near me, something of such importance my life depended upon it. Waiting!" She held to the last word as if it were part of an important formula.

"But the rest—"

"A place strange and yet not strange—I knew it and yet knew it not. Krip"— her head swung around —"when you ran as Jorth the barsk, did you not fear that in some ways the beast was becoming greater than the man?"

So did I at last learn her fear, as if she had described a vision of terror. I went to one knee and put my arms about that furred body, drawing it close. I had not thought that this fear would be hers, knowing that body change was a part of Thassa life. But perhaps she was no longer guarded by the safe checks they used on Yiktor.

"You think this may be true for you?"

She was very close to me, passive in my hold, yet still her mind held aloof. Perhaps she already regretted even that small reaching for reassurance.

"I do not know, no longer am I sure." Her admission was painful. "I try—*how* I try—to be Maelen. But if I become all Vors—"

"Then shall I remember Maelen for us both!" What I could offer her I did. And it was the truth! Let her slip back into the animal, yet I would make myself continue to see not fur but firm pale flesh, silver hair, dark eyes in a humanoid face, the grace, the pride, and the beauty of the Moon Singer. "And neither shall I let you forget, Maelen. Never shall I let you forget!"

"Yet I think of a failing memory—" If thought could come as a whisper, so did hers sink so low.

My wrist com buzzed, and I stripped back my mitten to listen to the click of code. Fortune was favoring us. Our off-world signal had raised an answer far sooner than our most optimistic hopes had dared suggest. There was a Patrol Scout coming in and we were now recalled to the *Lydis*.

The Scout set down in the night, braking rockets flaring in a valley near our own. Her crew would not try to reach us until morning, but in the meantime we beamed through to them a full report of all that had happened since our lift-off from Thoth. All except one matter—our find of the cat mask on the cliff.

In return the Scout had news of import for us. The rebellion on Thoth had flared high in Kartum, fed by a split within the loyalist party arising from the cursing of our ship. With priest turned against priest, and the solidarity of the ruling caste so broken, the rebels had found it easy to infiltrate and conquer. Those with whom we had had a contract were now dead. The rebels were demanding the return of the treasure. And there was talk that we had meant all the time to space with it as our spoil. We listened to this and then Foss spoke:

"It seems we now have another problem. Perhaps we did better than we knew when we cached the cargo here. Until we can sort out just who takes lawful custody now, let it remain where it is."

"It is contracted still for Ptah," Lidj pointed out. "We only cached it for fear of its possible influence."

"Our contract was given by men now dead. I want to know the situation on Ptah before we go in there—if the rebels have a foothold there too. Dead men don't own anything, unless you count their tombs. If the government is changed, what we have may be legally claimed elsewhere. To be caught on another planet with a cargo of uncertain origin can put a Trader out of business—perhaps permanently. Until we are sure of the present owners, we want to take no chances of being accused, as it seems we already are, of jacking it all ourselves. I am depositing second-copy contract tapes with the Patrol at once. That will cover us for a while. But we'll leave the cache as it is until we hear from the temple on Ptah."

"What about payment?" Lidj asked. "According to contract we were to take our pick *after* we set down on Ptah. We can't collect before delivery. And a dry run, with repairs unpaid for, is a setback we are not able to take now. We dumped cargo at Kartum to take this on."

"Interference claim—at least to cover repairs?" I ventured. "We can prove it was that box and the priest that brought us here. That ought to make a good claim—"

"Well enough," Lidj agreed. "But get to the fine points of stellar law and this can be argued out for years. If we pick up our pay at the end it will be too late to help us. We could be bankrupt or dead by the time the space lawyers got tired of clicking their jaws over it. We need that carriage fee. In fact, we have to have it if we are going to continue lifting ship!

"On the other hand, we dare not be accused of looting either. The best we can do at present is make a formal Claim of Interference, post our tapes, and ask for an investigation on Ptah—to be made by the Patrol. If they reply that everything is as usual there, are you willing to chance delivery?"

We agreed. I wondered a little at Foss's seeming reluctance to proceed without a solemn, signed crew agreement. Traders are always cautious, to a point. But Free Traders, especially on a Class D ship such as the *Lydis*, are not given to many second thoughts. We are of an exploring fraternity, willing to run risks in order to work among our own kind. Did Foss suspect something which was not clear to the rest of us? The fact that he even suggested that the ship not resume her voyage to Ptah after the necessary repairs was suspicious. Yet after we were alone, making a recorder copy of all matters pertaining to the contract, Lidj did not comment. And since he did not, I was silent also.

By early morning we had our tape ready as the

Patrol flitter came gliding over the barrier of the valley wall and stirred up ashy sand in landing beside the *Lydis*. The two men who climbed out of the small flyer appeared to be in no great hurry to join Foss, who stood at the foot of our downed ramp. Instead one knelt in the sand, setting up an instrument. And the other watched him closely. They could have been conducting an exploring survey.

Chapter 6

KRIP VORLUND

There is something about the cloak of authority which tends to put even the citizen with a clear conscience on the defensive. So it was when we fronted the representatives of the Patrol. As law-abiding and inoffensive space traders, making regular contributions to planetary landing taxes, all papers in order, we had every right to call upon their help. It was just that they eyed us with an impassivity which suggested that to them, everything had to be proved twice over.

However, we had the box taken from the Throne of Qur carefully disinterred after they admitted that their own instruments registered emanations of a heretofore unknown radiation. It was surrendered gladly to their custody, along with the body of the priest, which had been in freeze. And we each entered testimony on the truth tape, which could not be tampered with.

With relief we knew they had not asked all the questions they might have. Our find at the cat cliff was still our secret—though we did tell of the cargo cache. Lidj, armed with all the precedents of space law, explained that once repairs were made, we intended to continue our voyage and deliver the treasure to the temple on Ptah—providing we were sure that the priests to whom it was officially consigned were still in power.

"We have no news from Ptah." The pilot of the Scout displayed so little interest in Foss's inquiries it was plain our present dilemma was of no concern to him. "Your repairs, yes. Our engineer has checked with your man. We want visa-tapes of the damage for our report. We can lift you and your engineer off to our space base, where you can indite under League contract for what you need."

Indite under League contract was a suggestion to worry one, though here we had no alternative. Once we had so indited we would be answerable not to the Patrol, but to our own people. Not to pay up within the stated time meant having the *Lydis* put under bond. There was so great a demand for ships (men waited for frustrating years for some stroke of luck which would give them even the first step on the ladder of spacing) that bonds weighed heavily on those who had to accept them. They could mean the loss of a ship. So we had no way of recouping, saving that of delivering our cargo to Ptah, hoping to collect. That—or the wild chance that the cat cliff hid something worth the labor of breaking in. We had no time now to build a probe, nor could we do that without giving away the reason.

In the end it was decided that Foss and Shallard would lift with the Scout. But an armed party of Patrol, plus their flitter, would remain on Sekhmet, their first order being to search for our missing men. Since the Patrol flitter was a heavy-duty craft, armed and protected by every device known, it might have a better chance in a search. It carried a pilot, two gunners to man its shockers, and room for two more passengers. There was no drawing of lots this time. Before he took off for the Scout Foss spoke directly to me.

"You and Maelen will go. With her powers to search and yours to interpret—"

Of course he was right, though the Patrolman regarded his choice of what appeared to be an animal with open disbelief. However, though I gave no history of Maelen's past, I laid it out clearly that she was telepathic and would be our guide. Since no man may know all there is to be learned about alien creatures, they accepted my assurance of her worth.

For a full day after the Scout lifted with Captain Foss and Shallard, there was a storm lapping at the *Lydis*, raising the fine dust of the valley into an impenetrable fog, keeping us pent within the ship, the Patrolmen with us. There was no setting out in this murk, since we could not fly on any set beam but would be questing freely over an unknown area.

But on the second morning the wind failed. And though the ash-sand had drifted high about the fins of the ship and half buried the flitter, which was well anchored in what little protection the *Lydis* herself offered, we could take off. As we swung out over the knife-ridged country, the massed clouds overhead broke a little now and then, though the sunlight which came through was pale and seemed devoid of heat. Its radiance accentuated the general gloom of the landscape beneath us rather than dispersing it.

The pilot kept to the lowest speed, watching his instruments for any sign of radiation which might be promising. Maelen crouched beside me in the cramped cabin of the craft. It was seldom I was truly aware of her present form, but with the Patrolmen glancing at her as if she were a very outré piece of equipment, I was more conscious of her fur, her four feet, the glassia guise. And because I had heard her plaint of fear, that she might in time slide back too far into the animal to be sure of her identity as a Thassa, her unease was plainer to me. I myself had known moments when beast eclipsed man. What if my identity had been so lost?

Maelen was stronger, more prepared than I had been to overpower the flesh envelope she wore, since she knew well all its dangers. But if *her* steady confidence was beginning to fade—

She stirred, muscles moving with liquid grace under her soft fur. Her head pointed away in a quick turn.

"Something?" I asked.

"Not what I seek now. But—but there is that down there which is not of rock and sand."

I craned to look through the vision port. Nothing showed to my sight, but rocks twisted and eroded into such wild shapes could hide anything.

"Within—" she informed me. "But we are already past. I think perhaps another cache—"

I tried to memorize landmarks, though such seen from the air and from the ground were two different matters. But if Maelen was right, and her certainty of report suggested that she could be depended upon to be that, perhaps we had indeed come upon that which would redeem all debts we might incur through this trouble. A second cache! Was Sekhmet to prove as rich a treasure field as Thoth—perhaps more so?

However, Maelen reported nothing else as we flew

in a zigzag pattern, cruising back and forth over the broken land. The country was bad for visual sighting. There were too many of those deep, narrow valleys which might have swallowed up a grounded or crashed flitter, hiding it even from air survey. And we knew only the general direction.

Back and forth, as all the rocks took on the same look—though we did pass over several wider valleys where there were stands of withered vegetation. One held a cup of water in the form of a small, dark lake rimmed with a wide border of yellow-white which may have been a noxious chemical deposit.

Maelen stirred again, pressing more tightly against me, as she stretched her head toward the vision port.

"What now?"

"Life—" she signaled.

At the same time our pilot leaned forward to regard more closely one of the many dials before him.

"Reading—faint radiation," he reported.

Though we were already at a low altitude, he dropped us more, at the same time cutting speed nearly to hover so we could search with care through the vision port. We were heading over one of the valleys, which was roughly half-moon-shaped. At the upper point of that were the first trees (if trees one might term them) I had yet seen on Sekhmet. At least they were growths of very dark foliage which stood well above bush level. But the rest of the ground was covered only with the gray tough grass.

"There!"

There was no need for anyone to point it out—for it was as visible as if painted scarlet. A flitter stood in grass as high as its hatch. But there were no signs of life about it.

The pilot had been calling on his com, trying to

raise an answer. As yet he made no move to set down.
I did not wonder at his caution. There was something
about the stark loneliness of that valley, about the
seemingly deserted machine so plainly in sight,
which chilled me.

"Do you pick them up?" I asked Maelen.

"There is no one right here." By that she seemed
to contradict her earlier report.

"But you said—"

"It is not them. Something else—" Her thought-
send faltered, almost as if she were now confused,
unable to sense clearly.

And my uneasiness, which had been triggered by
the sight of the parked flitter, was fed by a suspicion
that perhaps this was what Maelen had obliquely
warned me of earlier, that she could no longer be
sure of her powers.

"Snooper picks up nothing," the pilot reported. "I
don't get any ident reading. By all tests there's no one
aboard."

"Only one way to make sure," commented the Patrolman at the port-side defense. "Set down and
look."

"I don't like it. Looks almost as if it were put out
for someone to come and see it." The pilot's hand had
not yet gone to the controls. "Bait—"

That was a possibility one could readily accept.
Though who would be using such bait? With the Patrol insignia plain on our own craft, it would be top
risk for anyone to spring a trap. Perhaps my faith in
the force of the Patrol was right, for we did come
down. Though both gunners stayed at their posts as
we flattened the high grass not too far from the
parked flitter.

The grass was not only close to chest-high, but

tough and sharp-edged, cutting any hand put out to beat it down. Yet it also gave us a clue as to what might have happened to the two we sought. For the flitter was empty of any passengers. Not only that, but their supply packs were still stowed within, as if Sharvan and Hunold had never expected to leave the flyer for long.

Out from the trampled and crushed section of grass immediately around the hatch a trail led straight for the stand of trees. The path was deeply indented, as though it might have been made by the transportation of heavy cargo. Yet here and there along it tougher patches of stem and leaf were lifting again.

I searched the flitter carefully, triggering its report tape. But that repeated nothing more in its last recording than a description of what we ourselves had seen during our morning's passage over the broken lands. Then it stopped in mid-word, the rest of the tape as bare as if it had been erased. For this I had no explanation at all. Whatever had brought them to land here remained a mystery. Still, all the instruments were in working order. I was able to apply full power and raise to a good height in testing before I set down again. There had been no failure of the craft to force a landing.

As I made my examination one of the Patrol gunners and the pilot, Harkon, went for some distance down the trail leading to the trees. Maelen remained behind, hunkered down at the edge of the slowly rising grass. And as I emerged from the hatch I had one question for her.

"How long?"

She sniffed the ground in the trampled space, using glassia gifts now.

"More than a day. Perhaps as long as they have been missing. I cannot be too sure. Krip—there is a strange scent here—human. Come—"

A swing of her head beckoned me to one side and there she used the unsheathed claws of one forepaw to pull aside the tall grass. The tuft did not come easily and I put out my mittened hands to help. Then I found the vegetation had been woven into a blind, forming a screen about a space where the ground had been grubbed clear. Upon the patch of soil was the impression of a square which might have been left by a heavy box.

I had knelt to examine this depression as the Patrolmen returned. Harkon joined me. He held a small detect and I heard a revealing chatter from that.

"Small residue of radiation. Could be left from something like a call beam," he commented. Then he studied the woven grass curtain. "Well hidden—this could not have been spotted from above at all. They could even have produced engine failure and at the same time blotted out a distress signal—"

"But why?"

"You people have already claimed sabotage. Well, if your men had reached the beacon they could have spoiled any game to be played here. It was only by chance we picked up your space call, one chance in five hundred, really. Whoever is in hiding here could not have foreseen that. Or even that your com-tech had the knowledge and equipment to try it. If they have a reason to keep you pinned here, the first step would be to cut you off from the beacon. And they must believe that by taking your flitter, they have done that effectively. And as to who 'they' are—" He shrugged. "You ought to have some guess."

"Outside of jacks with inside knowledge about our

cargo—no. But what about Sharvan and Hunold?"

I meant that question as much for Maelen as Harkon, and I thought she might have the more reliable answer.

"They were alive when they left here," she replied.

"No attempt made to conceal the trail. I don't think they believed anyone would be after them in a hurry," Harkon replied when I passed along Maelen's report.

"You have this much reassurance," he added. "The Free Traders' loyalty to their own is a known fact. They might keep your men alive to bargain with."

"Exchange." I nodded. "But we had had no offers—nothing. No one we could detect has been near the *Lydis*."

"Which is not to say that they won't show up with a ransom deal sooner or later."

I arose, brushing the dead grass wisps from my thermo suit. "Maybe not now. Not if they saw your ship land."

Yet jacks are not timid, not when they have such a rich take as the *Lydis*'s cargo to consider. The Patrol ship was a Scout, and it had gone off-world again. Three Patrolmen in an armed flitter, and the reduced crew of the *Lydis*— This might be the very time the enemy would select to make such a move, if they did have us under observation. I said as much.

"We'll follow the trail to the woods anyway," Harkon answered. "If there's nothing beyond"— he shrugged again—"nothing to do then but wait for reinforcements. We can't stand up to a jack gang with only three men."

I noted that he apparently did not class the Free Traders as part of his fighting force. But perhaps to the Patrol any outside their own close company was not to be so considered. Just another of the things which made them less than popular.

We left one gunner on guard and tramped along the grass track once more, Maelen with me now, Harkon ahead, his fellow bringing up the rear. As we drew near that wood I saw that the growths could indeed be termed trees, but they lacked any attraction, their limbs being twisted and coiled as if they had once been supple tentacles flung out in a wild attempt to embrace something and had solidified in such ungainly positions. The leaves were very dark and thick-fleshed, and there were not many to a limb. But they were still able to form a heavy canopy which shut out that pallid sunlight and made the way ahead a tunnel of deep dusk.

But the path we followed did not enter there. Instead it turned left to run along the edge of the stand. Here there was little grass, but the gray soil showed scrapes and scuffs, being too soft to retain sharp prints. Having skirted the woods, the way came to the very point of the valley. Maelen, who had paced by my side, drew away to the sharp rise of the cliff.

She sat up on her haunches, her head swaying a little; she might almost have been reading some inscription carved on that rugged wall, so intently did she regard it. I took a couple of strides to join her, but I could see nothing, though I searched, believing that she must have come upon something such as the cat mask.

"What is it now?" I ventured to break her concentration.

For the first time she made no answer. Her mind was closed as tight as any defense gate barred to the enemy. Still she stared, her head turning a fraction right, left, right again. But I could detect nothing to keep her so scanning stone.

"What is it?" Harkon echoed my question.

"I don't know. Maelen does not answer." I touched the raised crest on her head.

She drew back from even that small physical contact. Nor did she open her mind or show that she was aware of me. Never before had this happened.

"Maelen!" I made of her name a challenge, a demand for attention. And I thought that even so I had not reached her. That fear she had implanted in me, the suggestion that she might surrender to her beast body, was sharp.

Then that swinging of the head, the unblinking stare, broke. I saw her red tongue flick out, lick her muzzle. Both her forepaws scraped upward along the sides of her head in a gesture which aped the human. She might have been trying to close her ears to some sound she could no longer stand, which was racking her with pain.

"Maelen!" I went to my knees. Our eyes were now nearly level. Putting out my hand, I caught those paws holding her head, urged her face a little around to meet my gaze. She blinked and blinked again—almost as one rousing from sleep.

"Maelen, what is the matter?"

There was no longer that solid barrier. Rather I was answered by a flood of confused impressions which I could not easily sort out. Then she steadied her chain of thought.

"Krip—I must get away—away from here!"

"Danger?"

"Yes—at least to me. But not from those we seek. There is something else. It has prowled at the edge of my thoughts since first we set foot on this dark world. Krip, if I do not take care there is that here

86

which can claim me! I am Thassa—I am mistress—"
I felt she did not say that to me, but repeated the
words to herself to steady her control. "I am Thassa!"

"You are Thassa!" Straightway I hastened to say
that, as if merely repeating my conviction would be
a life line thrown to one struggling against dire danger.

She dropped her forepaws to earth. Now her whole
body was shaken by great shudders, such as might
result from violent weeping. I dared to touch her
again, and when, this time, she did not repulse me, I
drew her close for such companionship as that hold
might give her.

"You are Maelen of the Thassa." I held my thought
firm. "As you will ever be! Nothing else can claim you
here. It cannot!"

"What is the matter?" Harkon's hand was on my
shoulder, giving me a small shake as if to summon my
attention.

"I do not know." I told him the truth. "There is
something here that threatens esper powers."

"Harkon!" The other Patrolman, who had gone
along the cliff, now stepped away from it. "Set-down
marks here. A flitter—big one by the looks of them."

Harkon went to see; I remained with Maelen. She
had turned her head, was nuzzling against my jacket
in an intimacy she had never before displayed.

"Good—good to have you here," her thought came.
"Keep so, Krip, keep so with me. I must not be less
nor other than I am—I must not! But it is calling—it
is calling me—"

"What is?"

"I do not know. It is like something which wishes
help that only I can offer. Yet I also know that if I
do go to it—then I am no longer me. And I will not be

not-Maelen! Never while I live will I be not-Maelen!" The force of that was like a shout of defiance.

"No one but Maelen. Tell me how I can aid. I am here—" I gave her quickly what I had to offer.

"Remember Maelen, Krip, remember Maelen!"

I guessed what she wanted and built in my mind the picture I liked to remember best of all—of Maelen as I had first seen her at the Great Fair in Yrjar, serene, sure, mistress of herself, untroubled, proud of her little furred people as they performed before the awed townsfolk. That was Maelen as she would always be for me.

"Did you indeed see me so, Krip? I think you draw a picture larger and more comely, more assured, than I was in truth. But you have given me that to hold to. Keep it ever for me, Krip. When I need it—have it safe!"

Harkon was back. "Nothing more to do here." His tone was impatient. "We had better head back. They lifted in a flitter, all right, which means they can be anywhere on this continent. Can you pilot your own flyer?"

I nodded, but looked to Maelen. Was she ready, able, to return? She wriggled in my hold and I loosed her. Perhaps she was well pleased to be on the move again. She scrambled into the flitter, curled up in the second seat as I settled in front of the controls.

The Patrol flitter headed straight back toward the *Lydis* and I matched its speed. Maelen, curled still, seemed to sleep. At least she made no attempt at mind-touch. However, we were not to be long without a new problem. My com clicked and I snapped it on.

"Can you raise your ship?" was Harkon's terse demand. I had been so absorbed with Maelen I had not thought of sending any report to the *Lydis*. Now I pressed the broadcast button. There was a hum—the beam was open. But when I punched out our code call I got no answer. Surprised, I tried again. The beam *was* open; reception should have been easy. Surely with us out on search the ship's receiver would have been constantly manned. Still no reply.

I reported my failure to Harkon, to be answered with a stark "Same here."

We had set out in early morning, eating our midday meal of concentrates as we flew. Now began a fading of the pallid sunlight, a thickening and indrawing of the clouds. Also the winds were rising. For safety's sake we both rose well above the rocky hills. There was no way we could be lost—the guide beam would pull us to the *Lydis*—but strong winds make a blind landing there tricky. A blind landing? It should not have to be blind. They would be expecting us, have floodlights out to guide us down. Or would they? They did not answer—would they even know we were coming? *Why* did I get no answer? I continued to click out the code call, pausing now and then to count to ten or twenty, praying for an answer which would end my rising suspicion that something was very wrong.

Chapter 7

MAELEN

It was hard to fight this thing which had come upon me in the valley where we found the flitter. Never had I been so shaken, so unsure of myself, of what I was—of *who* I was. Yet I could not even remember clearly now that which had flowed in upon my mind, possessing my thoughts, struggling to eject my identity. I know shape-changing, who better? But this was no ordered way of Thassa doing. This had been a concentrated attempt to force me to action which was not of my own planning.

As I crouched low now in the second seat of the flitter, I was still trying to draw about me, as one might draw a ragged cloak against the stabbing air of winter, my confidence and belief in my own powers. What I had met there I could not trace to its source and did not know—save that I wanted no more of it!

I was thus so intent upon my own misery and fear that I was not wholly aware of Krip's actions. Until his thought came piercing my self-absorption in a quick, clean thrust.

"Maelen! They do not reply from the *Lydis*. What can you read?"

Read? For a moment even his mind-send seemed to be in a different language, one beyond my comprehension. Then I drew heavily on my control, forced my thought away from that dire contact in the valley. *Lydis*—the *Lydis* did not answer!

But at least now I had a concrete focus for my search. I was not battling the unknown. Though the ship itself, being inanimate, would not act as a guide to draw my search; Lidj would be best for that. I pictured in my mind the cargomaster, loosed my tendril of seek—

What I encountered was a blank. No—below the surface of nothingness there pulsed something, a very muted sense of identity. I have mind-sought when those I so wished to touch were asleep, even in deep unconsciousness produced by illness. This present state was like unto the last, save that it was even deeper, farther below the conscious level. Lidj was not to be reached by any seek of mine. I transferred then to Korde—with the same result.

"They are unconscious—Lidj and Korde—deeply so," I reported.

"Asleep!"

"Not true sleep. I have reported it as it is. They are not conscious, nor do they dream, nor are their minds open to under-thought as they are in true sleep. This is something else."

I tried to probe deeper, to awaken some response, enough to win information. But even as I concentrated I was—seized! It was as if I had been pushing toward a goal when about me rose a trapping net. This net had the same feel as that which had enhanced me for a space in the valley. Save that this time it was stronger, held me more rigidly in its bonds, as if another personality, stronger, more compelling, had joined with the first to bind and draw me. I could see Krip and the flitter. I could look down at my own furred body, at my forepaws, from which the striking claws were now protruding as if I were preparing to do battle. But between me and that sane outer world there was building a wall of haze.

Maelen—I was Maelen! "Krip, think me Maelen as you did in the valley! Make me see myself as I truly am, have been all my life, no matter what body I now wear. I am Maelen!"

However, my plea must not have reached him. I was dimly aware of a crackle of words from the com, words which had noise but no meaning.

Maelen—with all my strength of mind and will I held to my need of identity, besieged by rising waves of force, each beating upon me stronger than the last. Dimly I thought this a worse peril because I *was* one who had been able to change the outward coverings of my spirit—something which made me the more susceptible to whatever abode here.

But—I was Maelen—not Vors, no one else—only Maelen of the Thassa. Now my world had narrowed to that single piece of knowledge, which was my shield, or my weapon. Maelen as Krip had seen me in his memory. Though, as I had told him, I had never been so fair, so strong as that. Maelen—

All beyond me was gone now. I closed my outer eyes lest I be disturbed from my defense. For how long I continued then to hold Maelen intact I do not know, as time was no longer broken down into any unit of measure. It was only endurance in which I feared weakening more than any bodily death.

That assault grew in strength, reached such a

height that I knew if it advanced I could not hold. Then—it began to fail. With failure there came a secondary current, first of raging impatience, then of fear and despair. This time also I had held fast. That I could do so a third time with this strange power fighting against me, I doubted. And Krip—where had Krip been? What of his promise that he would stand with me?

Anger born of my great fear flared hot in me. Was this the true worth of what I might expect from him, that in my hour of greatest need he would leave me to fight a lone battle?

The influence which had tested me this second time was now gone, the remnants winking out as a lamp might give way to the dark. I was left so drained that I could not move, even once I had returned to an awareness of what lay about me.

Krip—he still sat at the controls of the flitter. But the flyer was on the ground. I could see from the vision port the fins of the *Lydis*, though the bulk of the ship towered far above us.

"Krip—" Weakly I tried to reach him.

Tried—but what I met was that same nothingness which I had encountered when I had sought Lidj and Korde! I pulled up on the seat, edged around to look directly into his face.

His eyes were open; he stared straight ahead. I reached out a forepaw, caught at his shoulder. His body was rigid, as if frozen, a piece of carving rather than blood, flesh, and bone! Had he been caught in that same net which had tried to encompass me, but more securely?

I began to fight again, this time to reach that which lay beneath the weight of nothingness. But I was too weakened by my own ordeal—I could not win to that secret place where Krip Vorlund had been imprisoned, or to which he had retreated. He sat rigid, frozen, staring with eyes I did not believe saw anything of the outer world. I scrambled off the seat, clumsily freed the catch of the door hatch with my paws.

Though the fins of the *Lydis* were bulky enough to show through the dark, the rest of the valley was well hidden in night shadows. I dropped over the edge of the hatch into the soft sand, which puffed up around my haunches, cushioning me by the edge of a dune. The hatch closed automatically behind me. Krip had not noticed my going, made no effort to join me.

Standing in the shadow cast by the flitter, I surveyed the valley. There was no boarding ramp out from the *Lydis*. She was locked tight, as we had kept her during each night on Sekhmet. Beyond the fins was the Patrol flitter. Around that was no stir. I padded through the sand to reach its side. There was a faint glow within, the radiance of the instrument panel, I thought.

Glassia can climb, but they are no leapers. Now I made a great effort, putting all I could into a jump which allowed me to hook my claws over the edge of the port, hang there long enough with a straining of my shoulder muscles for a look within.

The pilot occupied his seat with the same rigidity Krip displayed. His nearest companion was in position by the weapon, also frozen at his post. I could only see the back of the head of the second gunner, but since he did not move, I believed I could assume he was in a like state. Both the pilot and Krip had made good landings here, but now they seemed as truly prisoners as if they were chained in some dungeon in Yrjar. Prisoners of whom—and why? Still, since they had landed their flitters in safety, it was plain that the enemy did not yet want them dead, only under control.

That they would be left so for long, I doubted. And prudence suggested that I get into hiding while I could and stay so until I learned more of the situation. I might already be under surveillance from some point in the valley.

I began to test mind-seek—only to find it limited, so drawn upon by the ordeal I had been through that I dared not try it far. For the time being I was reduced to depending upon the five senses inherent in my present body.

Though it disturbed me to rely on the glassia abilities, I relaxed my vigilance and my control of my body, raised my head so that my nose could test the scents in the air, listened as intently as I could, tried to see as much among the shadows as my eyes would allow. The glassia are not nocturnal. Their night vision is probably but little better than a man's. But the contrast of the light-gray sand with the flitters and the tall bulk of the *Lydis* was enough to give me my bearings. And if I could reach the cliff wall, its rugged formation would offer me hiding in plenty. I squatted in the shadow of the Patrol flitter and mapped out a route which would give me maximum cover.

Perhaps I was wasting time; perhaps the valley was not under observation and I could have walked boldly enough. But that was too chancy. So I covered the ground with all the craft I could summon, alert to any sight or noise which could mean I was betrayed.

Then I found a crevice I thought was promising. It was so narrow that I must back into it. Within that I crouched, lying low, my head resting on my paws, taking up vigil to watch the ship and the two flitters.

As during that pallid day before, the clouds parted a little. There were stars to be seen, but no moon. I thought with longing of the bright glow of Sotrath, which gave such light to Yiktor, filling the night with blazing splendor.

Stars above me—or were they? For a beast, distances are altered, angles of vision changed. Not stars —lights! Those lower ones at least were lights, at one end of the valley. Three I counted. And in that direction was the spot where we had cached the cargo. With the crew and the Patrolmen caught now, were those mysterious others we suspected to be at the root of our troubles working to loot the treasure?

Having established the presence of the lights, I caught something else which came through the rocks about me—a vibration. Nothing stirred in the valley, there was no sign of any watcher. Perhaps whoever had set this trap had been so confident of its holding for as long as necessary that no sentry had been posted. I squirmed uneasily. I did not in the least want to do what I thought must be done—go to see if my suspicions were correct, that the cache was being looted—to see who was responsible. Stubbornly I hunkered in what seemed to me now to be a shell of safety, one I would be worse than foolish to leave.

I owed no allegiance to the *Lydis*. I was no Free Trader. Krip—Krip Vorlund. Yes, there was a tie between us I had no thought or wish to break. But for the rest— Yet Krip had as strong ties to them, so I was bound to their fate whether I would or no. Could a glassia have sighed, I would have done so then as I most reluctantly crawled out of my safe little pocket and began to pad along at the foot of the cliff, making use once more of every bit of cover.

When I had gone exploring with Krip we had suited our path to the demands of his human body. But I knew I could take a much faster way up and over the heights, since my powerful claws were well fitted to climbing this rock riddled with cracks and crevices. I worked my way around until I reached a spot which I thought directly in line with those lights. There I began to climb. The rock face was dark enough so that my black fur would not show against its surface as it would have on the light dunes. As I had hoped, my claws readily found and clung to irregularities which served me well.

I made better speed at this than I had skulking about on the ground, and so managed to pull out on top of the ridge hardly winded by my efforts. From this vantage point I could see my suspicions were in part true. Three lights, giving from here a greater glow of illumination, were at the point where Foss and the others had thought they had so well hidden the cargo. Yet the effort of breaking through the plug they had left there could not be an easy one. I guessed from the vibration in the rocks, and a faint purr of sound now to be heard, that some machine had been brought in to handle that task.

So intent had I been on that distant work I was not at first aware of what lay closer. Not until I moved a little aside and edged against that beam—Shock struck me with the power of a blow. Had I met it at a point of greater intensity I might actually have been borne back to crash into the valley.

It was pure force, delivered with such strength that one could believe such a beam should be visible. And it was mind force. Yet this was a concentration I had never experienced, even when our Old Ones merged their power for some needful action. That it had to do with the blanked minds of the humans below, I had no doubt at all. I was prepared now, wary, my defenses up, so that I could skirt the danger and not be once more entrapped. And that I must find the source, I also knew.

I did not want a second meeting with that deadly beam, yet I must somehow keep in contact in order to trace it. So I was reduced to flinching in and out on the edge, reeling away, shuffling on to touch again. Thus I came to a niche in the rocks. There was no light there, no one around; I summoned up enough mind-seek to make sure before I approached that pocket from the rear. It was very dark and whatever was in there was deeply set back in the niche.

Finally I had to pull my way to the top of the rock pile, since I had made sure that the only opening lay at the front. Crouched with my belly flat on the arch, I clawed myself forward. Then I bent my head down, hoping that the beam did not fill the whole of the opening, that I could see what lay inside.

It had seemed dark when viewed from a distance. But within the very narrow space was a faint glimmer, enough to reveal the occupant. I was looking, from a cramped, upside-down position, into a face!

The shock of that nearly loosed me from my precarious hold. I regained control, was able to concentrate on those set, grim features. The eyes of the stranger were shut, his face utterly expressionless, as if he slept. And his body was enclosed in a box which had been wedged upright so that he faced out over the valley. The main part of the box was frosted, so that only the section of cover directly over his face was clear. The face was humanoid enough, though completely hairless, without even brows or lashes.

And the skin was a pale gray.

The box which enclosed him (I believed the sleeper to be male) was equipped with a front panel which might have been transparent had not the frosted condition prevailed, for it looked like crystal. This was banded by a wide frame of metal flecked here and there with small specks of color I could not see clearly.

At the foot of the box was another piece of equipment. And while the sleeper (if sleeper he was) resembled nothing I had seen before, what sat at his feet was familiar. I had seen its like employed only a few days ago in the *Lydis*. It was an amplifier for communication, such as Korde had rigged when he made the off-world distress call.

Seeing it where it now was left only one inference to be drawn. The mind-blast was coming from the boxed body, to be amplified by the com device. Also, its being here could have only one purpose—that of holding Krip, the Patrolmen, and presumably the crew of the *Lydis* in thrall. Could I in some manner disconnect it, or abate the flow of current, they might be released.

About the boxed sleeper I could do nothing. I was not strong enough to handle the case—it had been too tightly wedged into that niche. My eyes, adjusting to the very faint light emitted from the frame, showed the rocks had been pounded in about the large box to pin it in place.

So—I might not get at the source of the mind-thrall, but the amplifier was another matter. I remembered well how cautiously Korde had adjusted the one on the *Lydis*, his constant warning that the slightest jar could deflect the line of force beam. But this was a task I had to push myself to. For, just as I had tired under my battle in the flitter with that which had tried to take over my mind, so now did my body send messages of distress through aching muscles, fatigue-heavy limbs.

I withdrew to the ground below and moved in cautiously from the side, creeping low and so hoping to elude the full force of the beam. Luckily it did not appear to sweep the ground.

Having made this discovery, I found it easy to wriggle closer. I could see only one possible way, and success would depend upon just how clumsy this animal body was. Backing off, I went to look for a weapon. But here the scouring winds had done their work far too well. There were no loose stones small enough to serve me. I padded along, nosing into every hole I saw, becoming more and more desperate. If I had to return to the floor of the valley to search, I would. But I still hoped.

Stubbornness rewarded me in the end, for in one of the hollows I found a rock which I worried at with my claws until it loosened, so that I could scrape it out into the open. When one has always been served by hands, it is difficult to use one's mouth. But I got the rock between my teeth and returned.

Once more I edged in as flat as I could, and with the stone between my teeth I hammered away at the top of the amplifier, until that was so battered I did not believe those who had left it could ever use it again.

I did not approach the box of the sleeper. But from that seeped a dank chill, like the worst blast of highland winter I had ever met on Yiktor. I believed that had I set paw to that frosted front, I might well have frozen a limb by that unwary touch. There was no change in the face, which could have been that of a carven statue. Yet the sleeper lived, or had once lived. Looking up at the entombed stirred a confused feeling in me.

Quickly I not only glanced away from those set features, but also backed out of the line of sight of the closed eyes. The other, added presence I had sensed in the flitter—I felt a stirring of that. And the sensation caused such alarm in me that I loped away without heeding the direction of my going.

When I had my emotions once more under control, and that hint of troubling influence was gone, I discovered I had headed not back to the ship valley but toward the lights and the purr of sound. It might be well for me to scout that scene of activity. I hoped that now that the broadcast had been stopped, those in the *Lydis* and flitters would be free. And it could be to their advantage if I were able to supply information upon my return.

The strangers had no guards or sentries about. Perhaps they were so certain of that which they had put to work in the heights that they felt safe. And it was easy enough to slip up to a good vantage point.

Busy at the cache they were, with flares lighting the scene, brighter even than Sekhmet's daylight. Robos, two of them, were at work on the plug we had set to seal the crevice. But the Traders had done so good a job there that the machines were not breaking it down in any hurry. They had various tools, flamers, and the like fitted into their work sockets and were attacking the fused stone with vigor.

The robos of the *Lydis* were mainly for loading, although in extreme need they could be equipped with a few simple working tool modifications. These looked larger and different. They were being directed to their labor by a man holding a control board. And, though I knew little of such machines, I thought they seemed chiefly intended for excavation work.

As far as we of the *Lydis* knew, there were no mines on Sekhmet. And casual prospectors did not own such elaborate and costly machines. We had found traces of what might be treasure deposits here. Could these robos have been imported to open such deposits?

The men below—there were three of them—looked like any spacers, wearing the common coveralls of ship crewmen. They appeared completely humanoid, of the same stock as the Free Traders. The two who were not controlling the robos carried weapons, blasters to be exact, an indication that they could well be outside the law. The sight of those was warning enough for me to keep my distance.

I stiffened against the ground, my breath hissing between those fangs which were a glassia's natural weapons. A fourth man had come into sight. And his face was very clear in the flare lamps. It was Griss Sharvan!

There were no signs of his being a prisoner. He stopped beside one of the guards, watching the robos with as much interest as if he had set them to work. Had he? Was it Sharvan who had led this crew to the cache? But why? It was very hard for anyone who knew the Traders to believe that one of them could turn traitor to his kind. Their loyalty was inbred. I would have sworn by all I knew that such a betrayal was totally impossible. Yet there he stood, seemingly on excellent terms with the looters.

From time to time the robo master made adjustments on the controls. I caught a feeling of impatience from him. And when that reached my conscious attention, I thought that the weakening of my power had passed. Which meant I might just dare to discover, via mind-probe, what Sharvan did here. Settling myself to the easiest position I could find, I began probe.

Chapter 8

KRIP VORLUND

It was very quiet; there was no *thrum* in the walls, no feeling of the usual safe containment which a ship gave. I opened my eyes—but not upon the walls of my cabin in the *Lydis;* instead I was facing the control board of a flitter. And as I blinked, more than a little bemused, recollection flowed in. The last thing I could remember clearly was flying over the broken ranges on my way back to the ship.

But I was not flying now. Then how had I landed, and—

I turned to look at the second seat. There was no furred body there. And a quick survey told me that I was alone in the flitter. Yet surely Maelen could not have landed us. And the dark outside was now that of night.

It took only an instant or two to open the hatch and stumble out of the flyer. Beside me rose the *Lydis.* Beyond her I could make out a second flitter. But why could I not remember? What had happened just before we landed?

"Vorlund!" My name out of the night.

"Who's there?"

"Harkon." A dark shadow came from the other flitter, plowed through the sand toward me.

"How did we get here?" he demanded. But I could not give him any answer to that.

There was a grating sound from the ship. I raised my head to see the ramp issue from her upper hatch like a tongue thrust out to explore. Moments later its end thudded to earth only a short distance away. But I was more intent on finding Maelen.

The sand around held no prints; I could not pick up a trail. But if the ship's ramp had been up, she could not have gone aboard. I could not imagine what would have taken her away from the flitter. Except her strange actions back in that other valley made me wonder if some influence had drawn her beyond her powers of resistance. If so, what influence, and why would it affect her more here? Also, I could not remember landing the flitter—

I flashed out a mind-seek. And an instant later I reeled back, striking against the body of the flitter I had just quitted, going to my knees, my hands against my head, unable to think clearly, gasping for breath—for—

By the time Harkon reached me I must have been very close to complete blackout. I recall only dimly being led on board the *Lydis*, people moving about me. Then I choked, gasped, shook my head as strong fumes cut through the frightening mist which was between me and the world. I looked up, able to see and recognize what I saw—the sick bay of the ship. Medic Lukas was by me, backed by Lidj and Harkon.

"What—what happened?"

"You tell us," Lukas said.

My head—I turned it a little on the pillow. That

sickening wave of assaulting blackness mixed with pain ebbed.

"Maelen—she was gone. I tried to find her by mind-seek. Then—something hit—inside my head." It was as hard now to describe the nature of that attack as it was to remember how I had come earlier to land the flitter.

"It agrees," Lukas nodded. But what agreed with what, no one explained to me. Until he continued, "Esper force stepped up to that degree can register as energy." He shook his head. "I would have said it was impossible, except on one world or another the impossible is often proved true."

"Esper," I repeated. My head ached now, with a degree of pain which made me rather sick. Maelen, what about her? But perhaps to try mind-seek again would bring another such attack, and that dread was realized as Lukas continued:

"Keep away from the use of that, Krip. At least until we know more of what is happening. You had such a dose of energy that you were nearly knocked out."

"Maelen—she's gone!"

He did not quite meet my eyes then. I thought I could guess what he was thinking.

"She wasn't responsible! I know her sending—"

"Then who did?" Harkon demanded. "You stated from the start that she is highly telepathic. Well, this is being done by a telepath of unusual talent and perhaps training. And I would like to know who landed us here—since we cannot remember! Were we taken over by your animal?"

"No!" I struggled to sit up, and then doubled over, fighting the nausea and feeling of disorientation that movement caused. Lukas put something quickly to my mouth and I sucked at a tube, swallowing cool liquid which allayed the sickness.

"It was *not* Maelen!" I got out when I finished that potion. "You cannot mistake a mind sending—it is as individual as a voice, a face. This—this was alien." Now that I had had a few moments in which to think about it, I knew that was true.

"Also"—Lukas turned to Lidj— "tell them what registered on our receivers here."

"We have a recording," the cargomaster began. "This esper attack began some time ago—and you were not here then. It broke in intensity about a half hour since—dropped far down the scale, though it still registers. Just as if some transmission of energy had been brought to a peak and then partly shut off. While it was on at the top range none of us can remember anything. We must have awakened, if you can term it that, at the moment it dropped. But the residue remaining is apparently enough to knock out anyone trying esper communication, as Krip proved. So if it was not Maelen—"

"But where is she now?" I swallowed experimentally as I raised my head, and discovered I felt better. "I was alone in the flitter when I awoke—and no one can find a trail through that sand out there."

"It may be that she has gone to hunt the source of what hit us. She is a far greater esper than any of our breed," Lidj suggested.

I pulled myself up, pushing away Lukas's hand when he put it out to deter me. "Or else she was drawn unwillingly. She felt something back there in that valley where we found the flitter, she begged me to get her away. She—she may have been caught by whatever is there!"

"It is not going to help her to go charging out without any idea of what you may be up against." Lidj's

good sense might not appeal to me then, but since he,
Lukas, and Harkon made a barrier at the door of the
sick bay I was sure I was not going to get past them
at present.

"If you think I am going to stay safe in here
while—" I began. Lidj shook his head.

"I am only saying that we have to know more
about the enemy before we go into battle. We have
had enough warning to be sure that this is something
we have never faced before. And what good will it
do Maelen, Sharvan, or Hunold if we too are captured before we can aid them?"

"What *are* you doing?" I demanded.

"We have a fix on the source of the broadcast, or
whatever it is. On top of the cliff to the east-north-
east. But in the middle of the night we aren't going
to get far climbing around these rocks hunting for it.
I can tell you this much—it registers with too regular
a pattern to be a human mind-send. If it is an installation, which we can believe, working on a telepath's
level—then there should be someone in charge of it.
Someone who probably knows this country a lot better than we do. But we have our range finder out
now—"

"And something else," Harkon cut in crisply. "I
loosed a snooper, set on the recording pattern, as
soon as Lidj reported this. That will broadcast back
a pick-up picture when it locates anything which is
not just rock and brush."

"So—" Lidj spoke again. "Now we shall adjourn to
the control cabin and see what the snooper can tell
us."

The Patrol are noted for their use of sophisticated
equipment. They have refinements which are far
ahead of those on Free Trader ships. I had heard of

snoopers, though I had never seen one in action before.

There was a flutter on the surface of the small screen set over the visa-plate of the *Lydis*—a rippling of lines. But that continued without change and my impatience grew. All that Lidj had said was unfortunately true. If I could not use mind-seek without provoking such instant retaliation as before, I had little chance of finding Maelen in that broken country, especially at night.

"Something coming in!" Harkon's voice broke through my dark imaginings.

Those fluttering lines on the screen were overlaid with a pattern. As we watched, the faint image sharpened into a definite scene. We looked into a dark space where an arching of rocks made a niche. And the niche was occupied. It was the face of the man or being who stood there which riveted my attention first. Human—or was he? His eyes were closed as if he slept—or concentrated. Then the whole of the scene registered. He was not in the open, but rather enclosed in a box which, except for the space before his face, was opaque. That box had been wedged upright, so he faced outward.

At his feet was a smaller box. But this was broken, badly battered, wires and jagged bits of metal showing through cracks in it.

Harkon spoke first. "I think we can see why the broadcast suddenly failed. That thing in front is an alpha-ten amplifier, or was before someone gave it a good bashing. It's meant to project and heighten com relays. But I never heard of it being used to amplify telepathic sends before."

"That man," Lidj said as if he could not quite believe what he saw. "Then he is a telepath and his mind-send was so amplified."

"A telepath to a degree hitherto unknown, I would say," Lukas replied. "There's something else—he may be humanoid, but he's not of Terran stock. Unless of a highly mutated strain."

"How do you know?" Harkon asked for all of us.

"Because he's plainly in stass-freeze. And in that state you don't broadcast; you are not even alive, as we reckon life."

He glanced at us as if he now expected some outburst of denial. But I, for one, knew Lukas was never given to wild and unfounded statements. If he thought that closed-eyed stranger was in stass-freeze, I would accept his diagnosis.

Harkon shook his head slowly. Not as if he were prepared to argue with Lukas, but as if he could not honestly accept what he was seeing.

"Well, if he is in stass-freeze, at least he's tight in that box. He did not get there on his own. Somebody put him there."

"How about the snooper—can it pick up any back trail from that?" Lidj gestured to the screen. "Show us who installed the esper and the amplifier?"

"We can see what a general life-force setting will do." Harkon studied the dial of his wrist com, made a delicate adjustment to it. The screen lost the picture with a flash and the fluttering returned.

"It isn't coming back," Harkon reported, "so the life-force search must be at work. But as to what it will pick up—"

"Getting something!" Korde leaned forward, half cutting off my view of the screen, so I pulled him back a little.

He was right. Once more there was a scene on the

screen. We were looking into a much brighter section of countryside.

"The cache—they're looting the cache!" But we did not need that exclamation from Lidj.

There were excavation robos busy there. And they had broken through the plug we had thought the perfect protection. Three—no, four—men stood a little to one side watching the work. Two were armed with blasters, one had a robo control board. But the fourth man—

I saw Lidj hunch farther toward the screen.

"I—don't—believe—it!" His denial was one we could have voiced as a chorus.

I knew Griss Sharvan; I had shared planet leave with him. He had been with me on Yiktor when first I had seen Maelen. It was utterly incredible that he should be standing there calmly watching the looting of our cargo. He was a Free Trader, born and bred to that life—and among us there were no traitors!

"He can only be mind-washed!" Lidj produced the one explanation we could accept. "If an esper of the power Krip met got at him, it's no wonder they could find the cache. They could pick its hiding place right out of his brain! And they must have Hunold, too. But what are they—jacks?" He asked that of Harkon, depending upon the authority of one who should know his lawbreakers to give him an answer.

"Jacks—with such equipment? They don't make such elaborate efforts in their operations. I would think more likely a Guild job—"

"Thieves' Guild here?"

Lidj had a good right to his surprise. The Thieves' Guild was powerful, as everyone knew. But they did not operate on the far rim of the galaxy. Theirs was not the speculation of possible gains from raiding on frontier planets. Those small pickings were left to the jacks. The Guild planned bigger deals based on inner planets where wealth gathered, drawn in from those speculative ventures on the worlds the jacks plundered. If jacks had dealings with the Guild it was only when they fenced their take with the more powerful criminals. But they were very small operators compared with the members of that spider web which was, on some worlds, more powerful than the law. The Guild literally owned planets.

"Guild, or perhaps Guild-subsidized." Harkon held to his point stubbornly.

Which made our own position even more precarious, though it would also account for the sabotage and the elaborate plan which seemed to have been set up to enmesh the *Lydis,* both in space and here. The Guild had resources which even the Patrol could not guess. They were rumored to be ready to buy up, or acquire by other, more brutal means, new discoveries and inventions, so that they might keep ahead of their opponents. The boxed esper with the amplifier—yes, that could well be a Guild weapon. And the mining robos we saw at work here—

I thought at once of that cat mask on the cliff, of Maelen's assurance that other finds existed. Suppose some enterprising jack outfit, ambitious and farseeing, had made the discovery that Sekhmet had such finds. With such a secret as their portion of the partnership, they could get Guild backing. At least to the extent of modern excavation equipment, plus such devices as the esper linkage for protection.

Then one of their men on Thoth could have picked up the news of our cargo. And they might have prepared to gather that in as a bonus. The Throne of Qur would be worth any effort. I could not help but believe that was the answer.

But what other devices could they have? That which sabotaged the *Lydis* we still do not understand. And the esper was something entirely new. Nor were the Free Traders backward in hearing about such things.

"Look out!"

I was startled out of my thoughts by Harkon's cry. We could still see the scene of the cargo cache. The robos had started to bring out what we had stored there. But it was not that action which the Patrol pilot had noted.

One of the guards had turned about, was pointing his blaster directly at our screen. A moment later that went black.

"Took out the snooper," Harkon commented.

"Now they know—first, that their esper is no longer controlling us; second, that we have learned of their activities in turn," Lidj said. "Do we now expect an attack in force?"

"What arms do you carry?" Harkon asked.

"No more than are allowed. We can break our seal on the ordnance compartment and get the rest of the blasters. That's the extent of it. A Trader depends on evasive action in space. And the *Lydis* does not set down on worlds where the weapons are much more sophisticated than on Thoth. We haven't broken that seal in years."

"And we don't know what they have—could be anything," Harkon commented. "I wonder who took out that amplifier. Might that man of yours be operating on his own—the one you did not see?"

But I was as certain as if I had witnessed the act. "Maelen did that."

"An animal—even a telepathic one—" Harkon began.

I eyed him coldly. "Maelen is not an animal. She is a Thassa, a Moon Singer of Yiktor." The odds were that he had not the slightest idea of what that meant, so I enlarged on that statement. "She is an alien, wearing animal form only for a time. It is a custom among her people." I was determined not to go farther into that. "She would be perfectly capable of tracing the esper interference and knocking out the amplifier."

But where was she now? Had she gone on to the cache to see what was happening there? I did not know how the jack guard had picked the snooper off so accurately. They were programmed to evade attack. He could have been just as quick to dispose of Maelen, had he sighted her. They had probably been planeted on Sekhmet long enough to know most of the native wildlife, so they would have recognized her even in animal form as something from off-world, and been suspicious. I could imagine plainly the whole sequence of such a discovery.

If only I dared mind-search! But even though the amplifier was not of use, I knew I could once more bring upon myself that force I had experienced earlier. Until the stass frozen man—or thing—was rendered harmless (if he could be) I had no hope of tracking Maelen except by sight alone. And in the dark of night that was impossible.

"We can just sit it out," Korde was saying when I again paid attention. "Your ship"—he nodded to Harkon—"will be back soon with Foss. We have power enough to warn them once they come into braking orbit."

But Lidj was shaking his head. "Not good enough.

The jacks must have been watching us all along, even if we could not detect them—they certainly possess a protective field which blanks out even esper when they want, or Maelen would have picked them up earlier. So they know about us and that we are waiting for help. They could move fast now—pack up and be off-world before we get reinforcements. After all, their base may be half this continent away, hidden anywhere. We've got to keep on their tails if we can. But it won't do any good to try another snooper. They will be watching for that now."

"We haven't one anyway," Harkon commented dryly. "For the rest, I would say you are right. There is also this—if we stay in or around your ship, they may be able to pin us down, blank out an com warning, hold us just as tightly as they did before. I say, leave the ship with a guard and a locked-up boarding ramp. The rest of us will take to the country. It is rough enough to hide an army. We'll work our way northeast, starting at the cache, and see if we can at least locate the general direction of their base. They won't be able to transport all they are pulling out of there without making a number of trips. Also—that esper is still up there. If we find him before they come to see what is wrong, we may just be able to shut him off, or do whatever needs to be done to hinder them in using him again. And what about this Maelen of yours—can you contact her, find out where she is?" He spoke directly to me.

"Not as long as that esper is broadcasting. You saw what happened when I tried that before. But I think she is near that cache. It may be that if I get close enough she can perhaps pick me up, though I can't be sure. She is far more powerful than I am."

"Good. That makes you our first choice for the

scouting force." He certainly did not wait for volunteers. Not that I would not have been the first of those. But a Free Trader does not take kindly to any assumption of authority except from his own kind. And it was very apparent that Harkon considered himself without question to be the leader of any sortie we planned.

Lidj might have challenged him, but he did not. He went instead to break the seal on the arms locker. We took out the blasters, inserted fresh charges, slung on ammunition belts. E rations were in packets. And we had our thermo suits as protection against the chill.

In the end Korde and Aljec Lalfarns, a tubeman, stayed with the ship. Harkon's gunners from the flitter removed the charges from those crafts' defense to render them harmless and made ready to join us. It was still dark, though dawn could not now be too far away. We had a short rest and ate our last full ship's meal before we left.

It was decided we would try the more arduous climb up over the cliff, so we could find the esper and take action to insure he would not trouble us again. And climb we did, the blasters on their slings over our shoulders, weighing us back, making the climb more difficult, though the face of the stone was already rough enough. We had had to put aside our mittens in order to find handholes, and the chill of the rock bit deep, so that we must press on as quickly as we could before any numbing of our fingers could bring about disaster. I thought of Maelen's sharp-pointed claws and knew that this road must have been a fairly easy one for her. But her passing had left no traces.

We reached the top of the cliff, spread out in a

single thin line as Harkon ordered. From this height we could see the lights at the location of the cache. The workers there made no effort to hide their presence. And, having been alerted by the snooper, they could already be preparing a warm welcome.

Our advance had been very short when my wrist com buzzed. "To the right," clicked the signal which brought me in that direction, picking my way more by feel than sight.

Thus we gathered at the niche we had seen from the snooper. The smashed amplifier had not been moved. It was apparent that those who had installed it there either had not arrived to check on it, or had abandoned it. I stepped closer, flinched. For the first time in my life I experienced mind-send not only in my brain, but as an invisible but potent force against my body.

"Don't go directly in front of it!" I said sharply.

At my warning Harkon edged in from one side, I from the other. There was no sign of life on that face. It was humanoid, yet it had an alien cast. I might have been looking at a dead man, in fact I would have said so, had I not felt that strong current of send. The Patrolman stepped back, yielding his place to Lukas. Now the medic put out his unmittened hand and moved his fingers, held an inch or so away from the surface of that case, as if he were smoothing it up and down.

"Stass-freeze to a high degree," he reported. "Higher than I know of in general use." He unsealed the front of his jacket, drew out a life-force detect, and held that at the level of the sleeper's chest, though we could not see the body through that opaque opening.

In the very dim light radiated by the box I saw the

incredulous expression on Lukas's face. With a sharp jerk he brought the detect up level with the head, took a second reading, returned to heart level for another examination. Then he edged back.

"What about it?" Harkon asked. "How deep in stass is he?"

"Too deep—he's dead!"

"But he can't be!" I stared at the set face of the box's occupant. "The dead don't mind-send!"

"Maybe he doesn't know that!" Lukas gave a queer sound, almost a laugh. Then his voice steadied as he added, "He's not only dead, but so long dead the force reading went clear out of reckoning. Think about that for a moment."

Chapter 9

KRIP VORLUND

I still could not really believe that. A mind-send from a dead man—impossible! And I said so. But Lukas waved his detect and swore that it was working properly, as he proved by trying it on me and pointing to the perfectly normal reading. We had to accept that a dead body, linked to an amplifier, had managed to keep us in thrall until the machine had been smashed; that esper power, strong enough to upset anyone human (I could hope Maelen was beyond its control) who tried to use a like talent in its vicinity, was issuing from a dead man.

But the cache was still being looted. We dared not spend too long a time with this mystery when action was demanded elsewhere. The damaged amplifier was speedily disposed of, but we could not unwedge that box. So we left the strange sleeper there, still broadcasting, as he had—for how long? Though I was sure not from the same site.

The way over the cliffs was much shorter than the ground-level trail. We crept up, following all the precautions of those invading enemy territory, until we could look down at the cache. There the robos had emptied our hiding place. The glittering Throne stood in a blaze of harsh glory amid the boxes and bundles.

A flitter, perhaps double the size of our own, had grounded, was being loaded with the smaller pieces. The three jacks we had seen via snooper were studying the Throne. It was plain to see that that was not going to fit into the flyer, and its transportation must present a problem.

Save for those three there appeared to be no one else below. Sharvan had disappeared. But at the moment my own concern was for Maelen. If she had come here, was she hiding somewhere among these rocks, spying as we were? Dared I try mind-send again?

There was no other way of finding her in this rough terrain. Though one of Sekhmet's cloudy dawns was at hand and visibility was better than it had been when we had begun this trek. I made my choice for mind-seek, ready to withdraw that instantly if I so much as brushed the edge of any deadly broadcast. But this time I met none. So heartened, I fastened upon a mind-picture of Maelen and began my quest in earnest.

But I did not even meet with the betraying signal of a mind-block. She was not on the heights where we lay in hiding. Down in the valley near the cache then? Very cautiously I began to probe below, fearing to trigger some such response as I had before. They might well have a second sleeper at the scene of action as a cover.

I met nothing, and that in itself was kind of a shock. For all three of those I could see conferring about the Throne did not register at all. They were mind-shielded with a complete barrier against any probe. Perhaps because of the fact that they dealt with the sleeper, and only thus could they venture to use him. So there was nothing to be learned from them either. Nor did Maelen's answer come from the valley.

Having made sure of that, I began to extend my search—choosing south, the way from which we had come when we had first discovered this place. And, as my send crept on and on, I picked up the faintest quiver of an answer!

"Where—where?" I put full force into that.

"—here—" Very faint, very far away. "—aid—here—"

There could be no mistaking the urgency of her plea. But the low volume of the send was an even greater spur to action. That Maelen was in dire trouble, I had no doubt at all. And the choice I must make now was equally plain. The cargo had brought us here; it was the responsibility of the *Lydis*'s crew. We were eight men against an unknown number.

And there was Maelen—lost—calling for my aid.

The decision as partly dictated by my Thassa body, of that I am now sure. Just as I had once feared that Jorth the barsk was stronger than Krip Vorlund the man, so now Maquad of the Thassa—or that small residue of him which was a part of me—changed my life. Thassa to Thassa—I could not hold out against that call. But neither would my other heritage allow me to go without telling my own kind that I must.

Chance had brought me closest to Lidj. I crawled now until I could set hand on his shoulder. He jerked at my touch, turned to look at me. Dusky as this cloud-shrouded day was, we could see each other clearly.

"Maelen is in trouble. She is calling me for aid," I

told him in a whisper which I meant to carry no farther than this spot.

He said nothing, nor did any expression cross his face. I do not know what I expected, but that long, level look was one I had to force myself to meet. Though I waited, he continued silent. Then he turned away to gaze into the valley. I was chilled, cold, as if the thermo jacket had been ripped from my body, leaving my shoulders bare to the winds.

Yet I could not bite back my words; there was that in me which held me to my choice. I turned and crawled. Not only from the side of the cargomaster, but from that whole length of cliff where the others crouched waiting for Harkon's signal to attack, if that was the order he would give.

Now I had to force from me all thought of those of the *Lydis*. I must concentrate wholly on that thread, so thin, so far-stretched, which tied me to Maelen. And a thin, far-stretched one it was, so tenuous I feared it would be severed and I would have no guide at all.

It brought me down from the cliffs. And I could not mistake landmarks I had memorized. This was the way to the cat mask. I reached a point from which I ought to be able to see that pale and ghostly vestige of ancient carving. But this morning the light, perhaps the lack of sand to cling in the right places, did not aid me. I could trace nothing but the hollow which was its mouth.

And Maelen's desperate call led me there. I wriggled forward on my belly, expecting she must lie there in the shadows. But the pocket was empty! Only her call continued—from beyond the wall!

With my mittened hands I pushed and beat against the blocks, certain that there must be some concealed door, that one or another of them would fall or turn to provide me with an opening. How else could Maelen have entered?

But the blocks were as firmly joined as if they had been set in place but weeks before.

"Maelen!" I lay there, my hands resting against the wall. "Maelen, where are you?"

"Krip—aid—aid—"

Faint, far away, a cry fast fading into nothingness. And the fear which had been riding me since first I picked up her send now struck deep into me. I was certain that if I could not find a way to her soon there would be no reason to go at all. Maelen would be gone for all time.

I had but one key left to use. And by using it I might throw away a means for my own defense. But again I had no choice. I edged back, out of the mouth of that cleft.

I lay flat outside, sighting inward with the blaster. Then I dropped my head to my bent arm, veiling my eyes against the brilliance of the blast I loosed as I fired.

Scorching heat beat back against me, though the worst was absorbed by my thermo clothing. I smelled the crisping of my mittens, felt a searing lick across the edge of my cheek. Still I held fast, giving that inner wall top power. What effect it would have on the blocks I could not tell; I could only hope.

When I had used all that charge I had yet to wait, not daring at once to crawl back within that cramped space until it had a little time to lose some of the heat. But neither could I wait too long.

At last impatience won, and I was startled at what I found. Those blocks, which to the touch had had a likeness to the native rock of the cliff wall, were gone

—as cleanly as if they had only been counterfeits of stone. Thus I was able to enter the passage beyond.

Not that that was much larger. The cleft, or tunnel, or whatever it was, ran straight as a bore, with just enough room to wriggle. As I advanced I liked the situation less and less. Had I even been able to rise to my hands and knees, it would have given me a measure of relief. As it was, I had to edge on with a maximum of effort in a minimum of space.

Also, the farther I went, the less I liked the idea of perhaps coming up against a dead end and having to work my way out backward. In fact, so disturbing did I find that thought that I had to banish it as quickly as I could by holding to my mental picture of Maelen.

That journey seemed endless, but it was not. I used the blaster, now empty of charge, as a sounding rod, pushing it ahead of me through the dark, so feeling for any obstruction or fault which might cause trouble. And that did at last strike a solid surface.

I probed with the blaster in exploration, and it seemed that the passage was firmly plugged ahead. But I must make sure, so I squirmed on until my hand came against that surface. It did fill the space, and yet into my face blew a puff of air. Though hitherto I had not even wondered why I had been able to breathe in this tightly confined space.

As I slipped my hands back and forth, my fingers discovered a hole, through which flowed a distinct current of air. Hooking one hand to that, I strove to dislodge the whole plug. My effort moved it, though I found I must push instead of pull. It swung away from me and I shouldered through.

So I came not only to a much larger space, but to one with dim lighting. Or perhaps it was dim only in comparison with the outer world. To my eyes, used now to total dark, it seemed bright.

The hole of my entrance was some distance above the floor of this other space. I entered in an awkward scramble, half falling to the lower level. It was so good to stand erect again.

This chamber was square. And the light came through a series of long, narrow cuts set vertically in the wall to my left. Save for those, there appeared to be no other opening, certainly no door.

When I advanced to the light, I discovered a grating in the floor against the wall, wide enough for an exit if there were some manner of raising the grating itself. Just now I was more intent on looking through one of the slits.

It was necessary to squeeze very close to that narrow opening. Even then the area of vision was much curtailed. But I was looking down into a room or hall which was of such large proportions I could view only a fraction of it. The light came from the tops of a series of standing pillars or cases. And a moment's inspection of the nearest, though I must do that from some distance above, suggested something familiar. By almost grinding my face against the frame of the slit, I made a guess. These had a close resemblance to the box which had held that dead man above the valley. I was looking into a place for beings in stass-freeze!

"Maelen?"

Nothing moved below among the pillar-boxes. And —I had no answer to my call. I went on my knees, shed my charred mittens so I could lock fingers in the grating. And I had to exert all the strength I could summon before that gave, grudgingly. However, I was able to raise it. How I longed for what I did not have—a torch, for there was only dark below once more.

Lying flat, I tried to gauge what did lie below by letting the blaster dangle from its carrying strap. Thus I discovered what appeared to be a narrow shaft, its floor not too far below. And I dared to drop to that. Once down, I explored the wall which faced the sleepers' hall and was able to trace a line. Pushing outward brought no results. It was when my hands slipped across the surface of that stubborn barrier that it moved to one side and I was able to force it open a crack. Then the barrel of the blaster inserted there gave me leverage enough to force it the rest of the way.

How large that hall was I could not guess. It appeared to stretch endlessly both right and left. And there was such a sameness to those lines of boxes one could not find any guide.

"Maelen?"

I fell back against the very door I had just forced open. As it had happened before, my mind-seek brought such an answer as nearly struck me down. This response was no concentrated beam, but still it was a daunting blast, filling my mind painfully. So I crouched there, my hands raised to my ears in an involuntary response as if to shut out thundering shouts.

It was a torment, worse than any physical pain. A warning that here I dared not use the only way I had of tracing her whom I sought. I would have to blunder along, depending on the whim of fortune.

Shutting out mind-seek, I staggered forward in a wavering way between the boxes in the row directly before me. Now and then I paused to study the faces of those sleepers. There was a sameness about those.

They might all have come from some uniform mold, as there appeared to be no distinguishing marks to make one case differ from the next. Then I became a little less dazed by that mental bolt which had struck me and noted that there was a change in the patterning of color sparks about the frame of each box.

I counted at first, but after I reached fifty, I decided there was no need for that. Beyond the rows where I walked now were more and more and more. It might be that the entire army of some forgotten conquerer was here laid up in stass-freeze. I laughed then, thinking what an excellent way to preserve troops between one war and the next, assuring a goodly supply of manpower with no interregnum living expenses.

Such a find as this had never been made before. In fact the treasure discoveries on Thoth had had no conjunction with the remains of bodies, a puzzle for the archaeologists, since it had previously been believed that such furnishings were placed with rulers as grave goods. So—was this the cemetery of those who had left their treasures on Thoth? But why, then, cross space to bury their dead on another world?

And if they were dead, why were their bodies in stass-freeze? It was a condition known to my own kind in the past, used for two purposes. In the very early days of space travel it had been the only way to transport travelers during long voyages which might last for centuries of planet time. Secondly, it was the one hope for the seriously ill, who could rest thus until some future medical discovery could cure them.

Nations, peoples, even species did entomb their dead, following beliefs that at the will of their gods, or at some signal, these would rise whole and alive again. Was this so profound a belief here that they had used stass-freeze to preserve their dead?

I could accept such preservation, but I could not accept the fact that, although dead, they apparently still used their esper powers. My mind shied away from the horror that a live mind could be imprisoned in a dead body.

There was an end at last to the hall. In the faint light of the boxes I could now see another wall, and in that an archway framing a wide door. A closed door. But I was so filled with a loathing of that place that I halted, fumbled for another charge for the blaster, determined to burn my way out if I found that portal barred to my exit.

However, at my urging it rolled aside into the wall. I looked into a passageway. It was lighted, though by what means I could not see, save that the walls themselves appeared to give off a gray luminosity. With the blaster ready I went along.

There were doors in this corridor, each tightly closed, each bearing on its surface a series of symbols which had no meaning for me. And where in all this maze could I find Maelen? Since my sharp lesson in the hall of the sleepers, I dared not risk another call. There was no help but to look within each of the rooms I passed.

The first door opened on a small chamber holding but two sleepers. But there were also chests ranged about its walls. However, I did not wait to explore those. Another room—three sleepers—more storage containers. Room three—two sleepers again—more chests.

I was at the end of the hall and here the way branched right and left. I chose the right. The hall was still lighted and it ran straight, without any break. How many miles did this burrowing run? I wondered. It might be that Sekhmet was half honeycombed with these tunnelings. What a find! And if those chests and boxes I had seen in the smaller rooms contained such treasures as had been found on Thoth —then indeed the jacks had uncovered a mine which the Guild would not disdain to work. But why had they jeopardized their operation by sabotaging the *Lydis?* They could have worked here for years and never been discovered, had we not been forced down and they overplayed their hand by the attack on us. Was it a matter of being over-greedy?

The corridor I now followed began to narrow; soon it was passage for one only. There—I paused, my head up as I sniffed. Some untrackable system of ventilation had supplied all these ways. But this was something different—it was an odor I recognized. Somewhere not too far away cyro leaves had been recently burned. There were other faint scents also —food—cooked food—but the cyro overlaid most of that so strongly I could identify little else.

Cyro is mildly intoxicating, but it is also used as a counter to both body fatigue and some nervous depressions. As a Free Trader I was and am conditioned against certain drugs. By the very nature of our lives we must keep ourselves alert and with top powers of reaction. Just as we are conditioned against a planet-side interest in intoxicants of any type, gambling, women not of our kind, so we know the drugs which can spell danger by a clouding of mind, a slowing of body. So well are we armored against such that the use of any can make us violently ill.

Now I felt myself swallowing, fighting the nausea that smell induced in me. But such an odor could mean nothing less than that somewhere ahead were, or had been, others than the sleepers. After such a warning my progress was doubly cautious.

The hall ended in a blank wall, but then I saw an opening to my right, framing a brighter glow some distance ahead. And so I came out on a low-walled balcony overhanging another large chamber. This in turn was partly open to the sky. And beyond, in that daylight, I caught a glimpse of a spacer's fins, as if one side of this cavern opened on a landing field.

There was no way down from the balcony. But from this perch I had a good view of all which lay below. And there was plenty to see. To one side was heaped a pile of such chests and boxes as had been in the rooms. Many of them had shattered lids as if they had been forced. And not too far away two servo robos were fastening up a shipping crate.

Off to the right was a plasta-bubble, the kind of living quarters used by explorers as a base camp. This was sealed. But two men sat on upturned boxes outside it. One was speaking into a wrist recorder. The other held a robo control board on his knee as he watched the two busy at the crate. There was no one else in sight.

I tried to gauge the ship's size from what I could see of its fins, and decided it must be at least equal to the *Lydis*, perhaps larger. But there was no doubting that I witnessed a well-established and full-sized operation, and that it had been going on for some time.

The last thing I wanted to do was attract their attention. But Maelen—had she wandered in here, to be caught in some trap? Indecision held me fast. Dare I mind-call? There were no sleepers visible. But that did not mean that the jacks might not be using one as a defense or a warning.

I was still hesitating when a man came in from outside. Griss Sharvan!

Griss—I still could not accept that he was a part of this, or that he had of his own free will gone over to the enemy. I had known him far too long, and he was a Free Trader. Yet he moved freely, gave no sign of being a prisoner.

He joined the two by the bubble. The one recording got to his feet hurriedly, as did his companion. They gave the response of underlings in the presence of a leader. What—what had happened to Griss?

Suddenly his attention turned from them. His head came up, he stared straight up—at me! I fell behind the low wall edging the balcony. His actions had been those of a man alerted to danger, one who knows just where to look.

I began to crawl back to the passage which had brought me here. Only I never reached it. For what struck me then was something I had never experienced before, in spite of my many encounters with different kinds of esper power.

The command of my own body was taken from me. It was as if my mind was imprisoned in a robo which was obeying commands broadcast by a board. I got to my feet, turned around, and marched back into the sight of the three below, all of whom now watched me.

Griss raised his hand, pointed a forefinger at me. To my complete amazement I was raised from the stone under my boots, lifted above the wall, carried out and down, all as if I had antigrav on me. Nor could I struggle against that compelling force which held me captive.

That energy deposited me, still on my feet, on the

floor of the cavern. I stood there, a prisoner, as the two who had been checking cargo advanced on me. Griss remained where he was, that pointing finger aimed at my head, as if his flesh and bone had become a tangler.

The man who still held the robo control reached out his other hand and snatched the blaster from my hold. Even then my hands did not change position, but remained as if I still gripped barrel and butt with them. But the other jack brought out a real tangler, spinning its web of restraint around me. When he was done, Griss's had dropped and that compulsion was gone, though now I had no chance at freedom. They had left my legs unbound, and the jack with the tangler caught my shoulder and gave me a vicious shove toward Griss.

Chapter 10

KRIP VORLUND

Only it was not Griss Sharvan who stood there. Though he—it—wore Griss's body as one might wear a thermo suit. The minute those eyes met mine, I knew. Nor did that knowledge come as too great a shock, since my own experiences had taught me such shifts were possible.

However, this was no shift for the sake of knowledge, nor for the preservation of life, such as the Thassa practiced. The personality which had taken over Griss was alien to our kind as the Thassa could never be. I had a swift mental picture of a terrifying creature—a thing with a reasonably humanoid body but a head evilly reptilian, a mixture which repelled.

Only for an instant did I hold that mental image; then it was gone. But with its disappearance there was also a flash of incredulous surprise, not on my part, but from the alien. As if he—it—was astounded that I had been able to pick up that image at all, as its true nature was so well concealed it never revealed itself.

"Greeting, Krip." Griss's voice. But I knew well

133

that those slow, toneless words carried another's thoughts. I did not attempt any mental scanning, being warned by instinct that such would be the most dangerous thing I could do. "How many are with you?"

He held his head a little to one side, giving the impression of listening. A moment later he smiled.

"So you are alone, Krip? Now that was very foolish of you. Not that the whole crew could take us. But if they had been so obliging as to come it would have saved us much trouble. However, one more is a good beginning."

His eyes searched mine, but I had been warned enough to draw on the full resources of my talent, erect a mind-shield. Against that I could feel his probing, but surprisingly, he did not try to force it. I feared, guessed, that had he wanted to, he could easily have stripped me of any defenses, taken over my mind to learn all I had been trying to hide from him. This was a master esper, such as perhaps were the Old Ones among the Thassa, far beyond my own talent.

"A beginning," he repeated. Then he raised his hand in an arrogant gesture, crooking his finger to beckon me. "Come!"

I had not the slightest hope of disobeying that order. As before, I walked helplessly after him across the cavelike chamber. Never once did he turn his head to see whether or no I was behind, but wove a path in and out among the boxes.

So we came to another door and into a passage beyond. The light faded once again to that gray gloom which I had seen above, and the passage made several turns. Along its walls were open doors, but all the rooms were empty.

That this creature wearing Griss's body meant me no good was evident. I believed that my only defense against dire and instant peril was to dampen all esper talent, to depend only on the five senses of my body. But those I used as best I could to give me some idea of the territory through which we passed.

There were traces of odors from the cyro, but they were soon gone, leaving only an indefinable scent I could not name. Sight gave me the passage and the empty rooms along it. Sound—there was the faint rasp of two pairs of space boots against the stone floor, the fainter pulsing of my own breathing—nothing else.

And where was Maelen? A prisoner perhaps in the bubble? As quickly as I thought of her I thrust that thought again from my conscious mind. If she had not been discovered, I must not betray her.

My captor turned his head to glance back at me. And I shivered. He was laughing silently, his whole body quivering in a horrible travesty of the honest mirth my species knew. And his face was a mask of unholy and frightening joy—worse than any rictus born of torture or wrath.

Yet he made no effort to speak, either orally or by mind-touch. And I did not know whether that made his unseemly laughter, that silent gloating laughter, better or worse—probably the latter. Still laughing, he turned from the hallway into one of those rooms, and still helplessly in thrall, I followed.

The gray light of the corridor held here, but the room was empty. My captor stepped briskly to the left-hand wall. Once more he put out his hand, pointing a finger even as he had used it to make me prisoner. If he did not touch the surface of the stone, he came very close to it. So he began to trace a series of complicated lines. But as his finger moved there glowed on the wall a glistening thread, weaving in and out.

I knew that it was a symbol. We have devices such as persona locks which can be opened only by the body heat and thumb pattern of the one setting them. It could be that what I now saw was a very sophisticated development of such a safeguard, coming to life when will alone was focused on it.

He drew a design of sharp angles, of lines which to my eyes not only were distorted, but bothered me to look upon, as if they followed rules so alien that the human eye found them disturbing. Yet I could not look away.

Finally the alien seemed satisfied with the complicated pattern of line-cross-line, line-upon-line. Now his pointing finger indicated the very heart of the drawing. So he might have opened a well-concealed lock.

Sound answered, a grating—a protest, as if too long a time had passed since certain mechanisms had been activated. The wall split, a straight-edged crack down through the center of the design. One portion moved to each side to form a narrow doorway. Without hesitation he stepped within, and again I was drawn on.

There was no light here, and what sifted in from the chamber behind was sharply cut off as that crack closed. Where we stood now, in another chamber or a corridor, I had no idea. But that pressure kept me walking ahead. By the faint sounds, I deduced that he whom I trailed went as confidently as if he traveled a lighted and well-known road.

I fought an imagination which was only too ready to picture for me all which might lie underfoot, on either side, even overhead. There was no way of escape. And I had best save my energy, hold my control, for a time when I might have some small chance against that which walked in Griss Sharvan's body.

To travel in utter darkness, and by another's will, distorts time. Minutes might have been stretching, or else they were less—I had no way of telling. It seemed to me that we went so for a long time, yet it may not have been that at all.

Then—light!

I closed my eyes against what seemed to be a wild burst of eye-hurting color. Blinked, closed, opened—

The chamber in which we stood was four-sided with walls which sloped inward, to meet at an apex well over our heads. And those walls were also transparent, so we might have been inside a pyramid-shaped room of crystal.

Through the transparent walls we looked into four rooms. And each had its occupant, an unmoving, unbreathing occupant, who yet seemed no statue but a living creature, or once-living creature, frozen into complete immobility.

I say "creature," for while these preserved beings beyond the walls were humanoid to at least the ninth degree outwardly, I had, as I looked upon them, the same sensation of an indweller wholly alien. For three I had that sensation. For the fourth—I gazed the longest at him—and knew, shocked into applying mind-probe to learn the truth.

Griss—that was Griss! As tightly bound within that body as I now was in the tangler's cords. He was only dimly conscious of what had happened to him, but enough so that he was living in an endless nightmare. And how long his reason could so endure—

I wrenched my eyes away, fearing to draw the crushing burden of his fear just when I needed a clear mind. Such would be no aid to him. Instead I made myself examine more closely the other three who waited there.

The rooms themselves were elaborately furnished, the furniture carven, inlaid with gems. Two had narrow beds, the supporting posts of which were the bodies of strange animals or birds; two, chairs which bore a small likeness to the Throne of Qur. Tables with small boxes; chests.

Then—the inhabitants. Whereas the bodies I had seen in the freeze boxes had been bare, these all wore helmets or crowns. They also possessed eye-lashes and eyebrows. Each crown differed also, representing grotesque creatures. I shot another quick glance at that body now holding Griss's identity.

The crown it wore was a brown-yellow in the form of a wide-jawed saurian thing which was akin to the head I had seen in the mental image I had picked up earlier. It sat in a chair, but the one behind the next wall reclined on the narrow bed, head and shoulders supported by a rest of decorated material. The third was seated again. The crown of the second was a bird, and that of the third a sharp-muzzled, prick-eared animal.

But the fourth of that company was a woman! None of those behind the walls were clothed except for their crowns. And their bodies were flawless, akin to the ideal of beauty held by my species. The woman was such perfection as I had never dreamed could exist in the flesh. From beneath her diadem flowed hair to clothe her almost to her knees. That hair was of a red so deep and dark as to seem nearly black. Her crown was not as massive as those which seemed to weigh down her companions, but rather a band from which sprang a series of upstanding but uneven and unmatched filaments. Then I saw more clearly that each of these bore on its tip a small head like that mask of the cliff face. And each of those heads was equipped with gem eyes.

I gasped. When I had looked directly at the woman those cats' heads of her crown had begun to move, to turn, to rise, until they were all stiffly upstanding, pointing outward as if their jewel eyes were looking back at me in alert measurement.

But her own eyes stared beyond me as if I were so far outside her inner world that I had no existence for her.

A hand on my shoulder brought me around—to face the seated alien with the animal crown. And in my ears, Griss's voice:

"Attend, you! A great honor for this puny body of yours. It shall be worn by—" If he had meant to utter some name, he did not. And I think he cut short his words because of caution.

There is a belief, found mainly among primitive peoples, that to tell another one's true name puts one at his mercy. But that such a superstition would persist among aliens with manifestly so high a level of advancement I could not altogether believe.

However, that he intended now to force such an exchange as there had been for Griss, I had no doubts at all. And I was afraid as I never remembered being before in my entire life.

He caught my head from behind, held it in a vise grip, so that I had to look eye to eye with that one behind the wall. There was no fighting for freedom. Not physically. But still I could fight, I would! And I drew upon all the reserves of esper I had, all my sense of being who and what I was. I was only just quick enough to meet the attack.

It was not the harsh blanketing which had served as the knockout blow I had met in the ship valley, but rather a pointed thrust, delivered with arrogant self-confidence. And I was able to brace against it without bringing all my own power to bear.

Though I did not then catch any surprise, there was a sudden cut-off of pressure. As if he of the animal crown retreated, puzzled by resistance where he had thought to find none at all, retreated to consider what he might actually be facing. While I, given that very short respite, braced myself to await what I was sure would be a much stronger and tougher attack.

It came. I was no longer aware of anything outside, only of inner tumult, where some small core of my personality was beaten by smothering wave after wave of will; trying to breach my last defense and take that inner me captive. But—I held, and knew the crowned one's astonishment at such holding. Shock after shock against my will, still I was not engulfed, lost, borne away. Then I felt that other's growing rage, uncertainty. And I was sure that those waves of pressure were not so strong, that they were ebbing faster and farther as a tide might withdraw from a shore cliff which was mercilessly beaten by the sea but which still stood.

Awareness of the room returned. My head, still in that hold, was up, eye to eye with him beyond the wall. His face was as expressionless as it had ever been. Yet those features seemed contorted, hideous with a rage born of frustration.

"He will not do!" It was almost a scream within my head, bringing pain with the raw emotion with which it struck. "Take him hence! He is a danger!"

My captor jerked me around. Griss's face before me, but the expression was not his, an ugly, raw menace the real Griss had never known. I thought that he might well burn me down. Yet it seemed he might have some other use for me, for he did not reach for the blaster at his belt but rather sent me sprawling forward, so that I skidded up against the crystal surface of the wall behind which lay the woman, if woman she had ever been.

The cat-headed filaments of her crown quivered, dipped, their eyes glinting avidly as they watched me. I slid to my knees as if I were offering some homage to an unresponsive queen. But she stared unseeingly above my head.

The alien pulled me up, sent me on, with another push, toward the narrow slit of a doorway near one corner of the room. Then I was for the second time in the full darkness of that passage, this time ahead of my captor.

Nor was I to make the full return journey; for we were not far along that tunnel, in a dark so thick one could almost feel it, before I was again propelled to the right. I did not strike against any wall there, but kept on, brushing one of my shoulders against a smooth surface.

"I do not know what you are, Krip Vorlund," Griss's voice rang out of the dark. "'Thassa,' says that poor fool whose seeming I wear. It would appear that you are a different breed, with some armor against our will. But this is no time for the solving of riddles. If you survive you may give us an entertaining puzzle at a later hour. *If* you survive!"

Painfully alert to whatever guides I could use in this dark, I thought his voice sounded fainter, as if he no longer stood close by. Then there was only the dark and the silence, which in its way was as over-powering as the blackness blinding me. No compulsion to follow; I was as free as if a cord had been cut. But my arms were still tightly bound to my sides by the constriction of tangle cords.

I listened, trying even to breathe as lightly as I could so that would not hide any possible sound. Nothing—nothing but the horrible weight of the smothering dark. Slowly I took one step and then another from the wall, which was my only point of reference. Two more—three steps—and I came up against another wall. If I had only had the use of my hands, it would have been a small relief, but that was denied me.

Exploration, so hindered, told me at last that the narrow space in which I stood must be the end of another corridor. I found I could not return the way we had come—if my sense of direction had not altogether failed me—for that had been cut off, though I had not heard the closing of any door. There were left only the three walls, with the fourth side open. Leading perhaps to a multitude of possible disasters. But these I must chance blindly.

It was slow progress, that blind creeping, my right shoulder brushing ever against the wall, since I had to have some reference. I found no door, no other opening, always the same smooth surface against which my thermo jacket brushed with a soft rustling. And it went on and on—

I was tired—more, I was hungry, and thirst made my mouth and throat as dry as the ashy sand of the valley. To know that I carried at my own belt the means of alleviating all my miseries made it doubly hard. There was no fighting the grip of the tangle bond. To do so would lead to greater and more dangerous constriction. Twice I slipped to the floor of the passage. It was so narrow I had to hunch up with bent knees to rest, for the toes of my boots grated against the other wall. But then to get up again required such effort that the last time I did so, I thought I must keep on my feet and going, with a thin hope of survival. For if I went down again it could well be I would never have the strength to rise.

On and on—this was like one of those nightmares in which one is forced to wade through some muck which hinders each step, and yet behind comes a hunter relentlessly in chase. I knew my hunter—my own weakness.

Action held much of a dreamlike quality for me now. The four crowned ones—Griss Sharvan who was not Griss. Maelen—

Maelen! She had receded from my mind during that ordeal in the crystal room. Maelen! When I tried to see my mind-picture of her she flowed into someone else. Maelen—her long red hair, her— Red hair! No, Maelen had the silver hair of the Thassa, like that now close-cropped on my own skull. RED HAIR—the woman of the cat crown! I flinched. Could it be that some of that compulsion which had been loosed against me back there was still working on me?

Maelen. Laboriously I built my mental picture of her in the Thassa body. And despairingly, not believing I would ever again have any reply from her, I sent out a mind-call.

"Krip! Oh, Krip!"

Sharp, clear, as if shouted aloud in joy because, after long searching, we had come face to face. I could not believe it even though I heard.

"Maelen?" If thought-send could whisper, then mine did.

"Krip, where are you? Come—oh, come—"

Clear; I had not been mistaken, misled. She was here, and close, or that call would not be so loud. I pulled myself together, made answer quickly as I could:

"I do not know where I am, except in a very dark and narrow passage."

"Wait—say my name, Krip. Give me a direction!"

I obeyed, making of her name a kind of mind-chant, knowing that here perhaps there was power in a name. For upon such a point of identity could a mind-send firmly anchor.

"I think that I have it. Come on—straight ahead, Krip."

I needed no more urging; my shuffle quickened. Though I still had to go with my shoulder along the wall, since I could not bear to lose that guide in the dark. It was good that I kept it so, for there was another sudden transition from the dark to light, enough to blind me temporarily, so I leaned against the wall with my eyes closed.

"Krip!"

So loud she could be there before me!

I opened my eyes. She was. Her black fur was grayed, matted with dust. She wavered from side to side as if she could hardly keep her feet. There was a blotch of dried blood along one side of her head. But she was alive.

I slipped down by the wall, edging out on my knees to bring me closer to her. But she had dropped to the floor as if no reserve of strength remained in her. Forgetting, I fought my bonds, then gasped as the resulting constriction punished me.

"Maelen!"

She lay, her head on her paws, flattened to the

stone, much as she had laid on her bunk in the *Lydis*. But now her eyes were fast closed. It was as if the effort of guiding me to her had drained her last strength.

Food, water—by the look of her, her need for those was greater than my own. Yet I could not help her, not unles she first freed me. And I did not know if she could.

"Maelen, at my belt—the cutter—"

One of those tools which were the ever-present equipment of an adventurer on an unknown world.

Her eyes opened, looked to me. Slowly she raised her head, as if to do so was painful, or so fatiguing she could hardly manage it. She could not regain her feet, and she whimpered as she wriggled on her belly to my side.

Bracing herself against my body, she brought her head higher; her dust-caked muzzle rubbed my side as she nosed against my belt. While she had once been so graceful of body, she was now clumsy and awkward, taking a long time to free the cutter from its loop, though I turned and twisted to give her all the aid I could.

The tool lay in the dust for a long time (or so it seemed to me) before she bent her head to mouth its butt, bring it up to rest against the lowest loop of the tangle bond. Twice the cutter slid away to thud to the stone before she could bite down on the spring releasing its energy. My frustration at having to watch her efforts and not be able to help made me ill.

But she kept to it stubbornly and finally she made it. The energy blade snipped into the thick round of the tangle well enough so that my own struggles parted it. Once broken, after the way of such, it shriveled away and I was free, though my arms were numb and I found it difficult to lift them. A return of circulation was painful, but I could grope for the rations in my supply bag. And I had those at hand as I pulled Maelen's body closer, supported her head against me, trickling water into her parched, dust-rimmed mouth.

She swallowed once, again. I put aside the water container, licking my own lips, to unscrew an E-ration tube, squirt the semiliquid contents into her mouth. So I fed her half of that restorative nutriment before I slaked my own thirst, fed my hunger-racked body.

For the first time, sitting there, holding the tube to my mouth, Maelen resting against my knee, I really looked about me. This was another of those pyramid-shaped chambers, though it did not rise to a point but was sliced off midway up with a square ceiling much smaller than the floor area.

Nor were these walls crystal, but rock. The ledge where we sat was about halfway between roof and floor. I turned my head to see the doorway through which I had come. But there was nothing—nothing at all! I remembered that quick transition from dark to light, as if I had pushed through a curtain.

There was a very steep stair midway along the ledge, descending to the floor. And that floor supported a series of blocks, some tall, others shorter, in uneven heights. Cresting each of these was a ball of some opaque substance which was not stone. And in the inner heart of each ball was a faint glimmer of light.

The balls were colored—red, blue, green, yellow, then violet, orange, paler shades, those closest to the walls the palest hues of all, deepening as one approached the core. The center one there was very dark indeed, almost black.

On the surfaces of the brighter and lighter-colored ones were etched patterns. And as I studied them I recognized some—there was a reptilian head resembling the crown of the body that now imprisoned Griss; I saw the animal one, the bird one, and, farthest away, a cat mask. But the meaning of this display or its use I could not guess. I leaned back against the wall; Maelen lay unmoving. I thought that she slept now and I had no desire to trouble her rest.

Rest—I needed that also. I shut my eyes to the dull light. Undoubtedly I should keep watch, for we must be in the very heart of enemy territory. But this time I could not fight the demands of my body. My eyelids closed against my will—I fell asleep.

Chapter 11

KRIP VORLUND

Now Maelen stood before me, not in animal shape, but as I had known her first on Yiktor. In her hand was that white wand which had been her weapon in those days, and which the Old Ones had taken from her. She was looking not at me, but rather at an inclining stone wall, and I knew that we were still in the burrows beneath the crust of Sekhmet. And she was using that wand as those with certain esper talents might to search out the presence of water, or any object worked by men, underground.

Save that her wand did not point down but stretched in a straight line before her. Holding it so, almost as if it were imbued with energy of its own to draw her after it, she walked forward. Afraid to lose her once again, even in this dream, I followed.

The wand touched the wall, and that barrier was gone. Now we passed into a space which had no boundaries, in which there was no substance. Until once more we stood in a chamber. Looking around, I knew where we were, though this time I was on the opposite side of the crystal wall.

There was that narrow bed, upheld by four cat creatures, on which lay the woman. And the gem-eyed heads of her diadem arose straight on their fine filaments. They did not all face Maelen; rather they twisted and made quick darts here and there until brought up short by the threads which attached them to the circlet about that red hair. It was as if they were alarmed.

Maelen paid no attention to the darting, almost frenzied activity of the crown. Rather she advanced to the end of the couch, her wand pointed at the other's body, her own gaze intent, measuring—

She glanced once to me, showing that she knew I had followed.

"Remember this one in time of need—" Her thought was faint, as if we were far separated, yet I could have put out my hand and laid it on her arm. Although I knew that I must not.

"Why?" Her words were too ambiguous. That they were of import I did not doubt, but for me they had no meaning.

She did not answer, only gave me a long, level look. Then she turned once more to the woman with her now wildly writhing crown, as if she must imprint that image so firmly in her mind that a hundred years hence she would still see it in detail.

The wand trembled, wavered from side to side. I could see that with both her hands Maelen fought to hold it steady. To no avail, for it leaped from her grasp.

I opened my eyes. My neck and shoulders were stiff where they rested against the stone of the wall. I felt an inner chill which my thermo clothing was no proof against. My hands moved over fur engrimed with dust and grit. I looked down. The glassia head rose from its pillow on my arm.

"Maelen?" So vivid had that dream been that I half expected to find her still as she had been moments ago.

"Look yonder!"

She used her nose as a pointer to indicate the globes. Some of those were glowing brighter, giving more light to the chamber. It took me only a moment or two to be sure that not all of them had so awakened —just those with the reptilian design.

"Griss!" I put the only name I knew to that menace.

"Griss Sharvan?" Her thought was surprised. "What has this to do with him?"

"Much, perhaps." Swiftly I told her of what had happened to me since I had been taken captive by that thing wearing Griss's body, and of the visit to the crystal-walled chamber where he had endeavored to give my body to his fellow being.

"She is also there, is she not?" Maelen asked.

I did not mistake her. There was only one "she"— the woman of the cat crown.

"Yes! And, Maelen, just now I dreamed—"

"I know what manner of dream that was, since it also spun me into its web," she interrupted again. "I had thought that no one could surpass the Thassa in inner powers. But it would seem that in some things we are as children playing with bright pebbles, making patterns on the earth! I think that these have slept here to preserve their race against some great peril in the past. But only those four you have seen survived, able to rise to full life again."

"But if they can be revived, why do they want our bodies?"

"It can be that the means of revival on their own cannot now be used. Or it may be that they wish to pass among us as beings of our own kind."

"To take over." That I could believe. Had the seeming Griss Sharvan concealed his alienness, posed perhaps as a captive among the jacks, we would have been deceived and so in saving him could have brought disaster among ourselves. I thought of the men I had left behind on the cliff. They were facing worse than jack blasters—and now I was impatient to be away, to warn them.

I had found Maelen. Now we must find our way out, return to the *Lydis*, or to the force of our men. What was happening here was vastly larger and worse than any jack looting!

"You are right." Maelen had followed my thoughts. "But as to discovering the path out—that I do not know. Can you even now find the door which you entered?"

"Of course!" Though I could not see any opening, I was sure I knew just where I had come through to this ledge. Gently I lifted her aside and arose. To make certain I would not miss what I sought if the opening were disguised in some manner, I put my fingers to the surface of the wall and edged along back toward that place where I thought I had entered.

I reached the far end of the ledge. There was no opening. Sure that I had made some mistake, yet somehow equally certain I could not have, I made a slow passage back, this time reaching both above and below my former tracing of the surface. I returned to Maelen. There had been no break in that solid wall.

"But I *did* come through!" I burst out, and my protest echoed hollowly through that space.

"True. But where?" Her question seemed a mockery of my vehemence.

Then she continued. "Such an experience is not unknown here. This has happened to me twice. Which is why I have been so completely lost."

"Tell me!" I demanded now.

So I learned how she had made her way from the ship valley, found the sleeper with the amplifier, how she had come to witness the looting of the cache, even as I guessed it might all have happened. But for the rest it was a tale of a strange journey, of her will battling that of another reaching out for her. Not, she felt, for her personally, but as one might fling a net in hope of catching something within it. But that compulsion was not continuous in its powers and she was able to fight it at intervals. It had brought her to where the ship of the jacks was finned down, and through the cavern there into the passages beyond. But there, bemused by the ebb and flow of the current which held her, she had been lost. Then she had contacted me, had been drawn toward my call in turn.

"I had believed that Thassa could not be so influenced," she admitted frankly. "Always I have been warned that I was too proud of my powers. If that was ever so, it is no longer. For here I have been as one played with by something infinitely greater, allowed to run a little, then put under restraint again. Yet this is the strangest of all, Krip—I will swear by the Word of Molaster that this power, this energy, whatever it may be, was not as conscious of me as I am of it. It was rather as if it flexed muscles in exercise so that it might be ready to use all its strength at a future call."

"The four of that inner place?" I suggested.

"Perhaps. Or they may be only extensions of something else, infinitely greater still. They are adepts, without question—very powerful ones. But even an adept recognizes something above and beyond himself. We name Molaster in our petitions. But that is only our name for what we cannot describe, but which is the core of our belief. These others are—"

What she might have added to her speculations was left unsaid. Those yellow globes with the reptilian masks, which had been glowing so much brighter, now gave off a low, humming note. And that sound, subdued as it was, startled us into immobility. We crouched, breathing only shallowly, our heads going right to left, left to right, as we went on guard against what this change might herald.

"Where is the door out?" I demanded.

"Perhaps you can guess better than I have been able to. Even as you, I went from dark to light, found this ledge, but no return. When your mind-send came I hoped it would direct me to an exit. But that was not to be. You came to me instead."

"Where did you come in?"

Her nose pointed to the other end of the ledge, well away from the spot where I was still sure my door existed. I went there, again running palms and fingers along the surface, hunting the smallest hint of an opening. I still had the cutter which Maelen had used on the tangler cords. Perhaps with that, or one of the other tools from my belt, I could force a lock, were I able to find it. A forlorn hope, but one clings to such.

The humming from the globes was continuous now. And it did something to my hearing. Or was there a more subtle outflow rising beyond the range of audibility to affect my thinking? Twice I found I had halted my search, was standing, gazing down at the globes, my mind seemingly blanked out. It could only have lasted a second or two, but it was frightening.

Now I believed that the globes were generating a haze. The forbidding representation of the designs on them was fading. However, that concealment acted in a strange way, just the opposite of what one might expect. One could no longer see those monsters, their elongated jaws a fraction open, their formidable fangs revealed, yet there was the feeling that so hidden, they were more alive!

"Krip!" Maelen's thought-cry dispelled what was building in my mind. I was able to look away, turn my head back to the wall. But now I feared that a danger worse than imagination presented was threatening us.

Solid wall. I thumped it now with my fist as I went, my blows faster, more savage. All they brought me was bruises and pain. Until—I had carried in mind so sharply the thought of a door, the need for a door— my fist went through!

To my eyes the stone was solid, as solid as it had ever been. But my hand had sunk in up to the wrist.

"Maelen!"

She needed no call. She was already padding towards me. Door—where had the invisible door come from?

"Think *door*—think it! See a door in your mind!"

I obeyed her. Door—there was a door there—of course there was. My hand had gone through the opening. There might be an illusion to deceive the eye, but there was nothing now to baffle touch. I rested my other hand on Maelen's head and we moved resolutely forward together into what appeared solid, unbroken stone.

Again we passed abruptly from light to dark. But

also, as if a portal had slammed shut behind us, the humming was instantly silenced. I gave a sigh of relief.

"Is this your way?" I asked. Though how she could be certain of that in the dark, I did not know.

"I cannot be sure. But it is *a* way. We must keep together."

I left my hand on her head as she crowded against me. So linked, we went on, very slowly and cautiously, my other hand outstretched before me to warn of anything which might rise in our path.

Shortly thereafter I found a wall, traced along it until there was another way open to the left. Long ago I had lost all sense of direction, and Maelen confessed to a similar disability. We could do little until we found some lighted way. That we might not do so was a horror we refused to give mind-room to.

Whether the Thassa shared the ancient fear of the dark with my own race, I did not know. But the sense of compression, of stiffling pressure, returned. Save that this time I did not walk with my arms bound to my sides.

"Left now—"

"Why? How do you know?"

"Life force in that direction."

I tried mind-probe for myself. She was right—a flicker of energy. It was not the high flow I associated with the aliens, but more like such as I could pick up when not too far from a crew member. And there was an opening to the left.

How far we were from the chamber of the globes now I could not guess. But a lighting of the way cheered us—and that grew ever brighter.

Only now there was sound also. Not a mutter of

voices, but rather the clank of metal. Maelen pushed against me.

"He, the one who wears Griss's body—ahead!"

I tried no probe. I wished I could do just the opposite, reduce all mental activity so far down the scale he could not pick up any hint of us in return. I had not forgotten how easily he had found me out when I had spied on the jacks.

"He is one-minded now," Maelen told me, "using all his power for something which is of very great importance to him. We need not fear him, for he puts all to one purpose."

"And that?"

She did not reply at once. Then—

"Lend me of your sending—"

It was my turn to hesitate. To strengthen any mind-seek she might send out could make us more accessible to discovery. Yet I trusted her enough to realize that she would not suggest such a move unless she thought we had a fair chance. So I yielded.

Her probe sped out, and I fed my own energy to it. This we had not often done, so it was a relatively new experience for me, bringing with it an odd sensation of being pulled along in a current I could not fight. Then a blurred mind-picture came.

We seemed to be hanging in the air over a pit, or rather we were in the apex of one of those pyramid chambers. Below a robo was blasting away at the foot of one wall. There was already a dark cavity there; now the machine was enlarging that.

Behind the worker stood Griss. He did not hold any control board. It would appear that he was able to keep the robo at work without that. And his attention was completely absorbed by what he was doing. But that feverish desire which drove him was like a broadcast. He did not hold his defenses now, but fastened avidly on what he sought—an ancient storehouse of his kind, perhaps containing machines or weapons. His need was like a whiff of ozone. A whiff, I say, because I caught only the edge of it. Around the chamber, well above the level at which the robo worked, was another of the ledge ways. This ran across one wall, leading from one door to another. And without needing to be told, I recognized that this was the path we must follow.

Whether we could do it without attracting attention from below was another matter. But now that hole the robo battered was larger. The machine wheeled back, became inert. And the alien hurried to the break, disappeared through it.

"Now!"

We sped along the lighted corridor, and it was only a short distance until we ventured out on that ledge. It was so close to the apex of the pyramid that the opposite wall leaned very close. Maelen found it easier to take that route than I, for I could not stand erect but had to go on hands and knees.

Nor did I waste any time looking back at the hole the robo had opened. To reach the door on the other side, scramble within, was all I wanted.

"We made it!"

"For now, yes," she answered me. "But—"

She swung around, her head down. Her dusty body quivered.

"Krip! Krip, hold me!" It was a cry for help, coming so suddenly, without warning, that I was startled. Then I half threw myself over her, grasping her tightly around the body, holding on in spite of her struggles for freedom.

It was no longer Maelen whom I held so, but an

animal that growled and snapped, struck out with unsheathed claws. Only by pure chance did I escape harm. Then she collapsed against me, her breath coming in deep gasps. There were flecks of white foam at the corners of her jaws.

"Maelen, what is it?"

"The calling—it was stronger this time, much stronger. Like—like to like!"

"What do you mean?" I still held her but she was far from fighting now. As if her struggle had exhausted her, she was in nearly the same condition in which I had earlier found her.

"The dream—she of the cat crown." Maelen's thoughts did not make a completely coherent pattern. "She is—akin to Thassa—"

But I refused to believe that. I could see no resemblance between her and the Maelen I had known.

"Maybe not to the sight," Maelen agreed. "Krip—is there more water?" She was still panting, the sound of it close to human sobbing. I found the flask, poured a little in her mouth. But some I must save, for we did not know when we could replenish that small supply.

She swallowed greedily, but she did not press me for more.

"The mind-call—the dream—I knew their like. Such are of Thassa kind."

I had a flash of inspiration. "Could it be adjusted? That is—having discovered you, could the pattern be altered to a familiar one, thus with a better chance of entrapping you?"

"That may well be so," she admitted. "But between me and that other there is something—Only when I face her, it will be on my terms and not hers, if you will give me of your strength as you did this time when she called."

"You are sure it was she? Not the one we just saw?"

"Yes. But when I go it will be at a time of *my* choosing. Which is not yet."

Having taken a mouthful of water myself, I brought out an E-ration tube, which we shared half and half. Made for nourishment during times of strain, it was high in sustenance and would keep us going for hours to come.

There was no sound from the chamber where the robo must still be on guard beside that hole. I wondered very much what the alien sought beyond the battered wall. But Maelen did not mention that as we went. On the contrary, she asked a question so much apart from the matters at hand I was startled.

"Do you think her fair?"

Her? Oh, I realized, she must mean the alien woman.

"She is very beautiful," I answered frankly.

"A body without blemish—though strange in its coloring. A perfect body—"

"But its mind reaches for another covering. That which walks in Griss was also perfect outwardly, yet its rightful owner saw fit to exchange with Griss. And I was taken there to exchange with another one. Are they in stass-freeze, I wonder?"

"Yes." She was definite. "That other one, he whom they used on the cliff top—"

"Lukas said he was dead—long dead. But those four, I am sure they are alive. The one in Griss *must* be!"

"Perhaps it may be that their bodies, once released from stass-freeze, will truly die. But I do not think so. I believe that they wish to preserve those for some other reason. And they seek our bodies as we would put on meaner clothes which may be soiled and thrown away once some dirty job is finished. But—she is very beautiful!"

There was a wistfulness in that, one of those infrequent displays of what appeared to be human emotion on Maelen's part. And such always moved me the more because they came so seldom. So I believed her a little subject to the same desires as my own species.

"Goddess, queen—what was she, or who?" I wondered. "We cannot guess her real name."

"Yes, her name." Maelen repeated my thought in part. "That she would not want us to know."

"Why? Because"—and I thought then of the old superstition—"that would give us power over her? But that is the belief of a primitive people! And I would say she is far from primitive."

"I have told you, Krip"—Maelen was impatient—"belief is important. Belief can move the immovable if it is rightly applied. Should a people believe that one's name is so personal a possession that to know it gives another power over one, then for them that is true. And from world to world degrees of civilization differ as much as customs and names for gods."

My head was up now, and I sniffed, alerted once again by a scent rather than a sound. Maelen must have been quick to catch the same trace of odor.

"Ahead—others. Perhaps their camp."

Where there was a camp there must also be some communication with the outer world. And I wanted nothing so much as to be free of these burrows, to return to the *Lydis*. At least my sojourn here had given me knowledge enough to warn and arouse my fellows to such danger as we had not known existed.

So—if we did want to escape the heart of the enemy's territory, we must still push on into what might be open danger.

But I had not realized that my own wanderings must have been in a circle. For when we came to a doorway we were looking out into the cavern of the pack camp. The looted chests were piled about, and we could see, in the outer air before the entrance, a portion of the ship's fins.

There was a line of robos, all idle now, to the right. No sign of any men about. If we could keep to cover behind the boxes we might reach the outer opening—

But one step, or at the most two, at a time. Maelen was slinking, with her belly fur brushing the floor, along behind that line of empty chests. And I crouched as low as I could to join her. There was no sound; we could be totally alone. But we dared not depend on such good fortune. And it was well that we did not, for the side of the plasta-bubble tent parted as its entrance was unsealed and a man came out.

When I saw him I froze. Harkon—and not a prisoner. He carried a blaster openly, had turned to look back over his shoulder, as if waiting for someone else. Had the party from the *Lydis* taken, by some miracle of fortune, the headquarters of the jacks? If so, they must be speedily warned of what wore Griss's body. I had no illusions as to what would happen if that confronted them. The odds might be ten to one against that alien and yet he would come out the winner.

Chapter 12

MAELEN

We are told that all the universe lies on the balance of Molaster's unseen scales--good weighs against bad, ill against well. And when it seems to us most likely that fortune has turned, that is the time to be most wary. I had met much which was new to me since I had put on Vors's body and come to be one of this band of off-worlders. Yet I had always supposed that the core of the balance remained the same and that only the outer forms differed.

However, in these underground ways I had avoided challenges and learned things which were so outside the reference of all I had known before that many times I could only make blind choices. And to a Moon Singer of the Thassa a blind choice is an affront and a defeat.

Twice I had dreamed true—I could not be deceived in that—of her whom Krip had actually looked upon. Why was she so familiar to me when I had never seen her like before? There were no women on the *Lydis*, and those I had met on the three planets we had visited since first I raised from Yiktor were no

162

different from the females of the plains people—never more than pale copies of what their men desired, creatures without rights or many thoughts.

But she—there was in me such a longing, a drive, to go and look upon her in body even as I had a dream, that I ever struggled against that compulsion, nor did I reveal it wholly to Krip. But that he had shared my second dream was to me proof that danger lay in actually facing her and I must not risk a confrontation yet. For what he had to tell me of the fate they had intended for him was a warning. I believe that it was perhaps that small bit of Thassa lurking in him which had defeated the takeover they had planned.

During the months we had voyaged together I had realized that Krip was a greater esper than he had been at our first meeting. It was my thought that this slow awakening of power, this development of his talent, was influenced by Maquad's body. Though I did not know how or why. Which again gave me to think about what a long indwelling in my present form might do to *me!*

I knew that the aliens had not been able to dispossess him, that the encased creature had ordered him taken away as a possible danger. And that small fact was the only favorable thing I had to hold to—save that we were together again and had found the door to the outer world.

It was pleasing that Krip did not move at once into the open when we saw the Patrolman. His care to remain in hiding, willing to accept nothing and no one unproved, reassured me. So we lay behind the boxes watching. Nor did either of us use mind-send. For if this Patrolman was not what he seemed, we would be thus betrayed to greater peril than we had lately been in.

Harkon moved away from the bubble and another came out—Juhel Lidj of the *Lydis*. He, too, carried his weapon; still, about both of them there was no sign that they feared any enemy. They were too much at their ease. And yet they were both men who had faced danger many times over, not foolhardy adventurers.

Together they passed us, moving toward the back of the cave and the mouth of one of the dark ways there. Still Krip did not stir nor try to hail them, and I waited his lead. But he edged around to watch them go. When he could be sure they were out of sight his hand touched my head for a close communication which could not be heard.

"They—I have a feeling all is wrong—not right."

"So do I," I was quick to answer.

"Could they have been taken over also? It is best we try to reach the *Lydis*. But if I have guessed wrong, and they are walking straight into what lies there—" I felt him shiver, his fingers on my head tremble slightly.

"If they are as you fear now, then they are masters here, and should they discover us—But if the others are still free from such contamination they must be warned. For the present we can hope such domination is confined to Sekhmet. Have you thought what might happen if their ship out there lifts off, carrying those who can change bodies as easily as you change the clothing on your back—spreading the contagion of their presence to other worlds?"

"Such evil as has never been known before. And there could be no finding them once they were off this planet!"

"Therefore—carry your message while still you may." In this I was urging what I had decided was the greater good. There was nothing one man and one glassia could do in these burrows to overset such enemies, but there was much which we could accomplish elsewhere.

"They could already have started it," he said then. "How do we know how many there are of them—how many voyages that ship out there has made?"

"The more reason why a warning must be given."

We were on the move again, using the looted chests as a shield as long as we could. Then we came into the pallid daylight at the cavern's entrance.

The cargo hatches of the ship were sealed, but her passenger ramp was still out. Krip looked up at her. He was far more knowledgeable of such than I. To me she merely seemed larger than the *Lydis*, and so I said.

"She is. We are D class; this is a C class ship, also a freighter, a converted Company freighter. She is slow, but can lift far more than the *Lydis*. And she has no insignia, which means she is a jack ship."

There were no guards to be seen, but we still kept to cover. And the broken nature of the country seemed designed to aid such skulking. That and the fact that the clouds were very dense overhead and a cold, ice-toothed rain began to fall. Shivering under the lash of that, we found a place where we could climb the cliff. We thought prudence dictated such an exit rather than use of the rough road beaten by many robo tracks.

Aloft, I could trust for our guide to the sense which was a part of Vors's natural equipment, and we headed in the direction where I was sure we would find the *Lydis*. But it was a nightmare of a journey, with the sleet sluicing around us and the dark growing thicker. We crawled where we longed to run, afraid of missteps which would plunge us over some rock edge.

There was a wind rising. I unsheathed claws to anchor me and crept close to the ground under the beating of its force and that of the sleet.

"Krip?" Here four clawed feet might manage, but I was not sure that two booted ones might do as well. And the fury of this storm was like nothing I had felt before. It was almost as if the natural forces of this forsaken world were ranged on the side of those who looted.

"Keep on!" There was no weakness in his reply.

I had come to a down slope where the water poured in streams about me as I twisted and turned, using every possible hint of protection against the worst blasts. As I went I began to doubt very gravely if we could press on to the *Lydis*, wonder whether it would not be much more prudent to seek shelter and wait out the worst of this storm. And I was about to look for a place where we could do so, when the stones my claws rasped were no longer firm, but slid, carrying me with them.

Over—out—into nothingness! An instant of knowing that I was falling—then a blast of pain and darkness.

Yet that dark was not complete, and I carried with me an instant of raw, terrifying knowledge—that it had been no normal misstep, no chance which had brought me down. I had been caught in a trap I had not suspected.

And, recognizing that, I knew also why it had been done and the full danger of what might follow.

But with Sharvan, again with Krip on Yiktor, there

had been an exchange of bodies. Why need my present one be destroyed—why?

How better to enforce slavery upon an identity than by destroying the body which it inhabited?

Pain! Such pain as I had not believed could exist in a sane world. And in no way would my body obey me.

"Cannot—can never now—"

The message reaching me was erratic, such as a faulty line of communication would make.

"Leave—come—come—come!"

"Where? For what purpose?"

"Life force—life force! Live again—come!"

I made the great effort of my life, trying to cut off the pain of my body, to center all my energy and will on that which was the core of my identity.

"Come—your body dies—come!"

Thereby that which called made its grave error. All living things have a fear of being blotted out, of nonexistence. It is part of our armor, to keep us ever alert against evil, knowing that we have a certain way to walk and that how we walk it judges us on Molaster's scales. We do not give up easily. But also the White Road has no terrors for the Thassa, if the time has come for us to step onto its way. This which had entrapped me played upon the fear of non-existence, as if those with whom it had had earlier dealings could visualize no other life beyond what men call death. Thus it would readily gain what it wanted by offering life continuation quickly at the moment when that death approached.

"Come!" Urgency in that. "Would you be nothing?"

So I read its great need. My identity was not what it wished to take to itself, nor did it seek another's body. For to it its own covering was a treasure it clung to. No, it wanted my life force as a kind of fuel that, drawing upon this force, it might live again on its own terms.

"Maelen! Maelen, where are you?"

"Come!"

"Maelen!"

Two voices in my head, and the pain rising again! Molaster! I gave my own cry for help, trying not to hear either of those other calls. And there came an answer—not the White Road, no. That I could have if I willed it. But such a choice would endanger another plan. That was made clear to me as if I had been lifted once more to the cliff crest and a vast scene of action spread before me. What I saw then I could not remember, even as I looked upon it. But that it was needful, I knew. And also I understood that I must struggle to fulfill my part in that purpose.

"Come!" No coaxing, no promises now—just an order delivered as if it could not possibly be disobeyed. "Come now!"

But I answered that other call of my name, sent my own plea.

"Here—hurry!" How I might carry out the needful task I did not know. Much would depend now upon the skill and resources of another.

I could not make the glassia body obey me or even give me sight. To keep my mind clear, I had to block off all five senses lest pain drive me completely forth. But my mind—that much I had—for a space.

"Krip!" Whether he was still on the cliff top or beside me, I had no means of knowing. Only I must reach him and give him this last message or all would fail. "Krip—this body—I think it is too badly broken —it is dying. But it must not die yet. If you can get it into stass-freeze—You must! That box with the sleeper—get me to that—"

I could not even wait for any answer to my message. I must just hold grimly, as long as I could. And how long that might be—only Molaster could set limit to.

It was a strange hidden place where that which was the real "I"—Maelen of the Thassa, Moon Singer once, glassia once—held and drew upon all inner resources. Did that other still batter at my defenses, crying "Come, come—live"? I did not know. I dared not think of anything save holding fast to this small stronghold which was under attack. Weaker grew my hold so that at times the pain struck in great punishing blows. Then I tried only to form the words of singing, which I had not done since they took away my wand. And the words were like dim, glowing coals where once they had been leaping flames of light. Yet still there was a feeble life in them and they sustained me, damping out the pain.

There was no time in this place—or else far too much of it. I assured myself, "I can hold one more instant, and one more, and one more"—and so it continued. Whether Krip could accomplish that which would save me, or *if* it would save me—But I must think of nothing save the need to hold on, to keep my identity in this hidden place. I must hold and hold and hold!

But I could no longer—Molaster! Great were the powers once given me, much did I increase them by training. But there comes an end to all—and that faces me now. I have lost, I cannot remember that pattern of life which I was shown. Though I know its importance and know that not by the will of the Great Design was it interrupted for me. Yet it would seem that I have not the strength to finish out my part of it. I—cannot—hold—

Pain rushed in as a great scarlet wave to drown me.

"Maelen!"

One voice only now. Had that other given up? But I thought that even yet, were I to yield, it would sweep me into its web.

"Maelen!"

"Freeze—" I could shape only that one last plea. And so futile, so hopeless a one it was. There came no answer.

None—save that the pain grew less, now almost bearable. And I had not been cut free from the body. What—

"Maelen!"

I was in the body still. Though I did not command it, yet it served as an anchor. And there was a freedom from that pressure which had been upon me. As if the process of my "death" had been arrested, and I was to be given a short breathing space.

"Maelen!" Imperative, imploring—that call.

I summoned up the dregs of my energy.

"Krip—freeze—"

"Yes, Maelen. You are in the case—the case of the alien. Maelen—what—"

So—he had done it. He had taken that last small chance and it was the right one. But I had no time for rejoicing, not now. I must let him know the final answer.

"Keep freeze—Old Ones—Yiktor—"

My hold on consciousness, if one could term that state of rigid defense "consciousness," broke. Did I walk the White Road now? Or was there still a place for me in the great pattern?

Chapter 13

KRIP VORLUND

The wind could not reach fully here, still my hands were numb. I watched the box. How I had ever mastered its catches, opened it long enough to pull out the body it had contained and put the broken, limp, bloodied bundle of fur in its place, I did not know. I shook with shock more than with chill, weak with the effort of transporting what had been Maelen across the rocky way, sure that she—that no living thing could survive such handling in the state I found her after that terrible fall. Yet she had lived, she was in freeze now. And I swore she would get to Yiktor— to the Old Ones—that she was not going to die! Though how I might do this I did not know.

I edged around. There stood the *Lydis* far below, the two flitters. No sign of life about them. Something else lay here among the rocks. I stared, and my shudders grew worse. The alien I had pulled so hastily from the freeze box—

But no body lay there—only a crumbling mass. I covered my eyes. Lukas had said it was dead, and his words were being proved now. Not that it mattered

171

—nothing did, save Maelen. And the warning which must be delivered. Harkon, Lidj—were they still men or—And who else? All those who had gone out against an enemy infinitely stronger than we had suspected?

I put out my hand to the freeze box as gently as I might have laid it on a furred head.

"I cannot take you with me now," I thought. Perhaps I could still reach her, perhaps not. But I had to try to make her understand that I was not deserting her. "I shall be back—and you shall see Yiktor, the Old Ones—live again. I swear it!"

Then I set about wedging that box even more tightly among the rocks, making very sure that it could not be shifted by any freak of wind or storm. If she was safe now, that covering must endure until I could fulfill my promise.

Having done what I could to ensure her protection, I descended through the lashing of wind and sleet to the floor of the valley. Reaching there, I used my wrist com, clicking out the code which ought to open the *Lydis* to me, waiting tensely for some sign that the call had been heard within the ship.

My answer came, not from the ship, but out of the night. A flash beam cut the black, pinned me against the rock wall of the cliff. Jacks—they had beaten me here!

I was so dazzled by that ray that I could not see who was behind it, though I believed they were moving in for the kill. I had no weapon now. Then someone stepped out into the light beam and I saw the uniform. Patrol! Only now that could be no reassurance either. Not since I had seen Harkon and Lidj in the cavern and knew what walked in Griss's body.

I tried to read in his face whether he was what he seemed or one of the enemy, but there was no clue in either eyes or expression. He motioned with his hand. The howling of the wind was far too loud to allow speech, but his gesture was toward the *Lydis*. Then the beam flashed downward, pointing a path to the ship, the upper edge of it catching the slow descent of the ramp. I went.

The *Lydis* had been my home for years, and I had felt privileged that that was so. But now, as I climbed her ramp, using handholds to drag myself up against the sweep of the wind, it was as if I approached something alien, with a whiff of trap about it. It could be just that, if the contagion of the aliens had spread this far.

I found myself sniffing as I came through the lock, the Patrolman behind me, as if I could actually scent that alien evil I feared to find here. But there was only the usual smell of a star ship. I began to climb the ladder to the control cabin. What would I find there?

"Vorlund!"

Captain Foss. And beyond him a Patrol officer with the stellar sword badge of a commander. Others— Though it was on Foss I centered my attention. If it *was* Foss. How could I be sure? What might have happened during that endless time I wandered under ground? I did not answer but only stared at him, searching his face for any hint that he was not the man I knew.

Then one of the Patrolmen who had followed me up the ladder took me by the arm, turned me a little as if I were totally helpless, and pushed me down into the astrogator's chair, which swung as my weight settled in it. I dared to try mind-probe—for I had to know if there was yet time.

173

"You *are* Foss!" My voice sounded thin, hardly above a whisper.

Then I saw his expression change, recognized that slight lift of one brow—something I had seen many times in the past.

"You were expecting someone else?" he asked.

"One of them." I was near to babbling, suddenly so tired, so drained of energy. "Like Griss—one of them—inside your body."

No one spoke. Had I said that at all, or only thought it?

Then the captain turned to the emergency dispenser on the wall, twirled its dial, brought out a sustain tube. He came over to me. I tried to raise my hand to take that restorative. My body would not obey. He held it to my mouth and I drank. The stuff was hot, fighting the chill and shaking weariness in me.

"One of them—inside my body?" he said as if that were the most natural condition. "Perhaps you had better explain."

"Back there." I gestured to the wall of the *Lydis*, hoping I was indicating the direction of the burrows. "Aliens. They can take over our bodies. They did with Griss. He's—he's in the alien body now—behind a wall. He—" I shut out that memory of Griss imprisoned in the motionless body wearing the reptilian crown. "I think maybe Lidj, Harkon, too. They were too much at ease there in the cavern, as if they had nothing to fear. Maybe others—They tried to do it with me—didn't work. The alien was angry, said I was dangerous—to put me in the dark—Then I found Maelen."

Maelen! In that freeze box—on the cliff. Maelen!

"What about Maelen?" Foss had taken the pilot's

seat so that his eyes were now on a level with mine. He sat forward, and his hands took mine from where they lay limp, holding them in a firm, warm grip. "What happened to Maelen?"

I sensed a stir, as if the Patrol officer moved closer. Foss frowned, not at me.

"What about Maelen, Krip?"

"She fell—onto the rocks—all broken. Dying—she was dying! Told me—must freeze—freeze until I could get her home, back to Yiktor. I took her—all broken, broken—" I tried to sever the compelling stare with which he held me, to forget that nightmare of a journey, but he would not let me. "Took her to the alien—opened the box—took the alien's body out—put her in. She was still alive—then."

"These aliens." Foss's voice was level, clear. He held me by it as well as by the grip on my hands and wrists. "Do you know who they are?"

"Lukas said dead—a long time. But they are esper. And the crowned ones are not dead. Bodies—they want bodies! Griss, for sure, maybe the others. There are four of them—I saw—counting the woman."

"He doesn't make sense!" cut in an impatient voice.

Again Foss frowned in warning. "Where are these bodies?"

"Underground—passages—rooms. The jacks have a camp—in a cavern—ship outside. They were looting—rooms with chests." Memories made dizzy, whirling pictures in my head. I had a bitter taste in my mouth as if the restorative was rising now to choke me.

"Where?"

"Beyond the cache. I got in through the cat's mouth." I tried to control that nausea, to remain coherent. "Passage there. But they—Griss—can hold men with thought alone. If the rest are like him, you have no chance. Never met an esper like him before, not even Thassa. Maelen thought they could not take me over because I am part Thassa now. But they did take me prisoner—Griss did—just by willing it. They used a tangler on me after."

"Korde." Foss gave a swift order. "Scrambler on—highest frequency!"

"Yes, sir!"

Scrambler, I thought vaguely—scrambler? Oh, yes, defense against probes. But would it work against the thing in Griss's body?

"About the others." The Patrol commander had moved around behind Foss. "Where are the others—my men—yours?"

"I don't know. Only saw Griss, Harkon, Lidj—"

"And you think that Harkon and Lidj may also be taken over?"

"Saw them walking around in jack camp, not taking any precautions. Had the feeling they had no reason to fear discovery."

"Did you probe them?"

"Didn't dare. Probe, and if they were taken over, they would have taken us, Maelen and me. Griss—he knew I was there even before he saw me. He made me walk out into their hands. But—they acted as if they belonged in that camp. And there was no sign of the others with them."

I saw Foss nod. "Perhaps the right guess. You can sense danger."

"Take you over," I repeated. The restorative was no longer working. I was slipping away, unable to keep my eyes open. "Maelen—" They must help Maelen!

Chapter 14

KRIP VORLUND

There was no night or day in the interior of the *Lydis*, but I had that dazed feeling that one has when one has slept very heavily. I put up one hand to deliver the usual greeting rap on the side of the upper bunk. If Maelen had slept too—

Maelen! Her name unlocked memory and I sat up without caution, knocking my head painfully against the low-slung upper bunk. Maelen was still out there —in the freeze box! She must be brought in, put under such safeguards as the ship could give. How had I come to forget about her?

I was already on my feet, reaching for the be-grimed thermo clothing dropped in a heap on the floor, when the door panel opened. I looked around to see the captain.

Foss was never one to reveal his thoughts on his face. A top Trader learns early to dissemble or to wear a mask. But there are small signs, familiar to those who live in close company, which betray strong emotions. What I saw now in Foss was a controlled anger which I had known only once or twice during the time I had shipped on board the *Lydis*.

Deliberately he entered my cabin without invitation. That act in itself showed the gravity of the situation. For privacy is so curtailed on board a spacer that each member of the crew is overly punctilious about any invasion of another's. He pulled down one of the wall seats and sat in it, still saying nothing.

But I was in no mood to sit and talk, if that was his intention. I wanted Maelen as safe as I could make her. I had no idea how long I had slept, leaving her exposed to danger.

Since the captain seemed in no hurry to announce his business with me, I broke silence first.

"I must get Maelen. She is in an alien freeze box—up on the cliffs. I must get her into our freeze compartment—" As I spoke I sealed my thermo jacket. But Foss made no move to let me by, unless I physically pushed him aside.

"Maelen—" Foss repeated her name, but there was something so odd about the tone of his voice that he caught my attention in spite of my impatience to be gone.

"Vorlund, how did it come about that you weren't with the rest—that you found your own way into that chain of burrows? You left here in company." His eyes held mine in intent measuring. Perhaps, had my mind not been largely on the need for reaching Maelen, I might have been uneasy, or taken partial warning from both his question and his attitude.

"I left them on the cliff top. Maelen called—she was in trouble."

"I see." He was still watching me with a measuring look, as if I were a piece of merchandise he had begun to suspect was not up to standard. "Vorlund—" Suddenly he reached up and pressed a stud. The small locking cupboard sprang open. As the inner side of the door was a mirror, I found myself staring at my own face.

It always gave me a feeling almost of shock to see my reflection thus. After so many years of facing one image, it takes time to get used to another. My skin was somewhat browner than it had been on Yiktor. Yet it in no way matched the dark space tan which all the other crew members had and which I had once accepted as proper. Against even the slightest coloring my silver brows, slanting up to join the hairline on my temples, and the very white locks there, close-cropped as they were, had no resemblance to my former appearance. I now had the delicately boned Thassa face, the pointed chin.

"Thassa." Foss's word underlined what I saw reflected. "You told us on Yiktor that bodies did not matter, that you were still Krip Vorlund."

"Yes," I said when he paused, as if his words had a deep meaning to be seriously considered. "I am Krip Vorlund. Did I not prove it?"

Could he possibly think now that I was really Thassa? That I had managed to masquerade successfully all these months among men who knew me intimately?

"Are you? The Krip Vorlund, Free Trader, that we know would not put an alien above his ship—or his duty!"

I was shaken. Not only because he would say and think such a thing of me, but because there was truth in it! Krip Vorlund would not have left that squad on the cliff top—gone to answer Maelen. Or would he? But I *was* Krip. Or was it true, that shadowy fear of mine, that something of Maquad governed me?

"You see," Foss continued, "you begin to understand. You are not, as you swore to us, Krip Vorlund. You are something else. And this being so—"

I turned from the mirror to face him squarely. "You think I let the men down in some way? But I tell you, I would not have dared use esper—not around what controls Griss Sharvan now. Only such as Maelen might dare that. And *his* change was certainly none of my doing. If I had not acted as I did, would you have your warning now?"

"Only you did not go off on your own for us, to do our scouting."

I was silent, because again he was speaking the truth. Then he continued:

"If enough of Krip is left in you to remember our ways, you know that what you did was not Trader custom. What you appear to be is a part of you now."

That thought was as chilling as the fear I had faced in the burrows. If Foss saw me as an alien, what did I have left? Yet I could not allow that to influence me. So I turned on him with the best argument I could muster.

"Maelen is part of our safeguard. Such esper powers as hers are seldom at the service of any ship. Remember, it was she who smashed that amplifier up on the cliff, the one which held us all prisoner while you were gone. If we have to face these aliens it may be Maelen who will decide the outcome for us. She is crew! And she was in danger and called. Because I can communicate with her best, I heard her and I went."

"Logical argument." Foss nodded. "What I would expect, Vorlund. But you and I both know that there is more standing behind such words than you have mentioned."

"We can argue that out later, once we are free from

Sekhmet." Trader code or not, I was ridden by the need to get Maelen into what small safety the *Lydis* promised. "But Maelen has to be brought to our freeze unit—now!"

"I'll grant you that." To my vast relief the captain arose. Whether he accepted my plea that Maelen was crew, that her gifts were for our benefit, I could not tell. It was enough for the present that he would go to her aid.

I do not know what arguments he used with the Patrol to get them to help us, because I left him behind as I climbed to the cliff crest. There was no alien face behind the frostless top plate now. Maelen's small body took so little room in the box it was out of sight. My quick inspection of the fastenings proved that the container had not been disturbed since I had left it. And where I had put the alien body, there was nothing at all. The winds must have scoured away the last ashy remains hours ago.

Getting the box down the cliff face was an awkward job, one which we had to do slowly. But at length we brought it up the ramp of the *Lydis* by hand, not entrusting it to the robos. And the Patrol ship's medic waited to make the transfer to the ship's freeze unit.

Every stellar voyaging ship has such a unit to take care of any badly injured until they can be treated at some healing center. But I had not realized, even when I labored to take care of Maelen, how badly broken her glassia body was. And I think that the medic gave up when he saw that bloody bundle of matted fur. But he got a live reading, and that was enough to make him hurry to complete the transfer.

As the hasps locked on the freeze unit, I ran my hand along the top. There was the spark of life still in her; so far had her will triumphed over her body. I did not know how long she might continue to exist so, and the future looked very dark. Could I now possibly get her back to Yiktor? And even if I tracked down the Old Ones of the wandering Thassa and demanded a new body for her, would they give it to me? Where would such a body come from? Another animal form, to fulfill the fate they had set on her? Or perhaps one which was the result of some such case as gave me Maquad's—a body from the care of Umphra's priests, where those injured mentally beyond recovery were tended until Molaster saw fit to set their feet upon the White Road leading them out of the weary torment of their lives?

One step at a time. I must not allow myself to see all the shadows lying ahead. I had Maelen in the best safekeeping possible. In the freeze unit that spark of life within her would be tended with all the care my people knew. A little of the burden had been lifted from me, but much still remained. Now I knew that I owed another debt—as Foss had reminded me. I was ready to pay it as best I could. And I went to the control cabin to offer to do so.

I found Foss, the Patrol commander Borton, and the medic Thanel gathered around a box from which the medic was lifting a loop of wire. From the loop a very delicate collection of metal threads arched back and forth, weaving a cap. He handled this with care, turning it around so that the light glinted on the threads. Captain Foss looked around as I came up the ladder.

"We can prove it now. Vorlund is our top esper."

"Good enough. I am a fourth power myself." Thanel fitted the cap to his own head, the loop resting on his temples, the fine threads disappearing in his fair hair.

"Mind-send," he ordered me, "highest power."

I tried. But this was like beating against a wall. It was not the painful, shocking task it had been when I had brushed against the broadcast of the alien or faced the crowned one; rather it was like testing a complete shield. I said as much.

Borton had been holding a small object in his hand. Now he eyed me narrowly. But when he spoke he addressed Foss.

"Did you know he is a seven?"

"We knew he was high, but three trips ago he tested only a little more than five."

Five to seven! I had not known that. Was that change because of my Thassa body? Or had constant exchange with Maelen sharpened and raised my powers?

"You try this." Thanel held out the wire cap and I adjusted it on my head.

All three watched me closely and I could guess that Thanel was trying mind-send. But I picked up nothing. It was an odd sensation, as though I had plugged my ears and was deaf to all around me.

"So it works with a seventh power. But another broadcasting body with an amplifier, and this alien able to exchange identities, may be even stronger." Borton looked thoughtful.

"Our best chance." Thanel did not reach for the cap I still wore. Instead he took out four more. "These are experimental as yet. They held up under lab testing; that's why they have been issued for trial in the field. Sheer luck that we have them at all."

"As far as I can see," Borton observed, "we have little choice. The only alternative is to call in strong arms and blast that installation off Sekhmet. And if we do that we may be losing something worth more than the treasure the jacks have been looting—knowledge. We can't wait for reinforcements, either. Any move to penetrate their stronghold has to come fast, before these body snatchers can rise off-world to play their tricks elsewhere."

"We can get in through the cat's mouth. They may not yet know about that." I offered what I had to give. "I know that way."

In the end it was decided that the cat's mouth did give us the best chance of entering the enemies' territory. And we prepared to risk it. Five men only, as there were only five of the protect caps. Captain Foss represented the sadly dwindled force of the Traders, I was the guide, and the medic Thanel, Commander Borton, and a third from the Patrol force, an expert on X-Tee contacts, comprised our company.

The Patrol produced weapons more sophisticated than any I had ever seen before—an all-purpose laser type which could serve either as a weapon or as a tool. And these were subjected to a very fine adjustment by the electronics officer of the Patrol Scout, so that each would answer only to the finger pressure of the man authorized to carry it. Were it to fall into strange hands it would blow itself apart at the first firing.

Wearing the caps, so armed, and with fresh supplies, we climbed back over the cliffs. Though I could not be aware of any sentries while encapped, we moved with caution, once more a patrol in enemy country. And we spent a long number of moments watching for any sign that the wedge opening of the cat's mouth had been discovered. But the Patrol's persona reader raised no hint that any ambush awaited us there.

I led the way to the opening, once more squirming on my belly into that narrow passage. And as I wriggled forward I listened and watched for any alarm.

Though the first time I had made this journey I had had no way of measuring its length, I began now to wonder about that. Surely we must soon come to the barrier I had opened to allow me into the chamber above the place of the bodies. However, as I crawled on and on, I did not see it—though I carried a torch this time. Doubts of my own memory grew in my mind. Had I not been wearing that cap I would have suspected that I was now under some insidious mental influence.

On and on—yet I did not come to the door, the room beyond. The walls appeared to narrow, though I did not have to push against them any more than I had the first time. Yet the feeling of being caught in a trap increased with every body length that I advanced.

Then the torchlight picked out, not the door I had found before, but a series of notches in the walls, as the surface on which I crept slanted upward. This *was* new, but I had seen no breaks in the original tunnel wall. I was completely lost, but there was nothing to do but keep on. We could not retreat without great difficulty, strung out as we were without room to turn.

Those handholds in the wall allowed me to pull myself along as the incline became much steeper. I still could not understand what had happened. Only one possible explanation presented itself—that I had been under mental compulsion the *first* time I invaded this space. But the reason for such confusion?

Unless the aliens had devised such a defense to discourage looters. There were warping devices. Such were known; they had been found on Atlas—small there, to be sure, but still working—a device to conceal a passage from the eye or other senses. There had been tombs on other worlds which had been protected by all manner of ingenious devices to kill, maim, or seal up forever those who dared to explore them without knowledge of their secret safeguards.

And if this was so—what did lie before us now? I could be leading our small party directly into danger. Yet I was not sure enough of my deductions to say so. There was a jerk on one of my boots, nearly strong enough to drag me backward.

"Where," came a sharp whisper out of the dark, "is this hall of the sleeping aliens you spoke of?"

A good question, and one for which I had no answer. I might only evade until I knew more.

"Distances are confusing—it must still lie ahead." I tried to remember if I had described my other journey in detail. If so, they must already know this was different. Now I attempted to speed up my wormlike progress.

The torch showed me an abrupt left turn in the passage and I negotiated that with difficulty, only to face just such a barrier as I had found before. With a sigh of relief, I set my fingers in that hole, tugged the small door open. However, as I crawled through, my hopes were dashed. This was not the chamber overlooking the hall of the freeze boxes. Rather I came out in a much wider corridor where a man might walk upright, but without any other doors along it. I swung out and tried once again to relate my present surroundings to what I had seen before.

Certainly if I had been under the spell of some hallucinatory trick the first time, I would not have been led straight to one of their places for freezing their army. That should have been the last place to which they would have wanted to guide any intruder. Perhaps the Patrol caps, instead of protecting, had failed completely—so that *this* was the hallucination?

I had moved away from the entrance. Now, one by one, the others came through to join me. It was Captain Foss and Borton who turned upon me.

"Where are we, Vorlund?" Foss asked.

There was nothing left but the truth. "I don't know—"

"This hall of boxed aliens, where is it?"

"I don't know." I had my hand to that tight cap. If I took it off—what would I see? Was touch as much affected as sight? Some hallucinations could be so strong that they enmeshed all the senses. But almost desperately now, I turned to the rock wall, running my finger tips along its surface, hoping touch would tell me that this was only an illusion which I could thereby break.

I was allowed very little time for that inspection. The tight and punishing grip of Foss's hand brought me around to face the four I had led here.

"What are you doing?"

Could I ever make them believe that I was as much a victim now as they? That I honestly had no idea of what had happened or why?

"This is not the way I came before. It may be an illusion—"

I heard a harsh exclamation from Thanel. "Impossible! The cap would prevent that!"

Borton cut in on the medic. "There is a very simple explanation, captain. It would seem that we have been tricked by your man here." He did not look at me at all now, but rather at Foss, as if he held the captain to account for my actions.

But it was Foss's hand which went swiftly to my belt, disarmed me. And I knew in that moment that all the years of our past comradeship no longer stood witness for me.

"I don't know *who* you are now," Foss said, eyeing me as if he expected to face one of the aliens. "But when your trap springs shut, I promise you, we shall be ready to attend to you also!"

"Do we go back?" The other Patrolman stood by the tunnel door.

"I think not," Borton said. "I have no liking to be bottled up in there if we have to face trouble."

Foss had put my weapon inside his jacket. Now he made a sudden move behind me, caught my wrists before I was aware of what he planned to do. A moment later I found my hands secured behind my back. Even yet I could not believe that I had been so repudiated by my captain, that a Free Trader could turn on a crew member without allowing him a chance to defend himself.

"Which way?" he said in my ear as he tested my bonds. "Where are your friends waiting for us, Vorlund? But remember this—we have your Maelen. Serve us ill and you will never see her again. Or was your great concern for her only lip-deep and used as an excuse?"

"I know no more of what has happened than I have told you," I said, though I had no hope at all that he would believe me now. "The difference in the passages is as big a surprise to me as it is to you. There are old tales of tombs and treasures guarded by clever devices. Such a one could have been set here—perhaps this time defeated by our caps—"

"You expect us to believe that? When you told us that your very first explorations here brought you to a tomb, if tomb that hall was?" Foss's incredulity was plain.

"Why would I lead you into a trap, when I would also be caught in it?" I made a last try.

"Perhaps we have missed connections somewhere with the welcoming party," was Foss's answer. "Now —I asked you, Vorlund—which way?"

"I don't know."

The medic Thanel spoke up then. "That may be true. He could have been taken over, just as he said those others are. The cap might have broken that." He shrugged. "Take your choice of explanations."

"And choice of paths as well," Borton said. "Suppose we head right."

Borton and the Patrolman took the lead, Foss walked beside me, Thanel brought up the rear. The corridor was just wide enough for two of us to walk abreast. As was true elsewhere, there was breathable air introduced here by some ingenious method of the constructors, though I never sighted any duct by which it could enter. Underfoot there was a thick carpet of dust which showed no disturbed marking— proof, I thought, that this was no traveled way.

The passage ended abruptly in a crossway in which were set two doors, both closed. Our torches, shone directly on them, displayed painted patterns there. Each I had seen before, and perhaps I made some sound as I recognized them. Foss spoke to me.

"This—you know it!" He made it an accusation rather than a question.

What was clearly there in bold lines inlaid with strips of metal (not painted as I had first thought) was the narrow cat mask of the cliff. The slanted eyes of the creature were gems which caught fire from our torches. The other door bore the likeness of the crown of another alien—that which resembled a prick-eared, long-muzzled animal.

"They are the signs of the alien crowns!"

Thanel had gone to the cat door, was running his hand along the portal's outline.

"Locked, I would say. So do we use the laser on it?"

Borton made his own careful inspection. "Don't want to set off any alarms. What about it, Vorlund? You're the only one who knows this place. How do we open this?" He looked to me as if this was some test of his own devising.

I was about to answer that I knew no more than he, when Foss gave an exclamation. His hands went to the cap on his hand. He was not the only one to receive that jolt of force. Thanel's lips twisted. He spoke slowly, one word at a time, as if he were repeating some message to be relayed to the rest of us.

"The—eyes—"

It was Borton, now standing closest to the panel, who cupped one palm over each of those glittering gems. I wanted to warn him off; my effort to cry out was a pain in my throat. But my only sound was a harsh croak.

I threw myself forward, struck the weight of my shoulder against his arm, striving to dislodge his hands. Then Foss's grip dragged me back in spite of my struggles.

There was a grating sound. Borton dropped his hands. The door was moving, lifting straight up. Then it stopped, leaving a space through which a man, stooping, might pass.

"Don't go in there!" Somehow I managed to utter that warning. It was so plain to me, the aura of danger which spread from that hole like an invisible net to enfold us, that I could not understand why they did not also feel it. Too late; Borton had squeezed under the door, never glancing at me, his eyes so fixed on what lay ahead that he might be walking in a spell. After him went Thanel and the other Patrolman. Foss pushed me forward with a shove which was emphatic. I could not fight him.

So I passed under the barrier with every nerve alert to danger, knowing that I was a helpless prisoner facing a great peril I could not understand.

Chapter 15

KRIP VORLUND

I did not know what to expect, except that this place was so filled with a feeling of danger it might have been a monster's den. But what I saw looked far from dangerous, on the surface at least. I believe we were all a little dazed at the wonder of our find. The Throne of Qur, yes, that had been enough to incite cupidity as well as enchant the beholder. But that artifact was akin to a common bench in an inn compared to what was now gathered before us. Though I had not seen the temple treasures unpacked, still at that moment I was sure that all here outshone those.

There was a light which did not issue from our torches. And the contents of the chamber were not hidden from view in boxes and bundles, though there were two chests against the wall. The wall itself was inlaid with metal and stones. One section was formed of small, boxed scenes which gave one the illusion of gazing out through windows upon landscapes in miniature. I heard a sharp catch of breath from someone in our party. Then Borton advanced to the central picture.

That displayed a stretch of desert country. In the

middle of the waste of sand arose a pyramid, shaped like those two rooms I had seen here. Save that this was out in the open, an erection of smoothed stone.

"That—that can't be!" The Patrol commander studied the scene as if he wanted someone to assure him that he did not view what his eyes reported. "It is impossible!"

I believed that he knew that building in the sand, that he had either seen it himself or viewed it on some tri-dee tape.

"It's—it's incredible!" Foss was not looking at the picture which had captured the commander's attention. Instead he gazed from one treasure to another as if he could not believe he was not dreaming.

As I have said, the contents of the room were all placed as if this chamber was in use as living quarters. The painted and inlaid chests stood against a wall on which those very realistic pictures were separated by hangings of colored stuffs, glowingly alive. Those possessed a surface shimmer so that one could not be sure, even when one stared at them, whether the odd rippling shadows which continually flickered and faded were indeed half-seen figures in action. Yet the strips hung motionless.

There were two high-backed chairs, one flanked by a small table which rested on a tripod of slender legs. Carved on the back of one chair was the cat mask, this time outlined in silver on a dead-black surface. The second chair was of a misty blue, bearing on its back a complicated design in pure white.

On the floor under our dusty boots lay a pattern of blocks, black as one chair, blue as the other, and inlaid with more symbols in silver. On the tripod table were small plates of crystal and a footed goblet.

Thanel crossed to the nearest chest. Catching his

fingers under its projecting edge, he lifted, and the lid came up easily. We saw that the box was filled to the brim with lengths of color, green which was also blue, a warm yellow—perhaps garments. He did not take out any of them.

Chests, the two chairs, the table, and, directly facing the door, not another wall but a curtain of the same material as the wall panels. Foss started toward that and I followed close behind— It was beyond— He must not!

I was too late. He had already found the concealed slit which allowed one to pass through. I went closely on his heels, though I had already guessed what lay beyond. Guessed? No, *knew!*

And knowing, I expected to be met by a blast of the freezing air of stass-freeze— Come to think of it, why had we not already felt that in the outer chamber?

She lay with her head and shoulders supported by a thick cushion, gazing away from us, out through the crystal wall. But the tendrils of her crown swayed and entwined, moved, their cat-headed tips turning instantly, not only facing us, but making sharp jerking darts back and forth. It was as if those heads fought to detach the ties which held them to the circlet about the red hair, that they might come flying at us.

If she was not in freeze, then how had she been preserved? She could not be asleep, for her eyes were open. Nor could one detect even the slightest rise and fall of normal breathing.

"Thanel!" Foss went no further in. At the sound of his summons the cat heads spun and jerked, went into a wild frenzy of action.

I was shoved aside as the medic joined us.

"Is—is she alive?" Foss demanded.

Thanel produced his life-force detect. Making some adjustments, he advanced. And it seemed to me he went reluctantly, glancing now and then at the whirling crown. He held the instrument up before the reclining woman, studied its dial with a gathering frown, triggered some button, and once more took a reading.

"Well, is she?" Foss persisted.

"Not alive. But not dead either."

"And what does that mean?"

"Just what I said." Thanel pushed the button again with the forefinger of his other hand. "It doesn't register either way. And I don't know of any life force so alien that this can't give an instant decision on the point. She isn't in freeze, not in this atmosphere. But if she is dead I have never seen such preservation before."

"Who is dead?" Borton came through the curtain now with the other Patrolman, stopped short when he saw her.

I could no longer watch the woman. There was something in the constant motion of her cat-headed coronet which disturbed me, as if those whirling thumb-sized bits of metal wove a hypnotic spell. I made my last effort to warn them.

"Dead or alive"—my voice was harsh, too loud in the confinement of that room—"she reaches for you now. I tell you—she is dangerous!"

Thanel looked at me. The others stood, their attention all for her as if they had heard nothing. Then the medic caught at the commander's arm, gave a sudden swift pull which brought Borton around so he no longer eyed her squarely. He blinked, swallowed as if he had gulped a mouthful of some potent brew.

"Move!" The medic gave him a second push.

Borton, still blinking, stumbled back toward the curtain, knocking against Foss. I was already on the other side of the captain, had set my shoulder against his, using the same tactics Thanel had, if in a more clumsy fashion. And once shoved out of direct line with the woman, he, too, seemed to wake.

In the end we all got back on the other side of the curtain and stood there, breathing a little heavily, almost as if we had been racing. I was aware that the cap on my head was warm, that the line of wire touching my temples was near burning me. I saw Thanel touch his own band, snatch his fingers away. But Foss was at my side.

"Turn around."

I obeyed his order, felt him busy at my wrists. A moment later my hands were free.

"I can believe," he said, "in anything happening here, Vorlund. After seeing that, I can believe! She is just as you described her. And I believe she is deadly!"

"What about the others?" Thanel asked.

"There is one there." I rubbed my left wrist with my right hand, nodding in the direction where the next compartment must lie. "Two more on the other two sides. One held Griss when I was here before."

Borton went again to that picture of the pyramid. "Do you know what this is?"

"No. But it is plain to guess you have seen its like before, and not on Sekhmet," Foss returned. "Does it have any importance for us now?"

"Perhaps. That—that was built on Terra in a past so distant we can no longer reckon it accurately. By accounts the archaeologists have never agreed on its age. It is supposed to have been erected by slave labor at a time when man had not yet tamed a beast of burden, had not discovered the wheel. And yet it was a great feat of highly sophisticated engineering. There were countless theories about it, one being that its measurements, because of their unusual accuracy, held a message. It was not the only such either, but one of several. Though this particular one was supposed to be the first and greatest. For a long time the pile was said to be the tomb of a ruler. But that theory was never entirely proved—for the tomb itself might have been a later addition. At any rate, it was built millennia before our breed took to space!"

"But Forerunner remains," Thanel objected. "Those were never found on Terra. None of the history tapes records such discoveries."

"Perhaps no remains recognized as such by us. But—" Borton shook his head. "What do we even know of Terra now except from tapes copied and recopied, some of them near-legendary? Yet—and this is also very odd indeed—in the land where that stood" —he pointed to the picture—"they once worshiped gods portrayed with human bodies and beast or bird bird heads. In fact—there was a cat-headed goddess Sekhmet, a bird-headed Thoth, a saurian Set—"

"But these planets, this system, were named by the First-in Scout who mapped them, after the old custom of naming systems for ancient gods!" Foss interrupted.

"That is true. The Scouts gave such names as suited their fancies—culled from the tapes they carried with them to relieve the boredom of spacing. And the man who named this system must have had a liking for Terran history. Yet—he could also have been influenced in some way." Borton again shook his head. "We may never know the truth of the past, save this is such a find as may touch on very ancient mysteries, even those of our own beginnings!"

"And we may not have a chance to learn anything, unless we get to the bottom of a few modern mysteries now!" Foss retorted.

I noted that he kept his head turned away from the curtain, almost as if she who waited beyond it might have the power to pull him back into her presence. The wires of my cap no longer were heated; but I was unhappy in this place, I wanted out.

"That crown she wears—" Thanel shifted from one foot to another as if he wanted to look at the woman again. I saw Borton shake his head. "I would say it is a highly sensitive communication device of some sort. What about it, Laird?"

"Undoubtedly—" began the other Patrolman. "Didn't you feel the response of your protect? The caps were close to shorting, holding against that energy. What about the crowns the others wear?" He turned to me. "Are they alive—moving—also?"

"Not that I saw. They aren't shaped the same."

"I want to see the alien body holding Griss," Foss broke in. "Is that in the next chamber?"

I shook my head. And I had no idea of how one reached either the interior of the crystal-lined pyramid room or the other chambers which formed its walls. There had been another door beside the cat one. But side by side—when the rooms were at right angles—how—

Foss did not wait for my guidance. He slipped under the outer door and we were quick to follow. Thanel brought down the cat door, it moving much more easily to close than it had to open. Foss was already at work on the other door. It yielded as reluctantly as the first had done, but it did go up. However, we did not look now on a room filled with treasures, but on a very narrow passage, so confined one had to turn sideways to slip along it. This made a right-angled turn and then there was a second curtained doorway ahead.

"This one?" Foss demanded.

"No." I tried to remember. "Next, I think."

We slipped along that slit between walls to a second sharp turn, which brought us so that we must now be facing directly across from the chamber of the cat woman, if we could have seen through solid walls. Once more there was a door, this one patterned with the bird head. A third turn and we found what I had been searching for—the saurian.

"This is it!"

The door panel was doubly hard to dislodge because there was so little room in which to move. However, it gave at last, Foss and I working at it as best we could.

Once more we were in a furnished room. But we spent no time in surveying the treasures there, hurrying on instead through the curtain to the fore part. I could see now the crowned head, the bare shoulders of him who sat there, staring stonily out into the space beyond the crystal.

Foss circled to be able to see the face of the seated one. There was no moving part of this crown, no stirring to suggest that we had found more than a perfectly preserved alien body. But I saw the captain's expression change, knew that he could read the eyes in that set face and felt the same horror I had felt.

"Griss!" His whisper was a hiss.

I did not want to view what Foss now faced with grim determination, yet I knew that I must. So I edged forward on the other side of the chair, looked into the tortured eyes. Griss—yes—and still conscious, still aware of what had happened to him! Though I had passed through body change twice, both times it had been with my own consent and for a good purpose. However, had such a change been wrought against my will—could I have kept such knowledge and remained sane? I did not know.

"We have to do something!" The words exploded from Foss with the force of a blaster shot. I knew that he backed them with that determination which he had ever shown in the face of any peril that threatened the *Lydis* and those who called her their home. "You"—he spoke directly to me—"have tried this body exchange. What can you do for him?"

Always in such matters I had been the passive one, the one who was worked upon, not the mover in the act. Maelen had sung me into the barsk body when the Three Rings of Sotrath wreathed that moon over our heads, when the occult powers of the Thassa were at their greatest height. And I had passed into the shell of Maquad in the shelter of Umphra, where the priests of that gentle and protective order had been able to lend to Maelen all the aid she needed.

Once only had I seen the transfer for another— that in a time of fear and sorrow when Maelen had lain dying and one of her little people, Vors, had crept to her side and offered her furred body as a refuge for the Thassa spirit. I had seen them sing the exchange then, two of the Thassa, Maelen's sister and her kinsman. And I had found myself also singing words I did not know. But that I alone could make such an exchange—no.

"I can do—" I was about to add "nothing" when a thought came from my own past. I had run as Jorth the barsk; I now walked as Maquad. Could it just be— If Griss tried, overcame his horror and fear of what had happened to him, could he command his new body, rule it until he could recapture his own? But I must get through to him first. And that would mean setting aside the protect cap.

I explained, not quite sure whether this could be done, even if I dared so break our own defenses and put us all in danger. But when I had made this clear Foss touched the butt of the laser.

"We have our defenses. You know what I mean— will you risk that also?"

Be burned down if I were taken over—no, I did not want to risk that, but want and a man's duty are two different things many times during one's life. I had turned aside from what the Traders considered my duty once already, here on Sekhmet. It seemed that now I had a second chance to repay old debts. And I remembered how Maelen had faced exile in an alien body because she had taken up a debt.

"It may be his only chance."

Quickly, before I could falter, I reached for the cap on my head. I saw them move to encircle me, weapons ready. They all eyed me warily as if I were now the enemy. I took off the cap.

My head felt light, free, as if I had removed some burden which had weighed heavily without my even being aware of it. I had a moment of hesitation, as one might feel stepping out into an arena such as those on Sparta where men face beasts in combat. From which direction could an attack come? And I believe those around me waited tensely for some hideous change in me.

"Griss?" The impression that time was limited set me directly to work. "Griss!" I was not a close comrade of this poor prisoner. But we were shipmates;

we had drawn matching watch buttons many times, shared planet leaves. It had been through him I had first learned who and what Maelen was. And now I consciously drew upon that friendship of the past to buttress my sending.

"Griss!" And this time—

"Krip—can you—can you hear me?" Incredulous thankfulness.

"Yes," I came directly to the importance of what must be done. "Griss, can you rule this body? Make it obey you?" The question was the best way I knew of trying to make him break down a barrier which might have been built by his own fears. Now he must try to direct the alien husk, even as a control board directs a labor robo.

I had had a hard time adjusting to an animal form; at least he did not have to face that. For the alien, to our eyes, was humanoid.

"Can you rule the body, Griss?"

His surprise was easy to read. I knew that he had not considered that at all, that the initial horror of what had happened to him had made him believe himself helpless from the first. Whereas I had been helped through my transitions by foreknowledge, and also by the aid of Maelen, who was well versed in such changes, he had been brutally taken prisoner in such a way as to paralyze even his thought processes for a time. It is always the unknown which carries with it, especially for my species, the greatest fear.

"Can I?" he asked as might a child.

"Try—concentrate!" I ordered him with authority. "Your hand—your right hand, Griss. Raise it—order it to move!"

His hands rested on the arms of the chair in which

he sat. His head did not move a fraction, but his eyes shifted away from mine, in a visible effort to see his hands.

"Move it!"

The effort he unleashed was great. I hastened to feed that. Fingers twitched—

"Move!"

The hand rose, shaking as if it had been so long inert that muscles, bone, flesh could hardly obey the will of the brain. But it rose, moved a little away from the support of the chair arm, then wavered, fell limply upon the knee. But he had moved it!

"I—I did it! But—weak—very—weak—"

I looked to Thanel. "The body may be in need of restoratives—perhaps as when coming out of freeze."

He frowned. "No equipment for that type of restoration."

"But you must have something in your field kit—some kind of basic energy shot."

"Alien metabolism," he murmured, but he brought out his field kit, unsealed it. "We can't tell how the body will react."

"Tell him—" Griss's thought was frantic. "Try anything! Better be dead than like this!"

"You are far from dead," I countered.

Thanel held an injection cube, still in its sterile envelope. He bent over the seated body to affix the cube on the bare chest over the spot where a human heart would have been. At least it did adhere, was not rejected at once.

That body gave a jerk as visible shudders ran along the limbs.

"Griss?"

"Ahhh—" No message, just a transferred sensation of pain, of fear. Had Thanel been right and the restorative designed for our species proved dangerous to another?

"Griss!" I caught at that hand he had moved with such effort, held it between both of mine. Only my tight grasp kept it from flailing out in sharp spasms. The other had snapped up from the chair arm, waved in the air. The legs kicked out; the body itself writhed, as if trying to rise and yet unable to complete such movement.

Now that frozen, expressionless face came alive. The mouth opened and shut as if he screamed, though no sound came from his lips. Those lips themselves drew back, flattened in the snarl of a cornered beast.

"It's killing him!" Foss put out a hand as if to knock that cube away, but the medic caught his wrist.

"Let it alone! To interrupt now *will* kill."

I had captured the other hand, held them both as I struggled to reach the mind behind that tortured face.

"Griss!"

He did not answer. However, his spasms were growing less; his face was no longer so contorted. I did not know if that was a good or a bad sign.

"Griss?"

"I—am—here—" The thought-answer was so slow it came like badly slurred speech. "I—am—still—here—"

I detected a dull wonder in his answer, as if he were surprised to find it so.

"Griss, can you use your hands?" I released the grip with which I had held them, laid them back on his knees.

They no longer shook nor waved about. Slowly they rose until they were chest-high before him. The fingers balled into fists, straightened out again, wriggled one after another as if they were being tested.

"I can!" The lethargy of his answer of only moments earlier was gone. "Let me—let me up!"

Those hands went to the arms of the chair. I could see the effort which he expended to use them to support him to his feet. Then he made it, stood erect, though he wavered, kept hold of the chair. Thanel was quickly at one side, I at the other, supporting him. He took several uncertain steps, but those grew firmer.

The restorative cube, having expended its charge, loosened and fell from his chest, which arched and fell now as he drew deep breaths into his lungs. Again I had reason to admire the fine development of this body. It was truly as if some idealized sculpture of the human form had come to life. He was a good double palms' space taller than either of us who walked with him, and muscles moved more and more easily under his pale skin.

"Let me try it alone." He did not mind-speak now, but aloud. There was a curious flatness to his tone, a slight hesitation, but we had no difficulty in understanding him. And we released our hold, though we stood ready if there was need.

He went back and forth, his strides sure and balanced now. And then he paused by the chair, put both his hands to his head, and took off the grotesque crown, dropping it to clang on the seat as he threw it away.

His bared skull was hairless, like that of the body in the freeze box. But he ran his hands back and forth across the skin there as if he wanted to reassure himself that the crown was gone.

"I did it!" There was triumph in that. "Just as you thought I could, Krip. And if I can—they can too!"

Chapter 16

KRIP VORLUND

"Who are *they?*" Foss asked.

"Lidj—the Patrol officer—there and there!" He faced the outer transparent wall of the room, pointed right and left to those other two aliens on display. "I saw them—saw them being brought in, forced to exchange. Just as was done with me!"

"I wonder why such exchanges are necessary," Thanel said. "If we could restore this body, why didn't they just restore their own? Why go through the business of taking over others?"

Griss was rubbing his forehead with one hand. "Sometimes—sometimes I know things—things they knew. I think they value their bodies too highly to risk them."

"Part of their treasures!" Foss laughed harshly. "Use someone else to do their work for them, making sure they have a body to return to if that substitute suffers any harm. They're as cold-blooded as harpy night demons! Well, let's see if we can get Lidj and that man of yours out of pawn now."

Borton leaned over the edge of the chair, reaching

for the crown Griss had thrown there.

"No!" In a stride Griss closed the distance between them, sent the crown spinning across the floor. "In some way that is a com, giving them knowledge of what happens to the body—"

"Then, with your breaking that tie," I pointed out, "they—or he—will be suspicious and come looking—"

"Better that than have him force me under control again without my knowing when that might happen!" Griss retorted.

If the danger he seemed to believe in did exist, he was right. And we might have very little time.

Borton spoke first. "All the more reason to try to get the others free."

"Which one is Lidj?" Foss was already going.

"To the left."

That meant the bird-headed crown. We returned to the anteroom. Griss threw open one of the chests as if he knew exactly what he was looking for. He dragged out a folded bundle and shook it out, to pull on over his bare body a tightly fitting suit of dull black. It was all of a piece including footgear, even gloves, rolled back now about the wrists, and a hood which hung loose between the shoulders. A press of finger tip sealed openings, leaving no sign they had ever existed.

There was something odd about that garment. The dull black seemed to produce a visual fuzziness, so that only his head and bared hands were well-defined. It must have been an optical illusion, but I believed that with the gloves and hood on he might be difficult to see.

"How did you know where to find that?" Borton was watching him closely.

Griss, who had been sealing the last opening of his

clothing, stopped, his finger tip still resting on the seam. There was a shadow of surprise on his handsome face.

"I don't know—I just knew that it was there and I must wear it."

Among them all, I understood. This was the old phenomenon of shape-changing—the residue (hopefully the very *small residue*) of the earlier personality taking over for some actions. But there was danger in that residue. I wondered if Griss knew that, or if we would have to watch him ourselves lest he revert to the alien in some more meaningful way.

Thanel must have been thinking along the same lines, for now he demanded: "How much do you remember of alien ways?"

Griss's surprise was tinged with uneasiness.

"Nothing! I was not even thinking—just that I needed clothing. Then I knew where to find it. It—I just knew—that's all!"

"How much else would he 'just know,' I wonder?" Borton looked to Thanel rather than to Griss, as if he expected a better explanation from the medic.

"Wasting time!" Foss stood by the door. "We have to get Lidj and Harkon! And get out before anyone comes to see what happened to Griss."

"What about my cap?" I asked.

Thanel had passed that to the other Patrolman. And in this place I wanted all the protection I could get. The other held it out to me and I settled it on my head with a sigh of relief, though with it came the sensation of an oppressive burden.

We threaded along that very narrow passage to the next chamber, where the alien with the avian crown half-reclined on the couch. Having freed one "exchange" prisoner, I now moved with confidence. And it was not so difficult, as Juhel Lidj had greater esper power.

Then we retraced our way and released Harkon also. But I do not believe that Borton was entirely happy over such additions to our small force. They had put aside their crowns, and they were manifestly eager to move against those who had taken their bodies. But whether they would stand firm during a confrontation, we could not know.

We returned to the cat door. There I lingered a moment, studying the mask symbol. Three men, one woman—who had they been? Rulers; priests and a priestess; scientists of another time and place? Why had they been left here? Was this a depository like our medical freezers, or a politically motivated safe-keep where rulers had chosen to wait out some revolution they had good reason to fear? Or—

It seemed to me that the gem eyes of the cat held a malicious glitter, mirroring superior amusement. As if someone knew exactly the extent of my ignorance and dismissed me from serious consideration because of it. A spark of anger flared deep inside me. Yet I did not underrate what lay beyond that door and could be only waiting for a chance to assume power.

"Now where?" Borton glanced about as if he expected some guide sign to flare into life.

"Our other men," Lidj answered that crisply. "They have them imprisoned somewhere—"

I thought that "somewhere" within these burrows was no guide at all. And it would seem Foss's thoughts marched with mine, for he asked:

"You have no idea where?"

It was Harkon who answered. "Not where they are. Where *our* bodies are now, that is something else."

"You mean you can trace those?" Thanel demanded.

"Yes. Though whether mere confrontation will bring about another exchange—"

"How do you know?" The medic pursued the first part of his answer.

"I can't tell you. Frankly, I don't know. But I do know that whoever is walking about as Harkon right now is in that direction." There was no hesitation as he pointed to the right wall of the passage.

Only, not being able to ooze through solid rock, I did not see how that knowledge was going to benefit us. We had found no other passage during our way in (I was still deeply puzzled about the difference between my first venture into the maze and this one).

Harkon still faced that blank wall, a frown on his face. He stared so intently at the smoothed stone that one might well think he saw a pattern there—one invisible to us.

After a moment he shook his head. "Not quite here —farther on," he muttered. Nor did he enlarge on that, but started along close to the wall, now and then sweeping his finger tips across it, as if by touch he might locate what he could not find by sight. He was so intent upon that search that his concentration drew us along, though I did not expect any results from his quest. Then he halted, brought the palm of his hand against the stone in a hard slap.

"Right behind here—if we can break through."

"Stand aside." Whether Borton accepted him as a guide or not, the commander seemed willing to put it to the test. He aimed his weapon at the wall where Harkon had indicated, and fired.

The force of that weapon was awesome, more so perhaps because we were in such a confined space.

One moment there had been the solid rock of this planet's bone; the next—a dark hole. Before we could stop him, Harkon was into that.

We had indeed broken through into another corridor. This one was washed in gray light. Harkon did not hesitate, but moved along with such swift strides that we had to hurry to catch up.

That passage was short, for we soon came out on a gallery running along near the top of another pyramid-shaped chamber. This one was triple the size of the others I had seen. From our perch we looked down into a scene of clanking activity. There was a mass of machinery, installations of some sort, being uncrated, unboxed by robos. Pieces were lifted by raise cranes, transferred to transports. But those carriers ran neither on wheels nor—

"Antigrav!" Borton leaned nearer to the edge. "They have antigrav in small mobile units."

Antigrav we knew. But the principle could not be used in mobile units, only installed in buildings as a method of transport from floor to floor. Here these carriers, loaded with heavy burdens, swung along in ordered lines through a dark archway in the opposite wall.

"Where's the controller?" The other Patrolman peered over.

"Remote control, I would say." Foss stood up.

We had all fallen flat at the sign of the activity. But now Foss apparently thought we had nothing to fear. And a moment later he added:

"Those are programmed robos."

Programmed robos! The complexity of the operation here on Sekhmet increased with every discovery we made. Programmed robos were not ordinarily ship workers, like the controlled ones we had earlier seen and used ourselves. They were far more intricate, requiring careful servicing, which made them impractical for use on primitive worlds. One did not find them on the frontier. Yet here they were at work light-years away from the civilizations producing them. Shipping these here, preparing them for work, would have been a major task in itself.

"In a jack hideout?" Foss protested.

"Look closer!" Borton was still watching below. "This is a storehouse which is being systematically looted. And who would have situated it here in the first place—"

"Forerunners," Lidj answered him. "But machines —this is not a tomb, nor—"

"Nor a lot of things!" Borton interrupted. "There were Forerunner installations found on Limbo. The only difference is that those were abandoned, not stored away. Here—perhaps a whole civilization was kept—both men and machines! And the Forerunners were not a single civilization, either—even a single species. Ask the Zacathans—they can count you off evidence of perhaps ten which have been tentatively identified, plus fragments of other, earlier ones which have not! The universe is a graveyard of vanished races, some of whom rose to heights we cannot assess today. These machines, if they can be made to work again, their purposes learned—"

I think that the possibilities of what he said awed us. Of course, we all knew of such treasure hunting as had been indulged in on Thoth—that was common. Lucky finds had been made all around the galaxy from time to time. The Zacathans, that immensely old, immensely learned reptilian race whose passion was the accumulation of knowledge, had their libraries filled with the lore of vanished—long-vanished—

stellar civilizations. They led their archaeological expeditions from world to world seeking a treasure they reckoned not in the furnishings of tombs, in the hidden hoards discovered in long-deserted ruins, but in the learning of those who had left such links with the far past.

And parties of men had made such finds also. They had spoken of Limbo—that had been the startling discovery of a Free Trader in the earlier days.

Yet the plunder from here had not yet turned up on any inner-planet market, where it would logically be sold. Its uniqueness would have been recognized instantly, for rumor of such finds spreads quickly and far.

"Suppose"—Foss, plainly fascinated, still watched the antigravs floating in parade order out of the storeroom—"the jacks, even the Guild, began this. But now it has been taken over by those others."

"Yes," came the dry, clipped answer from Lidj. "It could be that the original owners are now running the game." He raised both hands to his bald skull, rubbed his fingers across it. There was still a mark on his forehead from the weight of the crown.

"You mean—" Borton began.

Lidj turned on him. "Is that so strange? We put men in stass-freeze for years. In fact I do not know what has been the longest freeze time ending in a successful resuscitation. These might be awakened to begin life at the point where they left off, ready for their own plan of action. Do you deny that they have already proved they have secrets which we have not? Ask your own man, Harkon—how can he explain what has happened to the three of us?"

"But the others stored here—at least that one in the box above the valley—was dead." My protest was weak, because too much evidence was on Lidj's side.

"Perhaps most of them did die, perhaps that is why they want our bodies. Who knows? But I will wager that they—those three who took ours—are now in command of this operation!"

Harkon had drawn a little apart, perilously close to the edge of the balcony. Now he spoke in the same husky tone our cargomaster used.

"Can you set an interrupt beam on these lasers you have?" I did not understand what he meant, but apparently his question made sense to Borton, who joined him.

"Tricky—from here," the commander observed.

"Tricky or not, we can try it. Let me see yours—"

Did Borton hesitate for a moment before he passed over that weapon? If so, I could understand, since lurking at the back of my mind was a shadowy suspicion of these three. It is never easy to accept body exchange, even for one knowing the Thassa.

But Borton appeared willing to trust the pilot and passed over the laser. Harkon squatted against the sharply sloping wall, which made him hunch over the weapon. He snapped open the charge chamber, inspected the cartridge there, closed it once more, and reset the firing dial.

With it in his hand he went to peer down, selecting a victim. There was a robo to his left, now engaged in shifting a metal container onto one of the waiting transports. Harkon took aim and pressed the firing button.

A crackle of lightning sped like a whiplash, not to touch the robo itself, but to encircle its knoblike head. The robo had a flexible tentacle coiled about the container, ready to swing it across to the platform. But that move was never completed. The robo froze with the container still in the air.

"By the Teeth of Stanton Gore, you did it!" Borton's voice was almost shrill.

The pilot wasted no time in waiting for congratulations on his skill. He had already aimed at the next robo and stopped that one dead also.

"So you can knock them out," Lidj observed. "What do we do now—" Then he paused and caught at Borton's arm. "Is there a chance of resetting them?"

"We can hope so."

The robos I knew and had always used were control ones. Free Traders visited only the more backward worlds where machines were simple if used at all. I had no idea how one went about reprogramming complex robos. But the knowledge of a Free Trader was not that of a Patrolman. Plainly Borton and Harkon hoped the machines could be made to work in some manner for us.

Which is what they proceeded to find out. When the six robos were halted we came down from the balcony. The antigrav transports still moved at a slow and even pace, though those now edging away were only partly loaded. Foss and the other Patrolman went into action, turning their lasers with less precision but as great effect on the motive section of those. The carriers crashed to the floor with heavy jars which shook even this rock-walled chamber.

The Patrolmen gathered about the nearest robo. Harkon was already at work on the protective casing over its "brain." But I was more interested in the transports. Basically these were nothing more than ovals of metal, with low side walls to hold their loads in place. The motive force of each lay in a box at the rear. The principle of their construction was unlike anything I had ever seen before.

"Something coming!" At that warning from Griss we all went to ground. But what loomed into view out of the opening was an empty transport back for another load. Foss had raised his laser to short it when Lidj jerked at his arm to spoil his aim.

"We can use that!" He made a running jump, caught the edge of the carrier's wall, and swung up on it. It did not halt its forward movement, proceeding steadily down a row of boxes until it came to a stop beside a motionless robo, still holding a crate aloft between clawed appendages.

Lidj was squatting before the controls, trying to make sense of them, when we clambered on board to join him. Unloaded as it was, the carrier bucked a little under our movements and shifting weight, so we had to take care.

"Could be set either of two ways," he said, "ready to go either when there is a certain amount of weight on board—or after a predetermined time. If it is the latter it's more risky. We'll have to either knock it out or let it go. But if it is a matter of weight—"

Foss nodded. "Then we can use it."

I could guess what they planned. Build a row of boxes around the edge of the carrier, then take our places inside that and have transportation out without fear of getting lost. We would, of course, be heading toward the enemy. But we would have the element of surprise on our side.

"Time it," Foss continued.

I looked around. A second empty carrier was now coming in, heading, not to where we waited, but to the loading site, where the Patrolmen now had the upper casing of the robo free.

"Look out!"

Those workmen scattered as the carrier swung in, just missing the upraised load arm of the robo. Then the platform halted, waiting to be loaded. The men arose to tug at the squat robo, pulling it out of the way to where they could get at it without any danger of being knocked out by a transport.

Lidj still knelt by the motive box. He had stopped trying to find any lever or control button. Foss had said to time it, and we were all counting furiously during long minutes as we stood tensely alert for the first sign that the carrier was preparing to move. But it hung there, still waiting. I heard the captain's sigh of relief.

"One hundred," he repeated aloud. "If it doesn't start up by five, now—"

His lips shaped the numbers visibly. The carrier did not stir.

"So far, so good. Weight must be what triggers it."

While we had conducted our crude test a third carrier had come nosing back. Counting the three which had been immobilized, there were now six. How many could there be in all? And how soon would someone come looking if they did not return?

Foss and Lidj went to one of the loaded ones which had been halted. Part of a cargomaster's duty is the judging of cargo loads, an ability to estimate, by eye, bulk and weight for stowage. Lidj was an expert. I was not so experienced, but I had had enough general training under his stiff tutelage to be able to come close to guessing the weight load on the downed platform.

Once we knew that, we moved along the still-racked boxes to pick out those which would give us protective bulk without too much weight—weight which our bodies must partly supply.

Having made our choices, we began to load by hand, a wearying process which was foreign to usual ship work. But in times of stress one can do many things he might earlier have thought impossible. We stacked our chosen boxes and containers as a bulwark running along the edges of the platform, leaving an open space between. Borton came to inspect our labors and nodded approval.

"Just let us get one of those boys going"—he nodded to the robos—"and we'll move out."

What he intended the reprogrammed cargo handler to do, I could not guess. Nor did we take time from our own labor to watch their struggles. There came a whir of sound. The robo brought down its upright arm, dropped the box it held. It turned on its treads to face the wide doorway.

"Now—" Harkon was moving to a second robo as if he planned to use that also. Then his hands went to his head.

"Time's just run out." His voice lacked the jubilation of seconds earlier. "If we make a move—it must be now!"

Chapter 17

KRIP VORLUND

No other carrier had returned for some time now. But Griss, Lidj, and Harkon all faced the doorway as if they heard some call.

"They are uneasy, those who wear our bodies," Harkon said to Borton. "We shall have to move fast if we would keep any advantage."

Borton triggered the robo and it moved out, heading for the door. With it as a fore guard, the rest of us took to the carriers. And as those edged away from the loading sites, picking up speed as they went, I could have shouted aloud in my relief. Our calculations had been proved right so far. Weight sent the carriers on their way.

Once airborne, I longed for the speed of a flitter. But there was no hurrying the deliberate pace, any more than we could urge on the robo rumbling ahead. Perhaps it was just as well we did not approach too near that. For as it went it came alive. It had been using two long, jointed arms, ending in clawed attachments. And it was also equipped with flexible tentacles, two above and two below those arms. Now all six of the appendages flailed the air vigorously, whipping out and around.

Though men have depended upon the services of machines for such countless ages that perhaps only the Zacathans can now reckon the number of those dusty years, yet I think deep inside us all there lingers a small spark of fear that some day, under some circumstances, those machines will turn on us, to wreak a mindless vengeance of their own. Long ago it was discovered that robos given too human a look were not salable. Even faint resemblances triggered such age-old distaste.

Now as I lay beside Foss and Lidj on the carrier and watched the wildly working arms of the robo, which seemed to have gone mad, I was glad that ours was not the first transport riding directly in its wake, but the second. Let the Patrol enjoy—if one might term it that—the honor of the lead. The farther I was from that metal monster seemingly intent on smashing the world, the better.

"They are not too far ahead now." Lidj's words reached me through the *clank-clank* of the robo.

"How many?" Foss wanted to know.

"My powers are not that selective; sorry." There was the ghost of Lidj's old dry humor in that answer. "I just know that my body is somewhere ahead. My body! Tell me, Krip"—he looked to me then—"did you ever stand off and watch yourself, back there on Yiktor?"

I remembered—though then the transition had been so great, my own adaptation to an animal's body had put such a strain on me, that I had been far more concerned with my own feelings at the moment than with what was happening to the body I had discarded.

"Yes, but not for long. Those men of Osokun's took me—it—away. And at the time I was, well, I was learning what it meant to be a barsk."

"At least we did not have that factor. It is hard enough to adapt to this covering," Lidj commented. "In fact, I must admit it has a few advantages over my own. Several aches and pains have been eliminated. Not that I care to remain in my present tenancy any longer than I have to. I fear I am conservative in such matters."

I marveled at what seemed my superior's almost complacent acceptance of a situation which might have unseated the reason of a less self-controlled man.

"I hope," he continued, "that the one wearing *me* has no heroic tendencies. Getting my body smashed up before I can retrieve it would be a disappointment —to say the least!"

With that he resurrected my own worries. Maelen —her present body could not continue to live, not long, if we roused her from freeze. And could it last, even in that state, long enough to get her back to Yiktor? How— I tried to think of ways that journey could be accomplished safely, only to reject each idea, knowing all were such wild plans as could be dreamed by graz chewers, and as likely to be realized.

The light ahead was brighter. Now the robo clanked on into the source of that, the first of our carriers closely behind him, ours drawn after without our guidance. We had our weapons and the protection of the bulwarks we had built about the edges of the platforms. Though those now seemed very thin shells indeed.

Here were piles of goods out of the storage place.

And moving among them were the common controlled robos, sorting and transporting to a cargo hoist which dangled from the hatch of a ship. A single glance told me that we were in that landing valley and that this was the same ship Maelen and I had seen when we fled the burrows. How long ago had that been? We had eaten E rations, gulped down sustain pills until I was no longer sure of time. A man can exist long on such boosters without even being aware that he must rest.

Our carriers kept on at the same even pace, but the robo was not so orderly. Its path was straight ahead, and it did not try to avoid anything in its path. The whiplash of its tentacles, the battery of its arms crashed into the cargo awaiting stowage, sweeping away battered and broken boxes, some to be crushed beneath its own massive treads.

The surprise was complete. I heard shouting—saw the lightning fire of lasers, bringing down more of the cargo, melting some of it. And the shock of those energy waves did their work. Men toppled, to lie clawing feebly at the ground, their minds knocked out for a space by the back fire of such force. We tumbled from our transports, took to cover among the cargo.

Producing tanglers, the Patrolmen moved in toward those feebly moving jacks while we slipped ahead, searching for more humans among the working robos. The reprogrammed one smashed on and on until it came up with a crash against one of the ship's fins. There it continued to whir sullenly, not backing away, unable to move on. An arm caught in the dangling chains of the hoist. Having so connected, it tightened hold with a vicious snap. Before whoever was running the crane could shut it off, the robo had been lifted a little. Then the strain of its weight told, broke the hoist chain. That small shift of position had been enough to pull the robo away from the fin. Dropped to the ground again, it still moved—though its assault on the fin had damaged it, and it proceeded with an ear-punishing grating noise. One of its arms hung limply down, jangling back and forth against its outer casing; the other clutched and tore with as much vigor as ever as it rumbled on the new course.

I saw Lidj as I rounded a stack of boxes. He was heading, not toward the scene of action, but away from it, crouching low as if he expected blaster fire. And there was that in his attitude which drew me after him. A moment later Harkon closed in from the left, his black suit conspicuous here in the open. Then came another dark figure—Griss. They were running, dodging, their empty hands held a little before them in an odd fashion, with the fingers arched, resembling the claws of the robo still engaged in senseless destruction near the ship. And they did not look right or left, but directly before them, as if their goal was in plain sight.

Watching them, I knew a rise of old fear. It could be that they were again under the command of those aliens who had taken over their bodies. And it might be better now for all of us were I to use the side wash of my laser to knock them out.

I was beginning to aim when Griss shot forward in a spring, launching himself into the mouth of the cavern where the jack camp was. By that leap he barely avoided a burst of greenish light. Another of those bursts flowered where Harkon had half-crouched as he ran—but the pilot was no longer there. His reactions were quicker than human. It was almost as if he sensed danger and his fear brought about instant teleportation. Yet I saw him only a little beyond where that green bubble had burst.

That the aliens must be in there was plain. I did not have the same agility which the three ahead of me possessed; yet I followed. What a meeting between the three and their alien enemies would bring about, no one could tell. It might well be that confronting them would reduce our men to puppets. If that were so—well, I held a laser and knew what to do.

But, try my best, I could not keep up with the three. I did see them by the plasta-bubble. The piles of loot had been much reduced since I had last seen them—there was not enough left to provide much cover. But the three were not trying for any concealment now. Instead they had drawn together, Harkon in the center, my two shipmates flanking him. Were they under control? I could not tell and, until I was certain, I must not venture too close. I lurked in the shadows by the entrance, berating myself for my own indecision.

Those whom the three sought were there, back in the greater gloom under the overhang of the balcony where I had once been trapped by him who wore Griss's body. Lidj, Harkon, Griss—yet they were not the men I knew. *Those* were the three apparent aliens advancing toward them. There were others there also, those with whom I had begun that scouting patrol, the men from the *Lydis* and the Patrol.

They were ranged against the wall, standing very still, staring straight ahead, no sign of emotion on their set faces. There was a robo-like quality to their waiting. Nor were they alone. Other men, jacks probably, were drawn up flanking them. All were armed, blasters ready in their hands, as if their alien leaders had nothing to fear from any revolt on their part.

Yet they did not aim at the three advancing. Slowly that advance faltered. The black-clad alien bodies came to a stop. Wearing the protect cap, I received only a faint backwash of the struggle in progress. But that the aliens were striving for control over their bodies was plain.

Of the three, Griss was the first to turn about and face outward, his expression now as blank as those of the men under alien domination. Then Harkon—and Lidj. With the same uniformity with which they had entered the cavern, they began to march out, and behind them the rest of the controlled company followed.

Perhaps the aliens thought to use them as a screen, a way of reaching us. But if they did so, they were not of the type who lead their own armies, for they themselves did not stir away from the wall.

Had I waited too long? Could I use the laser with the necessary accuracy the Patrolmen had shown? In any case even death, I believed, would be more welcome to those I saw under control than the life to which these others had condemned them.

I sighted over the heads of the three at the fore and fired.

The crackle of the released energy was twice as spectacular here. Or else I had not judged well and set the discharge too high. But those over whose heads it passed cried out, loosed their weapons, staggered, and went down. The three at the van marched on a step or two, and I thought I must have failed to knock them out, save that their strength did not hold for long and they wilted, going to their knees, then lying prone. Yet their outstretched hands scrabbled on the floor as if they still sought to drag their bodies on.

At the same time that backwash of compulsion I had felt, even when wearing the cap, strengthened. The enemy did not have to seek me out! They knew where I was as well as if I stood in the open shouting for their attention. But it was by my will alone that I came out of cover, walking through the prone ranks of their stricken attack force to face them.

Their arrogance, their supreme confidence in themselves and their powers, was not betrayed in any expression on the three faces which I knew well but which now wore a veil of strangeness, as if the Terran features formed a mask for the unknown. No, their belief in themselves and their powers was an almost tangible aura about them.

Still I did not surrender as they willed me to. Or perhaps they were striving to launch me, as they had those others, as a weapon for the undoing of my own kind. Instead I walked steadily ahead.

They had depended so much on nonphysical power that they were late in raising material weapons. I fired first, another blast of that shocking energy, aiming above their heads, though I longed to center it on them. But I thought that must only be done as a last resort; those bodies must not be destroyed.

The energy crackled, died. I realized uneasily that I had now exhausted the laser charge. They was another cartridge in my supply belt, but whether I would have time to recharge—

I had never believed my reaction or my senses more acute than those of most other men. But, almost without thinking, I made a swift leap to the left. Yet I did not wholly escape the menace which had crept on me from behind. An arm flung out half-tripped me. I staggered, keeping my balance only by happy chance. And I saw that Griss had crawled on hands and knees to attack. But whatever small spark of strength had supported him now failed. He collapsed again, face down—though the length of his alien body twitched and shuddered, as if muscles fought will, will flesh and bone in return.

So I edged backward at an angle to give me vision of both the three by the wall and those they possessed. There was a writhing among the latter, as if they fought to get to their feet yet could not summon strength enough. As far as I could see, those who believed themselves masters had not changed position, save that they no longer raised their hands with the round objects I suspected were weapons. Instead those arms hung limply by their sides.

Then he who wore Lidj's body toppled forward, crashing to the hard stone of the floor, making not the least attempt to save himself. And the other two followed. As they did so, that tortured movement among their slaves was stilled. I could have been standing among dead.

"Vorlund!" Foss and Borton both shouted my name so that it sounded as a single word.

I looked around to see them at the cavern entrance. And I believe they, too, thought I had fought a fatal battle. For Borton hurried forward, went down on one knee beside the inert form of Harkon, then, having laid hand on the shoulder beneath that black covering, looked to the three by the far wall.

"What did you do?"

"Used laser shock." I holstered the weapon I still held.

Foss was beside Lidj. "Dead?" he asked, but he did not look at me.

"No."

They went on to the three by the wall, stopped to turn those over so they lay on their backs. Their eyes were open, but there was no hint of consciousness. It was as if the essence of the alien personalities had withdrawn—or else—

I had gone to look at them, too. Now I wondered. Could that shock have brought about a switchover? If so—or in any case—we should have both sets of men under guard before they returned to consciousness. I said so.

"He's right." Borton, rather than Foss, backed my suggestion. He produced a tangler, used it with efficiency. First he bound the three by the wall, then he attended to those in the alien bodies, putting all the others of that band under restraint as well for good measure. In addition the three aliens were given stiff injections to keep them unconscious—or so we hoped.

We were masters now of the jack headquarters, though we put out sentries and did not accept our victory as total. There was too good a chance of others' still occupying the ship or the burrows. And the whole nature of this site was such as to make a man very wary of his surroundings, only too ready to hear strange noises, start at shadows, and the like.

We made use of the bubble in the cavern as a prison, stowing there our blacked-out prisoners. Borton used the jacks' com to summon the rest of his men from the outer valley. The energy which sustain pills and E rations had given us was ebbing. This time we did not try to bolster it. Rather we took turns sleeping, eating rations we found in the camp.

There was evidence that the jacks had been here

for some time. Signs, too, by deep flare burns left on the valley floor, that there had been more than one ship landing and take-off over a period of perhaps a year, or longer, planet time. But after sleep-gas globes had made the ship ours, we discovered very little more of the setup which had been made to market the loot or otherwise do business off-world—there were only faint clues for the Patrol to follow up.

Our prisoners did not revive quickly and Thanel was loath to use medical means to induce consciousness. Too little was known of the stresses to which they had recently been subjected. In all there were some twenty jacks, and the men of our own party which had been taken—including Hunold. And our only safe control on the alien three was to make sure they could not use their esper powers.

Thanel ordered these three, plus their alien bodies, to be put in a separate division of the tent. There he spent most of his waking time keeping them under observation. They still breathed, all six of them. And the detect showed a life signal whenever he used it on them. Yet the vital processes were very slow, akin to the state of one in stass-freeze. And how this state could be broken, he admitted he did not know. After a certain time had passed he even experimented by taking off his protect cap (having first stationed a guard to watch him and move in at the first hint he might be taken over) and trying to reach them via esper means—with no result.

I had fallen asleep. And I did not know how long it was before I was shaken awake again. Foss was the one who had so abruptly roused me.

"Thanel wants you," he said tersely.

I crawled out of the pheno-bag I had found in the camp. Foss was already heading into the open where the darkness of night had largely concealed the standing ship.

But it was not the chill of the night wind probing now and then into the cavern which set me shivering as I watched him go. I have known loneliness in my life. Perhaps the worst was when I realized on Yiktor that I might never return to my human body, that it was possible I might be entrapped for years in animal form. Then I had literally gone mad, striking out into the wilderness, allowing the remnant of beast in me to take over from the human which had been transplanted. I had run, I had killed, I had skulked, I had— Today I cannot remember all that happened to me, nor do I wish to. That was loneliness.

And this—this was loneliness of another type. For in that moment when Captain Foss walked away I saw the wall which was between us. Had the building of that wall been of my doing? Perhaps, though looking back, I could not deny that given the same choices I would have done no differently. Yes, I was no longer of the *Lydis*. I could ship out on her, do my duty well, maybe better than I had a year ago. But for me she was no longer the sole home a Free Trader must have.

What had happened? I was as lost as I had been when running four-footed across the fields of Yiktor. If I was not Krip Vorlund, Free Trader born, who wanted nothing more than a berth on the *Lydis*, then who *was* I? Not Maquad—I felt no closer kinship with the Thassa than I did with the crew; even less.

I was alone! And I shuddered away from that realization, getting to my feet, hurrying to obey Thanel's summons, hoping to find forgetfulness in this task, if only for a short time.

The medic was waiting for me as I came into that inner section where the six bodies still lay on the floor, looking just as they had when I had helped to bring them in. But Thanel had the appearance of a man who had not had any rest. And to my surprise he was not alone.

Lukas, whom I had last seen lying in tangle cords, stood beside him. It was he who spoke first.

"Krip, you are the only one of us who has been through body switch. The Thassa do it regularly, do they not?"

"I don't know about doing it regularly. Anyone who wishes to train as a Moon Singer does it. But there are only a limited number of Moon Singers. And so it may not be well known to the others. They have their failures, too." My own present body was witness to that, if one was needed.

"The question is, how do they do it?" Thanel came directly to the point. "You have been through it and witnessed it done for that maelen of yours. Do they use some machine, drug, type of hypnotism—what?"

"They sing." I told him the truth.

"*Sing!*"

"That's what they call it. And they do it best when the moon there is three-ringed, a phenomenon which only occurs at long intervals. It can be done at other times, but then it needs the combined power of quite a few Singers. And the expenditure of their energy is such that it is only tried when there is great need. The rings were fading when Maelen was transferred to Vors's body—so there had to be more Singers—"

"Maelen was a Moon Singer, *is* one," Lukas said thoughtfully.

"Her powers were curtailed by the Old Ones when she was sent into exile," I reminded him.

"All of them? The fact remains that we have body transfer here and the only other cases known are on

Yiktor. It might be possible to load these"—he indicated the sleepers—"into a ship and take them there. But there is no guarantee that your Thassa would or could make the exchange. But Maelen is here—and if she knows what can be done—"

He must have seen my face then, understood to the full my reaction to what he was proposing.

"She is not an animal!" I seized upon the first argument he might be tempted to use. But how could I make him understand, he who had never seen Maelen the Moon Singer in her proper form, only as the small, furred creature who shared my cabin, whom he rated as lower than any wearing human guise—a *thing* expendable for the crew's good.

"Who said she was?" Thanel might be trying to soothe me, but I was wary. "We are merely pointing out that we do have on this planet, here and now, a being—a person who is familiar with our problem, who should be approached in the hope that we have a solution to it here, not half the galaxy away."

But the very reasonableness of his argument made it worse. I flung the truth at them.

"You take her out of stass-freeze and she dies! You"—I centered on Thanel—"saw her condition, worked to get her into stass. How long do you think she might have if you revived her?"

"There are new techniques." His low voice contrasted with the rising fury of my demands. "I can, I think, promise that I can retard any physical changes, even if her mind is freed."

"You 'think.'" I seized directly on that qualifying phrase. "But you cannot be sure, can you?" I pressed and he was frank enough to admit the truth with a shake of his head.

"Then I say 'no'! She must have her chance."

"And how are you going to give it to her? On Yiktor? What will they do for her there, even if you can get her so far? Do they have a reserve of bodies?"

Chapter 18

MAELEN

It is true that sometimes we can remember (though that memory is as thin as the early-morning mist) a way of life which is larger than ours, into which dreams or the desire to escape may lead us. Where did I roam during that time I was apart from my broken body? For it was not the nothingness of deep sleep which had held me. No, I had done things and looked upon strange sights, and I came back to the pain which was life, carrying with me an urgency that would spur me to some action I did not yet understand.

Returning, I did not see with the eyes of the body which held me now so poorly. Perhaps those eyes no longer had the power of sight. Rather did Krip's thought reach mine, and I knew he had brought about my awakening, and only in dire need.

That need worked upon me as a debt-sending, so that I knew it was one which I must answer. Tied are we always to right our debts so the Scales of Molaster stand even!

Only with that summons came such pain of body

as blotted out for a breath, or four, or six, my ability to answer. I broke contact that I might use my strength to cut off the communication ways between my body and my mind. I did this quickly, so that pain was lulled to a point where it could be endured, remaining as only a far-off wretched wailing of a wind which had naught to do with me.

So armored, I sought Krip once more.

"What would you?"

"—body—change—"

I could not understand clearly. Body change? In me memory stirred. Body change! I was in a damaged body, one for which there was no future. A new body? How long had I existed in that other place? Time was always relative. Was I now back on Yiktor, with a new body awaiting me? Had as much time as that passed in the real world? For now it appeared that I was no longer closely tied to Krip's world, though that had once been the one I also knew best.

"Body change for whom?"

"Maelen!" Even stronger his thought-send. As if he were trying to awaken some sleeper with a shout of alarm, as does the horn man on the walls of fort keeps, where death by sword can creep out of the night unless a keen-eyed sentry sees it to give warning.

"I am here—" It would seem he had not heard my earlier answer. "What would you have of me?"

"This—" His thought became clear and he told me how it was with those of the *Lydis* and their allies.

Part of that tale was new. And, as his mental pictures built in my mind, my own remembrance sharpened. So I was drawn yet farther from the clouding mists where lately I had had my being.

Body exchange—three humans for three aliens. But

235

—there had been a fourth alien. A fourth! Sharply clear in my mind she suddenly stood, her hair falling about her shoulders as a dark fire cloak, and on her head— NO!

My mind-touch broke instinctively. In her crown lay the danger, an ever-present danger. But she was there—waiting—ever waiting. She could not take over any of the others, even suck their life force, since they were male—she must have one of her own sex in order to exchange. That was it! She had called me (clear was my memory now). Yet while I kept apart she could not control me, force the exchange as her kin had—force the exchange? No, that had not been her desire as I had read it last—she had wanted my life force—not my body.

"Maelen?" Krip was sensitive to my preoccupation with the woman, though he may not have known my reason. "Maelen, are you with me? Maelen!" His call was stark now with fear.

"I am here. What do you want?"

"You changed me. Can you tell us how to exchange these?"

"Am I still a Moon Singer?" I demanded bitterly. This was no proper debt, for I could not supply payment. "Is Sotrath above our heads wearing Three Rings? Where is my want? And can animal lips, throat, bring forth the Great Songs? I am of no use to you, Krip Vorlund. Those upon whom you must call stand tall on Yiktor."

"Which means well beyond our reach. But listen, Maelen—" He began with the haste of one who has a message of importance, and then his thought wavered. But I caught what he would say. Perhaps I had known my fate from the beginning, in spite of all his efforts to save me from it.

"If you would say that this body I now wear so badly will not continue long to hold me—that I have already guessed. Have you any answer for me, since I have given one which is no help to you?"

"She—the woman of the cat crown—she is a body!"

Once more I drew upon my power, probed behind his words seeking her insidious prompting, the setting of that thought in his mind. So that was to be the method of her attack? She would use Krip to reach me with temptation. For it is very true that living creatures, offered a choice of life or the unknown ways of death, will turn to life. And in the past I think that those with whom she had had dealings were much lesser in power, so that she had grown very confident, arrogant, in her reckoning.

But I could not discover any such prompting in his mind. And I was sure he could not have concealed that from me; I knew him too well and too deeply. There was nothing there but concern and sorrow lacing around his mental image of Maelen as he had seen me on Yiktor when I had been so sure of *myself* and the powers *I* held.

Knowing that this was not an implanted idea, I began to consider it. I could surrender to the mist and darkness, release the anchorage which held me in his body which could not be repaired in spite of all their science. We of Molaster's people do not fear to take the White Road, knowing that this life is only the first stumbling step on a long way leading to wonders we cannot know here and now.

Yet it is also true that we *know* when the time comes for such release, and I had not received such a message. Instead there was that pattern of which I was a part and which was unfinished—of which I had been shown a glimpse. If I chose to go now out of pain, or timidity, it was not right. And so my time was not yet. But I could not remain in this body, and there was only one other—that of her who waited. For it I would have to fight, and it would be fair battle, my strength against hers; a fairer war, I believed, than she had ever fought before.

If I had had but one of the Old Ones by my side my fear would not have been so great. But this was my battle only. Had the whole rank of them stood behind me at this time I could have asked no aid from them. But where was my wand; who would sing? Suppose I entered into that waiting alien and found myself a helpless tenant—

"Maelen." Krip's call was tentative now, almost as if he only wanted to know if I could still be reached.

"Take me to the woman. Do not try to contact me again until we are there. I must conserve my strength."

Sing? I could not sing. We were not under a three-ringed moon whose glory could enhance my power. I had no one of the Thassa to stand with me. No one of the Thassa—Krip? But he was only outwardly Thassa. Yet—and now I began to consider the problem with objective concentration, as if this action did not affect me at all but dealt with others with whom I had no emotional involvement.

Exchange needed a linkage of power. Once I fronted the alien it would be my battle, but to bring her to bay I might lawfully call upon aid. There had been that dead man—or seemingly dead man—who had broadcast to keep the crew of the *Lydis* and the Patrolmen under control. He, or the will behind him, had made use not of the traditional tools of the Thassa, but of mechanical means. What one could do, could not another do also?

For long ages the Thassa have shunned the aid of machines, just as we long ago went forth from cities, put aside possessions. I knew not the way of machines. However, to say in any crisis "because I do not know this thing, it will not aid me" is to close the mind. And neither have the Thassa been given to such narrowness. Even though we withdrew from the stream of life wherein swim the plainsmen and these star travelers, we do not stagnate.

So—a machine to aid. And a machine of the *Lydis* or the Patrol that was on my side, not that of her who watched and waited. Also—she had not seen me in body. Let me be brought before her. Shock had value. And if my mind was seemingly lulled—could she so be pushed off balance, made more receptive to counterattack?

Having made my plans, I spoke to Krip again, letting him know my decision, what I would need, then as swiftly retreating once more into my safe-keeping silence, while I waited, storing up what energy I could summon. Also I must prepare for this new technique—no want, no songs. I would instead have to funnel what power I had through a machine. But behind me would be Krip and upon him I could depend, that I knew.

Though I had shut off contact with Krip, I became aware now of mind-send. That did not come boldly and openly, but was rather like the barsk, wily, untamed, prowling at the gate of a holding, scenting the uneasy herd within, working to find the best way of breaching the barrier between it and its victims.

I wanted to explore that skulking identity, but the need in my own plan for surprise kept me back. How great an adept did I now face? I am as a little child compared to some of our Old Ones. Would I now discover that the same held true here? I could only wait for the final confrontation, and hope the machine would aid.

Though I was not aware of any change in my own surroundings, I guessed, from the increased pressure from that would-be invading mind, that I must be approaching its lair. To hold barriers on two levels of consciousness is very difficult. As I allowed that invader to edge into my—as one might term it—outer mind, I had to stage that intrusion with more care than I had ever before taken in my life. For the enemy must believe that she was succeeding in her take-over—that there were no depths beneath which I marshaled forces, prepared a counterattack.

Perhaps I reached heights that day—or night—which I had not known were possible, even for a Moon Singer. But if I did, I was not aware of my feat. I was intent only on holding the delicate balance, lulling my enemy, being ready when the moment came.

There was a sudden cessation of that cautious invasion. Not a withdrawal, but further exploration had halted. Though I could see only with the mind's eye, I saw *her!* She was there in every detail, even as Krip had showed her to me, as she had been in my dream.

That had been blurred, filtered as it had been through his reaction to her. This was as sharp and clear as the Stones of Yolor Plain where they lie in the cruel moonlight of Yiktor's midwinter. Only she did not half recline on a couch as Krip had described. Rather in this place she sat enthroned, her cloak of hair flung back to bare her body, her head a little forward as if she wished to meet me eye to eye. And the writhing cats's heads of her diadem were not in play, but all erect on their thread-thin supports, their eyes turned also upon me—watching—waiting—

Diadem! I had had my wand, through which to center my power, when I had sung the small spells and the deep ones. Even the Old Ones possessed their staffs to focus and hold the forces they controlled. Her diadem served her so.

Perhaps I erred then in revealing my sudden enlightenment. I saw her eyes narrow. The hint of a cruel twist of smile about her lips vanished. And the cats' heads—a quiver ran along their filaments, a ripple such as a passing wind brings to a field of grain.

"Maelen—ready!"

Krip broke through the shield I did not try to hold against him. I saw the cats' heads twist, turn, whirl into a wild dance. But I turned from them to join Krip's guiding thought.

By some miracle of Molaster's sending, I could follow that mind-directive. I "saw" the machine before me. Its shape, its nature were of no interest to me, only how it was to act as my want, my own diadem. To it Krip must link me, since it was of his heritage and not of mine.

Link and hold—did he understand? He must, for the mental image of the machine was now clear and solid. I directed power to it.

Recoil—a frenzied recoil from that other—rooted in fear!

Even as she withdrew, so did my will and purpose flood behind her. Though I did not quite reach my goal. She steadied, stood firm. The diadem braced her—

Between me and my mental image of the box the cats' heads danced a wild measure. To look beyond those, focus on the box was almost too much for me. And pain—pain was beginning to gnaw once more.

I could not hold the blocks I had set up in that broken body, evade the spell of the cats' heads, concentrate upon the amplifier—not all at once!

Strength feeding me—that was Krip. He could not sing where there was no true Thassa to guide him. He could only support my link with the box. And then—more—small, but holding steady. I did not know from whence that came (Molaster's gift?)—I was only glad I had it.

She had driven me back a little from the advance point I had reached. But I was still ahead of where I had begun. Look not on the cats. The amplifier—use that! Feed it with a flow of will—feed it!

A broken image—that was a flash of physical sight. Blot it out! See only what is within, not out—this battle lies within! I knew now that the ending must come quickly or else I was lost. Once more—the amplifier, call all my resources—Strike!

I broke through some intangible defense, but I allowed myself no feeling of triumph. Success in one engagement does not mean battle won. What did face me now? Almost I recoiled in turn. I had thought that what I fought was a personality, one as well-defined as I saw myself—me—Maelen of the Thassa. But this was only will; a vicious will, yes, and a dark need for domination, but still only a husk of evil left to go on running—a machine abandoned by its one-time owner, left to "live" through the mists of un-numbered years. There was no inner self wearing the diadem, just the dregs of the will and forgotten purpose. So when I broke through the shell maintained by those, I found an emptiness I did not expect. Into that space I flowed, making it my own, then barricading it against the remnant of that other.

That remnant, robo-like, was far from being vanquished. Perhaps the many years it had been in command had developed it as a form of quasi-life. And it turned on me with vicious force.

The cats! Suddenly I could see nothing but the cats, their narrow heads, their slitted eyes, crowding in upon me! They began a whirling dance around and around—the cats! They were the focus through which this thing could act!

Dimly, beyond their attempt to wall me away from the world, I could see. Not with the mental sight, no, but truly. Forms, though I found them hard to focus upon, were there. Then I knew that I was not looking through the eyes which Vors had long ago given me. I was in another body. And I realized what body that was!

The pressure on me, the waves of enmity which were as physical blows against cringing flesh—those came from the cats. I was in a body, a body which had arms—hands—I concentrated my will. And all the way that other half-presence fought me. I did not feel as if I were actually moving; I could only will it so.

Were those hands at my head now? Had the fingers tightened around the edge of the cat diadem? I set my mental control to lifting the crown, hurling it from me—

The cats' heads vanished. My vision, which had been blurred, was now vividly clear. I knew that I had a body, that I was living, breathing, with no more pain. Also—that other presence was gone as if it had been hurled away with the crown.

They stood before me, Krip, Captain Foss, strangers in Patrol uniforms. There were others on the floor, encased in tangler cords: Lidj, Griss, the Patrol pilot —and three alien bodies.

Krip came to me, caught my two hands, looked

down into my new eyes. What he read there must have told him the truth, for there was such a lighting in his face as puzzled me. I had not seen that expression before.

"You did it! Maelen, Moon Singer—you have done it!"

"So much is true." I heard my new voice, husky, strange. And I looked down upon this new casing for my spirit. It was a good body, well made, though the flow of dark hair was not Thassa.

Krip still held my hands as if he dared not let them go lest I slip away. But now Captain Foss was beside him, staring at me with the same intensity Krip had shown.

"Maelen?" He made a question of my name as if he could not believe that this had happened.

"What proof do you wish, captain!" My spirit was soaring high. I had not felt this way since I had donned fur and claws back on Yiktor.

But one of the Patrolmen cut short our small reunion. "What about it? Can you do the same for them?" He gestured to the men in bonds.

"Not now!" Krip flung at him. "She has just won one battle. Give her time—"

"Wait—" I stilled his bristling defense of me. "Give me but a little time to learn the ways of this body."

I closed off my physical senses, even as I had learned to do as a Singer, sent my inner questing here and there. It was like exploring the empty rooms of a long-deserted citadel. That which had partially animated this fortress had occupied but little of it. My journey was a spreading out, a realization that I had new tools ready for my hands, some as yet unknown to me. But there would be time to explore fully later. Now I wished most to know how I who was Maelen could make best use of what I had.

"Maelen!" That call drew me back. I felt once more the warmth of Krip's grasp, the anxiety in his voice.

"I am here," I assured him. "Now—" I took full command of this new body. At first it moved stiffly, as if it had been for long without proper controls. But with Krip's aid I stood, I moved to those who lay in bonds, alien flanking Terran. And their flesh was like transparent envelopes to my sight. I knew each as he really was.

As it had been with the woman into which I had gone, those which now occupied the Terran bodies were not true personalities, but only motivating forces. It was strange—by the Word of Molaster, how strange it was! I could not have faced those who had originally dwelled therein. I doubt if even the Old Ones could have done so. Whatever, whoever those sleepers had been, that had once been great, infinitely more so than the men whom only the pale remnant of their forces had taken over.

Because I knew them for what they were I was able to break them, expel them from the bodies they had stolen. Krip, still hand-linked with me, backed me with his strength. And, once those aliens had been expelled, to return the rightful owners to their bodies was less difficult. The Terran bodies stirred, their eyes opened sane and knowing. I turned to Captain Foss.

"These wore crowns, and the crowns must be destroyed. They serve as conductors for the forces."

"So!" Krip dropped my hand and strode across the chamber. He stamped upon some object lying there, ground his magnetic-soled space boots back and forth as if he would reduce what he trampled to powder.

In my mind came a thin, far-off wailing, as if somewhere living things were being done to death. I shivered but I did not raise hand to stop him from that vengeful attack upon the link between the evil will and the body I had won.

It was a good body, as I had known when first I looked upon it. And I found in the outer part of the chamber the means to clothe it. The clothing was different from my Thassa wear, being a short tunic held in by a broad, gemmed belt, and foot coverings which molded themselves to the limbs they covered.

My hair was too heavy and long and I did not have the pins and catches to keep it in place Thassa-fashion. So I plaited it into braids.

I wondered who she had been once, that woman so carefully preserved outwardly. Her name, her age, even her race or species, I might never know. But she had beauty, and I know she had power—though it differed from that of the Thassa. Queen, priestess—whatever— She had gone away long since, leaving only that residue to maintain a semi-life. Perhaps it was the evil in her which had been left behind. I would like to believe so. I wanted to think she was not altogether what that shadow I had battled suggested.

But the exile of that part, and of that which had animated the three male aliens, opened a vast treasure house. Such discoveries as were disclosed will be the subject for inquiry, speculation, exploration for years to come. As the jack operation (so swiftly taken over by the aliens) had been illegal by space law, those of the *Lydis* were allowed to file First Claim on the burrows. Which meant that each and every member of the crew became master of his own fate, wealthy enough to direct his life as he wished.

"You spoke more than once of treasure." I had returned to the chamber of the one in whose body I now dwelt to gather together her possessions (the company having agreed that these were freely mine), and Krip had come with me. "Treasure which could be many things. And you said that to you it was a ship. Is this still so?"

He sat on one of the chests, watching me sort through the contents of another. I had found a length of rippling blue-green stuff unlike any fabric I had ever seen, cat masks patterned on it in gold. Now they had no unease for me.

"What is your treasure, Maelen?" He countered with a question of his own. "This?" He gestured at what lay within that chamber.

"Much is beautiful; it delights the eye, the touch." I smoothed the fabric and folded it again. "But it is not my treasure. Treasure is a dream which one reaches out to take, by the Will of Molster. Yiktor is very far away. What one may wish for on Yiktor—" What had I wished for on Yiktor? I did not have to search far in memory for that. My little ones (though I could not call them "mine" now, for I had sent them to their own lives long since). But—with little ones of their kind—a ship— Yiktor did not call me strongly now; I had voyaged too far, not only in space but somehow in spirit. Someday I wanted to go there again. Yes. I wanted to see the Three Rings of Sotrath blaze in her night sky, walk among the Thassa, but not yet. There remained the little ones—

"Your dream is still a ship with animals—to voyage the stars with your little people, showing others how close the bond between man and animal may truly become," Krip said for me. "Once I told you that you could not find treasure enough to pay for such a dream. I was wrong. Here it is, many times over."

"Yet I cannot buy such a ship, go star voyaging alone." I turned to look full at him. "You said that *your* dream of treasure was also a ship. And that you can now have—"

He was Thassa and yet not Thassa. Even as I searched his face I could see behind Maquad's features that ghost with brown skin, dark hair, the ghost of the young man I had first met at the Great Fair of Yrjar.

"You do not want to return to Yiktor?" Again he did not answer me directly.

"Not at present. Yiktor is far away, born in space and time—very far."

I do not know, or did not know, what he read in my voice which led him to rise, come to me, his hands reaching out to draw me to him.

"Maelen, I am not as I once was. I find that I am now in exile among those of my own kind. That I would not believe until here on Sekhmet it was proved. Only one now can claim my full allegiance."

"Two exiles may find a common life, Krip. And there are stars—a ship can seek them out. I think that our dreams flow together."

His answer this time came in action, and I found it very good. So did we two who had walked strange ways choose to walk a new one side by side, and I thanked Molaster in my heart for His great goodness.

Chapter 19

KRIP VORLUND

When I looked upon her who had come to me, who trusted in me (even when I had called her back to what might have been painful death, because I believed that a small chance waited for her) then I knew that this was the way of life for us both.

"Not exile," I told her. "It is not exile when one comes home!"

Home is not a ship after all, nor a planet, nor a traveling wain crossing the plains of Yiktor. It is a feeling which, once learned, can never be forgotten. We two are apart, exiled perhaps, from those who once were our kind. But before us lie all the stars, and within us—home! And so it will be with us as long as life shall last.

	89705	**Witch World** $1.95
	87875	**Web of the Witch World** $1.95
	80805	**Three Against the Witch World** $1.95
	87323	**Warlock of the Witch World** $1.95
	77555	**Sorceress of the Witch World** $1.95
	94254	**Year of the Unicorn** $1.95
	82356	**Trey of Swords** $1.95
	95490	**Zarsthor's Bane** (Illustrated) $1.95

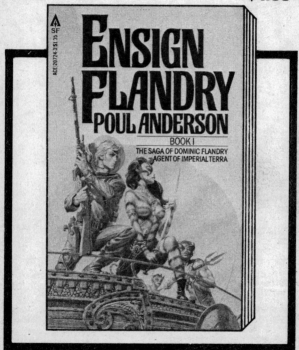

PROJECT PROMETHEUS WOULD STEAL THE FIRE OF THE SUN—
BUT THE PRICE MIGHT BE TOO TERRIBLE TO CONTEMPLATE.

A NOVEL OF THE NEAR FUTURE BY
HARRY HARRISON

SKYFALL

$1.95

Ace Science Fiction

Available wherever paperbacks are sold, or order by mail from Book
Mailing Service, Box 690, Rockville Centre, N.Y. 11571. Please add 50¢
postage and handling.